Praise for the Works of Richard Garfinkle

I0660582

Celestial Matters

"[A] remarkable fantasy . . . *Celestial Matters* is an exhilarating book, alive with energy and the wonder of discovery. Admirers of hard sf, historical fiction and fantasy alike should check it out."
--*Washington Post*

"*Celestial Matters* is a tour de force, a classic SF story set in an imaginative and highly consistent universe. . . . Highly recommended."
--*Aboriginal Science Fiction*

"Highly recommended for sf collections."
--*Library Journal*

"Weird, disconcering, fascinating, and original"
--*Kirkus Reviews*

"[P]lenty of intellectual play value."
--*Locus Magazine*

"For a student of the ancient world, much of its delight comes from the fact that its author plainly loves the civilizations that he has extrapolated into this alternative path of classical history. . . [I]t is delightful to watch him ring the changes. . . The complex history underlying the relationships of all these peoples is conveyed by suggestion, with considerable detail. . . . [E]xemplary for its whimsy and wit."
--*New York Review of Science Fiction*

"[A] hard science fiction novel of astonishing dimension . . . Rigorously conceived and outrageously executed"
--*The Magazine of Fantasy and Science Fiction*

"This very inventive, well written adventure story takes a very different view of the universe and speculates about the consequences. Good stuff!"
--*Science Fiction Chronicle*

"[B]rilliantly made up, with a constant stream of cleverly extrapolative details."
--*Aboriginal Science Fiction*

All of an Instant

"[R]eflects favorably on his historical and folkloric scholarship . . . [a] literate, cerebral exploration . . . of the concept of altering history"
--*Booklist*

"While at first the narrative may appear to be a simple fantasy plot cloaked in space-time physics, it develops a sophisticated consideration of the nature of consciousness, of the continuity of selfhood across a lifetime, and of ethnic conflict . . . stunning imagination, thrilling the reader with adventure, philosophy, and topological wonders."
--*Publishers Weekly* (starred review)

"[S]taggeringly metaphorical . . . [an] incredible exploration of temporal reality"
--*Starlog*

"[A]n intriguing tale even on the surface level. It is also heavily laden with metaphor and allegory, and it is perhaps even more intriguing on that level."
--*Analog Science Fiction and Fact*

Three Steps to the Universe: From the Sun to Black Holes to the Mystery of Dark Matter (with David Garfinkle)

"Science is often presented to the public as an unchanging and unchallengeable system of truths wrested by cabalistic means from nature. This book attempts something different. The authors' aim is to remove the aura of mystery by taking the reader into the back rooms of science -- showing how science is actually done -- and thereby fostering a better understanding of what lies behind the (sometimes inflated) accounts found in popular science articles and news reports. I really enjoyed reading this book."
--Werner Israel, University of Victoria, British Columbia

"With this insightful and enjoyable book, readers will enjoy a guided tour through the whole universe."
--Dorothea Samtleben, Max Planck Institute for Radio Astronomy

"[T]his smart, rewarding read is helped by a welcome voice, a feel for narrative and a useful glossary."
--Publishers Weekly

"[N]ot only an excellent introduction to the sun, black holes, and dark matter, but also a very good book about the scientific process. . . . The discussion of the scientific process is one of the best this reviewer has ever read. . . . [A]n excellent read for anyone interested in these topics. Summing up: Essential."
--Choice: Current Reviews for Academic Libraries

ALSO BY RICHARD GARFINKLE

Celestial Matters

All of an Instant

Three Steps to the Universe: From the Sun to Black Holes to the Mystery of Dark Matter (with David Garfinkle)

*Exaltations**

*Published by Achronal Press

WAYLAND'S PRINCIPIA

RICHARD GARFINKLE

www.achronalpress.com

This is a work of fiction. The characters, incidents, and dialogue are drawn from the author's imagination and are either fictitious or used fictitiously. Any resemblance to actual event or persons, living or dead, is entirely coincidental.

Wayland's Principia

Copyright © 2009 by Richard Garfinkle.

All rights reserved, including the right to reproduce this book, or portions thereof, in any form. No part of this book may be used or reproducd in any manner whatsoever without written permission of the publisher, except in the case of brief quotations embodied in critical articles and reviews. For information address Achronal Press.

ISBN 978-0-578-03514-7

Achronal Press

Achronal Press
Chicago, Illinois
www.achronalpress.com

First edition, August 2009

Cover art, author photo, and book design by Alessandra Kelley

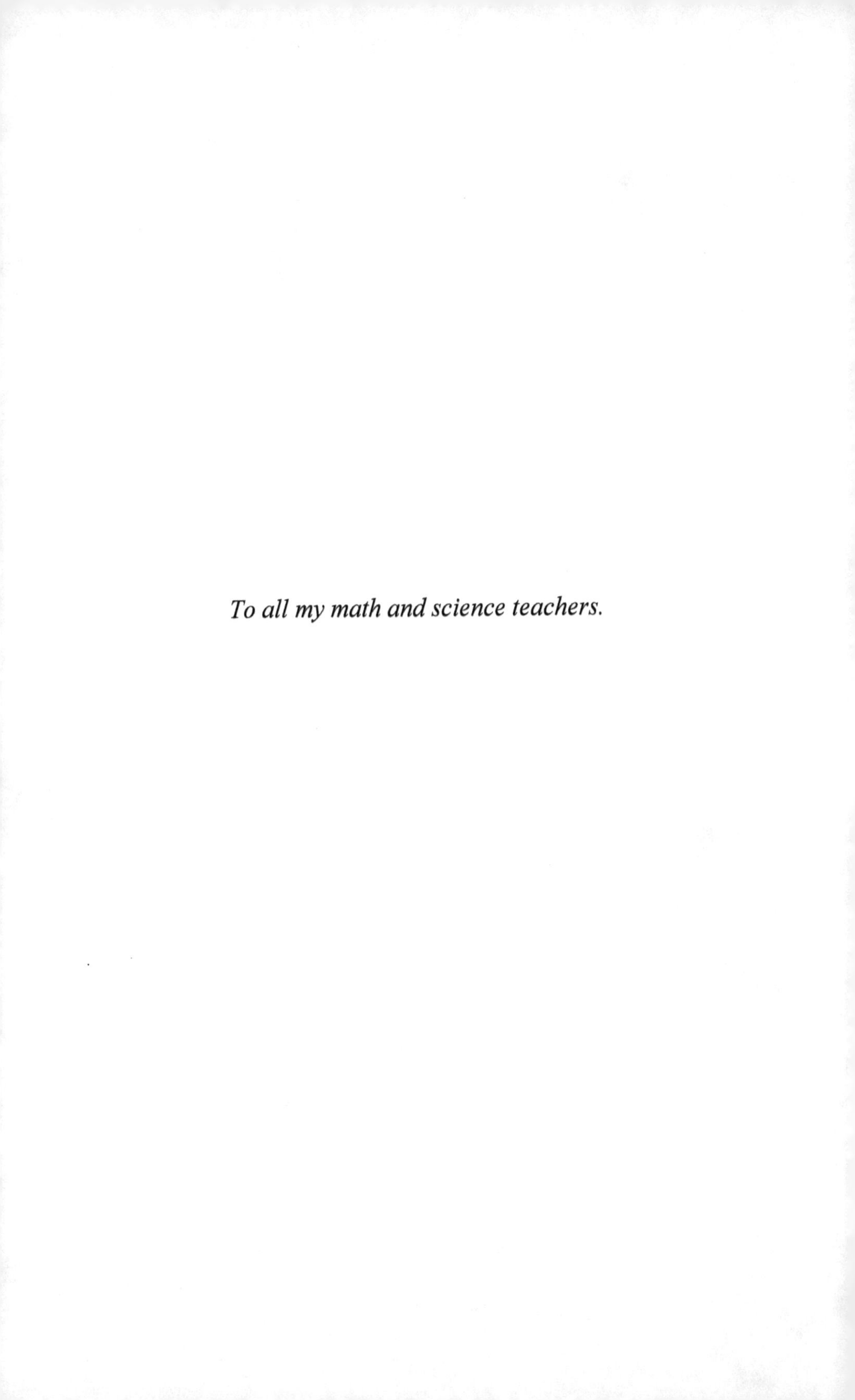

To all my math and science teachers.

Pronum

They were going to fail.

Again.

The computers, row upon row of them, neatly settled in their niches, flickered their calculations here in the University of Toronto's linguistics labs and in labs just like it all around the world, billions of processors committed in parallel networks to the unraveling of one riddle. All those powerful tools turned upon this single purpose, working upon it at their near lightspeed rates of calculation, and they were going to fail in this latest attempt, just as they had failed time after time in the last six years despite employing every translation and decryption program ever written.

Gisette D'Antibe watched the Professors and her fellow grad students staring with hope and dread at their screens, the human thoughts as readable upon their faces as the numbers were upon the panels. Please work this time, they were thinking. Please, they prayed to the screens as people had secretly prayed to the binary oracles since the first computer had shown forth an answer with no human mind doing the work. Human hope and fear displayed themselves before inscrutable screens on all but one face.

Professor Constance Marchant, Gisette's Professor, was the sole exception. On her spare but youthful face was an expression that could not be named or catalogued in the lexicon of human masks. The tilt of her eyes, the strain of a curious group of facial muscles and the gentle motion of Marchant's head spoke volumes, but in what language and to whom, Gisette could not say.

In an odd three-fingered grip Professor Marchant clasped a stylus. As she watched defeat scroll up her main screen she used the electronic pen to flick little markings on the faintly glimmering pad in her lap. To each notation the slim computer beeped its objection: "Unrecognizable characters: Delete, Define, or Save as Picture?"

"Professor?" Gisette said. "Would this help?"

She offered an antique fountain pen and a hand-bound pad of paper to Marchant.

"Thank you, Gisette," Marchant said. The words sounded distant and tinny. The linguist's attention remained riveted in the same strange way on one small section of the large screen. Her eyes did not move while her hands abandoned the small computer for the anachronisms she needed.

Gisette looked over her Professor's shoulder to see what held her fascinated. It was the most basic failure of the entire process. In a small window shunted to the side the computer displayed its continual inability to render the alien signal they struggled to decipher into any coherent digital or analog form.

Whatever means of communication the aliens had used to encode and send their message twenty-three light years defied all the categories and conceptions of human language and mathematics.

The creators of this alien-deciphering software had been so sure that whatever might be different about other intelligences, whatever oddities of culture and art might have been spawned on distant stars, they would share a mathematics with humans. Surely, they had thought, at root there could be only one way to count and measure the universe, and that any species that had developed itself enough to communicate across the stars would have devised that way, just as humans had when they sent forth their own signals.

So they had prepared. They had made their decryption keys. They had created their search programs to find all known forms of vital universal constants. They had created their solutions and waited for the problem to arrive.

When that great day came six years ago, they had struck their keyboards with satisfaction, letting their programs loose with a confident flourish. But the alienness of the aliens had defeated them, had crushed that confidence into desperate hope and prayer and a helpless trial and error which had soured the hearts of linguists worldwide.

Gisette D'Antibe knew with an awareness beyond logic or faith that though every other human would fail to unlock this mystery, Constance Marchant would succeed. Gisette had picked the Professor out of the thousands who had posted to the Web their ideas on cracking the alien's transmission. Professor Marchant had been vague in her page, had failed over and over to find words or metaphors to describe the means she intended to employ. Where the other linguists desperately echoed the boasts of the failing Information Age, Marchant had hemmed and hawed around what to Gisette D'Antibe were clear signs of incommunicable comprehension. Gisette had volunteered at once to assist, one of only two students who had lined up to help Professor Marchant.

Gisette had a serene, logically unjustifiable confidence in Marchant. She knew, because of the way Constance held her pen, the way a bit of Scottish 'rrr' showed up in her Québécois French, and the way she looked at people when no one else was looking at her, that Marchant and Marchant alone would come to understand what the aliens were saying to the human race.

But it would take the Professor much time to come to this understanding. Gisette feared -- and this fear had a thousand logical reasons -- that the moment of success would not be soon enough. The crowds at university and governmental gates across the world chanted their false hopes for alien intervention. "A ship is coming!" they chorused in their mobs.

They had leapt to that conclusion, jumped to it because it was what was expected of aliens. It was an expectation drawn solely from fiction, since no one had met or, before this, heard from an alien. The idea of aliens had been deeply planted in their minds by stories and prophecies, by the freedom art has when it need not depict reality. A ship is coming. That was certain in art. Reality would take much more care to unravel.

Yet in the Information Age expectation overcame patience like an Ace over a Deuce. The people of Earth had been promised knowledge all their lives. Anything could be known with a few taps on a touch-sensitive screen; that was the boast of the age. Any question could be answered. The world was connected at the speed of light and all understanding was available to all people.

But now another world had joined in the conversation, and that selfsame speed of light which trumped all other speeds was itself trumped by the unbreakable distance between the stars, a distance measured in crawl-slow light-years.

Light-year was a fancy phrase, a bit of advertising for great distances. But now it was hard reality. It takes light one year to go one light-year, and nothing can beat that rate. Communication between the stars takes years, and you can't do any better than that.

Years!

Humans no longer measured anything except their lifespans in years. All endeavors, all works to be done were a matter of days, hours, minutes, seconds, and the prefixes of seconds: milli, micro, and pico.

To ask the aliens what they meant by their dense unrepeating message would take a minimum of fifty-four years to elicit and receive a response. No one had that kind of patience anymore. The world demanded an answer of the linguists and the mathematicians, of the cryptographers and the psychologists, and of their world leaders. The people wanted the solution to this inhuman riddle and they wanted that answer not in years, days, hours, seconds, millis, micros, or picos. They wanted it, as the Information Age had taught them to want, now!

But they wouldn't get what they wanted.

In how many pieces would they break the world in the temper tantrum they would throw when they found out how fully their lust to know was thwarted? Gisette had no answer to that question. But this she did know, that when the world had fallen apart in that pique, she would be the one to find the people who could put it together again.

Part I
Geometry:
A Measure of Earth

1. Intervals

Times and means have changed.

The answer to all the world's problems was building thusly within an alien-schooled mind that for the moment called itself the ConCensor:

The American Manders lock into the north-south migratory footvolk, making one progress of cultural transformation. This progress interlocks with the tides of the sea footvolk and the orbits of the skyvolk to make one cultural umbrella. This umbrella interlocks with the retrovolks in Europe to create one Euro-American tension which interlocks with the many Asian, North African, South African, East African-Middle-Eastern and Australian tensions to create one world.

One Earth held in my mouth, good enough to eat.

"ConCensus is achieved," she said. In her mind the ConCensor struggled to put down the social package she had just created.

Drop the pack, Elsbet, she thought, drawing out her human mind and name from the veil of alien conceptions. Put away the papers, the lenticle-readers, the hand-scratched palm leaves, the dozen archaic forms of magnetic data used by traditionalists. Drop the ConCensus Takers, their personalities, tongues, stations and summaries of their work and posts. Stamp the seal of the ConCensor on the five year report, let go the alien mathematics and get some human rest.

Elsbet Chan-Dunlevy-DeMarnier-Tienh (and four other lineages she would not dignify with a place in her name) poured hot blue wax on the leather cover of her efforts and neatly pressed down the ceramic chop, imprinting the three-eye icon of the ConCensorship. Then with green wax and her personal seal she left a half-circle imprint of her name.

With a hot stylus she burned the words, *Sealed on the twelfth day of March, A.D. 2163, dated according to the reckoning of the sealer's people and religion.*

"Done," the ConCensor of the Dissociation said to the empty midnight of her office.

"Done," she said again as she stood up from her malachite-topped desk and stretched her back, letting her muscles arc up in longed-for flight, alien aches easing away her earthbound labors.

Elsbet Chan she now thought of herself as she stood up, her social, not formal, name. Elsbet Chan, she reminded herself, packing up the profession and unpacking the person. It was important to know her name at every moment. Otherwise the naming-counting-accounting she had learned from the Single-Sayers, the system of mathematics that kept the world recorded and delineated, would fall apart. If the ConCensor did not at every moment know her own name then no one she had reckoned could be known.

Elsbet Chan, thirty-nine years old, ConCensor for the last five years, having taken over for her father Michael DeMarnier after the last ConCensus (his seventh), tall from her paternal Aquitaine ancestry, but with maternally given eyes and face that spoke of drowned Hong Kong, and a mind that echoed thoughts from a world twenty light years from Earth.

Elsbet Chan, she reminded herself. And what counted to Elsbet Chan, what mattered, came out with the name as the vital efforts of Elsbet Chan-Dunlevy-DeMarnier-Tienh (and four other lineages she would not dignify with a place in her name) receded. Rest, she reminded herself. Food could wait until morning. Food and a visit to the Guesthouse to see her husband and children. A chance to talk to the Guests again, to remind herself of life within their fortress in the southern part of Toronto. Family and extended family, tomorrow she might be able to visit them, if the meeting with the Trustee took not too long. If not, the next day, or the next. They would be happy to see her whenever she came, and she delighted to see them.

"Good night," Elsbet Chan said to her private office. The door opened curtain-wise, the walls darkened, and a thin grey membrane grew over her desk and the work thereon, sealing in the sealed.

"And good night to you, Marc," Elsbet Chan said to the lone man seated in the public office.

"Bon nuit," the man said, not looking away from the rotating image of the Earth and its satellites that floated in the ball of image mist hanging above his desk. Dots of light marked the place of each ConCensus Taker on the planet, the eyes and ears, voices and reputations of the Dissociation.

During the day all twenty outer office desks would be occupied, but at night only one person was needed to handle emergencies, rare as they were. There had been fewer than fifty real emergencies since Elsbet Chan had taken up the post of ConCensor.

Marc Gerrand had night duty because he was swift of mind and tongue. The first was a good quality in anyone, the latter a social embarrassment. A deeper shame lay beneath that superficial characteristic, a shame for which he had been hired. Gerrand was a 'clever' man, capable of creating tricks that could temporarily defuse situations until others with more far reaching minds could apply long-lasting intelligent and wise solutions to the troubles his cleverness held at bay.

Uncontrolled cleverness had been the downfall of many, but put in its place it could do good work, so long as it was not given the freedom to run wild. Gerrand was grateful to the ConCensor for a job that used his abilities and kept him out of the laconic stream of society in which he would have to hold his tongue and check his repartee. Better to work in monastic isolation than to flare the collective temper of the volk.

Elsbet Chan left the young man to his intense, poised waiting, hoping as always that his skills and wits would go unused. The outside night was cool, March not yet having turned from leonine to ovine. Yet the ceramic plating of the streets, outer skin of the geothermal network that underlay Toronto, offered warmth enough and light enough, not so warm as to drive out awareness of the seasons, not so light as to deny the truth of night. Enough for a balance between comfort and reality.

The chill air around her head and the warmth at her feet revived Elsbet Chan, drove away the work-fog of alien mathematics applied to human society. Her thoughts and awareness flickered briefly into Tai Chi-thinking and she savored the illusion that the ground fed and energized her body as it in fact fed and energized the city.

Shunning the silent maglev tram that would

have taken her the kilometer and a half to her pied-a-terre in minutes, she decided to walk, to soak up the chi and the thoughts of human night.

Her route naturally took her through DeMarnier park and the memory of herself as a prattling child endlessly questioning her father.

"If it's your park why can't you have a playground put in for me?"

"It's not my park, ma petite, it's named for me. It's an honor the city gave me. If anything I have less choice about it than they do. Look at the city, Elsbet. Count the people, pack them up together into the city and see how it looks at the Dissociation."

Elsbet had complied, practicing diligently the mathematics of the Single-Sayers. Just nine years old, she had as yet learned only the basics of that strain of alien conception, but she could pack a city into a name and thought. "Toronto likes the Dissociation, likes being the capital, so they honored you."

"C'est vrai," said DeMarnier.

"But why you; why not Honor or the Trustee?"

"Because even here the people deal with the ConCensus Takers, and their good reputation is packed into mine. This park is a name for that reputation. If the park is ever neglected then you will know that we are no longer well thought of."

And what would you think of this, mon père? Elsbet Chan wondered as she came to DeMarnier Park with its mix of twenty-year-old maples and four-year-old cherry trees, with its warmed lanes and lighted fountains, with the immaculately trimmed dark expanse of Sky-Watch glade. What would you say this goblin market signifies?

Furtively scattered in the half-lit park, hidden under trees, beside bushes, down near the ponds, anywhere but next to the lit walkways, sat the traders, their unrolled blankets or unsealed carry-sacks upon the grass, waiting for custom. Their faces were in shadow, but their names were displayed beside their wares, some scrawled on paper, some carved on brick or slate. A few -- oh throwbacks to the past -- had bright signs displaying their names in running titles across screens, and a very few others, showing off wealth, let their signatures float in globes of image mist.

Next to each name were icons declaring what each would trade for: A bowl for food, a bed for lodging, coins for local currency, a hand for trading in kind (books for books, toys for toys, jewelry for jewelry), an open mouth for information, a square with a stamped seal for personal IOU chits, a square with two seals for Dissociation chits.

The customers of the goblin market flitted among the trees, eyes darting left and right, hoping not to be recognized, embarrassed to be buying goods from afar at night instead of local produce in the daytime shops. Some were seekers of curios, knickknacks from distant places to hide in the privacy of home and show only to friends dear enough to be invited inside. Others were refugees and émigrés, footvolk seeking news or souvenirs of their former homes.

Then there were the midnight gourmets who refused to adapt their distant-derived cooking to local goods. Elsbet saw one of these trading with a wine-seller. The gourmet was a tall, spare man whose face pinched when he talked about the quality of the Michigan wines drunk in Toronto. He wanted exotica from Napa or Islip, the coastal wineries. But the merchant, an elderly woman, dusky-faced and cool of voice, held up two rare prizes. "Real Burgundy," she said. "From the Rhine-Rhone collective. And Getariako Txakolina from the Basque Independency."

Elsbet Chan closed her eyes to take in the smell and feel of the goblin market, to find the Smooth blanket that underlay the Sharp counting of trade and custom. Remember to fly, she thought, remember the air and the wind, remember your four wings, remember the feel of the air. Forget all else, feel the air as you fly. Rough air, harsh with many crosscurrents and the smell of storm about it. A flyer in this weather notes where shelter lies, watches for good landing mountains, and keeps wings and tongues outstretched to taste all the sharp dangers.

Elsbet Chan opened her eyes, secure in the insecurity of the goblin market. Fear lay under her, the fear of those who trade without having much Reputation, who might be strung up from a tree at the first cry of "Deceiver" or stoned at a shout of "Predator."

So who was this striding boldly around? No, not boldly, defiantly, whistling-past-the-graveyard defiantly. The man's eyes flicked with fear but he would not let it stop him. Nor was he striding. He was taking purposeful steps because his feet were weary. Into the light he came, his face the complex tan and indeterminate features of the much-intermarried Americans. His carry-sack, a long cylinder of cloth strung over his shoulders, was a heavy weight to him, not quite a killing-load, but more than a short-carry, a life-burden and he had come a long way with it. But when he dropped the sack onto a patch of grass next to -- such bravado -- the lighted walk, it made no heavy sound. A non-physical weight lay in the pack.

The man ran a heat-scarred hand down the top of the carry-sack, unsealing it. The canvas unrolled into a polyglot display. A dozen or so small books, most plastic bound but a few hand bound in leather. Five black crystal lenticles, each with only one clear opening, single-reads, simple uses of the Band-Braider's information storage technology. Four hol-mem blocks, old fashioned technology requiring complex readers, not popular these days. A pile of unmatted drawings.

And five clear cubes, each containing a blown glass shape.

In front of the display, garishly lit by the red of the walkway, was this sign: *Feather's Monsters. Monsters Made, Traded, and Collected* and four icons: Bowl, Bed, Hand, and Ear. The last was rare. Whoever Feather was, he wanted to be heard and was willing to trade for that privilege.

Feather. He had one name in the manner of the Backlorn, those who had given up their pasts, their ancestors, their heritage and lineage. From what was he running and whom did he want to hear him?

Elsbet Chan was tired. She had spent weeks compiling the words and ideas, the counts and accounts of the entire world. No doubt somewhere in the sealed reports of her subordinates this man Feather would be found. She had only to open the ConCensus in the correct fashion and he would emerge in clear portrait. But the man recorded was not the same as the man seen, and the report of his imploring eyes and monstrous display would not be like the talking to him.

Elsbet Chan ambled over to the defiant young man, who looked younger with each step she took, who sat cross-legged and glared into empty space. No doubt he would have turned his look on passers-by if he did not fear the name 'Predator'. Closer now he looked very thin, as if all of his trading had been in kind or hearing and he had not known bed or board for a long time. A small keep-fresh-sack with two apples and a few dried cherries and a torn paper bag with the meats of a few walnuts were the only food he was carrying, and he had obviously husbanded this. Why had he not stopped to pick more of the wild foods? Most of the footvolk, the People of the Foot, knew enough to gather provisions as they traveled. There had been no major disasters that would have caused this man to leave whatever American Mander was his home without learning the ways of the road.

Elsbet was near enough now to see his goods in detail. The books were a scattering of what had once been called horror novels, ranging over the past three hundred and fifty years, from the time when foreigners were monsters to the epoch when body-parts and the dead corporeal and incorporeal were monsters to the introspection of people finding monsters in themselves to the Troth-Breaking when liars were the great horrors, to recent times when monsters were so out of fashion that nostalgia for horror was itself a creature of darkness.

The lenticles no doubt fed that nostalgia-beast. They were likely to be retellings of old stories, traditional to one or more cultures. The drawings were the work of many hands, nightmares put on paper by unskilled people and bought by Feather, but for what purpose?

The glass figures in the decimeter-on-a-side cubes, they were a different matter. An artist had blown them, had shaped them with care. They were not the crude figures of dream-stuff but the delicate working of hand and vision united, and they succeeded in being images of the horrible. One was a liquid mass with more than thirty pseudopods, each shaped into a different instrument of terror or torture, screws and saws, drills and knives, guns of a dozen kinds. The next was a tall hominid form with eyes that glowed deep red reflection at the walkway, its body made of threads wrapped into cords wrapped into cables. Then a ball of spines, barbed with barbs upon the barbs, and barbs upon that, and the hint of barbs beyond, down to an infinity of sharpness. Fourth was an armored horror low to the ground with a great-toothed lamprey mouth in its underbelly and smaller such mouths in its eight legs, a creature of tearing and chewing. And last, a winged monster, four bat wings, wide and splayed on a body that looked like the prow and keel of a boat, two wide green eyes, and a mouth that split the prow and prodded forth two tongues.

"Dec--"

Elsbet Chan bit back the word that had come unbidden to her throat. This poor man did not know he was a Deceiver. He would not have deserved what the goblin market would do to him if she shouted. He did not know his images slandered full five worlds with their art. The terror in his eyes as she had begun to speak told her all she needed to know about his sincerity. Whatever had driven him to make these, it was not malice, nor deception.

"I beg your pardon," Elsbet Chan said in Footsprach, the German-derived tongue used for trading between places, covering her expostulation with a cough. "I might like to purchase these five."

She waited as was proper. He waited, but not quite the proper length of time.

"They are my own work," he said. " I would not part with them for little."

"I will listen to whatever you wish to say," Elsbet Chan said after a decent wait. "And I will give you food and lodging for two weeks."

"I need monsters," Feather said. "For these I need new monsters."

"I have none," Elsbet Chan said. "But I can make these not be monsters."

"How?" asked Feather. "What do you know about what I've seen and heard about them?"

"Whatever you have heard I can find out," Elsbet Chan said. "What you have seen I will listen to. But I have also heard the aliens. And they are not monsters."

"How do you know?" The muscles in his face had tensed, his legs were poised to leap and flee. Say the wrong thing and he would run.

"I am a Guest," she said quietly, the wrong thing

but in gentle voice.

"I won't go to the Guesthouse," Feather said, his voice rising through an octave in that single outstretched word. "They tried to send me there when I was a boy. I ran away."

Elsbet Chan looked harder at Feather. What had Grandmère, she who found new Guests, seen in this young man? Which of the aliens had he seemed like? And why had she frightened him so much that he had become Backlorn?

"You don't have to go there to talk to me." said Elsbet Chan-Dunlevy-DeMarnier-Tienh and four other lineages she did not wish to dignify with a place in her name. She opened her small carry-sack and, putting aside her personal chit-pad, pulled out the official chit-pad of the ConCensor. She drew the stylus out from its sheath and wrote on top of the ceramic box, "To Feather. Give two weeks room and board at any Dissociation Hostel." She put back the stylus, then touched the authorization pad with her left palm. There was a brief tingle as the box touched deep into her cells, confirming her identity. Then a four-centimeter square of blue ceramic popped out of the box. Warm from just being made, it cooled swiftly in the air. The words she had written were sealed into the top of the chit; the underside bore both of her seals.

Feather stared at the chit in disbelief, then one by one he handed Elsbet Chan the five alien-monsters.

"The nearest hostel is on the north side of this park," Elsbet Chan said. "Get some rest and food. I'll come see you in the next few days." She held up her hand to cover the protest. "When I come I will listen to whatever you have to say. Go and rest."

Go and rest, Elsbet Chan said to herself as Feather packed up the remainder of his wares, a lighter load now, but still too heavy for flight. Go and rest.

Marc Gerrand spent the night without any calls upon him, poised and alert. In the morning when the rest of the staff replaced him, they found him, as always, wearied by the effort of thinking about the troubles that had not come in swiftness.

Late that morning, Elsbet Chan-Dunlevy-DeMarnier-Tienh etcetera (etcetera was a useful human creation, but dangerous for a Single-Sayer to rely on since it paved over the uniqueness of each thing with the assumption of commonality) returned to the Originate of the Dissociation, there to deliver ConCensus to the other three officials. The meeting took place in the semiprivate Rock Garden of the World, a ten-meter-high, twenty-meter-across disk with an artificial waterfall at the north end that fed a dozen meandering streams, waters that wandered in different ways but came together in a goldfish pond at the south end. Here and there a few trees and bushes poked up from the earth concealed beneath the carefully placed stones. Curved marble benches were severally laid down, always enough seats for four people. A coruscating mist covered the upper seven meters of the garden, separated from the breathable air by a transparent membrane. Occasionally a spark would show itself in the heavy fog or an image flicker into being, a momentary dream shape emerging from the nonconsciousness of the machines that waited to express themselves into the nimbus.

Elsbet Chan-Dunlevy-DeMarnier-Tienh, a little too tired to worry about all her names, met her colleagues beside one of the rivulets. They had been watching two frogs dance courtship or avoidance, it was hard to tell which, as the small animals hopped from bank to bank without ever entering the water.

"Good morning," she said.

"Good morning, ConCensor," said Mikhael MacLennan, Trustee of the Dissociation, friend of her father, Uncle Mikhael when she had been a girl and he had been Chief of Negotiations with Heads of State, a position under the Marshallate. Now he governed the Dissociation and she reported to him. Rarely, now, was he Uncle Mikhael. The last time had been at her son Sean's christening five years ago.

"Bongiorno, Elsbet," said Gabriello Benetti, Marshall of the Dissociation, risen from ConCensus Taker to the Marshallate by his deft handling of the Firenze-Vatican crises twelve years before. A restrainer Gabriello Benetti was, one who had to hold himself back and therefore had learned well when action was needed and when it was better to sit and wait.

"ConCensor," said Honor. That was the only name the small, youthful-faced woman had had for the last forty-eight years. She was the only one of the Dissociation's founders who remained. Backlorn in sacrifice, her name and past, her birth and presentments had been forgotten, so that the only Reputation she would concern herself with was that of the Dissociation.

The ConCensor held out the book she had sealed the night before. "Here is ConCensus," she said as she handed the document to the Trustee. Then she stood with arms crossed in front of her, holding the control pad that would call forth illustrations when needed. She looked up at the image mist overhead and waited. The Sealed ConCensus sat in the Smooth of her mind awaiting the questions and concerns of her Colleagues.

"Trouble marks?" The Marshall said.

ConCensus unpacked itself in the ConCensor's

thoughts, showing the world as a litany of sorrows, wars, plagues, and difficulties. She touched the pad in her hands and lights began to play in the mist above them. A map of the Caribbean islands appeared, as did images of hospitals overcrowded and people gasping in weariness. On the periphery of the mist were other images, of people restored to health but with an underlying green tint to their skin, lying in the sun, growing healthier as their new bioflora photosynthesized for them.

"The Green Fever epidemic in the islands is mutating faster than it can be adopted. Supplies of Organelle Adoptionase are nearly exhausted. I've spoken to the Guesthouse and the Method-Smith Guests have made a large batch of RNA Tractase which they hope will slow the trouble enough for the Adoptionase to replenish itself. But the Tractase has to be introduced soon."

"It will be attended to," The Marshall said.

"There have been seven gunflares since the last ConCensus," the ConCensor continued. "Continuing the trend of the last six ConCensuses, of five to nine gunflares worldwide. Five of them passed quickly through the usual cycle, leaving a residue of mistrust but little else of consequence."

The Marshall noted the locations. Gunflares were his especial concern. Home manufactories made the process of weaponsmaking so simple that a single manufactory could turn out an arsenal in a matter of a few days. Every so often some 'clever' person would realize that a small army could be mustered without much effort. The clever soul would arm his or her friends and try to conquer their home or a neighbor. Unfortunately for them the process worked for both sides, and the would-be-warlord would quickly find an armed opposition. Sometimes the warlord would win and then he would find armed neighbors and a subject people who did not trust him and would not work for him. It was usually only a matter of weeks before the warlord was toppled and the gunflare faded. There were only two known ways in which a gunflare could leave the gunbearers in power.

"One of the successful gunflares took place in the Idaho Manders," the ConCensor went on. Nothing more needed to be said about that. In that part of America the gunflare was an accepted rite of independence.

"The other one occurred in northern Madagascar and ended in public disarmament."

Images appeared in the mist. A line of men and women carrying long-barreled weapons marched one by one, led by a tall man of regal bearing and Bantu features to a manufactory where they ceremonially put their weapons in the hopper to be rendered down into metals and plastics, waiting to be made into more peaceful objects.

When the last gun was gone the leader stepped into the waiting crowd and offered himself in a gesture of trust to those he had liberated and wished to lead. The crowd swayed back and forth as he moved among them, the mistrust of those who carried guns pushing against the trust he had shown them in disarmament, wavering back and forth, until a cheer rose up and he was acclaimed among them.

The officers of the Dissociation nodded their approval as the images rolled away into the fog.

"The Israel-Judah-Palestine stalemate is boiling over," the ConCensor said, shifting her attention to another part of the list and changing the image mist to maps of the middle east and fortifications of stone, steel, light, and waving patch-fences. "All three nations are looking for help outside and are offering dangerous incentives to their neighbors.

"One side note of possible consequence. While

the High Priest in Judah was negotiating with the Peacock Throne for western Persian mercenaries, a Rabbi named Ephraim who has a high Reputation for learning and sanctity fell into religious discussions with one of the Shah's chief advisors, a Magus named Darius. The fruits of their talks on similarities and differences in practice are attracting attention from many well-regarded spiritual authorities in many parts of the world. I've sent Sister Anne, ConCensus Taker of Mount Athos, to see if she can expand the talks."

"I will see what can be done to lower the heat in the stalemate," the Marshall said.

"The only other major trouble mark is in China," the ConCensor said, making new images again. "The Four Kingdoms are all mustering armies on their borders. Conventional forces only, but they too are seeking allies. The East Kingdom is still drawing on Hokkaido for assistance, but only in terms of materiel." Since the undermining and sinking of Hong Kong, no one wanted to involve any of the Japanese volks in the Chinese civil war. "The North Kingdom has made overtures to the Mongols and that might be a serious problem; the Khanate has recently been recruiting many of the disaffected among the footvolk."

"I will attend to that part," said Honor. "I have Tale-tellers out among the footvolk, offering them different ways to live the unsettled life. And, of course, they have the Handyman to look up to."

"One more thing about China," the ConCensor said. "I offered the echo of Imperial China to the Path-Miner Guests, and they sang back that the echo would resolve itself in stone."

"Would you translate that into a human sprach?" said the Trustee, his voice commanding but with an avuncular undertone.

"It means the Four Kingdoms will not stay four kingdoms. The Empire of China will be restored, one way or another. It also means none of the four will resort to great destruction, and each will submit to the others before letting the whole of China fall apart."

"What about the other imperial echoes?" asked the Marshall.

"The echo of Rome is dulled," the ConCensor said. "The European volks are willing for the moment to be themselves. The echo of the Caliphate is similarly muted. The American echo is still strong but it is causing the Manders to distrust each other and rely more on us for their foreign needs."

The Marshall leaned back on his bench and took a sip of hot cider. He nodded, satisfied with the information.

"How is our Reputation?" Honor asked.

"There is considerable rise in Consent since five years ago," the ConCensor said. "Most of the volks, nations, states, and principalities accept our presence, and most resort to their ConCensus Takers when they need something not locally available, and everyone except the Professors uses the Marshallate for messages. Almost all the fear that we are Deceivers or Predators has disappeared. There are a few noteworthy exceptions."

The image changed again. "The Idaho Manders and the Free-Arms footvolk are still see-sawing. Whenever they become happy with our presence they become afraid of their happiness and remove their ConCensus Takers. Then a few months later they regret it and call them back. This pattern has not changed in the last four ConCensuses."

"They fear that we rule the world?" the Trustee said.

She nodded.

"Remarkably insightful," he said.

"The theocracies and closed community volks are as always worried about outside interference. Some of them distrust our recruitment and many are worried about our association with the Guests. But even that is fading. The largest problem is over our heads."

The mist turned blue and cloudy, then up and up the viewpoint rose to low orbit where the wisps of atmosphere met the rays and dusts of space. A flattened disk, pockmarked on top and grooved on the bottom, floated there. "There are now nineteen Stepping Stones," the ConCensor said. "The skyboroughs can now be easily reached from any volk on Earth that possesses space-planes."

The viewpoint rose and splintered into sightings of the nine great orbital habitats, spheres upon rings upon rings around spheres, cylinders by cylinders turning ever turning, their solar-catching Patches flying free to harvest energy then floating back to their abodes. The Guests' High-Talker orbited apart from the sky-boroughs, an amalgam of Patches, bending to receive, compacting to send, purely alien amidst the hybrid earthly habitats. The view refocused on the trian-gulated spheres of the stable Trojan point manufactories where anti-matter, the linchpin of interplanetary travel, was made; then the fledgling farskyboroughs, two orbiting Mars, three moving through the asteroid belt, and the half-built jewel-cascade that orbited Jupiter; and everywhere the nested spinning cylinders, matryoshka dolls of spaceships traveling the system to mine and explore, to build and find. All the things of space spoke of the grandeur of human striving. They glorified the skyvolk, height and bravery alone setting them above their earthbound progenitors.

"Except," said the ConCensor, "the skyvolk still cannot make a self-sustaining habitat. Time after time their farms fail and they need food from Earth. Time after time a vital piece of ecosystem previously unnoticed will be discovered and asked for, and time after time a machine best made in gravity will fail and they will need to trade for it. The Dissociation supplies these needs, and they resent us for filling their lacks. As long as they want to be People of the Sky and not human beings our Reputation will suffer among them."

"I will see what can be done," Honor said quietly.

There was a period of silence, during which the mist returned to waiting and the ConCensus resealed itself in the mind of Elsbet Chan-Dunlevy-DeMarnier-Tienh and four other lineages she did not care to recall. Cider was drunk, fruit, cheese, and bread eaten, so that a quiet mood came gentle over the late morning.

"ConCensor," the Trustee said as he put down an empty stem that had recently held concord grapes from Toronto-ruled Michigan. "What do the people do for fun?"

"Is the ravening horde ready?" called the alto voice of Theadora Coskun from the costume closet.

"Almost, Mother," replied her twelve-year-old son, Gregory Coskun-Alliende, from his seat at the stage design console behind the portable theater.

"It is not almost ready, Theadora," countered the professionally stern voice of Gregory's tutor, Professor Beatrice Van Leider. "Come out here and see how your son is mangling history."

"But Professor," Gregory said, "look at how smooth they move, and look at their faces. Scarier than the cyclops I did for *Polyphemus and Galatea*."

Professor Van Leider looked at the mob standing in the image mist on the stage. Young Gregory had a great talent for depictions, grotesques and glorifications. There were over sixty distinct figures moving in the scene, yet no two looked alike and their faces and postures betrayed a remarkable variety of dementias, perfect villains to ennoble the heroine of the piece (to be played by Theadora, of course). Flawless stagecraft, and yet Van Leider's stomach turned in fear at the falsehoods so perfectly displayed.

"Gregory," she said, caching her fears in her demeanor, "Canadian and American women in the middle 2040s did not wear below-the-knee skirts, nor did the men sport bell sleeves on their shirts. At that time people wore loose, short clothing no matter what the season, and the most common materials were not linen and cotton but shiny synthetics and twills. And look. Several of your hordevolk are waving carry-sacks, which hadn't been invented, and the one banging on the gate is using a chit-burner which of course did not exist. Haven't you paid any attention to your history lessons?"

"Now, Beatrice," Theadora said as she emerged from the cabinet -- not emerged, entered. Theadora always entered -- "We can't have all that much authenticity. After all, this is a staid New York audience. We can't shock them with too much flesh, no matter how accurate it would be."

"This is also the City of Shame," Van Leider said. "They won't tolerate Deception."

She had that day been to the burned-out, salt-sown wreckage of Columbia University, NYU, Rockefeller University and all the other obliterated havens of Academia that had once graced New York. No other city in the world had been so savage in driving out the Professors, but then no other city had as much to regret and as great a need to assign blame for the Troth-Breaking. New York had led the world in adopting the breakthroughs in psychology, sociology, statistics and genetics for the classification of people and discrimination according to the desires and fashions of business. New York had, in the early 2000s, wrested control of the business of answering questions from the upstarts in the Californias and provided the computers that held those answers and the software that offered the answers. The City had risen to new glories by becoming fortune teller to the world, and when fortune failed in the face of alien telling, New York had been most in need of people to blame.

"They tolerate certain deceptions," Theadora said, her tone a study in seeming carelessness. Theadora always seemed to be tracking her words to Van Leider's thoughts.

"Well, if you must do this," the Professor said, "for pity's sake, will you at least remove those technological anachronisms?"

"Gregory," Theadora said, gesturing broadly, "do as she suggests."

Gregory's hands reached into the large green box atop the console and embraced the landscape of static electricity that played over him, raising the hairs on his arms. His left hand flowed along the contours of the scene he had crafted until it reached the first carry-sack. His right hand dipped down below the flowing static of the scene to the shape well where precrafted images could be drawn up. He felt along the catalogue of tactile storage until he reached valises, duffel bags and purses, also anachronistic, but there were so few real records from the time of the Troth-Breaking and those had not been properly catalogued by theater workers. One hand flicked shaped feelings to another, which placed them as appropriate. The mists flickered and the carry-sacks were changed to other baggage.

"Now the chit-burner," said the Professor.

That was quickly replaced with a hunk of broken steel, evil with sharp edges, threatening in weight, a masterpiece of dangerous debris.

"Good," said the Professor. "Now for the large problem."

"La-a-ahrge problem," Theadora said, modulating menace into her voice with the practice of thirty years on the stage.

"Yes, large problem," said the Professor with a defiance rare for one of her low-regarded profession. She pointed into the mist where the horde leader was banging the corrected implement against tall walls flickering with electricity and swirling with mind-distorting lights. "That is the Guesthouse they are attacking."

"Of course. We are performing Siege of the Guesthouse, a true tale of bravery and sanity in the face of the madness of quickseekers."

"Yes, yes, and you are portraying Constance Marchant, the First Guest and the displayer of this bravery and sanity. Except that while she was certainly brave, she was not terribly sane, and whatever's left of her is so inhuman that the whole idea of sanity is inapplicable. But in any case, when Constance Marchant drove away the horde you are depicting, the Guesthouse was still the University of Toronto."

"I know that, Beatrice, but the audience will not recognize the University of Toronto. They know the Guesthouse when they see it."

Not recognize. Beatrice Van Leider soured those words through her mind. No one would recognize any university, no one but a Professor. No one would care about a university except a Professor. We fell so far, she thought, automatically identifying herself with those pre-Troth-Breaking academics. Then she pulled back. She was not like them. No modern Professor was. The Troth-Breaking had been a scourge of Academia, a sorrow and a suffering to the Professors, but it had burned away many sins of the past. Cautionary tales told in private among the Professors warned against the ways of the past, and essays written and hidden in libraries laid bare the nature of those errors.

Beatrice's essay, written down when the diploma was first burned in her wrist, contained these words that came back to her in the throb of her branding:

> *Five primary trends can be identified among the pre-Troth-Breaking academics as the causes of Predation and Deception among the ranks of the Professors: overspecialization, which led to lives spent on empty work; Post-or-Perish, which led to sloppy research; the solicitation of outside support, which led to deceit and favoritism based on governmental needs rather than academic concerns; the selling of credentials in the form of diplomas granted for test passage rather than actual understanding; and the culture of speed which stated that all answers must be immediately available. Because of these trends academics found themselves forced to either give up the Professorial life or lie and steal to survive. When the Troth-Breaking came and the Predation and Deception prevalent in those societies was revealed and reviled, people were needed to bear the brunt of the blame. Who better than the teachers to be brought forth and put in the noose?*

Her left wrist throbbed where her diploma had been branded into her skin. She had shown the scar with the name of her teacher and his teacher and the fields she had mastered to each university in Europe, but each had turned her away. No room at the inn, no space in the barely surviving shells of once great institutions. So she had traveled in Theadora's company, teaching her three children, at each stop hoping that she would part ways and come at last to rest in a university Chair.

"It's plausible stagecraft, I know that," she said, raising her eyes to meet Theadora's (her flashing eyes, her floating hair. Had Coleridge seen Theadora Coskun he would have known what a demon lover was). "Easily accepted, I know that as well. But do you really want to substitute easy acceptance for truth here in the City of Shame?"

"You worry too much, Beatrice," Theadora said, her words a challenge that seemed to pull Van Leider's thoughts into sharp relief, a whetstone for her mind. "You know actors weren't targeted in the Troth-Breaking."

Actors. Beatrice considered the word. Slow down, her teacher had warned her when she would run too swiftly from concept to concept, jumping from word to word without due care to the meanings and context of what she was saying. "If you change too quickly the words you are speaking," he had said, "if you leapfrog from synonym to synonym you will lose the character and fullness of the words. You will deceive yourself. Whenever you are unsteady in thought or word consider the fullness of the words you are using."

Actors presented appearances of other people. Not people. Characters, human-seeming things from tales, but not humans themselves. Even this depiction of the dead and mostly dead was not a tale of humans but a story of events and ghosts and half-ghosts, spirits made flesh. Acting was a shamanic magic, not a historical essaying. That was Theadora's point, but there was a flaw in it.

"Some actors were," the Professor said. "The ones who claimed their fictions were true. Remember four of the leading ufnecks were actors, three were writers, and six were directors or producers."

"Directors? Producers?" interjected Gregory.

"Stage governors," said Theadora. She made a gesture of concession, but Beatrice wondered if Theadora was getting what she had wanted in the first place. "Like you, dear. I suppose Beatrice is right. Do this authentically."

"Mother, that's an afternoon's work," Gregory said. "I wanted to look around the city."

"Look tomorrow," she said.

"But Father's coming down tomorrow."

"Then let him take you around the city. He grew up here, you know."

"Father, in New York? He never told me."

"I found him here the first time I came through," Theadora said, her voice growing deep. A shadow of allure played across her face and she became by actor's art alone thirteen years younger. Her words smoldered and for the first time ever Gregory Coskun-Alliende saw that his mother was a woman whom certain kinds of men could not resist.

"Dark eyes that always looked up, not willing to wear shame on his handsome face. He came to see me after we did the *Völundarkvi•a* on a bare stage. Back then we didn't have all these delightful alien gifts to augment pure acting. He came to me and I showed him the way out of shame, the way to wealth rightly earned. You came from that, and he left the City of Shame to become richer than the wealthiest man who had ever lived here."

"Because of you?" Gregory asked.

"Perhaps," Theadora said, lowering her face in practiced false modesty. "I am told that I inspire men to action."

Beatrice Van Leider laughed, using the dangerous tool of academic cynicism to break the actress' spell. As always it only half-succeeded. "If you want to inspire anybody to anything you will let your son do his work."

It took all afternoon as Gregory had predicted, but the scenes were ready when evening came and the downcast New York theater crowd made its way into Sheep's Meadow in Central Park where the mobile stage had been unpacked.

Between two five-hundred-year-old oaks, a banner had been stretched.

By arrangement with the Mander Council of New York, New York, New York, the Troop of Guisers presents a re-enactment from the history of our times: The Siege of the Guesthouse.

Dramatis Personae

Constance Marchant Theadora Coskun

Leader of the Ufnecks Obadiah Jones

First Graduate Student Patricia Coskun-Overus

Second Graduate Student Karl Coskun-Rainbow

with the Mist Puppetry and Stage Governance of Gregory Coskun-Alliende

Seal of history placed upon this production by Professor Beatrice Van Leider

In the interests of accuracy the characters are not decently attired.

The meadow filled with the crowd. They came in family clusters, seated themselves in family groups with large spaces between one patch of people and another. Here and there sat lone spectators, little motes of dust isolated between the clouds. The trees lined the meadow. The stars came out above them, many and bright, a clear night, a sky full of the inhabited heavens. Here and there the upward view was occluded by the few remaining skyscrapers, their empty windows reflecting the light of the streets, reminders of the city's shameful past, reminders of their contribution to the Troth-Breaking.

In the image mist of the stage another night appeared, a Toronto night, when that city too had skyscrapers, when city gleam still dimmed the stars. A lone woman, Theadora, stunning in the short blue skirt and blouse open to the waist of Constance Marchant, walked in another park, Queen's Park near the University of Toronto. She looked up at the sky, at one spot in the sky, one star subtly more visible than the others.

"Who are you?" she said. "What does your message mean? How long will it take us to understand you? I know you are talking to me. I have broken a little of your code, if code it is. I know there is something there I can understand, though most of your months-long message seems fit for minds terribly unlike ours. No one believes me. So many people have said they understand you. They say you are God and that you are coming to take us to the stars, or that you are evil and come to enslave or eat us. Every day another interpretation. Every hour the Deceivers spin out lies to get wealth for themselves. Every minute the Predators say they know the truth and that those who will serve them will share in the dreams to come. So fast, so fast they speak of you. But to truly learn what you have said is taking years and more years to come."

Enter the First Graduate Student, her image coming from down a far street, growing larger and closer until, deep in mist, Patricia Coskun-Overus, her face pure in intensity, stepped into the image and took its place, mist-puppet disappearing as human actress took over the role, Patricia, the teenaged image of her mother, save that Theadora's Mediterranean tone had been lightened by the Norwegian ancestry of Patricia's sky-dwelling father.

"Professor Marchant, come inside. There are riots in the city. Come inside where it's safe."

Her delivery needs work, Theadora thought. More practice on voice control when we leave this city. And she needs to look at me, not the stars.

The pair entered the University, into the tense laboratory where the work decoding the first alien message went on night and day in a fevered pitch the audience could not recognize or comprehend but knew their ancestors had enjoyed. The linguists (oh, strange age of specialization, Professor Van Leider thought) worked and worked, desperate though desperation was of no use in this struggle. They threw all the power of their computers, all the strength of their linguistic and cryptographic theories at the matter. But the transmission refused to be anything like a human language. They played hunches, devised new theories without any data to support them. Try after try they sought to understand, and all failed, all but Constance Marchant. But that was years in the future, years of work while the city and the world fell into the confusion of the Troth-Breaking, the spread of distrust that had destroyed the fragile infrastructure of global society.

The ufnecks were the crest of that wave of distrust, the only people more desperate than the linguists to know the meaning of the message. There were ufnecks everywhere, ready to believe any Deceiver, ready to follow any Predator, ready because all their lives they had been told that any question could be swiftly answered. All you had to do was touch a keypad and ask. Someone in the world would tell you what you wanted to know. That was the way of the times.

The ufnecks wanted the answer to the mystery from the stars. They pushed their keys. They were told what it meant by Predators and Deceivers, by the beasts that hide themselves in human form and prey upon humanity. The ufnecks were told. Picking up the lies given them, they ran shouting into the streets in every city of the world. Shouting they banded together and cried to the skies the words that were half prayer, half terror. "A ship is coming! A ship is coming!"

They came and shouted before the University of Toronto, and Constance Marchant came out and said,

"We do not know what it says. We are trying to learn, but understanding takes time. They lied to you when they said all the answers were out there. They lied to you."

"Open up and let us see," shouted the Chief Ufneck. "Open your doors."

"We can't," the Second Graduate Student said. "Keep them out."

"No, let them in," said Constance Marchant. "They want to see aliens. We have none. They want to see translations of the message. We have only inklings. Let them in. They will not find what they want, and they have not the patience to wait for the truth to unfold slowly over time."

As a fable it was claimed that the ufnecks found nothing and faded back into normal life. But in truth they thought that Constance Marchant was ignorant, unwilling to see the truth before her. They denounced her because she was cautious, seemingly uninspired. They did not know that real inspiration takes effort to manifest into reality. They left the University of Toronto and went seeking those who knew the truth. They never found them. And when another five years had passed and Constance Marchant had learned to hear the words the Method-Smiths had sent forth upon the starways, no one believed her. Everyone thought she was just another mad ufneck. It would be a long struggle before the Guesthouse was established and Constance Marchant proved herself right.

"But the exoneration and glorification of Constance Marchant, First of the Guests, is a tale for another day," said Theadora as the light faded from the stage and the actors disappeared into the mist.

Not far into the next morning, when the sun was just high enough to glint off the shimmer-fenced omniport that covered Toronto's islands, Elsbet Chan rode the tram to the Guesthouse. Only three other passengers shared the cabin of the swift and silent train with her. Elsbet marked them out as a visiting family, tourists, to use the archaic term. Mother, mother, and son, from one of the southern African volks by their language and attire. They had come to see the Guesthouse.

"The chit says we can walk all around the public places for six days," one of the mothers said.

"Do you think we'll see any Guests?" said the son, a boy no older than ten and probably a year or two younger. "Do you think the Path-Miners really have mouths in their hands? And the Band-Braiders, do they really change if you shine lights on them?"

Elsbet Chan bit back a laugh. Eavesdropping was a severe breach of manners, one she justified to herself by the demands of her job, but still it would not do to be caught at it. So much ignorance, so many confused tales. Even in the era of truth misconceptions ran wild through the minds of humanity.

The tram slowed to a stop. A hole melted itself for the four of them to step down the few steps into Marchant Park. The fortress of the Guests was sentried by two ceremonial guards dressed in heavy blue coats and carrying archaic foggers, the brown pulsing bladders that breathed in air and if need be could breathe out a variety of mists, from poison to light absorbing, from pyrogenic to cryogenic. Those were the first weapons that had come from the Guests' alien knowledge. Mercifully they had not been used much, nor had the much deadlier devices that had later followed.

"Good morning, Walter," Elsbet Chan said to the elder sentry, sixty-seven years old and proud of his position, though it had been decades since he had needed to take up arms.

"Bonjour, Elsbet," he said. "Welcome home."

A hole opened up in the solid wall of the Guesthouse to admit Elsbet Chan. The wall sealed up behind her as the boy said, "Home? Was she a Guest?"

Inside the fortress walls glowed in rainbow shades, savoring the many bands concealed within the sunlight. But the first thing that caught the eye of anyone who entered the Guesthouse was a freestanding column on which stood a statue of Constance Marchant staring up at the sky. Inscribed on the column in a spiral was a story written in Latin.

To Elsbet Chan the column and the story were the Seal of the Guests and reading the story brought her home. In a slow circle she walked through the narrative.

After her twelfth circuit the entrance melted into being and the family of visitors walked inside. "Remember not to leave the green pathways," Walter called after them.

"What does this say, Mother?" the boy asked the taller of his two mothers.

"I don't know, Fulumirani."

"It's a story from a book by a renaissance philosopher named Pico Della Mirandola," said Elsbet as she finished reading the story. "In brief it says that God made man capable of making his mind like that of any other creature. He could become fierce as a tiger, industrious as a bee, pious as a pelican. Constance Marchant used that method to teach us how to be Guests."

"You are a Guest!" said the boy, jumping up and down to get a better look at Elsbet Chan. Disappointed, he said, "You look human."

"We only change our minds, not our bodies," Elsbet Chan said, speaking with a confidence that sometimes flagged in her. "I was taught from childhood how to be a Single-Sayer. Though I don't have wings or two tongues or see through long strips on my prow, I think as they think, so what they tell us in the transmissions from their world I can understand and give to humanity."

Elsbet Chan turned to face the mothers. "Enjoy your visit. I hope your son won't be disappointed that there is not much to see here. But if you listen you might hear something."

Elsbet walked away, leaving the green public path for the lavender semi-private walks permitted only to the Guests. Eastward across the former campus she made her way, over the thrumming caverns of the Path-Miners where five families had striven for two generations to conform their thoughts to a species that had evolved underground, loved volcanoes, and had nothing that resembled individual words or ideas. The first generation had learned enough to bring out geothermal power and heat storage and transmission. The second had brought forth thermodynamic theories that rivaled humanity's centuries-striven mastery of electricity.

She continued past the patchwork house and quarter-mile-deep pool of the Moment-Keepers. Time to see her husband later. Quint would understand that she had matters to attend to first. They both had their duties, and as the first cross-Guest marriage they had long ago learned to accept each other's worlds and ways.

Two half-shadows crossed over Elsbet Chan's head, darkening the ground around her.

"Mamma, Mamma, come fly with us," called a cherubic voice that gained and lost volume as it swooped up and down.

"Later, Sean," Elsbet called, modulating her voice to meet the near and far of the boy's erratic flight.

The four paddle-wings and the wide, thin kite body of the flying suit had been adapted from a race that had learned aerodynamics long before it had given the slightest thought to fire. Much effort had been needed to adapt their technology to a nonairborne species on a planet with twice the gravity of the Single-Sayer homeworld. Elsbet had learned to fly only a little after she could walk and her sons were doing the same, Julian, the twelve-year-old, flying watch over the exuberance of his younger brother.

"Today, Mamma?" Sean said.

"Today, Sean. Now fly down and give me a kiss. I'll join you in the skies later."

She watched her sons resume their joy of the air, knowing that the skills to operate the flying suit and the nuances of understanding its air-movement sensors were helping them learn to see as the Single-Sayers did, and that was half the way to teaching them to think properly.

Elsbet had two places she had to go before she could find her husband and join her sons in the air. The first was the newly built Band-Braider lighthouse, a thing of lenses, mirrors, diffraction gratings, prisms, lenticles, and rooms of image mist. Some pieces of Band-Braider technology, particularly image mists and lenticle-storage, had been available to humanity for decades, but that was because all the other species used them as well, just as they all used Moment-Keeper patches and Method-Smith medicine. Actual communication with the Band-Braiders had only begun a dozen years ago, so there were few Band-Braider guests and they were still learning to think properly and struggling to translate the messages of this light-loving species with its curious evolution.

Elsbet waited on the crystal bench outside the Band-Braider house, enjoying the oddities of light and shadow which the building produced. After a time she was noticed and one of the Guests came out and signed greetings to her.

Elsbet signed back. The Band-Braider Guests were all deaf. It was hard to find deaf people with the commonality of cures, but Grandmère had found a few of proper body and mindset, here and there. Marie, the young woman who now silently greeted Elsbet, had been found orphaned on Fiji at the age of six. Where in the Pacific she was from no one knew, nor how she had made it to Fiji, nor what she had thought she wanted there. But Grandmère had found her, in a hospital, confused and incapable of speech, staring in fascination at an ancient electric lamp which flickered relentlessly. Grandmère had brought her back to the Guesthouse and she had learned the mind of the Band-Braiders so well that she had mastered and now governed the Guests' planetary communications systems, such a young woman to oversee the mist booths and image transmissions.

"Could you contact Grandmère and tell her I need to speak with her?" Elsbet Chan signed. "It concerns a young man named Feather she tried to recruit."

"Of course, Elsbet," Marie signed. "I'll send for you when she's ready to talk."

"Where is Grandmère today?" Elsbet inquired.

"Siberia."

"She'll like that."

Elsbet signed her farewells and walked through the tree-covered back ways of the Guesthouse to the first house, the former linguistics-department-and-school-of-communication-arts building of the University of Toronto, now adopted by the Method-Smith Guests. They had built an artificial pond next to the old stone edifice and stocked it with the building blocks of earthly life and the methods of alien living in order to produce the Tractases and Adoptionases which had revolutionized medicine.

Tradition dictated that the Guests be led by a Method-Smith. That position was currently held by Ali Mustafa, recruited by Grandmère for just this job. Naturally he had adapted to it quickly, and governed five half-alien groups with an efficiency that would have amazed any government on Earth, particularly considering Ali's mere twenty-five years.

Ali, much to Elsbet Chan's surprise, was waiting for her.

"I told Walter to contact me when you came," he said. "Come inside."

"Inside?" she said. "In the Method-Smith house?"

Ali opened wide his arms in the general 'my house is open to you' gesture recognized all across the world. Elsbet Chan considered the invitation and the spirit in which it was offered. Ali Mustafa needed to speak with her in private, that much was clear. He had something to say that could not be overheard even by the other Guests. Those were the uniquenesses, the Sharps of the situation. They were very Sharp indeed; there had never been secrets in the Guesthouse before. Did she know Ali Mustafa well enough to accept such an invitation? Privacy was a serious matter, and hospitality a great thing to offer. Were they close enough for this? That was the Smooth of the matter, the backdrop against which the work of Sharpness was to be performed. The simple answer was no. Ali had been a Guest for only seven years, not enough time to enter someone's house. But he had been chosen by Grandmère, and the Method-Smith house was hers as well. And he was their leader.

Elsbet Chan stepped around the outstretched arms and came to the sealed doorway. Ali's touch melted their way in then sealed the portal behind them.

The outer parlor of the house was decorated with

souvenirs Grandmère had picked up in her travels. Masks from all over the world lined the walls. Chairs of cane and couches covered in silk were strewn in an illusion of haphazardness, inviting, homey but exotic. A silver samovar sat next to a Turkish coffee urn next to a crystal brandy decanter. And--

Elsbet stopped surveying the room when she noticed Ali's discomfort at her roving eye and professional inquisitiveness. The regret he had for bringing her in and the news he was carrying prompted him to a shocking show of haste.

"Elsbet," he said. "A ship is coming."

2. Metrics

Handyman to the stars, thought Tomaso Alliende as he fitted the last of nineteen rerouting pipes into the infrastructure of Skyborough Hoshimachi. They call me up from Earth to correct their mysterious slowdown in spin and what do I end up doing? Fixing the plumbing.

Still, if they paid attention to the inner workings of their cylinder worlds, they wouldn't need me, the Handyman thought.

There. All done.

Alliende pulled up into a crouch as he made his way through the steel drum labyrinth of maintenance tunnels that lay around the pulsing labyrinth of air, water, sewage, electricity, heat, and light pipings that arteried the skin of the skyborough. The skyvolk inside did their best to forget this confusion just as people in cities tried not to think about where their water and power were coming from and where their waste was going. True, the skyvolk had maintenance workers to make sure the ducts were clear and unbroken, but they had no one who was thinking about how they worked. And wherever you were, on, below, or above the world, not thinking could be fatal.

Here not thinking could also be strange. They had summoned Alliende because there had been an odd rash of equipment failures in the understructure of Hoshimachi. It had taken Alliende three days of studying plans and changes to plans and jury-rigged corrections to the changes and reroutings around the jury-riggings to realize that the overall push of liquids around the outside skin was setting up areas of heavy vibrations that were cracking nearby conduits and breaking pieces of hardware on upper and lower layers of skin. Their sewer system had a riptide. Now that had been fixed, and all the Handyman needed was to be paid and go back down to Earth to see his son and his . . .

To speak rightly, Theadora wasn't his, any more than she was Winston Overus' or any of the others she had inspired over the years. Still, he wanted to see her, wanted to be . . . close to her. But in which way, in what way close to her? That he had never been able to discern.

Tomaso Alliende stepped out through the membrane that separated the skin from the body of the skyborough and emerged greasy and grimy into the light as sewer workers had since the first underground pipes had been laid millennia ago.

Out into the almost-but-not-quite fresh air of the skyborough, into the cool-blue lighting from the fore and aft caps, out to the point-eight g that came from the cylinder's spin. Up to look at the cylinder of stars projected in the tube of image mist that lined the axis of the skyborough.

"Look up to the stars, look in to see out," as the skyvolk said.

"Tomaso, come clean yourself up and I'll give you your pay," said the wiry, pale man waiting for him.

"Thank you, Winston," the Handyman said as he wiped the grime from his heat- and radiation-scarred arms and scraped his hands over the cleaning rag, his right hand calloused with years of labor and scarred by the jobs he had done and the monsters of fire and light, water and acids he used in his labors, and his left hand newly regrown and smooth as a child's. The rag grabbed every molecule of grease and dirt and pulled them from him. A few swipes and he was cleaned, a few more and his tunic, pants and tool brassards were equally immaculate.

Tomaso Alliende loped slowly after the tall and gracile form of Winston Overus, the Handyman feeling the ground as he walked, knowing that space lay only twenty meters beneath him -- or above him depending on which frame of reference you felt like using. The skyman walked unconcerned as anyone would in their home, disregarding the dangers native to his habitat.

There were no roads or paths in the skyborough, only open spaces punctuated by the conical towers used as homes and workshops by the skyvolk. Most of these dwellings were low to the hull, flat tipis that might house one person or a family. A few were long tapers that rose up toward the mist-shroud, places for the starwatchers who monitored the surrounding sky by studying the sky within. Other buildings were manufactories that played games with spin and false gravity in order to make materials impossible on Earth. There were also the four rings that made their own different spins, toroids that circled the stars slower or faster than the surrounding cylinder. Specialized work took place inside them, side by side with specialized recreation.

Near the edges of the caps were the farms of the skyborough, growing larger year by year as the skyvolk found they needed to grow an increasing variety of flora and fauna in order to mimic an ecosystem. Fully an eighth of the four-kilometer-long cylinder was occupied with farming. And such things they needed to farm: earthworms, bees, bacteria, all to keep going. The frustration of the skyvolk was clear in their voices each time they had to call the Handyman to fix something -- and also, so Alliende had heard, every time they had to call the Dissociation for some rare supply or the Guesthouse for some copy of alien technology.

"Here you are, Tomaso," said Overus when they reached the tipi that was the skyman's home and office as liaison of all affairs downward, across orbit, or up to the stars. "Hoshimachi's chit for five years' free travel up and down with my seal as guarantor."

"Thank you, Winston," said the Handyman. "How soon until we're over Stepping Stone Eight?"

Winston Overus looked up at the sky, at the mirror of the eternal clock of the heavens. "Two hours, seventeen minutes."

Only in space, Tomaso Alliende thought, could someone give so precise an answer and not be embarrassed by it.

"Then I should leave soon," he said.

"You're meeting the Guisers?" Overus asked.

Alliende nodded.

"Could you bring some things to Patricia?"

"Of course."

Winston Overus ducked through the dissolving membrane of his house and emerged before it had had time to reform. He handed a smooth, clear box with a stone inside it and a chit to the Handyman. Alliende put both of these into his carry-sack and sealed it with a touch of his new index finger.

"Anything else?" Alliende asked. There was a slight rise in his voice, the kind of vocal nudge that can only exist between two people who share some understanding not commonly possessed.

"Yes." Winston Overus looked back up at the stars and his face contorted into a bipartite mask of ache and satisfaction, of longing and yet having all that was needed. "Tell Theadora that . . . I see her every time I look up, but I would still like to see her again."

Tomaso Alliende nodded his understanding and left the skyman gazing up to the sky beyond sky, knowing well what he was seeing there.

The walk to the forecap of the skyborough was a quiet one, the clean-aired work section giving way to the low-fogged farm lands where a mist of water, air, and microbes did as best it could the work of the cycles of dirt and water. The grim-faced children who served as sky-farmers barely acknowledged the Handyman's presence as he passed through the croplands and reached the jitney portal.

Out through a membrane. Then another membrane sealed around him, dotting his skin with compressed air bulbs and action-reaction pods for maneuvering in unadorned space. Then out another membrane to where the rocket-jitney sat glued to the cap of the skyborough.

The jitney was a small vehicle capable of holding two dozen people at most. It used an old-fashioned chemical propulsion system, adequate for the task of going from skyborough to skyborough, or skyborough down to the just-above-the-atmosphere Stepping Stones.

To go up from the skyboroughs and out to the reaches of the solar system required the anti-matter powered caravels, carefully designed and carefully maintained technology, human in conception, skyvolk created (powered by anti-matter manufactured using alien processes, but never mind that).

To go down from a Stepping Stone required a space-plane modeled on Single-Sayer designs, again carefully engineered and maintained.

The jitneys by contrast were slovenly. They were always flightworthy, of course. No one would dare send out something that could not do its job; such a person would be executed as swiftly in space as he would be on Earth. But still, the jitneys lacked the precision and attention to formality and functionality that their higher and lower siblings enjoyed.

The jitney pushed off from Hoshimachi with a gentle release of gases. Then a few bursts of rockets aimed it down toward Stepping Stone Eight. The pilot and Tomaso Alliende were the only occupants, down not being a popular direction for the skyvolk. The pilot, Itsuko Lookdown, a middle-aged woman of Japanese descent, performed her duties more or less mechanically. She knew the routine, knew how much to burn when, knew which engines needed how much fuel to match the orbital velocity of the Stepping Stone. Dull routine the job was, but it had to be done until they could be independent from Earth. Then she could retire, or, hope of hopes, move up to work on the caravels, the true space ships, a job she could proudly pass on to her daughter, liberating young Britt from the child-labor of the farms.

Down to the Stepping Stone and rid of the ground-man, back up to the sky.

The maglev line did not go as far as the isolated township of Princeton, and Beatrice Van Leider had to hike through a few kilometers of woods to reach her goal. The maglev tram had been stopped and searched when it had crossed the recently established border between the North Jersey Collective and the Principality of Trenton. Van Leider, who had never been in the American Manders before, had been amazed to discover that Princeton had changed governmental hands seven times in the last ten years. She had known in theory about the ebb and flow of borders, the quick dissolution of trust and the cautious yet oddly swift establishment of new alliances that made up the liquid political landscape of south-of-Toronto America, but as always, theory was empty without practice and experience to connect it with reality. The soldiers who had come through, asked her business and studied her diploma suspiciously with mutterings of nooses under their breath, had given that drop of poignant reality she needed.

Already, as she hiked, she found herself composing a chunk of history.

> *The word Mander comes from Gerrymander and refers to a deliberate process of creating artificial borders to gain temporary political advantage. The American Manders are a curious artifact of the Troth-Breaking. While the initial process of volk-formation (groups of people who trusted each other banding together) was the same in America as in the rest of the world, the next stage of alliance formation occurred differently here.*

Van Leider broke through the last stand of trees and found herself suddenly faced with the streets of Princeton, an abrupt change from the wild fractal geometry of a hilly forest to the regular grid of an American city, a fall backward through almost three thousand years of geometric development, down from the heights of human and alien multi- and fractional dimensions to the basic lines, squares, and circles of Euclid.

Van Leider hesitated before stepping into the squares. She had come so far, traveled across Europe seeking a Chair to rest in, but finding none. The universities in Europe, ancient and modern, had each no more than a dozen Chairs, and those were held in the iron grips of old Professors, each with a chosen heir groomed and trained, awaiting only the moment when death would make an Emeritus of the sitter and dust would bring rest to the replacement.

But all through the universities and all along the roads where most of the Professors made their vagabond way, there were tales of Princeton, the university that had no limits on its Chairs, where one skilled enough in mind and voice could find rest and work in one seat. She had come following the trail of rumors (which must have been true since no Professor would dare speak falsely if a tree branch or a pole or any other lynch-worthy scaffold was nearby) to break through into this straightness.

One step from nature-cooled ground to heated pavement; she had arrived.

And was immediately challenged.

"Professor, student, or consult?" asked a grayish-skinned woman in a patched and faded brown uniform that billowed around her legs and forearms. She had spoken Footsprach, the language of the road.

"Professor," Beatrice said, extending her arm to show the burn of her diploma.

The woman glanced at it with a surprising swiftness. Should not Princeton's guards study credentials more carefully?

"Come to stay?" the guard asked, switching to archaic English.

"I hope to," Beatrice said, shifting her speech as

well. Among themselves Professors shunned the post-Troth-Breaking changes and admixes that had altered tongues across the world, preferring archaic English, Russian, or Chinese, or in pure indulgence ancient Latin, Greek, and Sanskrit.

"You can change chits for local currency at the exchange on Von Neumann Drive. Places to stay can be rented in the dorms. Copy your works into the Library in the IAS. Students can be found everywhere."

"Shouldn't I speak to the Dean before I take on students?"

The woman growled out a line clearly honed by many repetitions of this encounter. "You won't see the Dean until you have enough students."

Tomaso Alliende, left on the orbiting platform, did not bother to watch the jitney jump skyward. His concern was inside the half-kilometer disk of the Stepping Stone: his Pantechnicon van, his design, his creation, his constant work-project, the most custom-fitted of vehicles here amongst all the stored space planes. Each one of the other planes had been modified from the designs pervaded by the Dissociation. His Pantechnicon, by contrast, had been built from the ground up out of his thoughts and the work of his hands and his forge-manufactory now ensconced inside the vehicle.

Alliende floated through the vastness of the Stepping Stone, passing hangar after hangar, most empty, a few occupied with space planes. Most of those had not been used for some time, the skyvolk's fleet mothballed by disinterest in the lower world. Still, they continued to build Stepping Stones, acknowledging in their deeds but not their words that Heaven and Earth were not so easily sundered.

There you are.

Nestled in docking balloons was the flat-bottomed zeppelin shape of his Pantechnicon, its wings still outstretched (no need to reel them in until he landed in New York). A thing of layers one upon the other was his vehicle. Outermost was the protective skin made of the Path-Miner material doubly misnomered Forgediamond, which absorbed light and shed heat. In the creases of the Forgediamond were thin and narrow air and light readers copied from the Single-Sayers. These touched and felt space and atmosphere and gave a picture of the unique character of the Pantechnicon's environment. Interlaced throughout this outer skin was the recognition membrane which knew him down to his molecules in the way of the Method-Smiths, three alien technologies to make one membrane for the simple human purposes of comfort and security.

Beneath that transparent transplantation lay a shell of enameled ceramic painted over with pictures from smith-stories around the world. Here was Wayland avenging his imprisonment with two deaths and a seduction. Here was Gofannon tricked into slaying his nephew. Here were the svartalfar forging Mjölner. Here was Mwindo reforged in iron by his uncles that he might fight but not kill his father. Here was Hephaestus, falling, falling nine days to Earth.

The Handyman did not have nine days. His son was waiting for him. He touched his hand to the skin of the Pantechnicon. Membrane joined membrane. Adopted bacteria in his skin cells and the skin cells of the ship recognized each other. An opening dissolved in the first two layers, leaving the steel and aluminum hull beneath. In that was an archaic lock, a thing of wheels and tumblers, of keys and pressure, of two turns to the right and one to the left, a seal of doors that had hinges and seams.

Alliende floated through the open door, then closed its locks, both the human and the alien. The second skin he pulled off himself and tossed casually into the intake hopper of his forge-manufactory, which quickly broke its chemical bonds, adding or absorbing energy as needed, and sorted the atoms by charge and weight. It was an extravagance to have a hopper that broke things down to atoms. Most home manufactories simply sorted molecules and built using chemical processes. Few could afford the energy of building atom by atom.

Alliende checked over the forge as he did every time he entered the Pantechnicon. The storage bank was secure against the left wall. The customized home manufactory itself was solidly locked in place, just as it would be in the basement of any settled family on earth. The lenticle readers and the lenticles that stored the paradigms, the forms and instructions needed to create common parts and devices were locked up as normal. And his primary customization, the electrostatic box that read hand movements and translated them into internal shapes, was working perfectly.

It had been a simple thing to do. Connect an artist's tool to a manufactory and create an artisan's shop where whatever was conceivable in his imagination -- and realizable within six species' lexicon of materials -- could be made.

Sealed to the side of the manufactory was a single book, hand copied by the Handyman. It was the private journal of the woman who had invented the home manufactory using what had been the most advanced of human science and the deftest of engineering. She had thought to create the ultimate making machine from which anything wished for could be created. She had labored all her life and had pronounced her triumph a failure since it could not do what she wanted. The user of it, the programmer, had to know the character and properties of the materials put in it and had to know how the things were shaped on the molecular level. Anytime another atom was added to a molecule a surprise could result, strange macroscopic effects arising from a microscopic turning or a picoscopic quantum realization. Materials still needed to be studied, and even six distinct lines of research on six different worlds did not begin to exhaust the possibilities that lay in the structural permutations of a hundred plus elements.

Skill, in short, was still needed, and a deft hand and mind necessary for the sophisticated uses of the manufactory. As a result her wish machine had become a device to make what was known out of what was known. It had democratized manufacturing but had not removed the need for understanding.

Having checked out the forge, Alliende made sure the rest of his home was well. The library was still flight-sealed so that the books would not fall from their cubbyholes. The bed emerged from the floor when stroked, and remelded with the carpeting when again properly pressed.

The safe full of chits from all over the world had not been meddled with. Of course no one could use his chits, except for himself and Gregory. Tomaso had made sure all his wealth would be available to his son when the time came.

The kitchen and keep-fresh were also working, not that the bacteria that guarded his food were likely to go on strike or mutate away from their duties. Tomaso set some hot chocolate to steep and scraped in the seeds from a vanilla pod before sealing the cup against the twists and turns of travel. Theadora loved chocolate, though she could not get it very often. It would be ready by the time he reached New York.

The cockpit chair joined his skin, touching his

spine with the sensations of the outside. Tomaso twitched his index fingers and the balloons let go of the Pantechnicon. Out into the hangar, then down to the catapult and guide path on the underside of the Stepping Stone. A few deep breaths, lean back and let go.

Swift and sure, the four-winged vehicle was pushed out and down into empty space (the tides of solar activity having briefly shallowed the atmosphere to only nine hundred kilometers of air above the Earth's surface). Gravity, a few bursts of rockets, a turning downward, and the monster had him.

For Earth below him was a monster, a terrible ravenous beast, and gravity was its arms, its mouth, its grinding teeth. Terrible is gravity, and more terrible are the creatures it arms. Stars and planets are horrible beasts of mass and convergence, benders of space, distorters of time, monstrous corrupters of the void. Some are barren and simple in their cruelty, creatures of fall and crash. Some like Earth, sheathed in raging atmospheres, are monsters with breath of hurricane, with terrible heat upon the skins of the falling, burners of the things of space, destroyers of all who cannot make their way through the ever-increasing density of their auras.

Tomaso Alliende knew this monster well, knew her ways and her clutches, and his Pantechnicon was made to withstand her. Its skin could use and shed her heat, its body could bear her buffets, and its wings could play games with the consequences and air, and fall, fall, fall, to land safely upon mother Earth, monster no longer.

Earth. The Long Island Omniport where ships, submarines, hovercraft, zeppelins, maglev trams, strato-planes, and spaceplanes all congregated under the auspices of the Dissociation.

All omniports were at least partially under

Dissociation control. No fixed nations were seriously interested in international travel, and the footvolk had their own trails and ways of getting around. Only the Dissociation cared enough to maintain avenues of international access.

The Handyman withdrew the wings into the body of the Pantechnicon, membranes slithering into the parent skin of the van. Struts folded into struts into struts, the fractal skeleton of the four wings returning to four pods of seeds and methods waiting to be opened again when the Earth would let its child go.

A hoverskirt bloomed at the base of the Pantechnicon just long enough to carry it to the tracks, where the air-rider was replaced by superconducting ceramic skis. Then down the maglev line that led into New York, New York, New York. A quiet trip through the vineyards and sheepfolds of Long Island, then on to Manhattan where the hoverskirt again made an appearance so the Pantechnicon could travel through Central Park to rendezvous with its daughter vehicle in Sheep's Meadow.

It was late afternoon when the Handyman drove up to meet the Troupe of Guisers. His arrival interrupted rehearsal of a new play based on the fall of the Communist Dynasty and the founding of the Four Kingdoms in China. Theadora had chosen to play the part of the last Chairman of the Party and was in the middle of a tragic soliloquy punctuated by sound-puppetry that resembled the rebellious people banging on the gates.

"Why are they coming?" she said, raising her arms to the skies. "Are we worse than those who came before us? Will those who come after us be better? Or were the ancients we cast aside correct? Have we simply ruled past our time?"

There was a crash as the doors of the central committee chamber broke in and the mixed crowd of imperialists, democrats, ufnecks, and people who simply wanted the government to go away and let them have children and farm in peace, burst in to overwhelm the chairman with their polyglot cries.

"We serve the Daughter of Heaven!"

"Election! Election!"

"A ship is coming!"

"Bring back our sons! Give us back our daughters!"

As Theadora fell under the apparent weight of mist puppets, the stage went black.

"Brava, brava," cried the Handyman.

"Pater!" called Gregory as he pulled his hands from the control box and ran across the spring grass to his father's embrace.

"Uncle Tomaso," said Patricia Coskun-Overus as she emerged from the back of the stage, still wearing the silk robes of She-Who-Would-Be-Daughter-of-Heaven, back when she had been young and idealistic, not the canny old woman who now governed South China.

"Uncle Tomaso?" A fifteen-year-old boy with deeply brown skin, arched eyebrows, and a fluidity of movement that bespoke his actress mother and dancer father emerged from the wardrobe compartment of the Guisers' van. Karl Coskun-Rainbow waved. "Uncle, there's something wrong with the weave in the manufactory."

"I'll fix it before I leave, Karl," the Handyman said as he put his son down and held out the box and chit he had carried down from the skies. "Patricia, these are from your father. The rock is from the rings of Neptune, which should complete your collection, and the chit is for travel to Skyborough Uberton for the Fair in January."

Patricia Coskun-Overus took the box and stared at the plain stone which had circled the farthest giant child of Sol for billions of years. The rock held her attention in the same fashion that the sight of Theadora could hold Tomaso's. Patricia's face grew pensive and wise as if the age of the stone called to her and fed her upon its lasting. Then she looked at the chit and the enchantment of the ages broke. Her visage became young delight entire. "The Fair, and I can see Father. Mother, Father's invited me to the Fair."

"Then you must certainly go, Patricia," said Theadora Coskun as she stepped out from the stage. In the darkness she had changed her clothes. She emerged wearing a gown of glimmering beads sewn together by fiber-optic thread, so that when light struck one bauble it skimmed around and flowed through the whole dress. The shades of afternoon, the gleams of sun-yellow and cloud-filtered orange flickered and flew around her, deifying her appearance. On her head was a tiara woven of thin strands of gold and silver, platinum and copper, a crown fit for the queen of Heaven and Earth, gifts from the Handyman, the work of his hands and mind, the work of worship.

"Te adora," Tomaso Alliende said as he reached out his hand and drew the actress toward him. "Monster," he whispered into her ear.

"Muse," she whispered back.

"What's the difference?" he said as he led her arm-in-arm into the Pantechnicon.

"Rehearsal's obviously over for the afternoon," Karl said with the worldly wisdom of teenage. "Who's for a game of Go?"

"I'll play," said Gregory. "You want to play the winner, Tricia?"

"No, thank you," Patricia said. "I want to study about this rock. I wish Beatrice hadn't left."

"She said her pilgrimage was over," Karl said, and there was a distaste in his voice, a hint of objection to the notion that travel could ever be done with. "She was with us to get to Princeton. Now we won't see her again."

But Karl Coskun-Rainbow was wrong. As the sun set over Sheep's Meadow Professor Beatrice Van Lieder, her head downcast and her pace slower than stately, slower than weary, slow as sorrow, walked back across the grass to the two parked vans.

Tomaso Alliende and Theadora Coskun emerged from the Pantechnicon, arms around each other to drink in the evening. But their idyll was broken by the Professor's return.

"Hail, *homo habilis triumphalis,*" shouted Beatrice Van Lieder as she neared the Handyman's vehicle. "Hail to the victor. The People of the Hand have finally won out over the People of the Voice."

"Professor?" Gregory's voice quavered. He did not understand why his teacher was shouting at his father, and what he did not understand made him wonder and seek to know.

"They have a way," Van Leider said. "At the shrine of Einstein, they have 'clevered' a way to make many Chairs. If you have enough local students to support you, you can have a Chair. There were Professors in the streets begging to teach, poaching each other's students, fighting among themselves for enough followers to sit down. They were camped out in the Shrine of Einstein, savaging each other with words just to get in."

Her voice broke, and Theadora dashed to her, not too fast lest she disarray herself beyond proper appearance. The actress took the Professor's arm and led her to a seat on the stage.

"They accepted my lineage, acknowledged me an academic. The Librarian copied my works into their library, books into books, lenticles to lenticles, voice records to voice records, copied me as if I were already dead. Then he shooed me out into the streets with the other hopefuls."

She turned her blazing eyes upon the Handyman, her voice falling back into archaic English. "The Hand has conquered. No one cares enough about us. We are called to consult and paid a pittance in chits. We teach the young but are distrusted. You can go anywhere and are rewarded handsomely."

"Beatrice," Theadora said, her voice gentled to persuasion, "I'm sorry you couldn't find a place. But you can still travel with us. The children need a teacher and the troupe still needs a fact checker, and we'll reward you with much more then a pittance."

"I'll stay, Theadora," Van Leider said, her anger cracking into inarticulate despair. Her students, hers, Theadora's children, her students, gathered around her, young Gregory looking with almost religious distress at the weeping icon of her face. Patricia, her hand offering a steady resolve, and Karl with grim recognition, the eyes of one who has seen despair turn to suicide and does not wish to see it again.

"Is this really father's fault?" Gregory asked.

Van Leider hid her face in shame. In her anger she had falsely accused, and her student had taken her words as truth. In bitterness she had committed the unpardonable sin of Professors, to deceive for one's own gain.

"No, Gregory," she said, dragging her voice back to life. She turned reddened eyes toward the Handyman. "I'm sorry, Tomaso. This isn't your fault. We did this to ourselves. We broke troth long before any of you knew it. Just as I just did."

"But you learned better," said Theadora, and her voice carried forgiveness and hospitality.

Quint Hillard is in Burst.

Hanging from the World Tree.

Centered in the Fractal Mandala.

Seated [Lucifer-like {fear of sin and pride}] in the Chair of God.

Body in chair [left arm stiff - fingers relaxed; legs melded with chair membrane; head cushioned [throwback to pre-adoption of epilepsy [seizures as a child [operation put off by Grandmère {All memories of Grandmère}; adoption as Moment-Keeper Guest]]]] Guesthouse monitors [children still flying; Elsbet in the Method-Smith house {All memories of Elsbet [Princess Elsbet and her loyal knight Sir Quint] [Distance to Wave-Love ---]}] Meeting State [View of the universe as seen from High-Talker. Spherical view of all objects visible in all ranges known. Markers for stars of the known intelligent species. All transmissions being received [Moment-Keeper transmission {Status of Moment-Keeper world and the sender of this Burst [Disputes begun in the deep ocean between the Yet-to-be-made-young about whether Human Moment-Keeper Guests would be intelligent because they can Burst [But they can't really Burst, they have separate nerve and muscle tissue; their Burst is an illusion since they only turn part of themselves over to perception instead of having their entire physiologies turn into awareness and thought in a moment of Burst, then into all action in a moment of Wave.] [But they can create the perception of moments by their minds folding the memories into a single fractal.] [But [But [But]]] Meeting State produces nineteen offspring, youthens thirty of the elders, produces Burgeon Spike of growing dispute. Matings carry the discussion on to land and into space] [Pass through of the Long Wave. Gravity distortion, time confusion, occlusion of lens-patches] [New ocean poked into being on inner planet, colonists settling down] [Molecular details for Patch designed to sort heavy metals, also serves as neutron radiation shielding.] [Branching imposed on ideological Burgeon Spikes permits multiple interleaved structure for formulating mass views and |Model Failure: cannot Burst this fractal branch ?Political Parties? ?Artistic movements? ?Midwife techniques?|--]}]] [Cool day outside {Memories of every day of Quint Hillard's life, all the weather he had ever seen} Smell of tea brewed. Reach out arm.]

Arm moves. Quint Hillard is in Wave.

Or would be in Wave if humans had Wave.

Quint Hillard picked up his teacup with his left hand and his stylo-etcher with his right and stopped. One action at a time, one thought at a time, that was the way back to human thinking.

Sip the tea, tastes good. Put the cup down. Put the etcher on the pad and engrave. Start with the understanding given. That was the way, that was the way he had been taught to linearize the simultaneity of Burst-mind. First understanding, then the gifts, then anything else it was worth the effort to poke holes in the world about.

Not poking holes, writing:

> *A new aspect of fractal-thinking in Burst was presented. This branching relates to social groups and is intimately tied in with the still-not-understood Moment-Keeper social structures. Several new pieces of technology described, details encoded on accompanying lenticle. Suggest trading them to nations with major mining concerns. Still no closer to Meeting State.*

Quint Hillard stood up from the chair and stretched his limbs, moving each part of his body in turn. The inventory was necessary after the separation of voluntary and autonomic nervous systems which kept him from flailing around and hurting himself, as well as preventing every pain receptor in his brain from firing when Burst came upon him. He was all right, a little hungry perhaps and there was an ache in him -- oh, yes, Elsbet, he had seen her in the outside cameras. Elsbet, his wife was home.

"Elsbet," Quint shouted into the air where she flew with their sons. "My swan-queen, come down to your ground-bound knight."

Such a long way to go from teasing her as a child, calling her princess because her father was ConCensor. Now she had the job, so naturally a royal promotion came with it. He had even had a crown made for her, a towering coronation of gold-plated copper oak leaves with glass balls and carved crystal ornaments. She kept it, but only wore it for him.

Elsbet swooped down, brushing his shoulder with her left-fore wing, looped thrice and landed on the grass near the Moment-Keeper house.

"Children," Elsbet called to her sons. "Time you went in for your lessons. Sean, I want you able to count the bugs in the rose garden tonight. Julian, you need to be able to count all the stores downtown including everything they have to sell and the kinds of customers they let."

"Can't we fly more?" Sean called.

"Flying is the Smooth of the Single-Sayers, counting uniques is the Sharp. You need--"

"The Sharp upon the Smooth; the Smooth under the Sharp," Sean and Julian called as they flew across the Guesthouse and landed on the high roof of the Single-Sayer home.

Quint watched his sons with a touch of melancholy. Neither of them had inherited the defect adopted into gift needed to be Moment-Keeper Guests, so both had followed their mother's adopted species.

Alien to him was his family as he was alien to them, but still he and they were together. None of the other Guests had thought a cross-adoption marriage would work, none but Grandmère, who was never surprised at anything her adopted grandchildren did.

Elsbet Chan leaned her flying shell against the cushioned waiting couch that sat outside the Moment-Keeper house and embraced her husband groundling to groundling. Her grip was tight, something more than happiness at the reuniting.

"What's the matter, Elsbet?" Quint asked.

Elsbet looked around her just as an actor might in one of those old fashioned conspiracy plays. "Can we talk inside, Quint?"

"Of course," he said and took her in to the private rooms of the Moment-Keeper house. Balloon-padded walls and no sharp edges as was the custom, neutral tan colors, a quiet place to all appearances.

"Quint, did you know the Method-Smiths have interstellar ships?"

Quint considered the question carefully. He knew so much, but it was hard to get to what he knew when he was in Wave. All the beautiful fractal trees and passages that skeletally supported the omniscience of Burst turned into invisible connections of memory in the fallibility of human recollection. Interstellar ships. No one had those. There were too many logistical difficulties. First, there was the amount of antimatter it would take to get a good size ship up to an appreciable fraction of the speed of light [Up the Arch, as the Path-Miner image went], and second, the size of the ship itself, to travel from star to star, required having a portable ecosystem that would not be replenished. No, not possible.

But weren't there memories of visitors to the Moment-Keeper world from the four other alien kinds, and weren't there Moment-Keepers who had gone off on such expeditions? Yes, there were a few, two to five of them every -- [so hard to translate conceptions of time from the Moment-Keepers who did not truly measure it to the humans who had once been obsessed with the careful tracking of time] -- some stretch of time on the order of centuries. Yes, there were a few ships, and yes, only the Method-Smiths had invested the effort, physical and mental [Wave and Burst, though the Method-Smiths had their own thoughts as to what the real dichotomy was] and the planetary resources needed to make such ships. The Long Wave, that was a ship. It had been near the Moment-Keeper world only thirty-five years ago when the message Quint received today had been sent].

"Yes, apparently I do know that," Quint said. "How did you find out?"

"Ali told me. He said one of the ships is coming here. It should arrive in twenty-four years."

"That's not a lot of time to prepare the people," Quint said, remembering the history of riots and the simmering ufneck undercurrent. "What's the Dissociation going to do?"

"I haven't told the other officers yet. Ali asked me to wait until all the Guests know about it. Tomorrow evening he's bringing us together."

"Oh," All the Guests, all the human images of the five alien species, each coming from their own isolated existences learning to be unlike each other, coming together to learn from each other and decide upon a course of action. A seemingly impossible conjunction, yet the Method-Smith Guests had a way to forge the confabulation. "Shifting Speech always gives me a headache."

"Not me," Elsbet Chan said.

"I know. My queen is perfect and unflappable."

"Et mon chevalier est sans peur et sans reproche."

The lights in the room grew briefly brighter.

"Someone's waiting outside," Quint said as he released his wife from a long embrace.

A little while later, Elsbet Chan and Quint Hillard strolled out of the Moment-Keeper house to find Marie waiting and enjoying the afternoon shade of the great ash tree that rose to equal the house, the World Tree, the Moment-Keeper Guests called it. From its branchings they learned the basics of fractal thought needed to Burst properly.

"Grandmère awaits," Marie signed.

"Thank you," Elsbet responded.

In the semi-private house over the ancient bunker that had protected Constance Marchant and the other first Guests from rioters who would not listen to reason, Elsbet Chan stepped into the distant-meeting booth. Image mist filled the small room, lights played upon her, lenses gathered her reflection, sounding boards her speech. A moment, then an image sent from Siberia through the skyvolk's communication channels coalesced in the mists.

Elsbet Chan faced the thin woman whose grey-green skin and aqua hair bespoke the microscopic bargains she had made to retard the effects of age, to push back death until her chosen moment came. She was dressed in a light blue linen tunic that went down to her ankles. No doubt she cut a figure in the chills of Siberia just as she did everywhere else.

"Elsbet, for what have you called?" Grandmère said in tones sharpened over decades of choosing and teaching.

"For two things, Grandmère. First, Ali asks that you come home immediately."

"Immediately? I did not choose the boy for the methods of rudeness."

"Grandmère, it's important."

"Very well. Eh bien. And the other reason?"

"Grandmère, I met a young man named Feather.

He seemed to be from one of the Manders. It's hard to place his voice, but ConCensus indicates he came from one of the salvage towns around Ghost-Vegas. He claims you tried to recruit him and he ran away. He thinks the aliens are monsters. He thinks we're monsters."

"Was he very frightened?" Grandmère asked.

"Yes, and he was trading everything he had in order to be heard. He's desperate for others to listen to him."

"Splendid. Listen to what he has to say. I'll come and collect him soon enough."

"Grandmère, he's terrified of you."

"Of course, dear. The first of his methods is the person who runs and hides because there are monsters in the world. He's learned well. Now I can gather him in."

"He's to be a Method-Smith?"

"Wasn't it obvious? If you would stop counting the what of things and start watching the how, you would learn what we're doing."

"If you say so, Grandmère. I'll talk to him this evening. May I bring Quint?"

Grandmère shut her eyes for a moment and paced briefly through the room at the other end of the transmission. The image of her left side curved oddly outward as she came too close to one of the lenses.

"Take Quint. See how Franklin -- I beg your pardon. Feather, he's Backlorned himself. Good -- See how Feather reacts to him."

In the privacy of the Pantechnicon, Tomaso Alliende embraced the Muse who never left him, the inspirer of his life, the mother of his only child, hoping to find a human woman. But despite the touch and the conjoining, the mingling of breath and bodies, the joining of hands, feet, voices, and all the other human externals, still he could not find the woman in Theadora.

But she found him, as she always did, found him, touched him, raised him up, exalted him, reminded him in look and word and act of all the things he could be and was becoming, raised him and then commanded him.

"Talk to Beatrice," she said. "Tell her about the Crazy Old People. She needs a place to settle."

"You want her to live in my mind?"

"No, in the stage in your mind," Theadora said. "She will find her own settlement there."

"You're one of the spike-covered horrors from the deep?" Feather said as he stared at the gentle, almost-but-not-quite handsome face of Quint Hillard who had seated himself on the visitor's couch in the outer room of the hostel suite.

"When I can be," Quint said. "But it requires a lot of mental preparation and I have to trigger a seizure. Otherwise I'm far too human."

"How can you joke about it? Don't you know they made you a monster?"

"Tell us about the monsters," Elsbet Chan said. "That's what you traded for. So tell us."

"Do you know how hard it is to be human?" Feather asked after taking a few breaths and a drink of water. "It's like walking on a knife-edge. Every fault, every cruelty, every moment of desire or lust or melancholy can pull you away from humanity. Do you know how many people out there aren't people at all?

I've walked the roads with the footvolk, I lived with many groups of handvolk, I've even talked to some of the voicevolk. So few of them are human. They keep falling away into mindless animalism or angry demonism. A lot of them want to be gods."

"It sounds like you're talking about the Predators and the Deceivers," Elsbet Chan said.

"The Predators and Deceivers were monsters," Feather acknowledged. "And there are a lot of people who would be like them if they weren't afraid of the mob and the noose. But there are other monsters.

"For a year I was taught by a wandering Professor. He was so caught up in his theory of how my mind worked that he paid no attention to me. When my father found out that he was practicing psychology, he shot him. He was a monster of the Voice.

"My cousin when we were boys caught a muscle disease, debilitating. They gave him Adoptionases and the bacteria began to feed his muscles. He became a brute and a bully."

"But that wasn't the Adoptionase, that was him," said Quint.

"It was him succumbing to the temptation of his changed body. Monster-temptations are everywhere. And you, you Guests. You don't just give in to them, you embrace them, you take up inhumanity. You give your children to it. Do you understand me? Do you even hear me?"

"We hear and understand you, Feather," Elsbet said. "We don't see what we are as you do. But we have heard you. You can stay here until the chit runs out, and if you need to stay longer, contact me at the ConCensor's office."

Feather nodded numbly, as if the effort of speaking had drained all the spirit from him. He barely had the energy to see his guests out the door.

"He's a Method-Smith all right," Quint said as he took Elsbet's hand, warming it against the night air.

"Grandmère worked hard on him," Elsbet said. "He's Backlorn, but he talks about his family. She's made him want to belong to a volk and a family. Once he's turned he'll come to us."

"Maybe," Quint said. "But I think Grandmère's done something deeper there. Why the longing for family? It doesn't seem needful."

"You're asking why a Method-Smith does something?" Elsbet Chan said. "Why waste your mind on whys when all they care about is hows?"

"You're right. I wonder what his human-monster method will become when Grandmère's done with him. I wonder how he'll act."

"And on whom?" Elsbet said.

3. Boundaries

Long ago Constance Marchant went into the Ocean, there to dissolve her life into its methods. It had been hard to find the Ocean. Many years she had searched for it, envying the real Method-Smiths whose world's waters comprised one vast Capable Lattice -- not exactly a single living intelligent entity, but a composite means of creating and reabsorbing life and of choosing what to create and what to dissolve. When a Method-Smith had come to the extent of its actions, when it had done all that it had been generated for, it would go back into the Ocean, bringing the methods it had created to aid in carrying out its fundamental method and adjoining them to the lattice of life.

But Earth's oceans, though they had brought forth life as the Method-Smith ocean had in that circumstance when the interaction of molecules began the dance of evolution, had gone a different way, the way of cells and containment, of genotype and phenotype, of essence and manifestation. Although

Earth's waters held many forms of life that would have been happy to consume Constance Marchant, that consumption would have destroyed instead of preserving the means she had developed. Sharks might dine upon her body, but they would not emerge from the meal capable of translating alien transmissions to human speech, or of finding the proper kennings by which to convey the character of aliens to human hearers, nor would they speak in the Shifting Tongue.

For Constance Marchant and for every Method-Smith Guest who had come after her, finding the preserving Ocean consumed a great deal of their thought and time. Constance Marchant had finally made her Ocean. It was the satellite called the High-Talker. There the first Guest had gone in her old age, and there her body had joined molecule by molecule to the adopted viruses which encoded the messages of the alien peoples and to the living polymers which carried commands and contemplations from the Patch-antenna-transmitters into the methods of her mind. Her senses had slowly dimmed and the humanity had faded from her thoughts in the intervening decades since, until there was little left of Constance Marchant, the woman who had heard and understood and changed. But the methods of her mind remained, the speaking to the stars, the naming, and the Shifting Speech which she gave to the later Guests.

The Shifting Language was a means of listening to and a way of speaking with those whose thinking was vastly unlike one's own. At its base it required finding common ground of subject matter to act upon with different means of thought and word, and of accepting those means as coequal with one's own even if one did not comprehend the action of the other method.

Constance Marchant had found the seeds of the Shifting Language in simple human courtesy. She had nurtured these seeds in her half-alien mind and grown a tool by which one alien-human could comprehend an alien alien-human.

It was not hard to practice when two different kinds of Guests got together to talk through a matter. But when they all conjoined the images of five different species, then the Shifts and turns became a great strain, and the presence of Constance Marchant as overseer of the converse was needed. Then did she shine down by microwave transmission into the Shifting House and govern the meeting of all thirty-eight guests.

The light of Constance Marchant, pale blue on the seated Guests, deep gold upon whichever of them was to speak, shone upon the discussion. Her voice, old and distant, would occasionally interrupt from a voice-panel, offering a word here, a translation there, a bar or a bridge to discussion as the method demanded of the situation.

"The ship is a means of drawing the multiple adoptions closer," Grandmère was saying, her grey leathery skin showing a brilliant mottling under the Marchant light. "It is a Tractase, a smoothing out of every process of conjoining. We Guests are the Permiole of humanity. We must let in the Permiate of the ship and some of us must go out as Permiates to the alien worlds and enter their Permioles."

The flower-ringed room with its deep, comfortable couches was soaked in blue light. No one was designated to speak. Grandmère had pronounced.

All those present had been gathered by her, or their parents or grandparents had been. The Guests one and all found it hard to challenge what she said. There was a blue time of settling. Then the gold light settled upon Elsbet Chan, the shade pointing up one of her ancestries and hiding the others, making her look for all the world like a figure in Chinese Opera.

Marchant commanded Elsbet to take in the

Method-Smith words of Grandmère and respond as a Single-Sayer. Permiate-Tractase-Permiole. Elsbet folded this up in her mind and sealed it with the Shifting Language, then she opened the packet of thought, unsealing as ConCensor.

"To draw Earth closer to the others is good, but to participate in the ship we will have to build our own habitat. According to the instructions of the Method-Smiths we will need to make a small skyborough that will travel outwards. But this skyborough would have no access to Earth for needed supplies, no means of correcting errors in the ecosystem. I don't know if the undertaking is possible."

The gold light shifted to a boy, fourteen years old, and his father, a man prematurely grey with long supple hands calloused from much digging at rocks. Both were pale of skin from their Path-Miner underground lives. Neither had a name (the father having given his up, the son never having been so shackled), for the Path-Miners had no names -- in truth they had no words, no isolated ideas at all. Their thoughts were continuous flows, paths and hums through the world. They and the Moment-Keepers seemed the most alien of the aliens. However, unlike the Moment-Keepers, there were no genetic quirks lying about in the varietals of humanity that could create preformed Path-Miner Guests.

Only two means had been found to reach the Path-Miner continuous mind-work. The first had involved recruiting from Buddhist, Christian, and Taoist monasteries, searching among the contemplatives for those who were skilled in silencing their own minds, but not so good at going forth to great awareness or communion. Half-successful monks and nuns became the first generation of Path-Miner Guests. They had sat together in underground caves, their skins covered with adopted photosensitive lichens which had joined their nervous systems, giving them the full-body sight of the Path-Miners. They had sat and counted away their thoughts until they had heard a hum, a music in their minds. Then had they learned to move and act and hear and see with that hum as their guide.

Three years they had labored in the undoing of human thought and speech before they turned their ears to the interstellar hum of the true Path-Miner communications, and then what wonders had unfolded, what paths beneath and upon the crusts of worlds, what sorties to the savored heat of vulcanism, what glimpses of the stars above, what sculptings of terrain. They had followed the carved paths that taught the minds of those who traveled them and watched the smooth silences in forgetting and walking the untrod ways.

But the first generation paled in understanding before the second. The children born to the failed monks and nuns had never learned to struggle against words and individual thoughts. They had taken in the hum earlier than babies take in words. And when the time came, that time in development where what emerges from the new-formed mouth is a continuous hmmhmmummimmiiimmmemm, then were the babies taught the unbroken speech of the Path-Miners. And having learned this humming tongue, oh, what the children gleaned as they grew, understandings that their parents could not hear from a species deep in understanding who saw the world as a continuous echo from which little path-makers emerged and then returned.

The half-grown children gave much to humanity, computers that had not individual bits of data but smooth fields that flowed and changed and modeled weather and oceans and the four fields of the universe with a clarity that the ragged-edge of digitization could not approach. They crafted invisible guides and curves and channels that moved heat and cold around with the deftness with which wire moved electricity and fiber-cable carried light. They presented a panoply of materials so resistant to the elements that probes could be sent to the deepest parts of Sol's gas giants without being crushed and lanyards fashioned to tame and reign in comets.

But all of this was third-hand. The Path-Miners told the children, the children told their parents, and the parents told the world. There was hope that the children when they grew older would be able to learn the Shifting language and perhaps a measure of human speech with its isolated ideas, but for now they needed their parents to translate the mmnninnshhhhunnooon.

"The echo of the ship will grow loud as it comes near," the father translated for his son. "It will draw the people back into fear and noise. They will forget the times since the Troth-Breaking."

The light shifted to where the six Band-Braider guests sat. The eldest of them had been a Guest for but twelve years, not much time to acclimate to this society of alien societies. The six of them, normally deaf to the world, wore hearing induction membranes over their ears for this one occasion. Marchant's gaze settled on Marie and she spoke up, signing to focus her mind as she spoke.

"The ship is a lantern that will evolve our people. There must be guidance to the nurturing or sports will emerge and attack the settled groups. But also we must go on the ship. We must climb the Arch to see the world from above. Without that we cannot know light or truly evolve."

The light from above flicked to Quint, who was trying to keep his head from throbbing. Too many points of view to handle in Wave and he couldn't shift to Burst; he had to be at least partly human to handle the Shifting Language. Constance Marchant wanted him to speak, to give the Moment-Keeper perspective without becoming a Moment-Keeper. Take a deep breath, look at the big picture.

"We Guests need the ship to see those we are copying and become better at our tasks. But does Earth need the ship to come? Humanity has been kept from the effects of Species Shock because of us. We've given them the gifts of the stars without them having to see how truly alien the others are. We're not just a filter, we're a blind. When the ship comes the blind is going to fall and humanity will have all its hidden assumptions thrust in front of it like a harshly lit mirror."

"Species Shock is inevitable," Grandmère said, just as the light shifted to her. "And an Adoptionase is being prepared for it. You met him yesterday, I believe."

The light shifted to Ali Mustafa, who had been sitting quietly as was the custom. The leader of the Guests did not speak until a method of action was needed. "Grandmère is right about the inevitability of Species Shock, and if she is preparing to deal with the troubles we must take up the opportunity. Earth must be prepared to adopt the ship-method when it comes. That will take considerable effort. Elsbet, you must speak to the officers of the Dissociation and convince them that the work must be done."

Marchant's eyes looked down upon Elsbet Chan, studying her in her dual role as Guest and ConCensor. The Dissociation could not exist without a Single-Sayer Guest in that position. The government of the volks required that each group and each person on Earth be understood on its own terms. Only Single-Sayer mathematics could do that.

Up until this moment, the need for a Guest as one of the chief officers of the world government had been mutually acceptable to Guests and Dissociates.

Would that change when the Guests asked so much of the Dissociation, would all the gifts they had given to Earth be enough to pay for the social pressure humanity would muster against so much united work?

"I will speak to the others," said Elsbet Chan-Dunlevy-DeMarnier-Tienh and four lineages she did not care to honor. "But do you want me to threaten them with removal of our support if they do not help us, or do you want them to see the ship as good not just for the Guests but for the rest of humanity?"

Ali Mustafa sat still and thoughtful under the gold gaze. He was leader of the Guests. He was the method of Social Synthesis, the turning point of the Capable Lattice that was the Guesthouse, but his reach ended at the walls of the former university. Did he want to threaten? No. But he needed -- they needed -- the ship if the method of the Guests was to continue to live and grow.

"Earth will adopt the ship," he said at last, "if we can convince them that it will be a worthy stepchild and not a Reputation-ruining wastrel."

Roads are made by the People of the Foot, the precursors of the footvolk. The first such roads were game paths and migration routes. At that time every human being was a Person of the Foot. But then some settled down and became of the Hand or the Voice. They still had People of the Foot among them, but they did not realize they were of the Foot. They called them traders and bards, and said they were of the Voice. They called them itinerant workers and thought they were of the Hand. They called them soldiers and said they were the strength of the Voice enacted through the Hand. They called them beggars and said they were not People.

Outside the lands of the Hand and the Voice the true

People of the Foot still lived, but the People of the Voice called them barbarians. And since the People of the Voice wrote the histories, barbarians they were called ever after. The People of the Foot who lived outside simply added the countries and cities of the settled peoples to their migration routes and game paths. Sometimes they ignored, sometimes they traded, sometimes they raided, treating cities and villages as they would have treated a game-rich place, an oasis, or a sheltering cavern. What they did depended on what they needed, not what the things that lived there wanted.

For millennia power shifted back and forth between the Foot and the Voice and Hand. Barbarians raided, conquered, settled, became of the Hand and Voice, taking up the ways of the conquered. The Hand and the Voice spread until there was not one place on Earth open to the People of the Foot. Then . . .

Professor Van Leider's voice trailed off. For a little while the lenticle recorder waited for new words. When none came it turned itself off and sealed itself in its cocoon of silence and darkness.

Van Leider herself was watching in silence, looking out through the half-circle bubble at the front of the Pantechnicon, out at the wide, smooth road that wended its way westward from New York through the forests and orchards, farmlands and towns, through the ever-shifting political boundaries of the American Manders, now turning up along Lake Erie toward Detroit-Windsor, the southwestern gate of Toronto's hegemony. The road, this road, had been laid down by the Dissociation for the ease of the footvolk. Roads well-traveled the Dissociation made, and roads that were needed between places that could not be kept separate. Few of either kind of road were actually made. Most places were lacking the amenities of foot travel, being easily accessed by air or water alone. But the People of the Foot persevered. They walked all over the world, the peddlers, the itinerants, the homeless, the wanderers, the pilgrims, the bandits, the actors, singers, and dancers, and the Professors.

How could she write the irony without the words biting back at her? How could she record the Troth-Breaking and its results, how show that the folly of the People of the Voice had cost them their homes and powers, had sent them out to be among the People of the Foot, leaving the towns and cities to the Hands that made them?

She looked out at her fellows upon the road. The Guisers' van was ahead of the Pantechnicon, weaving its way through the many methods of the footvolk. Most of the travelers walked, some rode in hovercraft, a few on one-person tricycles pulling small cartloads of goods. Some few drove antique solar-autos -- slowly, of course, though the vehicles themselves were capable of much speed.

The Handyman slid the Pantechnicon to the left side of the road to avoid a family which had stopped to rest and eat. Van Leider looked at him driving quietly, alone with his thoughts, and wondered why he had asked her to ride with him, and why she had agreed. She had only met him a few times while she traveled with the Guisers. They had been cordial but not close, certainly not close enough for him to ask her into this mobile bastion that served as his home. Why had he invited? Why did she agree?

"Has Theadora ever talked to you about me?" the Handyman said, breaking the silence.

Theadora. That explained everything, the actress had primed Alliende to ask, and . . . Van Leider had to admit it, Theadora had convinced her to accept. Without saying an explicit word, without assertion or even insinuation, with her manner alone, Theadora had convinced the Professor to ride with the Handyman, the Voice to join the Hand upon the way of the Foot.

"A little."

"Did she ever tell you how I keep from getting lost in my work?"

"Lost in your work?"

"Like you do," Alliende said. "You're recording a history because you think it's important. The work alone matters to you, not what use anyone will make of it."

"Use is a thing of the Hand," she said, holding back the arrogance of centuries, modifying her voice down to a neutral tone.

"True, but it's also of the Voice, the Foot and the Mind. And if you don't think about the use of your work, aren't you only working for your own gratification?

"I know what being caught up in yourself is like. Before Theadora found me I was a kid who tinkered with things. I read all the books, studied all the manuals, went to hear the traveling Professors talk about the constituents of the universe and how they were arranged to make useful things. I talked to the ConCensus Taker in New York and got snatches of Guestsprach and alien thought, but all I was doing was playing. I was playing with thoughts and hands to get away from the village."

"What village?"

"The village where people live."

"Is this some story of Theadora's, one of those allegories she likes?"

"She didn't make this one up, I did. And up to now only Theadora and Gregory have heard it. It's how I remember who I am. The village is what I wanted to tell you about. Whenever I get lost in my work or my wealth, I remember who I am."

"Who are you?"

"I'm the Crazy Old Man who Lives with the Fire. I live north of the village in a cave with fire and metal and stone and charcoal. My back is bent and my legs are crippled. I live with monsters and the people think of me as a monster. But when they need shoes for their horses, axes for the trees, wheels for their carts, stones for their mills, plows for their fields, and swords for their wars they come north out of the village to see me. They're afraid or ashamed when they come, but they need me. And I go into my cave and embrace the monsters of fire and metal, I burn my hands and my throat, I hurt my feet, and I come out with what they need."

Van Leider considered the image. Fanciful, impractical, ahistoric, yet compelling. She could see Tomaso Alliende, his half-handsome, half-flare-mottled form stooped over an ancient forge instead of working the modern manufactory in the back of the van, could see the scars on him coming from a single fire, not a hundred little accidents.

And the image tickled her somehow. It was a simplification of the world, a model that fit well with his life and his efforts. It placed the important things, work, danger, and who he was working for, in front of him and hid the irrelevancies. It was a poetic model but it had much the same character as a mathematical one.

It was geometric. It measured and laid out the world as he needed it laid out.

"But I'm not the only Crazy Old Person around the village," The Handyman said. "East of the village is the Crazy Old Woman with the Plants and Herbs who feeds the people and heals the sick. South is the Crazy Old Man Who Talks to The Things No One Can See. And west of the village is the Crazy Old Woman Who Knows Everything, Both What Has Happened and What Will Happen."

Alliende paused and turned the Pantechnicon gently rightward to cross over a bridge.

"That's who you are," he said.

"A crazy old woman?" Van Leider said, exhaling

irony. "I'm only thirty-six."

"You became crazy and old as soon as you started traveling with your teacher, just like I became crazy and old the moment I put a stick in a fire and watched it turn to embers. You could have stopped, could have become sane and young again, until they put a library-pack on your back and branded a diploma on your arm, just as I could have stopped until I met Theadora."

Van Leider considered the elaborated drawing Alliende had just put before her. A village like a square with four points outside and lines of travel, roads drawn between each of the points and the center of the square. Four Crazy Old people doing all the strange work that the village required. The model was pretty, certainly, but could it be used for anything, was it a work of art or a work of work?

"So how does this help me?" the Professor said. "I'm sitting in a hut outside a village. I know everything that happened and I tell people what will happen. So what good does thinking like that do me?"

"Tell me," said the Handyman. "What happens if you take away the village?"

Beatrice Van Leider imagined the scene, though for some reason she saw Theadora playing the role of the Crazy Old Woman Who Knows Everything. The village went away. The roads vanished, leaving four isolated points, four dots in a plane. Two dimensions had been annihilated with the loss of the square. Isolation, isolated knowledge, isolated fire, isolated herbs, isolated gods.

No people would cross the emptiness to come to the Crazy Old Woman. No one wanted to know the past or hear about the future. No one brought food or clothes in return for knowledge. No one presented children to be taught. Eventually, in a display of sadness with gestures of bitter disappointment, the

Crazy Old Woman with Theadora's grace lay down and died.

"We depend on the village, on the people," she said at last.

"And they on us," said the Handyman. "But you forgot that. You thought they belonged to you, that their support was your birthright. That's why the People of the Voice have gone wandering. You over-claimed, you grew arrogant."

"That's not all of it," Van Leider said, her fingers poised over the lenticle recorder. "We were arrogant long ago. It's been thousands of years since we first claimed that the People of the Voice were the People of the Mind. We said we were thinkers and you doers. We didn't want to be just the workers of speech whose minds were tuned to words and meanings, while you were workers of things whose minds were turned to tools and purposes."

Van Leider realized that she had shifted to a lecturer's voice. With a caress upon the recorder, she began again to enunciate her thesis. Words of history came out while the Handyman drove on.

Patricia Coskun-Overus drove the Guisers' van while her mother rested and her brothers played Go in the surprisingly spacious living cubby that served as changing room when the stage was set up. Night fell as she drove and the stars came out over the road.

Patricia looked up to see and name the stars which seemed to circle the Earth, and the not-stars which truly did. Reality and appearance. Professor Van Leider talked a lot about them, warning that reality was the thing to pay attention to, that appearance was simply an accident. But when she taught Patricia how to look at the sky she dealt with its appearance, naming stars and constellations, projecting the four dimensions of reality into a two dimensional sphere.

Patricia's mother, on the other hand, refused to distinguish between the two.

"Appearance can change some of reality," Theadora had said after Patricia had talked to her about the Professor's lessons. "And reality always masks itself in appearance. Why worry about the difference?"

As with most of Theadora's rhetorical questions, this one seemed to have hidden depths of enigma. Patricia loved her mother deeply and knew her mother loved her, but she sometimes wondered what kind of life Theadora was preparing her and her brothers for. Theadora had taught them to act, had taken their talents and shown them how to use them on the stage (and in Gregory's case behind the stage), but she had also said that she did not expect them to stay with her and play the supporting roles in her life.

"Find your own stars," she had said.

Karl Coskun-Rainbow slid into the seat next to his sister. He moved so silently when he wanted to that she rarely heard him coming.

"Where's Gregory?"

"He beat me in a game, then I lowered his handicap one stone and he lost, so he's gone to do the reading the Professor gave him and think about his game."

"Do you think Uncle Tomaso can help the Professor?" Patricia asked.

"Mother says so," Karl said, then fell silent.

He looked out at the road while his sister scanned the stars.

In the back of the van, young Gregory read and reread the narrow bands of Euclidean proof and felt his hands itch, knowing in the feel of things and the experience of his father that no real thing was as thin as a line, as flat as a plane or as simple as a space. Everything in this ancient book met its limitations in reality. But he also knew that his father found much worth and help for his work in these ideas, so Gregory Coskun-Alliende settled down to learn these flat images, always remembering that they were as flawed as the puppets he made from light and mist, and as useful.

From her couch, Theadora watched, half-resting, but never fully sleeping, observing her children with satisfaction, but knowing they were not enough.

It was late at night when the two vans drove into Detroit-Windsor and settled down to camp near the bridge that joined two old cities into one.

The next morning the Troupe of Guisers was met by several local organizations that wanted to book performances and the Handyman was beset by a crowd of people with mechanical difficulties. In amongst these postulants was a smallish man with a bushy beard and a violet tunic that bore the seals of the Dissociation on it. He waited patiently until his turn came.

"I have a packet for you from the Marshall," he said to Alliende, holding up a seamless rectangle which unfolded itself at the Handyman's touch. Inside were a letter and a chit.

"Tell him I'll come soon," the Handyman said. The Marshall's Proxy nodded then faded into the crowd.

"I'm afraid I can't come with you to Gary-Chicago," Alliende said to the Troupe of Guisers as they dined al fresco that evening. "I have to go to Toronto in the next few days."

"What for, Father?" Gregory asked.

"I don't know. The Marshall's message was cryptic." The Handyman nodded to the Professor. "Beatrice, I forgot one. There's the Crazy Old Man Who lives in the Center of the Village and tells everyone else what to do."

Gabriello Benetti looked down at the listing of resources and in a wild mingling of Italian, Latin, and Friulian, cursed the day he had taken the position of Marshall. How could he be expected to muster the skills and dedication it would take to build a piece of interstellar craft in only a quarter of a century? He would have to construct three distinct volks to live on the ship which, thanks to the necessity of taking along an eco-system, would be large enough to allow the volks to follow their separate ways without too much mutual interference.

The logistics were nightmare-stuff. He would have to sort through the Professors to find those best skilled in the theories and he would have to deputize people to contact them. Under most circumstances the Professors refused to deal with the Marshallate even to the extent of avoiding the mail system. Their fear, well founded during the Troth-Breaking, of being absorbed by governments and changed into Predators and Deceivers for the ends of those governments could not be assuaged by any words of his, or even the Reputation of Honor.

Once he had found the Professors, he would have to hunt among the skyboroughs for the most practiced of mechanics and the wisest of skyfarmers and pilots. He would have to give the Handyman a chit of monumental worth in order to give him charge of the project. And was it worth it? Certainly the Guests thought so, but what else would they think? Honor wanted it as an enhancement of the Dissociation's Reputation -- if we can do this, the people will think we can do anything, she had said. The Trustee had agreed, since he saw this as an opportunity to consolidate the Dissociation and hopefully attract some of the Dissenting volks into Consent, though it was Benetti's opinion that the more likely result was heightened Dissent.

And what good would it do? It was not as if the aliens were coming to take them off to some stellar paradise, or to give them world saving devices, or to enlighten humanity as to its place in the universe. Benetti's parents had been ufnecks and he had grown up with their disappointment with the true messages from the stars. They had wanted gods to come down, not other -- very other -- people to speak to over the vast dark distances. They had wanted the human discoveries of the universe to be contravened by vastly more advanced beings, not essentially confirmed by others who thought radically differently and had wildly inhuman views of the world, but still confronted the same fundamental reality.

The ufneck retreat in the Friulian mountains had grown sour and embittered over the years of Benetti's youth as the Guests proved by communication, by dispensation of alien understanding, by the seemingly endless flow of new technology, that they did indeed understand the signals. One by one the ufneck families had left their cave-homes and gone down into the towns and cities of what had been Italy, Austria, Switzerland, and Slovenia.

They had expected to return in embarrassment to the lives they had left behind, or at least to find that the world was basically the same. Instead they confronted the reality of the Troth-Breaking, the worldwide failure of trust which had brought down nations, destroyed businesses, shattered religions, and broken illusions.

They had come out to find that the most basic of human societies, the volk, reigned everywhere. A volk was a group of people who trusted each other as individuals, not because they had grown up together or had the same ancestry or skin color or language, but because each had earned the other's trust.

Those ufnecks found that no one trusted them, and they had to slowly make their painful ways into the new societies, beginning with learning the new variations and meldings of language, the sprachs which had grown in a single generation of isolation.

Gabriello Benetti had come down at the age of fourteen, leaving his parents and sister behind, three of the nine stiff-necks who waited for the real aliens to come and vindicate them with holy guidance and miracle devices.

Benetti had come to Rome and, amazed at the wonders of the architecture and the delights of baroque design, had come to a church. He had not known what it was nor what the images of stone and glass, writing, and speech meant, but inside he heard this sermon from a priest who had gathered a volk around him.

"God made the universe to clump and cluster out of the primordial void. Within the clusters were smaller clusters, and smaller still within them, each formed by the hands of God. Clump upon clump the clay of God was molded, from super galaxies to galaxies to star systems, and in the systems clumping made planets, and on some of these planets there is life, and of those some are souled and blessed with the capability of looking out upon the world and seeing the handiwork of God.

"But between the stars was the trammeled emptiness, and God set down the speed of light as a boundary for all movement, saying this swift and no swifter. With that limitation he made the passage from star to star harder than any species would attempt, and he gave each band of souls safety, for no one could muster the forces of war to cross the star ways. Thus did God make nests for his fledgling souls.

But in the fabric of the universe, in the warp and weft of spacetime did he bring forth light, and light could bear words from nest to nest. Thus do we hear our fellows whose thoughts are strange to us, who see God as an echo or a state or a lattice of means. Thus are we enriched, and thus do we enrich them, for every view of the unknowable brings us closer to the knowing of it."

Except, Benetti thought, dragging himself from the past-moment which had freed him, that those who saw the whole of everything as a Capable Lattice (whatever that meant -- damn Guestsprach for its untranslatability) had built something that crossed the boundaries God laid down. And when they came, who would be there to greet them? Gabriello Benetti with a habitat to join their ship, maybe, if he could find amidst the ConCensus a Professor with proper understanding of ecology and among the skyvolk an engineer who could build a habitat that would not be permitted to spin (And why not? Nobody knew. The message had said it must not be spun for gravity). And if the Handyman would take the job of actually building the habitat. Such a marshalling of ifs.

Gregory Coskun-Alliende watched his father drive off with that strange mixture of longing and relief that he was, as yet, too young to understand. His father as a person was loving and instructive, but also painfully wounded by the work he did. The scars he bore hurt his son to see, and the concentration he gave to each matter before him was too fiery intense to be close to. But his father, as the Handyman, the richest man in the world, the greatest exemplar of what Professor Van Leider called the Dominion of the Handvolk, was easy to admire and worship.

Gregory's mother had taught him the effect of being worshipped. She was adored by everyone who watched her and loved intensely by his father, Patricia's father, Karl's poor sad dead father, and, Gregory had noticed, by Professor Van Leider. Each of them adored Theadora in their own way and strove to show her the value of their adoration. Gregory was confident that as he grew he would be able to give the Handyman that same manifest worship.

"Gregory." Professor Van Leider pulled him out of contemplation with the ancient voice of a schoolmistress. "Returning to the ellipse, we find many uses for this simple figure. The most famous is Kepler's law that planets orbit in ellipses."

Van Leider paused for two beats to let that sink in. "Provided," she said, "we ignore all other sources of gravity, the relativistic distortions of spacetime, and something the Path-Miners discovered which has not been well translated but which the Guests call white-stretching."

Guests and their alien teachings, Van Leider thought. How long would it be before they could be fully integrated into human thought? How long until we can profess them well enough to not need the Guests? Beatrice hoped it would be soon, but guessed that it would take decades at least, centuries more likely for the slow passages of light to bring species together and bring all understanding under the aegis of the Academia. Unless something happened to speed it up.

In the hostel room lay Feather, his every muscle twitching in fear, the sleep he hoped for dangling in front of him, tantalizing but beyond reach. The grandmother of monsters had come to see him, the grey-skinned horror with the voice that spoke Guestsprachlike French with a buzzard's caw, the breath that smelled like week-dead carcasses, and the words that cut into him.

"I adopted you long ago, Franklin Linder, or Feather if you wish. You are a Guest whether you know it or not, whether you Backlorn yourself or not. Wherever you have run you have done the work you were chosen for. You are the method of monster-making, and everyone you speak to has been touched by your method. Whoever you touch becomes a monster. Come into the Guesthouse and we will make you a greater method by far. You will be needed when the ship comes."

Monsters always said things like that. They always wanted you in their homes to work upon you, to eat you up, to chew your human bones and suck your mortal marrow. If you couldn't face them, couldn't slay them, then the only thing to do was run.

Feather pulled himself sluggishly from the bed, pushed his monster collection into his carry-sack along with the food he had been given (he had saved half of everything for travel), and left the hostel, out into the night. Back to the People of the Foot, back to the goblin markets. He had to warn everyone that a ship was really coming.

"Our messenger has left," Grandmère said into

the laser-sender that joined the Guesthouse to the High Talker. "He'll begin preparing the Earth for the ship."

Muted gold light played upon Grandmère, the comradeship of old friends.

"I'll collect him again in a few years. With his help I should be able to go into the Ocean at last. It's been too long a life, Constance, and with all the biota I've adopted it shows no sign of ending."

The light turned a sad green, and Constance's voice, modulated and clear but distant, distant as the ocean of the Method-Smiths, spoke. "We all end in the Ocean. You'll find your way."

"I wish I could see it before I go in." The younger Guests would have been amazed at the plaintive tones in Grandmère's voice. The iron tongue which had called them had softened to quicksilver.

"You will see it afterwards," Constance Marchant said from beyond the implements of life and death.

"But will I know I've seen it?" Grandmère said, hard metal back in her voice.

"Others will," Constance said, her voice fading into light then darkness.

4. Shapes

Two great bites had been taken out of the Chicago shoreline of Lake Michigan, and a thick promontory of green separated those bites.

"Once," Beatrice Van Leider lectured to her three students, "this was built up landfill. Tall buildings and roads covered this shore, the city stretched out to eat the lake. After the Troth-Breaking this piece of the city was itself eaten by scavengers who sought and dug up materials for their manufactories. But they left the park here."

"It would not have made a good scene for a play," Theadora interrupted, pulling her children's attention toward her. "The scavengers were civilized, worked in teams, gave way to each other. Some traded raw materials for manufactured goods. Very dull to look at."

"Dull is important," Van Leider challenged. "If you only study the exciting parts of history, you'll miss most of what actually occurred."

"That's one idea," Theadora said, her face a dismissive mask.

Why was she doing this? Van Leider wondered. Ever since Tomaso was called away she's been interrupting my lessons, undercutting the children. She didn't do this before.

Not for the first time Van Leider wished she could read Theadora's expressions and body language, read the manifestations of her mind. But Theadora never showed herself to anyone except the children. All the others got were appearances that were of use to her. That should have made her a Deceiver, but Van Leider knew that Theadora would never dangle from a noose. She was not engaged in trickery. She was doing something else. But what was it?

"Take a look around here and at the nearby parts of the city," Van Leider said to her three charges. "See what you can find. Look for the history in the stones, look for the archaeology in the bones. Talk to anyone who is being 'public', footvolk to civicvolk, and hear what they have to say about where they live. We'll talk more tomorrow."

Patricia set off purposefully southward to the broken shells of museums. Karl wandered along the streets, feeling the warmth of the underworld rising up. Gregory went off to see the sights.

"Theadora," Van Leider said, "do you want me to leave?"

"Only a little of you," the actress said, sibyl-faced, oracle-tongued.

"What little?" Van Leider braced herself for some turn of phrase, some show of cleverness that the actress could get away with where no one else could.

"The part that wants to be dead and gone," Theadora said in a voice that chilled and spoke of Romantic poets lingering in graveyards mooning over lost loves while the living mooned over them. "The part that lives in past glories."

"You -- you talk to me about past glories, you who dig up bones and wear them on stage, who make masks of skulls and call the ghosts back? You?"

"I give the famous dead a moment of life to remind the living of where they come from." As she spoke Theadora's face changed through a panoply of historical figures she had played, giving each of them a second's breath. "You wallow in the past and give your life to the dead.

"Besides, the dead you talk about are not the dead you've sacrificed yourself to. You've given your life to the past glories of Academe instead of trying to make new glories from the present."

"I tried that," Van Leider said. "They wouldn't let me in to make the glories."

"The dead past would not let you in. But the children, they can make your glories real if you teach them what the glories are. You give them the basic teachings of your books, but they could learn that by reading. You teach them as you would anyone else. Look at them individually. Teach Gregory what he needs to be Gregory, Patricia what she needs, and Karl what he needs. Teach me what I need."

"And what do you need, Theadora?"

"To know you."

The Crazy Old Man Who Lives with the Fire picked up his measure-stick. It had been a gift from the Things No One Can See Except in their Minds whom the Crazy Old Man Who Talks to the Things No One Can See talks to. They had given the Crazy Old Man Who Lives with the Fire three gifts: Fire, Iron from the stars, and the Stick.

"Here is One," they said through the Crazy Old Man who talks to things. "Lay this stick down on something and its length will be One. With One you can have Two and Three and One-Half and all the other numbers you care to make. With One you can measure any length."

The Crazy Old Man loved to make One with the stick. He had measured the length of the path that ran from his cave through the center of the village to the hut of the Crazy Old Man Who Talks to the Things No One Can See. He had done it by putting One after One after One and counting them up just as if they were a pile of stones. He had found the stones himself and learned to count by pulling them out of a pile one at a time and making a new pile of them. Counting stones was human, making one was divine.

Then he had put his stick up against a branch and cut a piece from that branch. He laid the two sticks next to each other, so their ends matched each other and said, "They are equals."

Then he had taken four equal sticks and had laid them together to make a square and said, "One stick by One stick is One square." With One square he could measure the size of the village.

One day he had tied a cord to the stick and tied a plate on either end. Then he took his favorite rock, a small smooth stone worn down by water, easy to carry and hard to chip. He called the rock 'One' and put it in one of the plates. Then he put some beans in the other plate. When the measure stick did not tip to one side or the other, he said, "This is One stone of beans."

Then he went on to find out how many stones everything weighed.

Later, the Crazy Old Man with the Fire took his stick, his equals, his square, his balance, and his rock and went to the Crazy Old Man Who Tells Everyone

What To Do and showed them off.

The Crazy Old Man Who Tells Everyone What To Do had had a problem. He had been given something by The Things No One Can See Except in Their Minds. This thing was called Justice and he was supposed to distribute Justice to the people of the village. But he had no idea how to allot Justice. The stick, the square, the stone, and the balance told him to mete out Justice evenly.

Well, except for him -- he was holding the stick after all -- and except for his friends. He could use a larger stone for them. That sounded good.

The Crazy Old Man with the Fire went back to his cave and looked for other things he could measure. He used twelve sticks and made a cube. He made a candle one stick in length. He lit it and measured time in the lifespan of the fire. He put sticks over candles to measure how fast things were. He put liquid in a tube one stick long and set it near the fire to tell how hot it was.

He discovered something in this making and putting together, that wherever he looked, whatever he measured there were still more complex things that needed more complex arrangements of sticks to measure. Every arrangement implied new arrangements, and still he could not exhaust reality now matter how ephemeral the measurements became.

Every so often the Crazy Old Woman Who Knows Everything would come and watch him work. Then she would go away and bring back ideas he could use. "It's called a line," she said. "It's a stick without ends. And this is a circle. You make it by holding the stick at one end and turning the other end around it. This is a sphere. You get it by spinning a circle around its center. This is differential calculus. By making very small sticks and very short candles, you can use it to measure the speed of things moving in curved paths.

This is integral calculus. You use it to find how many squares there are in funny-shaped objects."

The Crazy Old Man with the Fire found all these tools useful, but he was bothered by the fact that the Crazy Old Woman claimed that she had invented the ideas before he had the tools. Even worse, she had gone to the Crazy Old Man Who Tells Everyone What To Do and had given him some strange new measurements. "It's called statistics," she had said. "It allows you to count what you don't have."

Which was a strange thing to say, since both she and the Crazy Old Man with the Fire knew that statistics was a way to make your guesses better, not to count.

"This is actuary," she said. "It will tell you when someone is going to die. And this is called polling; it tells you what the people want to hear. This is computer modeling; it stops the need for actual experiment. These two are psychology and sociology; they let you measure the people completely so you never have to listen to what they are actually saying."

When she did that, the Crazy Old Man with the Fire hid in his cave, taking the Crazy Old Woman with the Plants and the Crazy Old Man Who Talks to the Things No One Can See. They waited while the village erupted in anger, while the hut of the Crazy Old Woman Who Knows Everything was burned to the ground with stolen fire and the Crazy Old Man Who Tells People What To Do was replaced with another Crazy Old Man.

This new Crazy Old Man Who Tells People What To Do liked to listen to the Crazy Young People Who Travel to Other Villages and ignored the Crazy Old Woman, who still knew everything but now was homeless.

The Crazy Young People had come back with new ways of doing things.

One had gone to the village of the Single-Sayers, the People who think everything is unique. The Things No One Can See had given these people the Pack and the Seal. The Crazy Young One had come back and said, "Sticks and stones are bad measures. Look at each thing on its own. Don't count how many squares there are in an acre. Instead remember when an acre was the amount of land a yoke of oxen could plow in a day. Remember that that would be different for each pair of oxen on each day on each plot of land. No sticks, no stones. Pack up what you see and Seal it with what you say."

One had gone to the village of the Moment-Keepers. The Things No One Can See had given them a Tree by which to look at the world. "Look at the whole world. Now put the Tree in it. The world-tree stretches everywhere, its trunks and branches, its leaves, the tiniest fibers that spread from it, each touches a thing and relates one thing to another. With the Tree you see how everything connects to everything else and everything measures everything else."

One had gone to the village of the Path-Miners. They had been given the Continuum. It was hard to understand what they said, but it seemed to amount to an unbroken journey through the twin terrains of world and mind, with the Continuum reconciling the two, carving world to be like mind and letting mind change to be like world. Each measured the other, and in the two there was the Echo of the Things No One Can See.

One of the Crazy Young People had gone to the village of the Method-Smiths. To them the Things No One Can See had given the Forge of Means. They made sticks and stones, seals and trees, all the methods of doing. They made the Tractation by which things were more easily brought together and the Adoption by which things were made familiar. With these two the cruelest of the world's things became Kind and Kin.

Most recently one of the Crazy Young People had come back from the village of the Band-Braiders. The Things No One Can See had given them the Mist and the Lens. With the Lens they could focus all the lights of the world as they needed. With the Mist they could select which light was shone and which hidden. To them all things were light, including evolution, the light of life. Down in their biochemistry was a Lens which told the stored light of their heritage what was valuable and what not, so that in the bands of their being they changed according to the dictates of the world around them.

The gifts of the Crazy Young People had made the people of the village pay less attention to the Crazy Old Man with the Fire and the Crazy Old Woman with the Plants. They were still called on occasionally, particularly when things started breaking down or when the village would send forth some new strain of life unlike any in the farther villages. The Crazy Old Man and the Crazy Old Woman managed to prosper in these circumstances.

But the people of the village had forgotten that the Old Men and Women were Crazy, because the Crazy Young People seemed so much Crazier. They had forgotten that the Crazy Old Man lived with monsters, that Fire, Iron, and One were monsters that could destroy or conquer, could consume and change. They had forgotten that the Crazy Old Woman Who Lived with the Plants knew everything about their bodies and their health, knew the cycles of life and growing, knew when to plant and when to reap, knew which herbs cured and which killed. They had forgotten that she was life and death among them.

Now the Crazy Old Man Who Told People what to do had called for the Crazy Old Man Who Lives with the Fire and said, "We need to grow closer to the other villages. They are sending a cart-train for us. We must make a cart to go with them. Can you make such a cart?"

Tomaso Alliende opened his eyes from long contemplation and nodded once to the Marshall of the Dissociation. "I can. I will."

Feather sat on the summer-warmed riverwalk under the artificial cliffs of the Chicago River. He opened his carry-sack and looked sadly at the meagerness within, only half a loaf of bread and a bunch of Michigan grapes. All his monsters were gone, traded to those who would listen on the roads and maglev lines from Toronto to Gary-Chicago -- No, Chicago-Gary. At this end of the road-girdling city it was important to put the western name before the eastern. That was the American Manders. Even in a supposedly united place regionalism reigned over all.

No monsters were left in the bag, but so many battled and roared in his head. If he could trade a glassmaker for time on their manufactory he could create some more. He wanted, badly, deeply, pleadingly to give form to the beasts that sat vivid in his soul, waiting for -- Not life, that they already had, but form so they could be seen for what they were: The Monster Grandmother, grey-spider with glowing eyes and reaching hands. The seizure-man, mental shapeshifter who turned from human to alien with a flick of thought. And the thousand armed, thousand-tendrilled ConCensor, each arm with a puppet ConCensus Taker, open handed with chits to lure the unwary and to tempt. In the corner of his carry-sack lay the tantalus-lure, a chit left for him in the Toronto hostel.

Give the Bearer, Feather, food, drink, and lodging.
Elsbet Chan-Dunlevy-DeMarnier-Tienh,
ConCensor of the Dissociation.

Doors to her lair lay open and baited everywhere the Dissociation touched. Here the office that held that door was only a little winding away, in the last skyscraper in Chicago-Gary, the black-glass, black-steel building, built like child's blocks rising high, visible far away, too much the city's symbol to be torn down. It ruled in majestic, terrible isolation now that all its competitors were gone, its height making a vast sundial of the flat ground. Each of the homes in the downtown had its shadowed hour when the reminder of commerce-past touched it.

The shadow lay across this stretch of the river, the reminder of what the city had been, second in commerce, second in the markets of illusion, but greater in the illusions of illusion. Trading in futures, they had called it. Feather had been told by his Nepalese-American grandmother how Chicago had exuded those shadows of nothing, taking money for promises. She had told him how the predictions and the predictors had risen so high in prestige that a dark market had been created to oppose them. In the undercurrents of guaranteed wealth had grown those who would take a person out of the actuarial trap laid down for them by genetics and statistics.

"The future forgotten," the Predators had promised, "for a price."

His grandmother had told him of those shameful little shops with their wafer-thin computers that would artistically obliterate aspects of one's life from all records.

"But how could that work?" Feather had asked. "Wouldn't people remember?"

"They relied on the computers to remember for

them. What came on the screen was realer than their own minds. If someone poked a false memory into their fragile networks it would be stronger than their own recollection. The future forgotten. For a price."

"Can you forget this future?" Feather roared at the black thing's shadow. "A ship is coming. Really coming this time. Monsters are coming, monsters who will mark out our future with alien measures and measurements. Can you forget that? Or will you pretend it's not happening?"

The few others on the riverwalk drifted away from Feather. He was unknown to them, so they did not intrude on whatever he was doing -- mad ranting, oration, play rehearsal, poetry creation, or a digitized discussion with someone a long way off (a shameful reminder of the years of swiftness).

Only one person remained watching him. Gregory Coskun-Alliende over the course of a few hours wandering had come to the riverwalk to watch the waters and think about mists and shapes of mists. Feather seemed to him an apparition of the city's past, a ragged creature from times when madfolk were made People of the Foot and the People of the Foot were named mad.

"Excuse me," Gregory said. "What monsters are you talking about?"

Feather turned eyes fired with hope toward the boy. "Do you want to know about monsters?" he asked.

"I already know a good deal," Gregory said, pride misting his eyes. "My father has a lot of monsters. He lives with them."

"Which monsters?" Feather asked. Could he have run from Toronto and found a Guest in Chicago-Gary?

"Fire, metal, the forge, desire," Gregory said. "My father says those are monsters. He told me a lot of stories about them. My mother's acted some of them as well. What kind are you talking about?"

"Monsters from outer space," Feather said.

"What's monstrous about them?"

"Do you really want to know?"

Gregory thought about it. Did he? Here was a crazy man telling him that aliens were monsters, which was ridiculous. But he was crazy and his father had told him to listen to crazy people, that madness was a different way of seeing things and that a smith had to learn to look in every different way in order to make and to fix. Gregory accepted this from the evidence of his senses. After all, both of his parents were Crazy Old People, and so was his teacher. Beatrice Van Leider had told him (in the dark of night, for to teach psychology was a hanging offense) that some madnesses were only physiological derangements and could be cured physically, others were mental confusions, and others, she admitted with reluctance, were simply signs that the madman was saner than the people judging him mad.

And his mother, echoing his teacher, had told him that the madvolk were sometimes kings in hiding, waiting for the moment they could come forth and take their thrones.

"I'd like to hear," Gregory said. He reached for his carry-sack where lay stored more wealth than most people could imagine. "What do you want in exchange for telling me?"

"What do I want?" Feather asked. Hunger pulled at him but the needs of his methods were different from those of stomach. "To be heard."

"Of course," said Gregory. "Everyone with a story wants to be heard. But the storyteller is still giving something to the listener. My mother wants to be seen on the stage, but the people who come to our plays still pay us to perform."

The simple doctrine and method of the strolling player burned itself into Feather's mind.

"Food, to start with," Feather said. "Maybe some clothing."

"I'd better take you to see Mother," Gregory said. "You can't bargain like a beggar if you have a tale to be heard. Come with me. We're camped in Grant Park beside the lake. I think mother will be very interested in you. She might even want to make a play of your monsters."

Theadora was doing a bare stage, one woman show as a matinee and to keep her acting skills in fine tune. The production was based on Paulina Vasillovna's fold-poem Regrets, the third of the tetrad Hopes, Follies, Regrets, and Passages. Vasillovna had been one of the first ConCensus recruiters, a founding member of the Dissociation. She had traveled all over the Troth-Broken Earth looking for potential ConCensus Takers. Along the way she had spoken to the old and dying members of the Troth-Breaking generation. Their recollections had formed the basis for the tetrad. Voices from before the world had changed now found face and form in the fluid acting of Theadora.

"When I was a child" she said in a voice that shifted across the whole world of accents, carrying forth how often Vasillovna had heard this regret unfolded, "Perfect Fertility Control was a gift from heaven, a blessing that gave life where it was barren or prevented it where it was not wanted. But when I was grown, just before the Troth-Breaking, it had become fixed in our minds that giving life was completely our decision. We were so confident of that that having children or not became a thing of fashion. One year you might have them, the next not, and that often depended on how you looked. Tall children were wanted one year, green eyes the next. But when I was old and the Troth-

Breaking happened, no one wanted to bring children into a world of fear. How could we feed them or clothe them? Who could we turn to teach them? How could we bring children into the world if no one would take payment to give them what they needed? So we didn't have them, even when the Baby Hunger took us and we wanted so badly to give more life."

Beatrice Van Leider watched Theadora with burning eyes, trying hard to see the woman beneath the role, and as all the actress' other lovers had, she failed to do so. Something was under there, something great and wonderful, something to worship and adore, but the woman, no, she was not there. Only her children saw the human Theadora.

She became an old man now, back bent, eyes bleared. "I kept going to the factory even after my son traded for a home manufactory. I thought the barter would go away. I thought we would have money again. We did, finally, but it was local stuff, plastic coins imprinted with the promises of the town leaders. It didn't seem real to me, so I kept going back to the factory and they kept paying me, upping the euros stored in my bank account. But no one would take my card. Even the selling machines were empty. But the numbers on the screen were so much more real than the copper cooking pots my son made at home in the manufactory. But the numbers didn't feed and clothe us, the bartered pots did."

Another old man, bright eyed, clear sighted, voice sharp with accustomed command thwarted. "The patients stopped coming because I demanded old money. I was a doctor. They needed doctors, so they had to do things my way. Yet they didn't. The kids, the young doctors, they traded, some of them even traveled. They had no respect for the traditions, but the sick went to them, not to me, and it was even worse when they had the alien medicines. When the Guests came round and taught the young doctors to turn plagues into benefits, I gave up."

Feather watched enthralled as the dead came back to life through the person of Theadora. He was captivated, unable to look away from the skill of performance or listen to anything but the voices from the past given breath by the actress. At last the playlet ended and Theadora disappeared into the Guisers' van to the thunder of applause. But Feather's enchantment remained.

He followed Gregory docilely to the rear of the van where the boy knocked on the door of the dressing compartment. "Mother, I have a man here with interesting stories to tell."

"Bring him to the public tent, dear," came the voice, low and thrilling. Her natural voice, Feather assumed, not yet knowing Theadora's ways. "I'll join you once I'm properly dressed."

"Yes, Mother."

The public tent was a collapsible room the Guisers pulled out when they had an extended engagement, like this two-month stint in Chicago-Gary. It had a table and two couches which dissolved into liquid storage when traveling, and a skylight that rippled with intermixed lilac and rose colored oils layered between clear membranes. The effect on a bright summer day like this was vividly alien, unearthing the inner landscape.

But even this did not trouble Feather. She was an actress, she liked the dramatic. That made human sense to him. He did not understand, even when Theadora walked in clad in a seemingly modest gown that covered her from neck to ankles but caught the light in such a way as to insinuate the figure beneath. Even then, even with all he was aware of he did not know he had entered a monster's lair.

"Welcome," Theadora said. "Sit and tell me your

stories."

Months later, Patricia Coskun-Overus stepped into Skyborough Uberton and waited impatiently while the protective membrane dissolved around her. The Fair was before her, in tents on the spinning floor of the skyborough, in bubbles in the air, in skydancers twirling around the rings and in a riot of stellar events played within the image mist.

Her visits to the sky were too infrequent for her taste. She could have lived here with her father, but that would have meant giving up the road and her mother. One day perhaps, but not yet, not until she had learned all she could about drama and enaction, not until her mother had given her all of Earth would she take to the sky.

"Tricia," her father's voice wafted down from the axis. Winston Overus darted and swooped through the light air above, his back adorned with feathered wings, a birdlike flying suit derived from but much more earthly than the Single-Sayer flyers. "Meet me under the first ring," he called.

"Anon, Pater," she spoke up in a voice Shakespearean in practice, delightfully intense like her mother's yet without that extra something that made it impossible to turn away from Theadora.

Patricia broke into a jog, bobbing her way through the games and booths set up by the visitors from other skyboroughs. Like a goblin market they had come, the makers of spatial oddities, the players with microgravity, the workers in emptiness.

"Perfect spheres, perfect spheres, all materia, perfect spheres, all sizes, perfect spheres."

"Superconductor line, spun superconductors."

"Solar dust clothes, impregnated with particles of solar wind, cut from real sailcloth. Solar dust clothes, just the thing for sky dancing."

Patricia stopped at that booth and looked at the star-shining gowns and robes, the capelets and shoes, made of shimmering materials that at a flicker of charge became nearly perfect black bodies. Band-Braider tech, the most recent delight of the sky-people.

"What will you take for two of those gowns?" Patricia asked.

"Star-cash chains only," the trader said, stiffening at Patricia's question. "Or chits from skyvolk."

Patricia bridled at the implications of his tone. That she was a hole-crawler -- as the skyvolk called the earth-bound -- would be obvious from the way she walked. She had grown used to, never happy with, the unsubtle contempt many of the skyvolk showed to her when she visited.

"Oh. Well. I'll have to wait. Could you set two of them aside? My father, Winston Overus, will come pay for them later."

The trader blanched. Overus was a powerful man in his skyborough and had connections all across the interlinked community of satellites and outer planet bases. A word from Overus could lose him his place in the Fair. "I'll set them aside, miss. They can be sized later."

Patricia reached the underside of the first ring. Its apparently swift rotation and the plumes of solar flares projecting from it set a dizzying wheel of fire over her head. The ring was actually spinning much slower than the outer cylinder, a low gravity workplace, and considerable effort was needed to move from the outer cylinder to that ring. Of all things in the universe, spin was the hardest to match and the most dangerous to miscalculate.

Patricia watched the image mist overhead. Visions of near and distant planetary, stellar, and galactic phenomena flickered in and out, the vibrant rings of the gas giants and asteroids where the miners of space worked, shots of antimatter manufactories and the free-floating habitat builders, vast factories that were the only large makers of things within Sol's system. There were pictures of many stars and galaxies, a brief moment of a dance of galactic collision, a mating that had begun long before any intelligence existed on the six known worlds and would still be at the beginnings of intimacy long after all these species were gone. A moment of the great wall of galaxies, a shot of the early universe seen in its roiling energy-ruled whiteness.

The scopes of the skyvolk looked out at the universe and brought the images in. Patricia, trained in the theater, knew these pictures to be images of stellar kinship for these people, a boast that they too were of the universe entire, not of any single world.

So why was there a lone unchanging image amidst the montage of spacetime? One star with a system of twelve planets. It had remained in view all the time she had been here. She recognized it, of course. Alpha Mensae, the star of the Path-Miners. It's true, Patricia thought. Feather is right.

"What's caught your attention, Tricia?" Winston Overus asked. He had shed his flying suit and was now garbed in the loose tunic and pants popular among sky-men.

Patricia looked into her father's eyes, studying his face as her mother had taught her, making sure she knew every detail of his visage before asking her question.

"A ship is coming from the Path-Miners, isn't it?"

There. The tell-tale flicker of his cheek, the

twitch of his left ear. She knew the answer before he gave it. "Yes. How did you know? You can't have seen Tomaso. He's too busy."

"Uncle Tomaso knows?"

"The Dissociation hired him to build a habitat for the ship. How did you know?"

"Mother picked up a crazy guy a few months ago. He's scared to death of the aliens and the Guests. He said a ship was coming. He said it's coming from the Path-Miner world, but that it's a Method-Smith ship."

"Your mother collects crazy people who know what they're talking about." Winston Overus gave a half-mocking smile. He couldn't muster the same ironic self-awareness of Theadora that Tomaso had cultivated, but he was working on it. He didn't want to end up like Rainbow, dying in a dance of self-awareness, Forlorn and Backlorn, Theadora's only failure.

"How long?" Patricia asked.

"It will come to Earth in twenty-three years. We're going to be ready for it."

"How?"

"That ship takes decades to go from system to system. The aliens know how to survive without a planet below them. The skyvolk have traded our co-operation and the use of our manufactories to the Dissociation for the secrets of independence. We're finally going to . . . When you say picked up, do you mean he's still with you?"

"Um-hmm. Picked up, took in, gathered, drew into our merry band the way she picked up you and Rainbow and Tomaso and Beatrice."

"I wonder what she's going to turn this one into," Winston said.

"I don't know," Patricia said. "But she and Beatrice have been talking about mysteries, initiation stories, monsters, Perseus and the Gorgon, Odin and

Ymir, Lugh and Balor, Osiris and Set, and a lot of other old stories. And they've been making him write down his ideas about the aliens and the Guests. They seem to be making a play, but Mother's not telling me about it, and I can't imagine they'd put his ideas on stage. We'd be hanged as Deceivers for slandering the Guests."

"Tricia, your mother knows what she's about, and she'd never put you children in danger."

Winston Overus fell silent, his mind drifting back to the time when he was a hole-crawler, when he lived in The Dominion of Eastern Cornwall and only dreamed of the stars. The Guisers had come. They were a much larger troupe then, and Theadora was only one of their actresses. She had played Wynona visited by the Manitou and giving birth to the four heroes of the Ojibwa. She had played Armstrong setting imperishable footprints upon the moon.

She had played Winston Congreve like a fish, luring him in and turning his soul inside out to find his true desires. When at last she had left, he had become Winston Overus on his way to the skyboroughs and she had been pregnant with this child. Child no longer, what are you becoming, my Tricia? What is your mother's presence and my absence making of you?

"Yes, she knows what she's doing," Patricia said. "Even if no one else does."

Neither Feather nor Beatrice knew why neither was jealous of the other. Theadora managed them, managed their domestic relations effortlessly, almost as if she were two different people, one for each of them. Or three if Tomaso came, or four if she saw Winston, or five if she talked about Rainbow.

Or one for her children, the born and the not-yet-born.

Beatrice Van Leider had tried to measure Theadora and had failed. The Professor had a saying handed down from her teacher by which she carefully measured the minds of others. She had told no one except Gregory about this tool, since even an aphorism of psychology could prove dangerous. The psychology was hidden in this aphorism, for it did not sound psychological, it sounded religious-philosophical, areas it was safe to Profess.

"Imagine a person in a war faced with a bomb that will blow up house and home," she had said to Gregory on a moonlit night when she thought none were around to hear them.

"If this person is Clever," and she spat the word, "he will break the connection between bomb and fuse."

"Will that work?" Gregory asked.

"If it doesn't no one will write of his cleverness.

"If he is Intelligent," Beatrice said -- she had caught the rhythms of dialogue from Theadora and had found the speechifying of Academia fading in the presence of stagework -- "he will find the plans for the bomb and learn how it works so he can defuse it."

"And if there isn't time to learn?" Gregory asked, knowing his cues in such a lesson.

"No one will write of his intelligence.

"If he is wise, he will call in expert bomb defusers."

"And if there are none about?"

"He will take his family and flee, though no one will write of his wisdom.

"And if he is perfect," Beatrice said (this was the line that made it philosophical), "he will stop the war."

"And if he doesn't?"

"Then he wasn't perfect."

But Beatrice thought, Theadora was none of these. When faced with a bomb she turned into the explosion that would end the world. When faced with a war she made it into a noble endeavor. When faced with destruction she would glorify it and emerge unscathed.

From his place in the Guisers' van, Feather had heard the lesson and catalogued in his own mind the monsters of Cleverness, Intelligence, Wisdom, and Perfection, as well as the monster who used these others to measure humans, and the monster who was learning the lesson.

Invisible to the scopes of the skyvolk, the awaited ship moved through the bitter emptiness between the warming stars.

Long Wave reached out to meet State.

The Echo-hole was traversed.

The Surrounder of aliens passed through the Surround of vacuum.

Sealed by the preeminent flyer between stars: Flying-Messenger, made by the Makers-of-Means and added to by each of the Races-that-can-if-only-tenuously-communicate-with-us left the star system of the Species-that-carves-memories-and-forgetfulness for the star system of the Species-that-is-ground-bound-and-teaches-generalization.

The Interstellar Adoptionase that cyclically lattices the nearby Species-using-languages adopted the mode of Tractase in journeying toward the means-of-survival and evolution of imitation-imagination-cogitation-manifestation-trial-naming.

The yet-to-be-named ship was coming.

5. Construction

"When the god Lugh came to the house of the Tuatha Dé Danaan, the gatekeeper challenged him, saying that only a craftsman practicing his art could enter.

"Lugh said, 'I am a bard.' The gatekeeper said, 'We have a bard, Ogma, greatest in the world.'

"Lugh said, 'I am a smith.' The gatekeeper answered, 'We have a smith, Goibhniu, maker of the weapons of the gods.'

"Lugh then declared himself a carpenter, a mason, a swineherd, and on and on, but for each declaration the gatekeeper could name one of the children of Dana who was the greatest of that art. Then Lugh said, 'But have you within one who is master of all arts?'

"The gatekeeper stroked his beard and shook his

head. 'Can you prove that you are such a master?' Lugh reached into a pouch on his saddle and from it pulled out an interstellar spaceship. 'Only a master of all arts could make that,' said the gatekeeper and he opened the gates."

The divine mist-play focused in on the bauble in the god's grasp, closing in on the many-lobed jewel as the image of the demiurge's smooth hands dissolved into the star-strewn softness of space, until after a span of breaths the man-crafted image was replaced by a live image of this greatest of human artifacts.

Spheres lobed by spheres it was, globes of spun polymer around metal; shining with reflection, black with absorption, color by color went the globes.

At first it seemed a drunken array of gems, a cascade of jewels conjoined by thin shivers of string. Then it looked like an overzealous' chemist's model of an atom's orbitals -- though the atom would have to have had an atomic number in the high two hundreds to account for all the spheres and teardrop shells of this construction. No such atom could last for even the drawing of a single breath, but this, this work was meant to endure not just the rigors of time, but those of space, and of the confusion between the two that the universe conceals at the upper limits of velocity and the deepest wells of gravity.

Like a darting hummingbird the mist's-eye-view flew between and around the bulbs and globes, the spheres and teardrops of the habitat. It swirled a loxodromic path around the kilometer-wide central sphere, a spiral around a ball to see the tracks and trails of the outside. Light from Sun, Earth and Moon played in a thousand ways of illumination and shadow, rainbow and ebon, reflection that glorified, absorption that energized.

The mistworker gauged his audience. They still savored the view. He could perhaps draw out that delight for a little longer, but he had learned well the value of want in those who watched. Time to change.

The view spun for a moment, twirling its gaze around the Earth-Moon system, encompassing the skyboroughs and satellites, ships and manufactories from horizon to horizon. Then down, diver-like, it struck the space ship and splashed into nine hundred and twenty-seven viewpoints, kaleidoscoping the central cylinder of Skyborough Hoshimachi.

Each view was from the center of one of the ship's orbs. Perspective rebelled in confusion as an object one kilometer wide seemed the same size as tens of decameter-wide ones and hundreds of meter-across balls.

There, in the habitats and cabins, in the living spaces and zero-g farms, in the apparatus and the applications, were the manifestations of a thousand theories, tests of hypotheses astronomical and cosmological, attempts to create materia that could not tolerate the least gravitational disturbance, studies of movement that insisted upon the absence of nearby stars and worlds, and laced all throughout micro-ecosystems in isolation that might give food to the travelers, controlled, so controlled. Out beyond the reach of the sun there would be less light than the darkest place of Earth. Not the most shadowed pits of the underground, not the deepest shafts, no locus on Earth would so lack the life-giving, life-burning radiations of a sun as would this tiny cluster.

Therefore did its designers ask, What does life truly need of light and heat and what can be made by chemicals, by artificial fusion, by the annihilation of matter and antimatter, and what of that can be regulated? There was data from the many aliens. Their lives and ecosystems were as sun-dependant as that of Earth, but that dependence had different constructions, different requirements, different aspects of spectrum and amplitude that must be preserved while others fell by the infinite expanse of interstellar wayside. Human theory also gave back many answers. Each one would need a trial, each trial a sphere. Lobe upon lobe of tests and proofs waited only the reality of interstellar travel to winnow true from false.

And light was but the beginning of wondering. The ship could not be spun for false gravity, that the aliens had warned them about. Spin, the Path-Miners had said in their strange way, translated through two tiers of Guests, was the deepest and first manifestation of the Echo. Out in the reaches, away from the worlds, rising up on the Arch, climbing up toward the speed of light (or rather as it seemed, all the world around you was so climbing), wayward spin could create a thousand strange dangers. Some were clear to human scientists, but other matters, such as what the risks of 'coruscating rainbows within the whiteness' could be, none of them could say.

Therefore the human habitat must not turn of its own, but would be made to dance in accord with the ship that was coming. Even the pretence of gravity had to be abandoned, and who knew what would happen to the gravityless over decades of travel? There were experiments in zero-g growing and medical labs set to study the effect of this lack on man and beast, plant, myco-growth and unicell.

On the outer baubles of the ship lay packages of experiments, tools created by longing Professors who had ached to test theory upon theory about the space between the stars, out there in the flatness, in the low energy, in the burble and bubble of the decaying vacuum. They had walked the paths of the world contemplating these queries, thinking never to test their wonderings. Now the ship would come and their devices would poke and prod the veneer of space-time in the realms where the constraint of matter on curve and curve on matter were rendered vivid by the lack of mass, out in the darks where most of matter and energy were unobserved virtuality, where the games of shifting eigenstates and naked quantum operators established the foundations of the universe.

The mist-worker reached his hands into the depths of the manifold images and yanked. The bubbles of view exploded, leaving only a single image, a sight gauze-wrapped, veil upon veil of strange filters coloring and confusing the light. The image grew and resolved in clarity. This was the center of the central sphere. The $1s^1$ of the orbital structure.

Here the ship was all cushions and momentum-distributing gauze, ten layers of onion skin, ten peels of membrane, each a hundred meters apart, spheres within spheres like an ancient model of the universe, though these were orbs of soft bandage instead of hard crystal. There were harder living spaces among the outer orbs, but within the center all was soft clouds and heavenly expanses. Here was the work and safety space of the crewvolk.

Gregory Coskun-Alliende reached into the image and pulled it inside out, everting in a dimension wholly imaginary, so that the core of the ship became the rind of the universe, the hard-bounded center became boundless infinity, and the raised up air of Earth became the star-strewn breath of the expanding universe shifting now in the glorious Dopplered blue of swift outrush. His father had built a world. Did he not deserve a tribute from the big bang itself, demiurgic fanfare from colleague to colleague, god of the Hand to man of the Hand?

The skyvolk caught that breath in unison and reveled in the opening of spacetime before them. Twenty years of labor done, twenty years under the whip hand and mind of the Handyman and now the work was accomplished. Now they had but to wait for the aliens to come and they would at last stretch out and become of the sky.

"Everything fails," Beatrice Van Leider said. She and her last student, the last of the Coskun children, stood within the mists of the stage, watching the universe fade and fail as matter either fell in upon itself or spread out too far for anything to be made of it. Spacetime became a thin sheet, flat save for the mutually fleeing black holes that had once held the life and action of the universe. Into darkness it all passed, darkness and flatness.

"Everything passes away," the Professor said. "Does that trouble you?"

Dominique Coskun-Feather considered the question with great care. Van Leider had been teaching her all the years of her life, teaching her from lineages of knowledge as old as writing, just as her mother had taught her from lineages older, and her father from no lineage at all.

Does that trouble you? Dominique turned the question over in her mind, turning it, stretching it, holding her tongue (clever, too clever), biting back the first few responses, so facile but so dangerous.

The Zen trick of asking 'does that trouble who?' she did not dare say, since she knew she did not understand the meaning of that counter question, and Beatrice would not tolerate mere manipulation of words.

"Never speak a thing you do not understand," the Professor had said over and over again. "People are hanged for doing that."

Nor did she dare ask the Professor to define 'trouble', knowing that ignorance of what she should have understood would be equally intolerable to Van Leider.

"No," she said at last. "It doesn't bother me. It's a beautiful theory that seems to fit reality, but it's not going to happen while any human being is still alive, so why should it trouble me?"

"Because," Van Leider challenged with a voice Dominique had long ago learned meant that the teacher was playing Devil's Advocate, "if nothing lasts, what is the worth of doing anything?"

"Professor?" Dominique said in a voice schooled to disarm. "Why are we playing philosophy?"

Van Leider smiled. "Because we can't avoid it. Everything the Professors do comes from philosophy. We can no more avoid the game of philosophy than your mother can ignore the holy origins of acting, or your father the fear of monsters."

Elsbet Chan-DeMarnier-Tienh and five other lineages she did not choose to honor with names weighed the books in her hands, on her left Consent, on the right Dissent. Both had grown heavy over the last score of years. Her fifth ConCensus awaited seal, but she could not close the books just yet.

Four times she had wanted to stamp her comprehension upon the leather, but each time she had withheld her chop. The alien logic of her thoughts defied her human hope that she was done. Each time she had unpacked the reports and studied anew the four hundred and seventy-two individual statements of the ConCensus takers, down fifteen from last ConCensus.

The first unpacking she had looked at work on the spaceship. She had checked the domains that were participating, from the least, the Malvinas Conventionality which had supplied some rare but potentially space hardy plants, to the largest, the United Kingdoms of Western and Northern China which had built most of the interior structure components of the habitat. All were working as hard as they cared to, all had been paid in actions or chits.

The second time she had unpacked as regarded the uplift of Professorial status that had come with this new effort. Universities had grown in size. Some had as many as thirty Professors. More people were hiring the traveling scholars and handing their children over to education. She had even noted reports of Professors teaching students without anyone else present to chaperone the intimacy of teaching. But there was still a watchfulness among the peoples, witnessed by nineteen lynchings of overconfident teachers who had tried to sway rather than instruct. The cry of Deceiver and the noose around the Predator still kept the People of the Voice in check.

The third time she had looked for views of the aliens. There she had found some hints of trouble. Six of the American Manders had openly declared themselves to be ufnecks and were, in a revival of ceremonies a century old, gathering to await the coming of the gods from the stars. There were also new ufneck communities in Kampala, Podgorica, the Diomede Islands, and, most annoying to the Guests, Toronto.

Two distinct groups of ufnecks had arisen in the capital of the Dissociation: the self-styled Siblings of Long Waited Justification, who were mostly made up of the grandchildren of old style ufnecks; and the Followers of the Secret Prophets. These last were personally irritating, as their doctrine declared that the Guests were servants of alien messiahs who had prepared the Earth for the coming of the true masters. The Followers listened to every public utterance a Guest made and interpreted it oracularly, sometimes with coding numerology, sometimes with Adopted Myco Trances, sometimes just with whatever struck them.

A troubling rise in alien-worship, but at least there had been a decline in the alien-monster stories since the last ConCensus. Something must have happened to Feather. She wondered what. Grandmère seemed pleased; she expected to see him soon. It was hard to believe he had not been near Toronto in the last twenty years. The Guests only knew about him from the trail of stories he left behind and the plays he had written in which the aliens took on the roles of creatures from the outer darkness and the Guests played their monstrous servants. Grandmère had been the central villain in a dozen well-written works. Elsbet and Quint usually served as her diabolical retainers.

As herself, Elsbet had been angered, but as a Single-Sayer watching a Method-Smith she had counted and folded up the means of displaying the monstrous character that lay dormant in each thing, and she had learned a little caution about the inhumanity within herself. Feather's alien gifts had done her some good, and he did seem to have mellowed lately. His most recent works implied that there might be some value in alien understanding. Perhaps . . . But she had to let the chain of thought drop while she returned to unpacking and repacking the ConCensus.

Finally, wearied to the bone from two sleepless nights, Elsbet had unpacked in a Smooth mind focused on Consent and Dissent, and there she had found her answer.

Her paternal grandmother had coined the terms Consent and Dissent for the first ConCensus. Back then Violette DeMarnier had gathered the reports of the first ConCensus Takers, gathered in direct speech person to person instead of written reports, eclectic, eccentric, often poetic, for Violette had needed impressions from which to formulate the Single-Sayer mathematics. The succeeding generations of ConCensus Takers had been taught the rudiments of that alien mind-work, enough to be able to count their overviews and seal them for the real Guest who bore the pack of their work. But in those days ConCensus Takers had been unskilled and could only report idiosyncratically. That untutored individuality had been reaped, threshed, milled, and baked by the Mental-art-worked-upon-by-every-flyer-and-thinker-of-the-Single-Sayers-for-longer-than-recorded-history-on-any-of-the-six-worlds idiosyncrasy of that first ConCensor.

Consent had marked how amenable a place was to the Dissociation, and Dissent how rejectionist they were. The character of Consent and Dissent had of course been individualized and the words were merely human labels, names to give to the other officers of the Dissociation. They had never had any reality in the Single-Sayer thinking.

Never until now. Consent and Dissent were suddenly palpable, real characteristics of every place on Earth. Every volk, dominion, kingdom, republic, Mander, principality, city-state, hegemony, and every other manifest form of human government was now strongly held by, strongly distant from, or battling internally over its relations to the Dissociation.

Elsbet looked again over the reports. Here in the Rhine-and-Rhone, the Elected Sieur of the Valleys had begun consulting with the ConCensus Taker on matters of policy. That ConCensus Taker had formerly been the Sieur's personal valet. Elsbet let the report sharpen in her mind. She could hear the two men talking about upcoming treaties with the United Republic of Kiev and its Protectorates. Tones of disapproval once given to choices sartorial were now being accepted as cautions in the laying down of borders.

The East Florida Mander had broken up since the

last ConCensus. That thin coastal province had split into a north and south, and the issue that divided it had been the city and omniport of Canaveral, its sacredness to the skyvolk, and its contributions to the spaceship work. North opposed (Dissented), South supported (Consented) and welcomed the skywork. The Spanish-English dialect of the southern Mander had now adopted a considerable amount of Skysprach, creating linguistic isolation as well as political dispute.

More examples presented themselves to Elsbet, enough to give report to the other officers, enough to be a satisfactory answer to a Single-Sayer. But not enough to satisfy her.

Elsbet dissolved the door of her office to address a man in his mid-thirties who sat at a desk that had only a control box and a mist cube on it. He sat staring at seemingly abstract mist flows, humming loudly. Elsbet held out her arms and curled her hands in a come-here gesture unknown outside the Guesthouse.

The man stood and turned his face toward her. As he did his expression changed smoothly, beginning with concentration and ending in puzzlement, with no sharp breaks between. Stoop-backed, he loped into the ConCensor's office.

The man had no human name. To Elsbet he was Second-Generation-Path-Miner-Guest-who-has-learned-a-little-human-speech-and-has-come-to-integrate-Path-Miner-thinking-into-Dissociation-work-given-to-me-because-I-can-talk-to-him-in-Shifting-Language. To the Path-Miner-Guests he was a hum-hmm-hi-hello-hee-humm-mmmnnnn which if translated might mean one who was presently new-carving human terrain.

Elsbet took a stylus from her desk and drew a circle. "Earth," she said. Then she drew two wobbly shapes around the Earth, touching each other at many points. "Consent and Dissent," she said. "Navigate."

The Path-Miner Guest stared at the drawing,

then slowly reached out his hands and trailed his fingers over the abstract space laid down. "Hmm-hhmm-huh-h-h-h-ng-han-hh-hu-ha-hh-mmmmm."

The focal point of his thoughts tunneled through the mantle of his undermind, through the complex caverns humanity had carved for itself and which he had only recently entered, cold places compared to the everwarms of Path-Miner thinking. Cold and overcrowded was human thought. There were too many thoughtless twists and turns, too many shortcuts that connected one kind of terrain with another. Human words were those shortcuts, slippery bridges over lava-filled rivers. Say the wrong word and fall in, burn up. Better to travel through the real terrain, through the continuous thought, not the confused word.

Consent and Dissent were side-by-side bridges that connected the whole political space of Earth, two bridges that covered over the tunnel-digs that the Dissociation had carved. Those tunnels were navigable, paths joining one land to another by discussion, seal, and copies of Single-Sayer terrain. Consent now spanned every happy smooth juncture, Dissent every jagged passage. The volks were becoming heavy places, overpassed, overtraveled, too laden with tracks to discern anything, places of forgetfulness where one could enter and completely lose the coming-from and going-to, places to get trapped or give up all things one knew, echo-shafts that bewildered, pulled up chaotic forgetting and cleansed the mind of all things past.

If only, if only one could truly and fully forget. But humans were cursed with constructed memory, not blessed with chaotic. The Path-Miner Guest reached the limit of Guest terrain and looked out over the uncrossable space at the other side where the true Path-Miners lived and carved, where they knew what was in the terrain they followed, and could forget all by passing through an echo-shaft.

"You . . . are . . . too . . . Loud," the Path-Miner said. "Consent . . . thinks . . . you . . . are . . . the . . . Echo. . . . Dissent . . . thinks . . . you . . . hide . . . the . . . Echo."

Elsbet Chan-DeMarnier-Tienh gently took the Path-Miner Guest by his shoulders and turned him around. As he spun his expression changed from concerned distress to relaxed interest. He glided from the ConCensor's office, followed by Elsbet who walked over to one of the emergency desks.

"Find Feather," she said to Marc Gerrand, who savored the urgency in his employer's voice. A hurry. What a wonderfully rare treat.

The wind of the Australian desert whirled and whipped its ancient dance across the back of Karl Coskun-Rainbow. He had come alone, alone on his pilgrimage to Uluru where his father had taken his own life long, long years ago. Karl had left his mother to follow his father as Patricia had followed hers to the skyboroughs and Gregory his out to the spaceship-works. But Karl had come to complete a longer journey, the path into darkness, night, and the dance of time. Rainbow's final dance.

Theadora had not known why Karl had gone. At least, Karl did not think she knew. She would not have let her son go to death without turning all her skills to sway him from the course. Karl knew that. He knew his mother's love. But he heard his father's call from the path beyond the grave where Rainbow danced in memory and trod the steps of dreamtime.

That was why Rainbow had come to Australia when Karl had been but a boy. The great dancer had promised to return to his son, to see him again. But he had danced himself to death in the stone and sunlight, his footsteps burning into the rock, the rock tearing his talented feet to ribbons. They had found his body the next day, and he had been mourned.

At the time Rainbow had been the most famous of the footvolk. His steps had revealed the world and called others away from home to take up the homeless way.

Karl knew that his father had once been staid and settled, a cloistered ballet dancer in Flanders, until Theadora had come to him in the guise of Terpsichore (or Terpsichore had come in the guise of Theadora) to set his dance free, to be all dances in all places. But the freedom the Guiser had shown him had eluded Rainbow. He had set out to dance everywhere and found that he could only dance in one place at a time, doing one step at a time. The infinite unfolding dance escaped him.

He had searched for it everywhere, seeking among the sacred places of Earth, until he had come here to climb and dance upon the back of the Rainbow Serpent, the dance of time eternal.

Karl pulled himself over the top of the wide stone and flipped to a stand. Someone else was there. A man of perhaps early middle age -- it was hard to tell with the variety of age-deniers available for adoption -- tall and narrow of build, but with a face rounded into a stiff-edged oval, sitting in absolute rigidity upon the rock. His eyes were frozen open. No muscle moved. Karl wondered if he was dead. There seemed to be breath coming in and out though his chest was still and his mouth unmoving.

Karl squatted down beside the seated man, knowing he would have to wait. He couldn't follow his father if there was anyone watching. A little time passed, hard to gauge how long under the hot sun where every second seemed to last forever. Then yes, an eyeblink, a drawn breath, a slow unfolding of limbs, one by one as if the sitter were inventorying his body.

"I beg your pardon," the man said in Footsprach lightly accented with something like Franco-English.

"Not at all," Karl said. That should have been the end of it, a distant apology, a distant acknowledgement, the propriety of the unknown upon the road, the manners of the footvolk who must temporarily share space without coming to any closeness.

But it was not all. Karl had come to end his life. He needed to know if this other had a life to return to. "Are you well?"

"Hmm." The man looked up. "I was only thinking I won't be here much longer, and I wanted to take a full look at the world before I left."

Karl violated all the manners he had been taught with his next question, but he had learned from Theadora how to break taboos and escape without harm. His tone betrayed neither curiosity nor intimacy. He simply asked as if it were proper to ask.

"Going where?"

"To the stars," the man said.

Karl withdrew his interest. Another Ufneck.

"No," the man said, easily telling Karl's thoughts. "I really am going. My name is Quint Hillard. I'm a Guest, and I'll be leaving when the ship comes."

Karl looked hard at Hillard. Yes, he looked familiar now. In the front rows of a performance in Toronto, a few years ago, young Dominique's first time on the stage, the Guests had been seated. This one had watched with interest the romance Feather had written (but not attended. Feather would not come to Toronto. He had waited for the Guisers in Kingston.). This man's, Quint Hillard's, eyes had fallen more often on the woman sitting next to him than they had lingered on Theadora. Karl had marked him, for the sight of such committed love was rare and pleasant to him.

"And you," Quint went on. "You are Karl Coskun-Rainbow, child of the actress Theadora Coskun and the dancer Rainbow. And you've come here to die, but you won't because I'll talk you out of it."

"How do you--"

"I see all, I know all," Quint said. "Except for what I can't see and can't know. I saw you come up. Your every step betrayed a failed intention to die. Whoever was here, whatever was here would convince you not to do it."

"Is this some alien thinking?" Karl asked. "Some monster-thought?"

"Some," Quint said. "Some alien, some human, some Burst, some Wave. Let us talk together. Tell me about monsters, and death, and dancing, and your father."

"I thought you knew everything."

"I do. Tell me anyway."

Dominique Coskun-Feather looked up from the Go board into her father's twitchy face and grinned with predatory glee. "Atari," she said.

"An understatement," Feather said, smiling at his teenaged daughter. "You have built a monster of black stones that will eat me all up."

Dominique curled her lips into an ironic ess, knowing that when her father spoke of triumphant monsters he was about to turn the tables. Sure enough, twenty stones later the ouroboros she had built had been cut into a dozen pieces, each fated to die. Even the snake's two eyes had been separated, looking helplessly at each other across a chasm of glittering white glass beads.

"How goes the game?" asked Beatrice Van Leider. The Professor's voice cracked with the rawness in her throat. The Arctic climate of Yellowknife did not agree with the Professor, but she had her charge to teach and she followed that student wherever she went. Van Leider had her hopes that Dominique would follow her along the lanes and paths of Academia.

Her other students, grown now, had all taken other ways. Karl had taken to the road, but for what purpose she could not say. Gregory and Patricia were off in the skyboroughs helping their fathers to build the spaceship. Van Leider had her own contributions to that work, but they were distant offerings, designs and experiments that could be worked on for months and then posted upwards from any office of the Marshallate. It had taken the Professor five years to accept the use of the mails, but she had at last acquiesced. Burned into her memory was the day she had walked into the central office of the local volk and nervous-handedly passed over the sheet of paper with plans for a device to gain accurate relative velocity readings on distant galaxies using the acceleration of the ship as it climbed the Arch as a measuring device. The Marshall's Proxy had taken the paper and sent the image without comment, an everyday event to him.

She had heard that most of the other contributing Professors had come to act similarly. The reality of the situation was that only the workers of the Hand had to be present at the making of the ship. Those of the Voice could not afford to go back and forth to the skyboroughs so they had to resort to the mail and the Marshall.

She had put a good deal of herself into the work -- as had so many Professors, but few of them really wanted to float through the physicality of their abstractions. Most disliked the idea of being in space. They had the Professorial ambition of settling in one place, and now that the Universities had expanded there were opportunities. Beatrice Van Leider had been surprised to discover that she no longer wanted one of those fortunate placements. She had been traveling with the Guisers for over twenty years and had acquired a grudging affection for the life of the Foot.

Besides, there was Dominique, that weirdling child of madness and inspiration, the focus of Theadora's love and Feather's fascination. As Dominique had grown from the helpless monster she was at birth into a human being, her father had come back from the reaches of desperation and had built in his mind a new relation between man and monster.

What that mental edifice was he had not been able to communicate to any of the others, but it had kept him satisfied and given him insights that had been turned into some of Theadora's most fascinating plays. Feather's version of Medea, who had gone from heroic lover to heroic lover and destroyed child to destroyed child, was a fascinating shadow odyssey through the darker reaches of Greek Mythology. And Theadora performing his Stalin's Soliloquies had terrified audiences across the world with the ease of monstrous self-justification.

"Father's beaten me again," Dominique said.

"Then let's work on your playing," Beatrice said as she took Feather's place on the bench in one of the many public recreation rooms of the farming community known as Under Yellowknife. There all the flora of the underworld grew, all the flavored diversity of the Kingdom Fungi which could grow on the savor of deep heat rather than the reach of high light. Yellowknife's underfarms were some of the most successful adaptations of Path-Miner food growth methods to Earthly physiology, and thus had attracted the attention of the ship-makers. Beatrice Van Leider had come to look at them and talk to the farmers about their means and methods, and the Guisers had come with her because they could play anywhere there was an audience.

Van Leider gathered up the white glass beads, each one made by Feather in the Guisers' manufactory, each one a work of art, distinct to eye and hand. The distinctions of eye were not so obvious in the artificial light of the underfarm. Still, the feel of the stones cascading over the hand, the hint of jagged tooth in one and the feel of serpentine smoothness in the next, gave a tension to the uniform role the stones played in the ancient game of Go.

Feather left his daughter and her teacher to their practice and wandered quietly around the recreation dome. High overhead there was a skylight where the dome jutted a bare meter above the ground. In emergencies a ladder would descend and permit escape. The people of Under Yellowknife could climb out from the warm world below to the cold one above, just as Feather's grandpaternal Jicarilla ancestors had climbed up from the world below to the Earth they knew.

The clear bubble was only a little poke into the sky, a glasslike prod and thrust. Just a bump above, the way many of the huge Fungi grown here might have expressed themselves in seemingly isolated mushrooms that concealed their kilometer-wide vastness.

"Your pardon," said a voice to Feather's right. "You are Feather?"

The question was purely formal. The Marshall's Proxy had a chit that bore Feather's image on it, and inside if need be were voice and retinal prints as well as a copy of his genotype and a history of all Feather's interactions with the Dissociation.

"I am." Feather noted a sealed package under

the Proxy's arm. What kind of mail could not wait for regular pickup? Feather, as did most people, went to the nearest Proxy's office once a week or thereabouts to receive any distant messages. All the Marshall's offices could access mail and make copies for the intended recipient. For a Proxy to be sent with a missive implied an unseemly haste.

The Proxy handed over the slate. The seal fell open at Feather's touch and he read:

To the Method-Smith Guest named Feather.
From the Office of the ConCensor.

Grandmère assures me that you have matured the youthful fear you showed when we first met many years ago and are now a proper Method for dealing with monsters. I realize that you are uneducated as to the customs of the Guests, therefore I will say only that I require your presence in my office immediately. I know that word may shock you, but there are times when we must be quick and I have a matter that requires your direct attention. The Proxy who delivers this will see you to the swiftest transport to Toronto.

Elsbet Chan, Single-Sayer Guest.
Elsbet Chan-DeMarnier-Tienh,
ConCensor of the Dissociation.

Feather stared at the missive, reading and re-reading at first in disbelief, then gradually in understanding, until the tenth time through he saw and laughed. He had been farmed, planted, nurtured, cultivated, and now he was being reaped. Grandmère, the spider-monster, had sent him out, sent him into the monster-filled world to learn and grow, and now Grandmère through the agency of another of her children was bringing him in.

"We shall come rejoicing, bringing in the sheaves," he sang.

"What, sir?" said the Proxy.

"Nothing," Feather said. He wondered for a moment if Theadora knew about this. But that flicker of paranoia faded. She did not know. She had been the fertile ground he had been sent to seek, and he would have found her eventually even if she had not been directly in his path of flight. Perhaps Grandmère knew where Theadora had been and had sent him off at the right moment. He did not know, could not guess at the details of the terrible old woman's methods, just as she would not be able to fathom the nuances of his.

Very well, he would go. There was no sense in running and no fear to lend him wings. He had been a Guest unknowing. Now it was time to learn what he was.

"Sir," he said to the Proxy. "Give me a minute to gather my things and tell my daughter and companions where I'm going."

"Everything fails," the Handyman said to the twenty-four men and women, his assistants, who floated through the center of the habitat with him. "One of the most broad-thinking men of the European Renaissance, a man named Alberti, warned that a society should not build things in the years of prosperity that it could not maintain if times became hard. The Earth is filled with examples of his wisdom, from the roads of Rome to the highways of America to the Space Elevator of the Ukraine to the seaward lands of Holland. If you can't maintain it, don't build it. So how do we maintain the habitat?"

A man floated forward, Muhammed Cecil who

had first caught Alliende's attention when he had been a boy of six in the Palestinian city of Hebron. Alliende had come to oversee the installation of the geothermal energy system and Cecil had followed him and watched and copied the movements of the Handyman's hands. Over the years whenever Alliende had come to Hebron, Cecil would be waiting, often trading for lessons or bringing problems (and later solutions) to the Handyman's attention. Alliende had picked him to work on the spaceship and had been pleased with his learning.

"We go with it," Cecil said. "To maintain it."

"All of us?" Alliende challenged.

"Two or three should suffice," Cecil said.

"Are you volunteering?" Alliende asked.

Cecil smiled and his face clearly said that he had volunteered a long time ago.

"And who else?" the Handyman asked.

A few others pushed themselves forward. Alliende pointed to Paula StarReach, knowing that one of the handvolk on the ship should be skyvolk as well, and StarReach had the best balance in her mind between the practicalities of survival in space and the longing to live there common to the skyvolk.

What remained of Constance Marchant was excited. For the first time ever communication with the aliens was coming with some swiftness. The ship, Interstellar Adoptionase that cyclically lattices the nearby Species-using-languages adopting the mode of Tractase in journeying toward the means-of-survival and evolution of imitation-imagination-cogitation-manifestation-trial-naming, was only four light-years away. Its signals were coming at last. It was descending the Arch, slowing down from the noisy bright universe of near-light-speed, pruning away the nines, as one of the skyvolk had coined the term, dropping to a high but no longer madly high fraction of lightspeed.

The Doppler shift of its transmissions was no longer so great as to make reception of signals impracticable. Frequency was down; wavelength could stretch out enough for variation to be noticed and read.

Close enough to begin to know the individual aliens on the ship, close enough for introductions to be made.

There was a pool of methods called Practices-culled-from-iterated-journeys and four Embodied Method-Smiths collectively named Covering-of-known-spatial-exigencies.

A single, slowly dying Moment-Keeper had sent all that it could send to be gathered up by Quint Hillard. He had for a time retreated into grave sadness and meditation upon Earth. Then he had come back from his journey and said, "I have to be on the ship to meet it. I saved one life here. I should save another out there"

There were seven Path-Miners who had only spoken of the echo-shaft of deep space forgetfulness.

There were nine Single-Sayers, only one of whom had identified itself, giving the name, Flyer-between-worlds-for-correction-of-future-historical-misprision-because-of-loss-sealers-also-unpacker-of-aliens-and-packer-of-known-disputes-over-alien-thought.

There were thirty-eight Band Braiders bred from the bands left by all previous expedition members. One was adapted to navigation, two to high gravity work, three to low gravity work, and one to interspecies communication. The last had taken the name Focus-of-Six-Lights for the purpose of talking to humans. What the others did the Band-Braiders Guests could not yet fathom.

Sadly, as yet Constance could not bear back any words from the Guests to their soon-to-arrive guests, for the ship was too small a target to hit with her signals. But as the ship neared and slowed its position could be determined. Then word-bearing lasers could reach out greetings to it. And at last, the Methods that had been Constance Marchant would be able to use those most ancient and sacred of human construction-means, the greeting to strangers and the offer of hospitality.

6. Dimensions

Feather reached out to grasp the hydra heads of the Dissociation. The monster that was eating the world had four hundred and seventy-two heads and one thousand six hundred and fifteen hands.

Each head had its fangs buried in one of the Consenting volks. Each seemed a normal citizen of that volk, a person of the people, native, accepted, known. That was the way of the ConCensus Takers, recruited from the common and accepted, taken from those of good repute and loyalty to their people, taken and turned into these backbiting heads.

The hands were different. The hands shuffled around, going from here to there, carrying things from place to place, bringing the necessities of one land to shore up the needs of another. That was the way of the Marshall's Proxies, mobile, swift (oh shameful word) travelers from place to place, bearers of messages from friends distant and kindreds foreign.

Above these heads and hands were the four faces of the monster:

The ConCensor, prow-headed, wing-faced, alien in visage.

The Marshall, whose elephant ears heard all things, whose eyes flamed with the dread of his gaze, and whose tongue was a sword that could burn a land by refusing it aid or blight crops by assisting undeserving neighbors.

Honor, whose glorious serpent-crowned head turned to mute adoring stone all those who looked upon her well-crafted reputation. Gaze not in her eyes lest you believe the deceits of the Dissociation. An ancient monster is she, a Deceiver of the old times, a curse upon her smooth voice and her acid-spitting mouth.

And last, that ironically named ruler of all, the Trustee. He is the Predator at their heart, he is the one who eats nations and in the fire-forge of his stomach makes the unification of the world. He will bite your sovereignty, take your throne and lands. He will transport your neighbors, steal the work of your hands. He has forces at his command, the Marshallate, and his secret workers among the footvolk, raiders and traders who will come and take all from you.

Feather let go of the hydra and turned to dance with the thousand-armed beneficent divinity of the Dissociation. She was tall and graceful, her arms fanning behind her in rainbow colors to form a peacock tail of actions. She danced upon the Earth and her head that looked in all four directions reached to the stars. A crown of spheres upon spheres upon spheres covered her head and its lights flickered among the orbs of heaven. Her tail-hands rearranged the Earth and sky for the benefit of humanity and she looked outward, waiting for the representatives of her alien comrades to come and bring the humanvolk together with its siblings of the stars.

Feather opened his eyes and looked sadly across the ConCensor's desk at Elsbet Chan. "You've grown too loud and glorious," he said. "You can't go back to being postmen and chit-brokers. You built the ship, something no one else could do. Something no mortal could do. The volks see you as more than human, as heroes or monsters depending on Consent and Dissent."

"And there's no way back?"

"Only one," Feather said. "Studied apathy. Don't do much of anything for a few decades and they'll forget all about you. But I don't see how you can do that and still be the Dissociation. Also, the first decades would be hard. The Dissenters will attack the Consenters, burn down your offices, lynch the Marshall's Proxies and the ConCensus Takers. And if you look too weak they'll probably band together and conquer the Consenting nations who rely on your support, which you won't be giving."

"I won't be here to attend to this," Elsbet Chan said. "My son Sean will have to."

"Where will you be?" Feather asked.

"On the ship," Elsbet Chan said, and a smile lit up her work-wearied face. "Bound for the Single-Sayer world, bound to learn all the unique things in the universe and all the ways to seal them up and unbundle them."

Feather grimaced and waved goodbye. But Elsbet Chan shook her head. "Don't bid me adieu," she said. "You are going as well. The Method-Smiths want you."

A bubble of fear rose in Feather's mind, a primal horror at confronting the monsters from the stars in their lairs. But as it rose the fear changed by some means that occupied his mind, was his mind, fear of this great unknown became --

Became what? He did not know what it was becoming, only that the bubble was growing and consuming all the manners of his thinking. He was not eager for its growth, did not want to meet these vastly other others, had no desire at all for them.

He had no desire at all, but still he would do this thing. He would go and meet them, and he would change, would change whatever came to be changed. Feather looked at himself in the reflective bubble of his thoughts and saw not the fearer of monsters, but the maker of them.

For two decades he had made monsters for Theadora, monsters of myth and story, of history and biography, monsters of Guests and aliens, monsters of humans. In the Guise of writing and acting, he had become monster-making.

Grandmère had sent him forth so that fear would become action, so that the method would rise in him and become him.

"I'll go," Feather said. He had no choice, he was what he . . . did.

The Marshall sifted through his choices. For two decades Benetti's mind had been split between Earth and sky. A thin channel had joined the two, Earth feeding the work of sky, sky controlling the thoughts of Earth, and he had been the fire of sacrifice that joins one to the other. Agni, one of the Proxies in India had called him, and he feebling the tongue of Toronto had responded, 'Agony.'

On his flames he had transported choice plants and animals, precious metals and goods to the voracious sky-god that was the habitat-in-making. Now he had to choose the human sacrifices. Who would have thought there were so many willing and eager to die, and so few places on the altar for them to die in?

Some choices had been made for him. The Guests, of course, decided for themselves. The Handyman had picked those who would maintain the ship, though there was wavering there and a hint that another might accompany them. Winston Overus had demanded a place for himself, but in return had permitted the Marshall to choose the remaining skyvolk who would go.

And the Professors had submitted their names with something like humility, not daring to press their risen status.

The skyvolk and the voicevolk knelt before him, asking who would go to eager death and who would stay in regretful life.

The Crazy Old Man Who Lives with the Fire appraised his work from every angle he could conceive of. He drew upon his millennia of experience to make a multitude of angles out of the lines lying in his cave. He had made the lines over the ages using his Stick, and had learned that by putting two sticks together so that they touched at one end he could make an Angle. Then all he needed to do was put the Angle up to his eye and it would become the focus by which he looked at things. Focus he understood well. Foci or burning points were the means of using glass and sun to create fire. Angles made fire and all fires were his.

He tried to look at every problem from as many angles as possible, since he had learned over the years the danger of making one angle pre-eminent. He had learned that lesson from the Crazy Old Woman Who Knows Everything and the Crazy Old Man Who Tells Everyone What To Do.

The Crazy Old Woman had at various times been obsessed with one or more angles. She called them theories and she had the habit of sticking them in her eyes and then forgetting they were there. She tended to forget her tools, leaving them in her eyes and ears and pockets. The Crazy Old Man Who Tells Everyone What To Do had a different problem with angles. He liked to do what he called 'working' the angles. By that he meant trying to get as much as possible out of the corners of things, trying to find the best approach to get what he wanted.

The Crazy Old Man Who Lives with the Fire had a different use for angles. He used them to find the flaws in his work. A thing might be perfect from the front but hollow behind, or strong above and undermined below. At one time he developed a whole art form from studying things with angles and finding the right angle from which to break them. He had called that art gunnery and it had made him very popular with the Crazy Old Man Who Tells People What To Do, but unpopular with most of the villagers.

This latest work of his, this habitat, looked good but had some troubling angles. First of all, it had no engines of its own. The strangers from the other villages would be providing motive power, but he did not know what that power was nor how it could accelerate gigantic structures to a percentage of lightspeed so high it could best be measured in the number of nines after the decimal point. The Crazy Old Man Who Lives With the Fire did not like to rely on the strangers. They were too differently gifted for him to comprehend their motives, if they could even be said to have motives.

The second trouble spot was the length of the journey. How could the crew remain human for decades away from Earth? How could they stay sane in the gravityless bubble sculpture he had made?

The most glaring flaw of all was that everything about it was an experiment. That meant he had had to build in ways of changing it to accommodate the results. But there were so many things that might need changing: power, light, food, atmosphere, shape, the people themselves. And he could only guess in what ways these things might need changing. He couldn't give instructions to someone else on how to do the changes since only the one who had set up the experiments could truly understand their results. It was his work. He would have to follow it through, ride with it to ensure that it accomplished its purpose. He would have to be a tool user, not just a toolmaker.

There was no choice. The Crazy Old Man Who Lives with the Fire would have to go with the experiment. And he would have to take the Crazy Old Woman Who Knows Everything with him, whether she wanted to go or not.

Tomaso Alliende looked out through the clear port wall of the caravel as it circled the interstellar spaceship for yet another inspection tour. Could he really go off on this piece of work, leave Earth, leave Gregory, leave his wealth, leave the chance to see Theadora in the flesh instead of her continual presence in his mind? Was even two decades of effort, even this masterwork worth the abandoning of his life?

But he had built it, built it for others to live in. He had made it to last and survive the journey. His reputation was wholly placed into this one tool. If it failed, what was he? If it failed because he was not on it would he not be a Deceiver? Would his reputation not fall to nothing, his wealth vanish? Better to leave with it and give Gregory all he had made, pass on his inheritance and go out. And, if he survived, when he came back in two or three centuries Earthtime, he might see what his son and his descendants had done with the legacy he left behind.

But still he would have the ache of Theadora's absence.

Could he leave her?

Would she forgive him if he did not go off?

No. She had made him great and she would not accept him if he turned his back on her gift of greatness.

From the cockpit of the caravel Winston Overus stared lovingly at the spaceship, thinking up names to christen it. No one had yet offered a title to this piece of work. Olympus, he thought, Hli•skjálf, Starcatcher, Dreamcatcher, Heaven Conqueror, Babel's Restoration.

No, none of those was right. Later, when the ship had been out among the stars for a time, they would find a name for it, something that was worthy of the skyvolk's glorification. He would be the one to name it, he would be the leader of the contingent of skyvolk on the ship. They would be the true masters of this vessel. The Guests and the others would be along for the ride, they who wanted to go to the other holes, the pits in space that were the stars and planets.

He and the sky people would stretch out into the void to ride the emptiness and stride the untrammeled flatness of interstellar space. The universe would be theirs to gaze upon, out there in the democracy of nothingness where no single planet or star could claim anyone by rights of birth or loyalty or love.

Theadora read the letters and smiled in triumph. They were all going, all her inspired delights: Tomaso, Winston, Feather, and Beatrice, all going to the stars. But her children, her loves were staying. Theadora studied her hands as they slid the etched letters into the inlaid teak box that carried her mementos. They had grown thin over the years and her skin had paled to translucency. Lines of blue and violet could be seen, the channels of blood through which life made its entrances and exits.

The time for choices had come. She had maintained her seeming youth throughout the years by drawing upon the subtlest of alien medicines. In her blood, oh red oh blue, were organisms that cleaned her cells, repaired her genes, and reset the clocks of her body. The treatments were expensive and few doctors could perform them. They had kept her on the stage and kept her fertile for decades longer than mortal span was allotted. But they had reached their limits. Other treatments could extend her life beyond this, she could look forward to another half century or more, if she were willing to lose her appearance, turn into a grey-withered creature that needed frequent infusions of unpleasant microorganisms. If she were willing to have her senses numbed and her skin harden, her bones soften and her muscles turn stony.

No, she had had enough of earthly life. Time to let the clocks of her body start anew and let age claim her mortal frame, leaving her immortal to the ages.

She had given birth to and nurtured four children, had performed and recorded many works upon the stage, and she had walked in the shadow of the muses, inspiring others to leap beyond their mortal confines and strive for heaven. Three forms of immortality were enough. The mere physical prolongation of life could be discarded in the face of these three vials of vital elixir.

Dominique Coskun-Feather helped her teacher pack for the long journey. It was a simple task. Eerily simple. Beatrice had been with her all her life, had taught her, had been her second mother, had traveled with the Guisers, who had room to store a lifetime of curios, keepsakes, and tools. But Beatrice had never picked up anything tangible. They had traveled the globe, seen hundreds of settlements and been seen by hundreds of thousands of people, but still Van Leider had gathered in nothing substantial. All that she had gleaned from her journeying were words imprinted and spoken, a weight of words. A Professor's baggage was a library in a backpack, mostly lenticles with a few books old and precious and a few special tools that marked out the members of Academe-in-exile.

"Not that," Beatrice Van Leider said, taking a small rod with a wire on one tapered end. It looked a little like an engraving stylo from a chit-burner, but it was not meant to burn plastics. "Not yet."

Dominique looked into her teacher's eyes, deep brown regarding sharp green.

"Dominique Coskun-Feather," Professor Van Leider said, "you have learned all I have to teach and you are not satisfied. Learning has left a hole in you that seeks to be filled. It will never be filled. The universe will not stop giving you things to learn.

"If you learn all there is to know about a certain thing, you will discover that objects of that study can be arranged to create a new level of things undiscovered in that first field, and that those original objects can be broken up to find new things only hinted at in the nature of those first things. The particles of matter in isolation can be learned, their nature and numbers known. But arrange them, arrange them and find elements, which have of a sudden new and undiscovered properties not found in the quantum numbers of the particles. Particle physics leads naturally to chemistry, but the small number of particles leads surprisingly to the diversity of materials in the world we live in. Chemistry leads naturally to biology, but tells you nothing of life. Biology leads to the study of animals and humans, which leads to the secret arts of psychology and sociology. Does this chain of increasing structure satisfy you?"

"I love to look at it," Dominique answered, finding herself speaking as a child. "It's very pretty."

"And very human," Van Leider said. "It is not how the aliens see things. I have taught you little of the alien thinking, because I know little of it. The Guests keep that understanding for themselves. They have not given it to us. That is why I am going to the stars, to see the alien firsthand."

"But you know something of how they think," Dominique said. Something stirred in her mind, something that echoed like her father's voice.

"A little. I know the Path-Miners make no distinctions of structure, seeing a continuum between the base of the universe and the most complex of biochemical phenomena. I know the Single-Sayers distinguish everything and do not even acknowledge an identity of particles. I know the Moment-Keepers see everything as one thing and each thing as distinct but connected. But I do not understand any of this. It all sounds metaphysical to me, but to them it is as concrete as fire and stone and metal and words are to us."

Dominique took in the challenge implicit in her teacher's words. She was being offered something, a direct line to one of the travelers (Two of the travelers.

Her father was going as well. But Feather was a Guest, an inhuman human. No matter how much she loved him and he her as child and parent, they were not of the same mind).

"I offer you the two-edged sword of Academe," Professor Van Leider said, "to learn and to teach, but never to think you know all and never to teach a thing until you have tried it and found it true. If you do nothing but pass on the words I have given you, you will be a Deceiver. If you alter your words out of pride or fear, you will be a Deceiver. If you try to force your words into another's mind you will be a Predator. If you give anyone a word by which others can be enslaved you will be a Predator. And if you forget people for words you will hang from the Tree of Knowledge and from a tree of reality as well. Do you ask for the brand?"

Wordlessly, Dominique held out her left arm. She had known this day was coming, known what Van Leider had prepared her for, with the compliance of her mother and the always slightly askew assistance of her father. They had made her. She had grown up with the notion that people were made by their parents and teachers. She had watched her brother Gregory in his worship of his father become an artist of images, seeking to sculpt a worthy form for the Handyman. She had seen Patricia go to the sky and take up the verve of the skyvolk, enlivening even the least of them with the notion that their work kept men in heaven. She had seen Karl follow the roads of the world, meeting the Guisers oftentimes in exotic places where he had befriended the footvolk and offered them understanding of the paths they followed, the dancer's son become the leader of a movement.

"You must answer with words," the Professor said.

"Mark me," Dominique quoted.

"I will."

"Here is how we shall become monsters," Feather said to the assemblage.

The Marshallate had brought the soon-to-be crewvolk together in an isolated hospital in Greenland. Five Guests were there, one of each kind; thirteen skyvolk who had been chosen by a combination of testing, verve, politics and the Marshall's seal, only seeming comfortable when inside the hospital where they did not need to face the chaos of weather; and five Professors selected by the Dissociation and one more Professor chosen by the Handyman. Beatrice Van Leider stood a little apart from her colleagues, who distrusted the manner of her selection. Even here in the final university she was not fully accepted. Beatrice growled internally. She had been chosen by the Hand and the Voice did not trust that choice. But she had grown to trust Tomaso Alliende and she would be his colleague even if the other Professors did not accept her as theirs. Beatrice flicked a glance at Tomaso, who stood beside his two apprentices, the man of Earth and the woman of Sky.

"First we will be made very ill," Feather said, his voice intoning according to Theadora's acting methods. As the Method-Smith Guest chosen to go, the adoption of crew to ship was his responsibility. "We need every useful disease known to man. Green Fever for photosynthesis. Thirty-some retroviruses for bodily defense. High- and low-temperature-loving bacteria to give us broader tolerances. Methanogens for atmosphere problems. Then anti-ageing treatments, the full gamut.

"Yes, your skin will turn grey, your eyes will lose

their color, your hormones will cycle wildly. At times you will feel so feverish and angry you'll want to break down the walls of the hospital. And that's only the beginning. Every medical development to stretch out our chances to survive will be used, and over the next two years we will all come to hate and curse the doctors who are altering us, and every one of us will change our minds and wish we had decided to stay on the Earth that bred us and knows our needs and weaknesses. Every one of us will wish we could be struck down by some common happenstance rather than dying in space."

"Not all of us are that bound to Earth," Winston Overus said, rising from his seat in the hospital's auditorium and challenging Feather with the same stage-presence and operation.

"More than you think," Feather said, turning the challenge into an opportunity for more oration. "Skyvolk, Guests, all of us who try to pull away, we move far in our minds, but our bodies are not isolated from the ebb and flow of biochemistry. Not a one of us is truly alone in the universe. The Earth and the ways of the Earth are always with us. In your skyboroughs, in the space ship, everywhere we go we must take the methods of Earth with us if we want to survive. But there are too many of those methods. We cannot have them all. So we try to broaden what we can carry within ourselves, try to arm our bodies against all the things we might lack, and in so doing we become monsters, and even after all that we will probably fail and die."

"Fail in what aspects?" Professor Saul Ben Isaac stood from his seat; his dry voice moderated with the oratory of teaching rose in tonal challenge to the actor who spoke from the stage. He coughed and pulled at the tight collar of his shirt where it bit into the old scar of a failed hanging. That lesson thirty-six years ago had taught him such caution and deliberation that he had been chosen unanimously as Dean of this first interstellar university.

Feather picked up a plaque, the contents of which had been relayed from the oncoming ship to the High Talker to the Guesthouse to his hand.

"Each of the other species had to send a first crew, a test crew if you will, to see what they would need to survive this journey. Of the original Method-Smiths only the sample of Ocean survived, but it had learned how to let its species live in space. Of the nine Moment-Keepers who left their world, none of the originals made it home. Three of their children did. None of the first crew of Band-Braiders adapted well enough to space, nor the second. Only their third made it. The Path-Miners routinely lose half their crews even now, though they have been nine times through the cycle of ship leaving and returning. Only the Single-Sayers have kept their mortality rates low."

Britt Lookdown, one of the skyvolk, piped up. The youngest of the crew by more than three decades, she had been recommended to the Marshall by Winston Overus for her piloting skills and her fervor for the sky. "If we die," she said. "the ones who come after will learn from us."

There was a slow collective sigh as the older crewvolk looked sadly at the young woman. Youth was too confident in its sacrifices. But perhaps she would learn.

"We will be gone a long time," Feather said. "And out there between the stars we will find what things of Earth we truly need to survive. Maybe some of us will come back, but Britt Lookdown is correct. We old and dying monsters will teach the people who come after us."

Sean Chan-Hillard (No other names were needed, for all that he had learned had come from his immediate forebears. There was no need to concern himself with further lineages.) looked around his new office. The ConCensorship had fallen on him as he had expected it eventually would. His brother Julian was too active a soul to sit and govern. But it had come earlier than he had anticipated. Both his parents were going on the ship. They would be gone much longer than his lifespan, longer than that of his own young children, perhaps even longer than their children's children. That would depend on choices made, and on the chances for survival in the depths of space.

Chances. At times Sean Chan-Hillard wished he could look at such a human concept and take it seriously. But there were no chances in Single-Sayer mathematics. The universe sealed something, then it was unsealed. Before that sealing there were what humans called causes, after the unsealing were effects. Even on the quantum level there was the seal of inobservation and the unseal of looking. Human mathematicians labeled such things with probabilities and distributions, the language of dice and cards. Quantum mechanics as humans spoke of it was the glorification of gamblers.

But the Single-Sayers talked differently of the matter. They said that sealing was the way of the universe, that only in hiding were things rearranged, that unsealing was the learning of the universe, but that the unsealer put his own view into the act of unsealing. They had suffered no problems, no trauma to their physics when they had learned the individualization of quantum phenomena. They had always expected such would be the case.

For them the ship was a simple matter. Seal up

the crew, send it out, unseal it when it returns and see what is inside. But Sean's parents were being sealed in, his past, his teachers, the two human-aliens who had taught him to be human and alien, and likely when they departed he would not see them again.

Likely. There was that alluring human mathematics again. No, seal them up, close the hatch, brand the doors with the names of the Dissociation, the skyvolk, and the Handyman. When the ship returned someone else would unseal it and look inside to see what his forbears had become.

And they were not going quite yet. They had another year of treatments in Greenland, and then two more years before the ship arrived. But in Greenland they had been isolated and were being sealed by Feather's Monster-Method into Solitaires.

Solitaires were a vital concept in Single-Sayer thinking. That which was alone became more what it was. It had been isolated Single-Sayers who had invented their mathematics, had created their languages, made their first tools. In isolation things became themselves. Every sealing was an isolation, a making of a new thing that existed alone, a Solitaire. Seal every Single-Sayer up and you had a new Solitaire. Each thing was alone. Everything (though the Single-Sayers had no concept of everything) was alone.

"Each thing is unique," Sean repeated to himself, back to first lessons. "Each view of each thing is unique. Each packing of each thing is unique, each unpacking unique. Each allotment is unlike every other allotment. See the uniqueness and you can count. Conjoin the uniquenesses and you can pack. See the packing and you can seal and unseal."

Sean touched the door that now recognized his uniqueness as it had until recently recognized his mother's. "Please bring me the seals of Consent and Dissent," he said to the workers in his office. Time to seal himself into his position.

The light ahead of the ship stretched and unkinked its Doppler-knotted wavelengths, relaxing into the lower reaches of energy. Radio and microwaves that had been pushed into the human-visible range now gentled down into the long wavelengths they favored. Common blues fell down from the excitation of hobnobbing with x-rays and gamma rays, and the latter, which had entered reaches not felt since the early energy-dominated universe, returned to their accustomed positions in the spectrum.

That, at least, was one perspective. Remarker-of-changes-in-light sealed its notice of the ship's arising slowness as they neared the star-of-newest-found-species-the-people-who-see-commonalities-but-express-proper-uniqueness. Remarker-of-changes-in-light flew back to the hollow mountain called natural-customs-of-home to become sealer-of-interstellar-reports. It was a long flight from filter-feeder-of-interstellar-gases, since he had to avoid any approach to highest-of-all-predators-that-yet-can-be-half-tamed-and-sustenance-taken-from.

Along the way Remarker-of-changes-in-light noticed that four of the species-that-digs-in-all-things-yet-sees-more-broadly-than-any-known had come out onto one of the flats that sat at all angles to their volcano of a habitat.

The Path-Miners had emerged to feel the first wisps of sunlight, the tenuous echo of nearing a star, the reminder of living on worlds. They had forgotten all of that in their journey across the Echo and their mining of the deepest heats of emptiness.

Now they rested, waiting to carve and be carved

by new experience in their unbounded minds.

Two bands of light shot forth from the filter of the ship, aimed for where the Earth would be when they struck. The Doppler games, the shifts and twists of gravity would distort each beam, but in the ratio of their frequencies lay a constant that would survive the distortions of the noisy universe, and in variations of that constant did the true Method-Smiths send tractation to their guestly surrogates.

The High Talker caught the beams and weighed their ratios in the scales of Constance Marchant's methods. Language, human in form if not intent, then cascaded down in a simple laser to reach the Method-Smith house where Grandmère waited to receive means from the stars.

For three weeks Grandmère studied the message, checking over the methods, editing, noting flaws and correcting. Like a smith at a forge she hammered away at the defects, tempered the extremes, sharpened the edges, until at last it was done.

"Constance," she called out and the room grew red with what attention remained to the first Guest. "We've done it. Here is an Option Lattice for choosing Guests. See, we've separated the scouting methods from the indoctrination methods. The scouting-Tractases have four classes with options between them. We can make specialist scouts to track through common groupings of people, isolated groupings, individuals, and with Feather's help, monsters. The indoctrination-Adoptionases have three classes: bringing in, driving off, and maintaining where they are. The Method-Smiths worked on the means I sent them and gave them back to me to finish so they can be passed on to others.

My methods can be given to others.

"And even if all the ones who come after us fail, the next time the ship comes it can recreate what we are. The Guests can return even if none of our followers live. Constance, it's done. I can join you in the Ocean."

The light went out and all that could be heard was the lapping waters of the method-pool, and for a few brief minutes, the beating of Grandmère's heart.

7. Injection and Projection

Once inside the solar system the alien ship began to feed. Filter-feeding at first, it savored the solar wind, slowing to dine upon the exhalations of a star. Light and matter, all were one to it. Only neutrinos passed uneaten through the four-kilometer disk of its filter; most of those escaped to the interstellar reaches, but those few that came too close to the monster at the ship's heart were eaten as well.

Relative to the star the ship was crawling inward, barely able to traverse the diameter of Neptune's orbit in a year, just another group of rocks falling down the well, tripping into Sol's gravity-maw. To the sun there was no sign that this little collection could escape it, nor that if it did capture and consume these morsels that it would die a much swifter and much stranger death than stars of its kindred could justly expect.

The monster in the ship ate the filter-food, but dining only made it hungrier. Wendigo-like, its growth induced starvation, but unlike that mythic monster of the earthly cold, this creature had a use for its hunger. Like a bear in summer it fed much upon much for the lean winter of interstellar travel yet to come.

Fortunately for the monster it did not have to rely upon the filter for most of its food. It had servants who would bring it meals more solid and substantial, bits of gas-giant ring ferried in on Single-Sayer wings, and closer in to its gleaming yellow cousin the savor of small asteroids. The monster would have delighted in the taste of planet or the too-swift absorption of plummeting into a star, but its servants guided it so that it came not close to any such storehouse of delectation.

No, the ship's handlers made sure that it dined sedately in its movable feast. They needed enough energy-fat for the journey to the next star, but not more, since too heavy a beast would not attain the swiftness they wished. The monster's diet was a delicate balance between the energy of travel and the inertial mass that needed to be moved.

All six of the species had come to the same troubling equivalence between matter and energy and the same troubling constraint of momentum and inertia. Some had come more swiftly than others.

The Path-Miners had never conceived of matter and energy as separate things, for to them it was the heat of a substance that made it important. Evolution had taught them to dig for heat, and they had dug deep and deep into the structure of things so they could draw heat from the emptiness of vacuum if need be.

The Single-Sayers had come grudgingly to the

equivalence, for they distrusted sameness. All they would acknowledge was the unbreakable seal that conjoined each thing to the space around it. They called it the Seal of Light and still yet wondered if it could be opened.

The Moment-Keepers knew that it was so, had seen that it was so, accepted that it was so, and created their actions accordingly.

The Band-Braiders had rejoiced in the simultaneous nature of matter and energy. It had affirmed their conception of the universe and they had taken up the lightness of matter and the heaviness of light with gusto.

The Method-Smiths had looked upon this as a means the universe used. They had studied its applications and concluded that interchangeability was a method of taking away and creating structure, that light was one of the fundamental Adoptionases of the universe, one of the deepest means of bringing things together. They saw that light adopted by becoming part of what it connected and then emerging changed to conjoin other things. Thus had they adopted light into their Option and Capable Lattices. Using light, they had found the baby monsters left over from the beginning of the universe and nurtured a few of them to large enough size to power their journeys between the stars. The capturers of light had become the means of imitating light in near swiftness, if not in all its fundamental characters.

And humans, well, humans had said that there is power in all things because energy is power and all things are energy. Therefore they hunted for power and eagerly learned all the alien ways of power, and therefore they awaited this demonstration of the power to cross the void.

Out from the well of Earth the human habitat sailed. Towed by twenty interplanetary caravels, riding a score of anti-matter torches, it fled the gravity of its birth until the Earth was but a trivial pull upon it and the grip of the sun had to remind it that it was still deep within the arms of a material body.

Once the habitat had been blessed with enough speed, ten of the caravels detached and returned to the skyboroughs, there to resume their commonplace in-system duties, while the remaining ten accompanied the habitat, waiting to become its workers out between the stars.

All over the Earth and in its over-dependencies there came an exhalation, a breathing out of the strange and a return to everyday matters. The aliens were not truly coming. Their ship would inject itself no deeper into Sol's system than the orbit of Mars. Nor would envoys come on alien wings to touch the ground of Earth and speak (if speak they could) to human or Guest.

The news of this non-landing had deflated many on Earth. The resurgent Ufneck volks had faltered in their rise, confused again as their forebears had been. Why did they not come? Why would they travel so far across the emptiness and not take the last few steps to meet humanity in its native habitat?

The Guests were besieged with these questions. But they too were at a loss.

At last Constance Marchant offered an explanation, eerily articulate as she had not been for many years. "They lack the methods of close approach. Next time they will know us well enough. Wait. It's only two or three hundred years until the next cycle."

Two or three centuries. The beyond-lifespans character of those numbers flew around the world, and for the first time since the Troth-breaking humanity felt the anger that comes from things going too slowly. The more radical of the Dissenting nations cried "Deceiver" against the Guests and the Dissociation. They tried to form a mob of volks to lynch the offenders. But most would not join in, and the eruption boiled down into simmering pools of anger.

The Consenting nations had hoped for some return for their donations to the effort, yet all the Dissociation could say was, "Wait. When those who have gone on the ship have learned the ways of the aliens better than the most advanced Guest, then we will be given the rewards of our efforts."

To this what could they do but Consent?

The wave of effort that had led the Earth to spawn, the contractions that had birthed the habitat rolled back upon the volks, Consenters and Dissenters alike. They had seen a child born, looked upon it, some with love, others with fear. They had stared at infancy and realized with terrible certitude that only time and experience would bring the new born to adulthood, and that the glowing face and first breaths of the baby told nothing of what kind of grown being it would become. The future stared them in the face, mewled for milk, and fell into inscrutable sleep.

At such times, parents turn to those who proffer glimpses of the future.

Five days out from Earth, Beatrice Van Leider decided to abandon 'up' and 'down' as useful concepts.

Seven days out she threw away 'day' and 'night'. Twelve days found her rejecting 'oriented' and 'disoriented'. At twenty days she teetered on the point of discarding 'here' and 'there', but that far she was not willing to go.

Professor Van Leider decided that she had destroyed enough of her old ways of thinking and that she should now build anew. Therefore she went floating from bubble to bubble, swinging from tether to tether, sliding along half-sticky, half-slippery membranes to reach the architect of this world and challenge him to produce a useful coordinate system.

The Professor found the Handyman in one of the telescope bubbles, studying the retreat of Earth. His sandpaper-rough grey hands rooted around in the empty box that controlled the scope. What he focused on appeared in a globe of image mist anchored by eight supple lines to the surrounding sphere.

"Look at Antarctica," he said. "The domes are already going up for the next test habitat. Three generations are going to live in there. Our image, our Guests left behind. Feather's right. We're already aliens to them."

Van Leider said, "Feather says we're monsters, creatures of the dark void, nightmares that go out and visit other nightmares. He thinks we'll be tales to frighten children by the time the ship returns."

"Whether or not there are any of us left alive," Alliende said, "monster ship or ghost ship, they'll be scared of us."

"And we of them," Van Leider said. "Who knows what Earth will be like when we return."

Alliende pulled his hands from the box and the image vanished into unintelligible fog.

"What can I do for you, Beatrice?" he said.

"What makes you think I need something?"

"Everyone is coming to me with problems.

Winston wants the caravel tugs made capable of more independent work. They can't last more than five months away from the ship. He wants them fitted out for a year away."

"Can you do that? Those are standard skyvolk caravels. I thought they were as good as we could make for now."

"They still have a lot of earthly comforts that take up space, comforts we don't need. We could also take the manufactories out of some of them. That would lighten the load but reduce their safety. And I can make the engines better, if we don't care about finesse in docking maneuvers."

"Don't we care about finesse?"

"The Path-Miner Guest says the Path-Miners will fit something onto the ship for docking. But there aren't any human words for hmmm-whirr-zzz-umm. At least not yet."

"Shouldn't you wait, then?"

"Of course. But Winston is shockingly insistent."

"Eager as an untrained child," Beatrice Van Leider said. "Who else has been bothering you?"

"Your colleagues want the experiment spheres up and running as soon as possible. I'm turning them on and testing them one at a time, but we still don't know what conditions will be like when we've joined the ship, so I have to test a broad range of possibilities for each one, slow work. And the Guests want all sorts of strange things. Hillard's the worst. He wants a space-capable membrane that can function underwater and can globally accept and send out electric impulses."

"Why?"

"He wants to 'really' talk to the Moment-Keeper when we get there. So what do you want, Beatrice?"

"A coordinate system," she said. "This ship is flying and turning so much I don't know which way is which. Why didn't you install directions in here?"

Alliende flashed a grin of sharp blue teeth, then stroked his jawline. The new-grown teeth with their ever-hardening enamel still felt strange where they gripped his skull. "Because what we say about where we are is your problem, not mine. You're the Crazy Old Woman Who Knows Everything."

"Then why didn't you suggest that I solve this before we took off?"

"Because you wouldn't have believed there was a problem until you experienced it. What good is a model that doesn't fit reality?"

Beatrice Van Leider paused to savor the question. What good is a model that doesn't fit reality? Maybe it fits something else important. She did not speak her answer, not needing to. Both she and the Handyman had experienced Theadora and knew that not everything important or useful was real.

"Very well," Van Leider said. "I'll work on the matter."

"If you will forgive me," the Handyman said. "I must start up the next five experiments for your eagerly abstracted colleagues."

With that he curled up, pushed off from the wall, and bounced out of the observatory, leaving Beatrice Van Leider to wonder whether Tomaso Alliende had come on this expedition to be the Handyman or to pay back the Crazy Old Woman Who Knows Everything for millennia of arrogance and disconnection from reality.

Or -- and this thought tingled Van Leider -- had he come to escape the bonds of his old assumptions? And had she come for the same reason? And what happened, she wondered for the first time, to the bonds when you escape them?

The walls of the Allways Hostel were perfect silent barricades as any living space on the grounds of an omniport had to be. The Allways was at the edge of the Haifa Omniport, gateway to Israel (and Judah and Palestine, and the Desert Disputed lands, and the seven Caliphates, but the locals did not care to discuss that). Ships of land and sea and sky and underworld all made noise, and none of those noises harmonized with any others. Only the maglev lines were silent, quiet functional workers amid the boister of alternative conveyances.

Karl Coskun-Rainbow looked out the window of his room in the hostel, looked out upon the noise and heard nothing but the socially inaudible sounds of his young sister Dominique in the next room. The builders of this place had silenced the music, but the dance of the road could be seen in the arrivals and departures.

The intense activity and heightened travel of the last twenty years had added an embarrassing bustle to the world's omniports, the transport of materia the (oh shameful word) importation of needed things had pushed the capacity of these places. But the ship, the human habitat was done, and already there was a slowing of effort and the people who knew the ways of the world and had been dragooned as navigators were returning the life of the road. The footvolk had been invited into the cities for a time. Now they were leaving again, after being reminded of the settled life.

"Any sign of their vessel?" Dominique said. She emerged dried and dressed in a hand-me-down gown of Theadora's, bright green silk embroidered with cranes.

"Not yet," Karl said. "But it should be today. Where will you go afterwards?"

"East China," Dominique said. "The University of Beijing has spoken with interest for me. They may only want me to wait for messages from Beatrice, but I will be able to work while I wait out the decades."

Karl nodded. His eye spotted a falling speck growing larger, larger. It swooped over the omniport, then lit upon the ground. Ovoid with wings, four times the size of its parent and much clumsier, still the second Pantechnicon landed with grace. The images on its sides, painted with love and attention by Gregory, showed forth the glory of smiths over the ages. It was not, as the first Pantechnicon had been, a working vehicle. Rather was it a traveler's luxury, and a reminder of the source of its owner's wealth.

A short time later the four children of Theadora Coskun met in the public restaurant of the Allways Hostel. There they spoke of their mother who had retired to her native Cyprus and their fathers who had all left the world, three together and one apart. And from there they made their disparate ways in the world.

Decades later much would be made of that meeting in the hostel, as if the fate of the Earth were plotted out and the aspects of humanity divided up, but the tales told did not fit the simple fact of two brothers and two sisters meeting together as family then departing each alone.

Thirty-eight days out from Earth, seventeen until rendezvous, Quint Hillard and Elsbet Chan lay cocooned together in a sleep-ball attached to the inside of the second membrane within the central sphere. Curled in each other's arms, they read through the gravings Beatrice Van Leider had distributed to the crewvolk.

"The central sphere will be called Home. The membranes around it will be numbered I to X from inside to outside. A gyroscope will be placed at the center of Home, tethered to the walls. Its axis will serve as the axis of the world. Its spinning disk will be the level of the world. All co-ordinates will be in relation to this axis."

Elsbet Chan, giddy from the long exposure to no gravity and the excitement of the trip, could contain her giggles no longer. Quint Hillard watched with pleasure. His Princess had so rarely giggled all the days of their lives that it was a joy to see. "Humans," she said. "What a messy way of thinking we have. Orientation, commutation, calculation. Why can't we just count things as they are? Central sphere, membrane-of rest, membrane-of-control, membrane-of-contemplation, membrane-of-mist . . . " She named all the parts of the ship one after another, implying connections where needed.

"Well, if you insist on doing that much work," Quint said. "I just took the whole place in."

"And what have you found of it, oh my omniscient lord?"

"That we have no idea what we're doing, so we've made a lot of guesses, and that our esteemed master builder has made sure he can change his design if need be, always assuming we have the materials and energy to make the changes."

Elsbet Chan nodded her head within the webbing, her body shivering slightly in response to the motion. "Yes, here we are, our bodies within the Seal of the Handyman and our lives within the Seal of Feather. I'm glad the children are still on Earth."

"They wanted so much to come," Quint said. "All the young Guests did. I heard from Britt Lookdown that many young skyvolk did as well. She's the envy of the skyboroughs, the only youth among us."

"They don't know what they'd be giving up," Elsbet said. "Now they can grumble that we took their chance from them. Better that than they see what the sacrifices are. I wish Winston Overus hadn't brought that child. But he did insist on the best pilot regardless of age and Gabriello had to agree."

"Poor girl," Quint said, "I hope she doesn't come to hate all of us when she realizes what she's left behind." He stroked Elsbet's cheek, roughened skin against roughened skin. He remembered himself as a boy, callow with superficial views. Even his Burst awareness had only touched the skins of things, not yet learning the adult means of spiking inside what he looked at. If in those days his Princess had once appeared grey-skinned, ciliated-and silicated-fronds for hair, eyes washed so clear that the blood in capillaries could be seen as red channels floating in the orbs, he would not have thought her beautiful as he did now, as he would for however long they had together. Whether they lived or died in space, they would be together, beautiful in each other's eyes.

The human ship decelerated to meet the alien vessel at a point that Mars had occupied eight months before, but which now was a stretch of unremarkable space. In this space, moving away from the sun at a few thousand kilometers per hour, was an assortment of mismatched oddities flying in perfect synchronicity. Luminous baubles, they gleamed, each in its own spectrum, marker buoys of the dark hazard in the center of them all.

The crewvolk had gathered in the elevation twenty-six degrees, nw-direction, secondary sphere, where Winston Overus was directing the ship's approach. The upper half of this sphere was filled with image mist that showed the course lines, vectors and arcs of travel, all plotted in overlay upon the image of the sky. Arrayed around the edges of the hemisphere were close views of the illuminated bodies.

"That looks like a mountain," Elsbet Chan said, pointing to a rich red-brown multispired cone, a tapering structure with clear balls on top of the spikes -- viewing nests, no doubt. She could almost smell the air of a Single-Sayer mountain, could feel the wind that would call a Single-Sayer to the life of solitude and observation. The crew of that habitat were Solitaires, then. Each of these Single-Sayers would have come to look upon the universe from this highest of perches. Each would be most like itself and have names folded within names, seals within seals. They would be deep in their thinking and clear in their vision. When would she be able to fly over and meet them?

"No," said the hesitant voice of the Path-Miner Guest. He had learned much of human speech since he had left Elsbet Chan's office and joined her crew. "That . . . is . . . a . . . mountain."

His hand gestured toward a carved and grooved surface, a flattened mesa in mid-space with a combination of slopes and craterings that bespoke volcano. Light played complexly from it, lines and swirls of arcs, meaningful only to him. Follow me, they said, travel down me. The edges of this edifice seemed to be ill-defined, as if they faded into the space around them without ever coming to a definite limit.

Quint Hillard stared at a pulsing patchwork ball covered with protrusions that opened and shut as needed. That was where his intended was, the one whom he had come to speak with, to meet with, to Meet State with. If he could, if the hardware worked, if he really was as much of a Moment-Keeper as he thought.

The eyes of Marie the Band-Braider Guest were intent on the cascade of lenses and mirrors that floated farthest from them. Light emerged from all its ways, lights and lights, all the shades. They were singing to her, the Band-Braiders were singing a welcome in a music no hearing human could ever appreciate.

Feather studied a simple ball that glowed beacon white. There is the Ocean, he thought. But what beasts of the deep has it spawned already, and when will it call me to my drowning?

And why am I so at peace with that flying death? Who has worked upon me? Grandmère, Theadora, myself?

Hesitantly, the caravel tugs reduced the human habitat's relative speed, bringing it in so that it and the other five habitats formed the vertices of an imperfect prism. At the center of this, more seen in the x-ray than the visible spectrum, was the monster, and around it orbited two matte dull pieces of hardware, one pitted by micrometeors, the other scarred by close approach to the black hole. The feeder and the harvester were the best translations from the Method-Smith language that Feather had been able to achieve. But they were enough for Tomaso Alliende to understand their purposes and instruct Winston Overus to keep the habitat well away from them.

The feeder brought solid food to the small black hole, and the harvester would dive into the ergosphere of the monster and extract energy that escaped the inescapable. From there the harvester would fly away and feed its bounty to the engine, one of the two ship components that flew in an orbit higher than that of the habitats, the other being the filter. All that was clear to the Handyman. What was not clear was how these disparate unconnected objects would be conjoined through the twenty-kilometer-radius region and be made to fly together.

From the ball of free-floating ocean emerged six black figures like flat-headed squid with fingers all up and down their tentacles. They had no minds, no thoughts of their own, but waiting on the opposite side of the membrane that held the ocean was a six-headed serpent that had all the mind they needed. Its heads fitted into sockets in their bodies, latticing their active functions to its mental ones. As one they slithered into the midsection of an almost-hourglass device. One end of it was rounded with half-sphere indentations, made to fit on the human ship. The other end was tapered and bell-like, its edges fading off into space. In the middle was a simple ring of maneuvering rockets and the minuscule store of anti-matter needed to move this device to the human habitat.

Four different crews, mixed Method-Smith, Single-Sayer, and Path-Miner working together, converged and attached the means of conjoining the new habitat to the ship, four pieces of hardware that would bring them all together. The Method-Smiths knew the devices as Adopt-the-Void, Catch-and-throw-small-ships, Tractase-through-Void, and Adopt-Conceptions.

In a brief time the methods were installed and the means of installing them returned to the ocean, bringing the taste of human materials and the feel and curve of human machining. These means the ocean absorbed and contemplated, adjusting its chemistry accordingly. The next methods spawned to deal with humans would fit their means more exactly.

"They're finished," said the Handyman, watching the retreat of the installation crews.

"What were those things?" Professor Saul Ben

Isaac asked.

"They were a means of building in space," Feather said.

"But they looked alive."

"I'm alive," he said. "Why shouldn't they be?"

"What's that humming sound?" Beatrice Van Leider asked.

"Testing . . . " said the Path-Miner Guest. "Sound . . . of . . . planet. Reminder."

"They're communicating with us?"

"The Path-Miners are," said Quint Hillard.

"What are they saying?" asked Saul Ben Isaac.

"The . . . path . . . to . . . leaving," said the Path-Miner Guest. "Prepare."

"When do we go?" asked Van Leider

"Path-Miners . . . have . . . no . . . when," said the Path-Miner Guest, straining at the human thought of time.

"What does that mean?" said Van Leider.

"It means get to launch stations," said Winston Overus. "We go when they decide. But we have to be ready now."

The crew made for the habitat balls and snugged themselves into their webbing. Feeder membranes slid into their skins to supply them with nutrients in case they were held down for long stretches. There the crewvolk floated, stuck to the webs of their own making. Patience they had aplenty, but even that exhausted itself as hours ticked by into days. All they could do was lie there and talk and let the multitude of adopted micro-organisms keep them fed and healthy and their muscles from atrophying, as well as suppressing the anger of their stomachs (though the empty feeling would not go away). Mist globes could show them images real and fictional, but even that began to pale in the face of the tension.

And then, at what seemed in retrospect like the

last moment they could have tolerated the suspense (though whenever it came it would have been the last such moment) there came a hum, then a push, a tautening of the webs, a directioning of space, a new up and a new down. There was a clear dizzy-ending recollection in their minds, in their bones, in their inner ears of apparent gravity.

"We have acceleration," Winston Overus' voice echoed through the ship. "Zero point six-two-seven gee. But we can't see anything outside. Our scopes just pick up white light, broad spectrum, all up and down from gamma to radio."

"We need some idea of what's happening out there," said Saul Ben Isaac. "Everybody out of the webs; let's go to work."

Sliding, grabbing, and swinging, the humans made their way to their various workplaces, all save the Path-Miner Guest who listened to the hum and watched the light with increasingly vacant eyes, and Marie the Band-Braider who looked out upon the white light and knew that it marked the beginning of their rise up the Arch toward the unreachable keystone of lightspeed.

Earth, mother of monsters, gave up her child. Into alien hands she commended her progeny. Out into the darkness and silence that spawned all things she let it go without regret. Let it live for a time among the stars, let it know what it was like to be isolated, to feed upon the simplicity of starstuff and from it try to form the complexities of life. Let it know what its mother did for it every second of every hour of every day of the whole span of earthly existence.

A little guilt was good for a child. Let it go. It would come back with a measure of respect that it would teach to the disorderly youngsters who stayed behind. Let it learn and come back, or not learn and not come back at all. That too might teach the little monsters.

Part II:
Analysis:
Rising Freedom

8. Gradient, Divergence, and Curl

"It's field," Beatrice Van Leider said, rolling the word around her throat. She had been speaking Footsprach for so long that the compromise between Footsprach, Guestsprach, Skysprach, and the birth languages of the crewvolk, the multi-pidgin that was becoming Shipsprach, still jarred at her. "They've excited and shaped the potentials of the unified field. That's what's holding the habitats and the other ship components together."

"How can you tell?" asked Tomaso Alliende

with annoying equanimity.

"Because whatever we shoot out there is affected," she said. "Whatever kind of particle we emit is attracted or repelled by that whiteness. Only the unified field affects everything in that way."

"Why is it white?" he asked.

"I don't know. It's doing something to the light."

"Have you asked our Path-Miner guest?"

"I tried. He said they were smoothing the echoes."

"What does that mean?"

"I don't know. All I know is that the ship's components are being held in fixed positions relative to the black hole and we're all accelerating uniformly."

"Have you tried asking any of the other Guests?"

"They're just as baffled. Why are you so complacent? There's a piece of hardware moving this ship around that we don't understand and can't fix if it breaks."

"Yes, but I expected that."

"You did? I thought they'd tell us what was happening before they did it."

"Why would you think that?"

"Because that's what we would do," Van Leider said, mustering patience and speaking in teacher-to-inattentive-student voice.

"That's what the voicevolk would do," the Handyman said. "The aliens aren't people, and if you'd paid attention to the Path-Miner Guest you'd know they aren't of the Voice."

"Very glib, Tomaso, but it still doesn't tell us what's happening or what else they can do with that hardware. Also, the Guests have always said that the aliens were not more advanced than we were, just differently developed."

Alliende laughed. Who but the Crazy Old Woman Who Knows Everything would want to put a measuring stick to a species' understanding in order to say which one was larger than another?

"Beatrice," he said after his laughter had died away and the ash-rose blush had faded from her face, "what do you want me to do?"

"Help us build testing apparatus. We want to know what it is and how it works. We're Professors. We want to learn."

"We?"

Beatrice turned away from Alliende. Her gaze roamed around the Pantechnicon. The securing membrane concealed the view of space, although of course without the membrane all she could have seen was white anyway. Her eyes at last found a convenient purchase in the webbed-down library shelving.

Such a span of books. No Professor would have collected so strangely. Translations of unearthed architecture notes dating back to the builders of Egypt's monumental works of worship, ancient Chinese alchemy texts, every fragment of Pythagorean writings that had ever been unearthed, the Book of Ezekiel but none of the rest of the Jewish or Christian Bibles, an account of the Mi'raj but not the Koran, mythologies from all over the world, two dozen medieval allegories all pointing toward heaven or love or money, all the surviving works of Leon Battista Alberti, a work by a Renaissance mining master called the Pirotechnia, a diary of a navvy who had helped build canals in England, and works on science and engineering from the nineteenth century through modern days.

"The other Professors are willing to include me in the work if I can get your assistance."

Tomaso held his tongue. He had been amazed that the snobbery of the Professors had survived the Troth-Breaking, had survived being overshadowed by the Guests, had survived the threat of the noose, and still manifested here. He had never asked Beatrice how that could be, not wanting to challenge her that directly.

Still perhaps it should not have surprised him. He had once overheard two Professors talking about the writing of history and the viewpoints of the writers, and he suspected that hidden in the conclaves and colloquies of Academe-in-exile was the knowledge that one day the voicevolk would write the history of this time. In that writing the world would be turned upside down and the homeless Professors would be made the heroes of the time, preservers of the light amidst the ragged tatters of non-civilization. And why not? They had done it before when they invented the myth of the Dark Ages.

His immediate reaction was to reject Beatrice's plea. But he hammered down the anger and quenched it in the waters of his mind. The crewvolk needed to know what was happening. And Beatrice needed to belong to this spaceborn University. At least for now.

"I'll help you," he said.

The Path-Miner Guest lay webbed against the Underbelly, the closest human word for the device that connected ship to field. The Underbelly had been constructed (carved in the fields that bound atoms together) to feel the way a Path-Miner's belly did as it slid through rock. Through its underbelly the warmth and thrum of the world beneath the world were open to a Path-Miner's mind. The underbelly was one of the two primary sense organs of the Path-Miners. It felt the underworld for them, just as their upper skins saw the world above. But to them the two were one, echoes of movement underground and echoes of light aboveground, all echoes in the terrain through which they dug.

Here out in space, a place they would never have gone if the Method-Smiths had not contacted them, they had needed to see and feel the terrain, for they could remember nothing without terrain to pass through. So they had dug down to the base of the universe, digging for warmth and nuance, and there they had found the Echo, the bubbling field, the decaying vacuum, the terrain within emptiness. They had made machines (Not machines. Humans made machines. Path-Miners made paths even if the paths had to be carved out of pieces fitted together) to find the hum of the Echo, to tune and thrum with the universe.

They had cast forth this understanding, and the Method-Smiths had caught the means they had thrown and adjoined it to the previously solid, compact ship. The Path-Miners had added space and emptiness, breadth and freedom to this interstellar Adoptionase, and because of that the Method-Smiths had been able to bring other species with them on their journeys.

But the Path-Miner Guest lay in hard hummed frustration. He could not feel the hum. He knew it was there, knew that the universe was singing to him in its underbreath, but he lacked the underbelly to feel it. His human body and human senses denied him the experiences of his adopted species.

Little by little mass was harvested from the monster and fed to the field which was mother to the monster, child feeding parent in reverse nursing. Little by little the ship's velocity grew relative to the star it was leaving and the star it sought. Up the potential gradient it rose, out of the pit of gravity toward the relative flatness between the stars.

And as its position rose from depression, so its

incommensurable velocity rose up the Arch toward the untouchable speed. Rising, the universe changed around it, the star forward gleaming into the blue of approach, the blue of newborn stars, and the sun behind it falling into the deep red of feeble old age. Distance shrank, time grew slow, all things distorted around the ship. Such was the terrible power placed in every moving object, to change all things within space-time by the exertion of acceleration. Each thing in the universe has this great ability to remold everything else by donning the mantle of relative swiftness.

"Have you found the communication method yet?" Elsbet Chan asked Feather.

"I believe so," he said. "It seems to be this pod connected to the Underbelly. "

"Why this pod?

"Because the material inside will conform to any earthly animal that enters it and touch their senses. I still don't know how to turn it on or signal any of the other components."

The Guests had been working for six months ship time, trying to comprehend the machinery attached to the human vessel. Their failure to do so had been a surprise to all of them. They had expected equipment similar to that which they knew of, but this had all been new.

The frustration had begun only a month after they had begun to study the ship. Failed attempts to understand the gifts of their correspondent species had brought Feather and the other Guests together. "The Method-Smiths did this deliberately," Feather had said. "They are fitting us into Species Shock before we actually meet the aliens

"Why?" Marie signed.

"Because we've been complacent," he said. We -- He was a Guest, had always been one, had finally accepted that he had always been one. "We've grown enough like them for interstellar communications, but not face-to- -- whatever -- meetings. They're slowing us down deliberately so we don't all go mad when we meet our counterparts."

"So we study the equipment slowly and learn what we can," Quint Hillard said.

"Exactly," Feather said. "There should be something here for each of us. Look around and find your methods."

Five more months of study and work had brought them a little understanding and a great aching void of bewilderment. Feather had found what might be the communications pod, but had not learned to use it. Elsbet Chan had discovered a Single-Sayer Seal on a complex array of rods, but had not been able to open it. Marie had found a store of lenticles, but could not find the correct light to shine through and read them. Quint Hillard had discerned the inner edge of a patch which now covered a region of spheres on the human habitat, but he had not been able to change its mode from passive to active. And the Path-Miner Guest had snugged up to the Underbelly, but still could not feel the universe.

Winston Overus had no interest in the frustrations of the groundlings, human or Guest. His concern was the imagined fading of the red star behind as it dwindled into a piece of stellar tinsel, just another bright night spot that faded into the whiteness of space. They had left the solar system behind and were now in the open sky. His time was spent in a clear bubble, looking out through the ivory expanse of the universe. Black or white mattered not to him. He knew they were free of the well, knew they were entering the embrace of the sky, knew it was calling to him, if only he could hear its words.

The white sky lured him with its variations, its flickers, its rainbows in the cloud-color and rainbows reflected in the reflections of the ship, scatterings from the eternal light-talk that the stars made through the lenses, prisms and diffraction gratings of interstellar gas. It was not all white out there, any more than the unaltered sky would have been all black. No matter what the artifact that filtered the cosmos for the delectation of the eye, be it atmosphere, cloud, smog, roof, telescope, radio telescope, x-ray telescope, patch, or this brightening, bubbling mass of whiteness, the sky would find a way to let you know it was there.

"We've mapped the field potential," Beatrice Van Leider said as she reached her hand into the control box, pulled the map out of the picture-well, and dropped it into the image mist.

The outline of a mountain appeared in the mist, or rather of a volcano, for there was a deep crater in the top of the mountain. Nestled in the crater was the human habitat. "The outer sides represent an attractive potential that pulls us down toward the black hole. It's primarily electromagnetic since the hole is too small to have much gravitational influence this far out. The cup at the top keeps us from falling toward the hole. That's mostly weak and strong force with some electromagnetic in case we drift too far. We are being held in a cup a fixed distance from the black hole and the black hole is accelerating, hence we are accelerating."

"And how are they doing this?" Alliende asked.

"We have no idea," Van Leider said. "Our basic method of studying fields involves tossing particles into them and seeing which way they go. We can generate fields around and between things. We could in theory build some sort of field strut or girders that would join one body to another, and that strut would have a field around it, but we can't sculpt field the way they do. We can barely solve the differential equations holding our habitat in place. We have no hope of solving them for all the habitats and the black hole and the other free-flying hardware of this ship."

"What do the Guests say?"

"They're all too busy doing the intelligence tests the aliens gave them to talk to me."

"You think the aliens are giving them tests?"

"There are puzzles in the hardware, one for each kind of Guest. What else could they be?"

Tomaso Alliende stretched out in the mist-theatre's audience webbing and considered. Van Leider assumed he was considering the problem of the ship, but his mind was much more occupied with her presumptions and his own presumptions.

They lived in such a small village, and they all thought so much alike, and they had so few tools which they used to cover all their jobs, so small so narrow in thought. How could he trust any idea any of them had about the other villages, particularly about their tools and their ideas of tools?

The Crazy Old Man Who Lives with the Fire had long ago learned that finding the right tool for the job was the most vital of his tasks. If he kept hammering where he should be sawing he would be wasting effort, materials, time, thought, life. So he had carefully built up a varied toolbox, but was it varied enough?

The Crazy Old Woman Who Knows Everything also had her toolbox, a small one, but enough for her because it appeared to be full of every tool imaginable. Each new problem that confronted her she would solve by rummaging around in the box and finding the tool that fit.

Everyone in the village had such a toolkit. Most of these tools had come from one of the Crazy Old people who had made or hunted down the needed object.

Sometimes those tools were stuck in obscure places and required digging out. Analytic geometry had been created by unearthing an ancient problem with ratios of intersecting lines. Non-Euclidean geometry had arisen from an annoyance with the aesthetics of one axiom. Computers arose in the coincidence of the brief fashion for truth-functional logic at the same time the electromagnetic revolution had been in full swing.

A few of the villagers had toolkits so small that it was easy to turn anything to fit their limited paraphernalia. Surgeons had only three tools: knives, needles-and-thread, and cauterizing torches. So simple to turn lasers into knives, polymerases into threads, and microwave-emitting catheters into torches.

Sometimes one tool was so big and beautiful that it was applied everywhere and could be found hidden in most of the toolkits. Calculus was the brightest of these. Ever since the times of Newton and Leibniz and Riemann, mathematicians and physicists had been so enamored of the sharp-edged saw of the calculus that they had tried to use it everywhere. How much, wondered the Crazy Old Man, had it blinded them to other tools that might apply to the same situation? Here was a field, here were centuries of practice solving differential equations, and here was frustration.

What tools were the people of the Path-Miner

village using that made this confusion easy for them to solve? For that matter, what tools were the people of the Method-Smith village using that looked to the voicevolk like intelligence tests, but almost certainly were not?

Feather let the communications pod get under his skin. One by one he twitched his fingers, then his wrists, then arms and so on through his body, teaching the thing the ways of his nerves and muscles.

The answer had come to him in his sleep, so obvious he could hardly believe he had missed it. The pod was not hardware as humans thought of it. It was a method. It had been grown in the ocean and had been merged with the lattice of equipment. It was a Method-Smith; they did not distinguish between themselves and their artifacts. It was a method of communication tailored to humans as far as the Method-Smiths understood speaking with humans. That meant it would be based on Constance Marchant's communications and her ways of interacting across the emptiness of space. It might also have a touch of Grandmère to it. The fact that it frightened him gave credence to that idea.

In any case it would be latticed with Tractases and Adoptionases that would interact with whatever he did inside it. It would learn him and he would learn it, and latticed together they would be the communications method. What he had to do was tractate it and let it tractate him until they were close enough to adopt each other. So he set about letting the older Method-Smith Guests get under his skin.

Quint Hillard is in Burst:

The Ship {Memories of training {memories of becoming a monster along with Elsbet [Their sons' growing distress at the sight of them]} and the first few months aboard} is more still more unmoving than any place he has ever been {all his tactile memories}, yet he is falling {memories of falls [terror when he had once tried cliff diving and flashed into Burst for the descent {the entire universe as a thing moving around him while he was completely still}] [first time in a spaceplane going to a skyborough as a boy]}. The falling varied as the Ship's acceleration changed {every shift in acceleration for the last eleven months}, gravity was changing [lessons of gravity given by other Moment-Keeper Guests, complete explanations laid out in mist which he learned in an instant of Burst then sorted out through months of Wave], the Ship was not moving. The Ship was moving {complete explanation of ship's path out of the solar system as plotted by the Professors including guesses as to when they would reach the Band-Braider world {all memories of Band-Braider guests [brief flirtations with Marie when they were much younger and she had first come to the Guesthouse while Elsbet [Elsbet had opened the Seal and unpacked a flying suit capable of traveling through the mini-system of empty ship space, but it could not be used as long as the Field was active] was seeing one of the other Single-Sayer Guests]}} the principle of Equivalence made it seem like gravity {life and work of Einstein and all later workers in relativity}

The Patch [Lecture from before he was adopted into being a Moment-Keeper: "Patches are the most widespread Moment-Keeper technology. Like the Moment-Keepers themselves they have two modes: Burst, in which they take in instruction and sensory data, and Wave, in which they act upon these instructions. Patches are to be found on all the alien worlds, most commonly as planetary satellites for communication and energy transmission purposes"] did not serve any of the known uses for patches [It did not transmit anything, it did not perform automated repairs, it did not shelter or filter out harmful materials or energy, it did not consume interplanetary matter . . . {all other known uses of patches}] but it does a great many things when signaled in Wave [Patch moving across surface of human habitat, patch forming itself into spiked ball {memories of models of Moment-Keepers drawn or sculpted by Moment-Keeper Guests and others [Feather's Moment-Keeper glass sculpture left behind for his children {Sean} {Julian}]}, patch accepting transmissions of Burst-to-Wave communications, but doing nothing with them, patch ignoring his transmission of contemplation of the patch]

|Model Failure {Universal Frustration} Model Failure|

[Watching floodlike aspects of some emotions {Frustration coloring all of Quint Hillard's memories, seeing every aspect of his life as one long string of frustrations |Memories of Model Failure when the human mind forced itself upon the Moment-Keeper Guest and would not let him approach the real STATE of things|} could also happen with love {memories of times when all of life was loveful} Anger { . . .} . . . [. . .] Use of Patch was outside his ability to be a Moment-Keeper. Patch marked the growth and branch limits. Patch was a Burgeon Spike, a growing marker of contention between Moment-Keeper Guest and Moment-Keeper. It would absorb the differences and bring them back to the Moment-Keepers who were still disputing the intelligence of Moment-Keeper Guests {recordings of those disputes he had listened to over the years} The patch was not for him but for those who waited for it to return on Long Wave].

Marie floated in the image mist, watching the lenticles play off each other, light going from one to the next. They were a symphony orchestra recorded by the Band-Braiders and arrangeable for different works by whoever laid them down. So far she had made over sixty different pieces of light-music depending on how the lenses were arranged and what light she shined in the four entry lenticles. They were a gift in greeting, a gift that could be arrayed around her in many different ways. Each configuration surrounded her with light and understanding. Each form was a light show meant to adapt her to the Band-Braider ways. And all the arrangements were beautiful.

"As near as I can translate the time references," Feather said to the assembled crewvolk, "we will be accelerating for another nine months ship time, after which the field will be turned off until we need to decelerate."

"How fast will we be going?" Beatrice Van Leider asked.

"I don't know," Feather said. "None of the aliens have a concept of speed."

"What?" the Handyman said. "How can they have physics without speed?"

"The Method-Smiths have notions similar to force and inertia," Feather said. "But they don't measure the relative rates of things. Their concern is what is being done, not the resultant change."

"The Moment-Keepers have passive and active states," said Quint Hillard. "The idea of a passive thing having an inherent action like velocity makes no sense to them. They acknowledge that things change between states but do not concern themselves with the rate of that change."

"The Single-Sayers don't measure anything the way humans do," said Elsbet Chan.

"The Band-Braiders have a concept of rate of transformation, which is most like our rate of chemical reaction or rate of gestation. But they don't see a moving object as changing," Marie signed.

"The Path-Miners move through the world," said the Path-Miner Guest, his voice and control eerily human. "They learn the world as they move through it, but do not concern themselves with the character of their own movements."

"Then how do they understand the speed of light?" asked Van Leider.

"They have agreed on the Arch," said Feather. "It came from the Path-Miners became a source for the Band-Braiders, is used as a marker by the Moment-Keepers, and has become a method in the Ocean of the Method-Smiths."

"So what is the Arch?" asked Alliende.

Feather flicked an image into the mist, half of an inverted archway rising high, asymptotically high as it curved upwards. Looking at it everyone in the crew could feel in their backs and their fingertips the strain of scaling that infinitely torturous climb. It would be easy at first to grasp the base and shimmy up, but then the backwards curve would bring dizziness and confusion and each new handgrip could lead to a fall.

"What a view from up there," Winston Overus said as his gaze rose higher and higher into the sky-vault of the Arch.

"We will be high on the Arch," said Feather.

"High enough for large relativistic effects. But how fast we'll be going relative to Earth, I can't say."

"We can find out when they turn the field off," said Beatrice Van Leider. "We'll just have to tailor a few of our instruments."

"I'll see to that," said the Handyman.

The Handyman made his way through spheres and spheres upon spheres, layer by layer going out from the center of the habitat until he reached the outermost layer of bubbles and slid through the membrane of one of the docking balls, the orb that held his Pantechnicon. He had not been able to spend much time in his vehicle since the ship had left Earth, a few visits with Beatrice but no time alone in his mobile home. So much work to do, so many projects.

Van Leider was expecting him to customize and calibrate the equipment for measuring Doppler shift and therefore relative velocity. But he needed a little time on his own first.

No concept of speed. How could that be?

Alliende dissolved the membrane around his bookshelves and began to pull down volumes of physics and mathematics. When those gave no help he reached for the older works of natural philosophy, architecture, and ancient geometry.

Movement and transformation need not be the same, he thought. Let me separate them. Consider transformation as the changing of one thing into another, either continuously or catastrophically, which is to say discontinuously. Now, a continuous transformation involves an evolution from one form to another. Evolution is movement.

Well then, discontinuous change involves a jump

from one state to another. Jumping is movement.

Movement, movement, movement. Change is movement. Physics is the measurement of motion. Everything moves. Measure speed with the stick and the water-drops. Speed is rate of change per unit time.

Are there devices without movement?

The simple machines are: the inclined plane (for moving things up and down without killing yourself), the lever (Give me a place to stand on and a lever long enough and I can move the world.), the pulley (Draw water out of a well with a bucket on a pulley.), the wheel (Spin as the universe seems to spin from the comfort of a planet. Why did I ever leave?), the wedge (Bang, bang, hammer, hammer, split, split, stroke by stroke, keep time with the rhythm, hammer at a steady rate.), and the screw (Turn it, turn it lads, pull up the water, empty it so we can dig our mines; turn it so we can move water across the land up from the lakebeds.).

Can't get away from it. Can't leave speed behind. How can I make anything, or fix anything without knowing how fast the fixed thing should work? If the gears aren't in sync the machine will break. If the pulley turns too fast, the lift will smash into the floor. If I can't turn, how can I tell time? How can I hammer out the iron if I can't measure the time it's in the fire? How can I change lines into circles and circles into lines without speed?

Alliende stared at his hands, turning, pulling, pushing, raising, lowering, holding, releasing. Everything, everything of the hand was movement. Hold them still, muscles creak and twitch, nerves flick commands to fingers, strong fingers, iron-gripping, delicate-holding, careful-moving. The hand, the hand is all motion. How can you act, how can you think of acting, how can you think without moving?

The hand: one palm, four fingers and a thumb, an opposable thumb, what was the opposition to the thumb? How many bones? Many bones, not his concern. How many bones? He could count them if he opened up his hand, x-rayed his hand, cut off his hand, peeled away the flesh, away the evolution, away the arising of the hand, strip away, strip away the hand, what is left?

The mind of the hand. Take away the hand and the mind remains. Consider the sound of no hands hammering. Hammering on the anvil, sound, sound, sound, tolling away the time, time, time in a regular beat. Movement is the hand, and I am the hand, and I move.

Four days later Beatrice Van Leider, in contravention of a hundred years of custom, entered someone else's dwelling without permission. She found the Handyman on the floor of the Pantechnicon, surrounded by three thousand years of treatises. He was banging his right fist into his open left hand in a simple rhythm, slap, slap, slap. The sound of the hammer in the forge. The strike of a clock chiming the hour. The spark-making tone of iron horseshoe on stone road, measuring the distance in the pounding of hoofbeats.

Carefully the Professor helped the Handyman to his feet and led him out of the Pantechnicon and rope by rope, membrane by membrane inward to the habitation sphere where they were met by Feather.

"Species Shock," said the Method-Smith Guest.

"What's that?" said Van Leider.

"Species Shock is the method of discovering that your prejudices and assumptions run much deeper than you thought possible. It's finding out that digging away the notions you were taught involves not just breaking down a few social lessons, but discarding the resultant thinking of all your species' history. Then discovering the assumptions that come from your senses and the way you move. Then seeing that there are assumptions buried in your species' biology. And if you get past those there are the assumptions implicit in the way your ecosystem works, the way evolution manifests on your world, the methods used down to the cellular level. Species shock is the eye opening and seeing only itself reflected in all the ways you are and all the means you use."

Feather paused, drew a breath like a conductor raising his baton. "Everyone on the ship will be struck be Species Shock."

Feather's manner and confidence, where had it come from? Van Leider had traveled with him, worked with him, helped rear and teach his daughter, and in all that time she had seen him intense and capable, fearful and careful, but never smoothly sure of anything as he was now. His confidence sounded distant and alien. How had this side of him been hidden for all that time? Or had it been concealed? Was this what Theadora had nurtured in him, this blazing able inhumanity?

Poke it, test it, challenge it, that was the way of the voicevolk, the way of analysis.

"Even the Guests?"

"Even the Guests."

"But haven't they already gone through this in learning to be Guests?" she asked.

"No," said Feather. "The Guests lived on Earth and absorbed the alien into the human. Now we're going outward, bringing the human to alien. As I said, you'll all be hit by it eventually."

"What do you mean 'you'? You're human also."

"Yes," said Feather. "I'm human, but I am also Species Shock. What do you think monster-making is?"

The terrible power of the ship sped up the universe in a cone around it. Before and behind it every movement accelerated, every action became blinding in rapidity, every reaction amazing in swift response. Yet the people of Earth were curiously incapable of seeing this change, they did not know that the rate of their actions was governed, controlled, dominated by the rapidly retreating mass of whiteness in the sky. They passed their lives in ignorance of the prime mover that lent them this terrible swiftness.

One lone frame of reference controlled the entire universe.

Just like every other frame of reference.

Beatrice Van Leider brooded upon Feather's words and the fire-eyed madness of the Handyman. Species Shock. She had never heard the phrase, but all the Guests knew of it, had expected it. None of them had spoken a word of it to the rest of the crewvolk.

Assumptions. Tomaso had collapsed because of his, because of humanity's assumptions. Hard to accept. Why was it hard to accept? Because the word, the word 'assumption' lacked strength, lacked force. It wasn't like 'pain' or 'sickness' or 'sorrow' or 'failure' or 'karma' or 'doom'. It was a quiet word, a useful word. You made assumptions when formulating hypotheses. Assume and see what follows. By this assumptions could be checked. That was the way of logic, the preformulation of science.

"Speak assumptions and find conclusions," Van Leider said out loud and listened to the words echo back from her recorder.

"Speak assumptions."

But wasn't Feather implying that there were too many assumptions to speak?

Assume he's right.

What follows?

What test can be made for Feather's presumption of assumption?

"What assumptions lie behind my assumptions?" the Professor spoke again.

"I assume that things can be understood."

Understand. Something to stand on, a solid ground beneath my feet. Out here in space, away from the solar system, flying in an alien ship. What stands beneath my feet?

"My knowledge, my awareness, my way of seeing and speaking."

Where do they come from?

Who asked that question? Why does it sound like Theadora yet feel like Feather?

Just a voice in your head. A voice you made up and assigned characteristics from the people you know. You're making me up as Devil's Advocate. Or Monster's Advocate, the Voice said, becoming more Feathery.

So where do knowledge, awareness, seeing and speaking come from? the Voice challenged.

Van Leider hesitated. Feather had himself given her an answer to that question when he discussed Species Shock. He had primed her to answer the image of him in her mind. Presumably this was part of the method. Follow the path he laid down and fall into Shock.

"They come from my mind, working upon the things I have seen and heard and the things I was taught," she said.

Aren't those assumptions? Feather-Theadora asked.

"If you expand the definition of assumption far enough," Van Leider said, beginning a rhetorical attack upon her own thoughts.

Never mind the word, the Voice said. Do you think the things you have seen and heard and been taught on Earth give a broad and deep enough understanding to encompass the alien you will be seeing soon?

"Why wouldn't they?" Van Leider said. "The Guests always said that the aliens are looking at the same reality as we are. They have different approaches and different minds, but the real world is our common ground."

But how much uncommon ground do you have on top of that common ground?

Van Leider smelled a trap. She had played Go with Feather many times, had watched him play against the Coskun children, had seen him teach the game to Dominique. She knew his ways of play, knew the monsters he built of simple stones, just as he had built this creature in her mind out of words spoken. How long had he been making it? Had the frightened Feather whom the Guisers had taken in always been some half-alien monster-maker? The other Guests had automatically accepted him among them, though he had never set foot in the Guesthouse, had never known them before. They knew he was a Method-Smith. How long had he known, how long had he been acting as one?

If he had been a Guest in disguise, acting as a Guest, mathematically constructing this voice, she could not trust it to be truly a part of her.

But if she couldn't talk to this image, this voice in her own head, this creation of her imagination (even if Feather's words had influenced that imagination), wouldn't she be forced to hide from herself, from her own mind? Wouldn't she become as Feather had been or seemed, someone who cowered from monsters?

"Very well, I will look at the uncommon ground," she said.

The voicevolk had ruled the Earth for as long as they said they had ruled the Earth. They told each generation what the previous generations had done. They wrote down what was important according to how they saw important things. They came together and talked and argued to settle what mattered and what did not matter, what was true and what was not true.

They created theories of how theories were made.

They made tests for tests.

They argued about argument.

They spoke rhetorically about rhetoric.

That's very 'clever', the Feather-Theadora voice said. Now try being intelligent, try being wise. Look hard at what you think you know about where you came from.

"I was taught by Academe-in-exile," Van Leider said, feeling the solidity of thousands of years of learning beneath her feet.

You were taught by one person.

"But what that one person taught me was checked by talking to others."

The Single-Sayers would say you were taught by one person, that the seal of that person is set hard upon your mind. And we humans would say that he taught you how to speak in a certain way, he taught you the academic voice and the academic manner. He taught you how to think and speak like a Professor.

"Are you saying that's only manner and image?" It was easy to imagine the Voice as Theadora making such a claim.

No, but manner and image are part of it. So are history and tradition. They aren't necessarily good or bad history and tradition, but they are a specific history and a specific tradition.

"Well, of course they are," Van Leider said. "What happened happened. What people said, they said. What they taught, they taught. You can't have a general history and tradition. Specifics are inevitable."

The Moment-Keepers have a general history and a non-specific tradition, if you can call what they have tradition. Have you analyzed the tradition you came from? Have you looked at it to see what you cannot see in it?

The ground beneath Van Leider's mental feet began to shake. Feather was tearing away the supports beneath her, and now with academic honesty she wanted to help him. He was right. There were assumptions in her, and if she truly wanted to see clearly she had to remove those assumptions. She had to fall.

Just as Tomaso fell?

If she fell did she have any cause to believe she would ever rise again?

Yes, she had one cause. She and Feather as person to person had been together for a long time, neither liking nor disliking each other, but always with regard for the other, and with regard for Theadora and Dominique's feelings.

They would never see Theadora or Dominique again. Why then would their feelings matter? They were cut off from the Earth. It was only the two of them, Beatrice and Feather neither liking nor disliking, never coming close enough, never knowing well enough to trust or mistrust.

No, she did not have even one cause to rely upon Feather.

Feather isn't here, said Feather's voice. This is just you talking to yourself. Now, will you have the courage to look at your understanding or not?

Van Leider stamped her foot.

And fell.

Into exile, learning around fires in campsites, reading the works of the ancients, testing hypotheses in words and thoughts, in equipment borrowed at Universities. Teaching the Coskun children, each of them in turn taking in her words and turning them according to their own minds. They would say things back about what she had taught them. Some of what they said fit the manners of academic speech, so those things were kept in her thoughts and her records. The other things said -- Gregory's glorifying words, Karl's half-mystic concerns, Patricia's almost military challenges -- these were shunted aside. Only Dominique always answered in academic voice, so she was chosen to rise to Professorship.

Falling through history into the Troth-Breaking. Universities broken into. Mass hangings, computers destroyed, but libraries not burned. Even the mobs of the Troth-Breaking knew that the people of the Voice were to blame, not the knowledge they preserved and added to. But the knowledge came from past people. The lynchers had been taught to respect the dead academics while they killed the living, killed them for abstract crimes. Crimes of abstraction. For the intelligence tests that condemned their children, for DNA screening that turned probability of death into sentences of unhirable life, for sociological classifications that locked up people for belonging to certain groups or exhibiting certain characteristics, for economic theories that praised debt and extolled poverty. But most of all they were killed for claiming to have the answers to everything and not being able to respond to the aliens.

Falling into the era of the Universities, to the fat centuries when education marked one out so much that it was guarded as privilege and sought after as a means of advancement. To the time when a Professor could hold a Chair knowing little beyond one narrow specialization. Earlier still, when a degree carried an odor of sanctity and an educated man was presumed closer to God.

Back and back through the time of no universities, when knowledge was not the province of the academics, when other voicevolk, monks and priests and players and singers, were esteemed.

Wait. Back up. That was only one lineage, only the tale of Europe that came to dominate the tale of Academe. There were other stories, the Muslim scholars who came close to Allah in their learning, and the Chinese lineages of learning whose works were later folded in and separated into the European classification of subjects. Dead masters had their works cut apart, one section classified as history, another as philosophy, a third thrown out as superstition.

And earlier, according to Academe's self-made history, to the time of the philosophers whose works became foundational.

But.

Almost Van Leider stopped her fall, almost her normal ways of thinking, the tools of analysis she had honed gave her a footing.

Here was the beginning of her lineage. But did she understand it? Those ancient academics came themselves out of other lineages and teachings that survived only in fragments. What assumptions were they making? What establishments were they adhering to or challenging? What was the context and what the reality of their words?

"Why Grammar? Why Rhetoric? Why Dialectic? Why Arithmetic? Why Geometry? Why Astronomy? Why Harmony?"

Why did these seven arts emerge from that era? Why not others?

Survival of the fittest.

But what did they fit?

"What did the voice of humanity fit before there were voicevolk? What was taught before words were written down? What was taught before words?"

"What was taught when RNA and DNA and protein chains and cells and multicells triumphed back in Earth's soup time?"

Feather carried Van Leider to a nutriating web and sealed her in. He listened to her recorder and wondered who she had been talking to in her own mind and why she seemed distrustful of the voice she answered. But he had little time to consider that as one by one the crewvolk came under Species Shock, fulfilling his prophecy.

The other Professors collapsed under the weight of their theories and the too many, many tests they needed to perform in order to sort one word from another, to declare yea or nay upon any concept.

The skyvolk fell like a house of cards when they found that no other species had any reverence for the sky. To the Single-Sayers and the Band-Braiders it was just another place to live. To the Method-Smiths it had its methods, but that was all. The Path-Miners saw no difference between sky and ground. And the Moment-Keepers felt it was too much work and hardship to live in space; they had patches to carry out their interplanetary works and they personally only left the ground when Long Wave returned.

The Guests fell one by one according to the manner in which human thought could not truly become alien thought, falling through the chasms, waves, gaps, and singularities of Model Failure.

The Handyman's two apprentices tripped themselves up when they found the habitat, alien added to human, too much for them, and their master lost. At first they poked and prodded what they did not understand. For a little time they reveled in the freedom that comes when no one is looking over your shoulders and checking your work. They briefly savored the moment when they carried the absolute ability to tinker as they saw fit. But that child's balloon of joy burst when they saw that all the crewvolk relied upon them and there was no help to be had anywhere. Then did their bravery confront their understanding and each found the limitations of the other. They fell, fell into the routine maintenance of what they understood. Muhammed Cecil wandered the habitat in mindless performance of the comprehensible and fearful disacknowledgement of the unknown. Paula StarReach looked at each object in turn, incapable of understanding its purpose yet knowing that even the smallest of the habitat's devices was vital to human survival in the terrors of the sky.

Until, alone among a ship full of the self-absorbed, the bewildered and the eternally frustrated, Feather emerged into the observation sphere to watch the sky return to its native black around them.

"We're free to move," Feather said, speaking into a lenticle recorder. He was chronicling his actions so that when they reached the Band-Braider system he would be able to send them home to the Guesthouse and to Dominique. "The time has come to pull them from Echidna's cave and see what monsters I have made."

9. Differentiation

Feather floated through the returned weightlessness, continuing his daily rounds of the monsters-to-be. Feather was waiting.

If asked by a non-Guest what he was waiting for he would have said, 'I'm waiting until things fit.'

In the words Constance Marchant had gleaned from the Method-Smiths he might have said, 'I am waiting for the Permioles to form so that I can inject the Monster-Making-Adoptionase.'

He had learned the Method-Smith Guest vocabulary in a matter of hours. Words incomprehensible to most people fit themselves into concepts which had always been in his mind. Once that had happened he had known, truly known, that Grandmère was right about him. He was a Method-Smith, had always been one.

A human might have said that Feather had a 'knack' for monster-making, but what he had was to a 'knack' what a planet is to a nest. Both nurture and protect, but one can give life to anything, the other can only protect the small and fragile. Feather had always had this planet-scale knack, and he had under Grandmère's distant guidance and fear-making absence evolved it as life evolved on a planet. When Grandmère had first touched him, his monster-nurturing was like the nurturing of primordial soup, but his two decades with Theadora had added two billion years of evolution to his ecosystem. Now he could nurture intelligence and bring forth the monster in anything.

Sometimes the means of doing so were subtle. Sometimes they were direct.

Feather punched the Handyman in his chest right over his heart.

Something was hammering, someone was beating on the silent forge. Who had dared to pick up the hammer in his cave? Who had come to the forge of Lugh/Hephaestus/Goibnhiu/ . . . ? What were they hammering?

Silence, the smith shouted in an empty voice. SILENCE.

But the beating went on, two beats, one outside, one inside. Hammer, hammer, hammer!

What was being beaten? Whatever it was was in great pain.

How does the iron feel in the fire?

How does the steel feel under the hammer?

It hurts to be forged, to be matter subject to the smith, to be someone else's subject matter. To be someone else's object-in-the-making.

Someone was hammering him, firing him, forging him.

That was only just. He had hammered and forged and struck everything that came to his hands. Now he was being forged himself.

Not for the first time.

There had been another fire, a fire of beauty that had burned him, smelted him, refined him from ore to metal. Now another had taken the metal of his soul and was working him into a tool.

"I am not a tool," Alliende said. "I am a toolmaker."

"Then make yourself," said Feather.

"Into what?"

"Monster Who Lives With Monsters," said Feather.

The Handyman heard the name, felt it fall into the cave of the Crazy Old Man Who Lives With the Fire, heard the Crazy Old Man accept it as another title. He knew he lived with monsters, knew he was a monster. All he had to do was accept the view of the villagers, accept that he was as alien to them as the aliens were to him.

No. Not as alien. That was not right, that did not measure up to reality. He was still too much of the Human Village to be equal to those of the other villages. But he could stand apart from the Human Village, could see the distance from his cave to the normal ways of humanity. Then he could look at the other villages, and get his hands on . . . the monsters they were giving to the Human Village.

"Can it be done?" he said, looking at his hands.

"Theadora used to talk to me about you," Feather said. He spoke her name with a reverence that turned the distance that separated them into a weight upon his heart.

"Te adora," Tomaso Alliende said.

"She told me how you created your reputation. How you forged the image and actions, the tool that is the Handyman so that you would be accepted anywhere in the world. She wanted to write a play about you, about your distillation of all the practical needs of humankind into a few broad-ranging skills, how you devoted yourself to learning the arts and practices of the smith and the engineer, how you sorted through libraries, culling away theories and finding what was truly useful in any work. But she couldn't write that play. She didn't know why until I told her."

"Why?" the Handyman said. Theadora's troubles were of greater moment to him than any disability of mind.

"Because all that was prologue," Feather said. "All your life on Earth, all your labors, your makings of tools and wealth. It all came before your real work, the work Theadora inspired you to."

"Inspired. That she did. Real work?" The sentences lay disconnected in the Handyman's mind but he strung them together and spat them out.

"This ship, this journey. You had already started building the habitat by the time Theadora told me about you. I knew you were meant to leave. You couldn't sit by the forge never knowing if your work had succeeded. You're too much a craftsman to just let it go."

"I was a fool," the Handyman said. "I should have let it go. Then I could pretend my hands were still capable of making and my mind of thinking. I know nothing, I can do nothing," he said.

"Not so," said Feather. "What human mind can conceive and human hand make you can conceive and make. But human isn't everything. Look at Theadora. How human is she?"

"She's a muse, a siren," Alliende said, his voice rising like a preacher in the pulpit. "She's Circe turning men into animals, she's Ceridwen brewing wisdom in a cauldron, she's a Sibyl prophesying."

Alliende paused and looked in his mind's eye at Theadora standing in the village pretending to be one of the villagers and he saw her mask slip, saw the invisible being beneath the actress' face.

"She's not human."

"Not with us," Feather said. "She's human with the children."

"True." The Handyman flicked his hands, releasing himself from the feed-webbing.

"Theadora sent you out here," Feather said. "She didn't know that that was what she made you for, but nevertheless she made you for us. For the sake of the play to be written about you, you have to get up and work."

"Work." The Handyman floated free, turning himself end over end in free fall. "How can I work? All my assumptions are just assumptions. There's no truth there."

"Are the assumptions useful?"

Tomaso looked at the mathematics, the physics, the chemistry, all the theories and justifications of his works, objects -- Did objects exist? Not if the universe was field bubbling and sloshing -- and motion. Was motion real? Not if the quanta flashed in and out in space-time in a ballet of teleportation. Were there materials to be worked and forged, hammered and fired? Not if matter was only bubbles in field. Did he exist, did his mind exist, did his hands or any thing else exist? Maybe, maybe not. But could he use them whether they existed or not? Did he have to be real to act upon reality?

Perhaps space was not a thing of lines, planes, curves, and surfaces. Perhaps space itself was an assumption (And it was. He had seen it laughing at him, gloating at the absurdity of presuming to see extent as a reality). But it was a usable assumption, an assumption that was a justified approximation to reality, just as the hammer was a justified assumption, just as the forge, and the fire. All were assumptions of human work and human thought, assumptions that came easily to the human hand.

Each of those assumptions was a beast, a monster let loose in the mental universe. They ravened and tore, eating anything that contradicted them, beating down contrary awarenesses.

Untamed they were nothing but monsters. But if he could yoke these bulls of iron he could plow the fields of mind, rein these nightmares and he could drive through the image of the reality, chain this dragon and he could forge ahead.

"Yes," he said simply, and all the thought behind those words came to Feather across the shared assumptions of two humans who know each other, know each other's work, and have known the same muse. It came to Feather and entered the methods of Monster-Making, as an argument enters a function to produce a result. Words came back from the method and left the equal-sign of his lips.

"Then use them. Use them as tools. But don't trust them any more than you'd trust a hammer, a sword, or a fire."

The Handyman closed his eyes.

The Crazy Old Man who lives with the Fire looked around his cave. There was the fire in his forge. Fire was the most obvious, most clear gift of the Things No One Can See. All the human villagers thought that to do anything you needed fire.

But not every village had fire. The Moment-Keepers didn't. The Single-Sayers didn't. The Band-Braiders had it, but only in the last few centuries had they developed any materials that burned very hot, so they had never smelted metals. They had worked light using carved crystals and only late had discovered glass.

Fire had been given to the human village. It had been given as a secret treasure hidden in the trees of Earth-village. Trees had wood, wood burned. More importantly, wood could be made into charcoal. Without charcoal there would have been no metal, no glass, no chemistry.

Fire and the Stick, those were the human gifts, Fire and the Stick to account for thousands of years of civilization. He could carry Fire and the Stick, he could hold all of human technology in his right and left hands. He could be the Handyman and meet the Handy-not-men.

Feather turned away satisfied. Monster Who Carries a Torch had been awakened.

The dictionary was poked full of needles, words threaded to words, each definition a reference to other definitions, each leading to each other, a knotwork, a matting of words, a tangle of empty sounds, a campfire surrounded by inarticulate grunts.

A campfire of hungry hunters who had not eaten for so long, hunters with hounds gone feral. Concepts and ideas were roaming untethered, a pack of back-to-the-wild dogs snarling through her thoughts. Reason, the master of mental hounds, had taken a vacation; no one knew when he would be back. Vacation was a euphemism. Reason had fled when it had been discovered that he had been covering up other tracks and leaving false scents for the hounds. Reason had his own way of going, step by step, pace by pace, sniffing the air carefully and guiding the dogs to the conclusion he wanted reached. Reason had his prey and would not wish that other beasts be hunted. His duplicity had been found out and he had been forced to escape. His hunting comrades, Definition, Rhetoric, Analysis, Argument, Axiom, Premise, Conclusion, Logic, and Syllogism, had also escaped the lynch mob of the mind.

One of the hounds began to bay in fear. Something was missing, something vital. There was a growling from somewhere, from a canine more ancient and primal than these domesticated creatures, something, some yawning horror from the pits of starvation.

That was it, starvation. The wolf was at the door.

Left alone too long the mind can starve. With nothing to hear, the ear can starve. With nothing to say, the mouth can starve.

Beatrice Van Leider was starving for words, meaningful words. It was as if she had been eating mist all her life, thinking the images in the mist were real. She had seen the emptiness, seen the mistiness of her thoughts and learning. Empty, all empty. What could she do with mists and empty images?

"Show a play." Feather's voice, Theadora's voice. Not inside, not from the campfire. Outside in the other world, the world she had thought mapped out, known, filled with meaning, filled with the nutrition and taste of words.

A play, a guise, a mockery. Half-synonyms whose mist-meanings could change like costumes. 'When I use a word . . .'

Use a word, convince with a word, Deceive with a word. All words were deceptions, all voicevolk Deceivers. Hang us from the trees, all of us, we have deceived ourselves and all others. Hang us all.

"The play does not exist," Feather's voice went on. "Someone wrote it, someone else acted it, a third person crafted the mist of scenery. It isn't real. But you see something in it. The words are not real, but you hear something in them."

"Literary criticism from a writer?" Van Leider growled, her tongue so used to disputation that the words came forth before her mind could find them empty, could see the Predation in them, could leash in the hound.

"Then the play does exist," Feather said. "I wrote it, you act in it. You are as much Theadora as I am."

Theadora. Theadora seeming to languish on a couch, but all the time acting. Her hand upon her brow was a source of twinkling amusement. Such games she had played with gestures and postures clichéd to the point of clowning, but alluring as well. Theadora had warned her about Reason. A good servant but a poor master, like Fire.

Theadora was always acting, always on stage. So was Beatrice Van Leider. Feather was right. They were both Theadora, both acting out roles, both costumed images concealing something within, something for which there were no full-words.

"Image of mist around something that sees and knows. That is what a monster is," Feather said. "Be the image when you act, be the hidden thing when you see and you will be the right monster."

"What monster? Which image?"

"What role are you suited to play?"

A howl rose in Van Leider's throat, a ravening in her ear-stomach. The hounds of her mind snarled and spit in savage hunger.

Beatrice Van Leider looked around her. She had been torn free from the feeding capillaries. Feather was berating her as she had berated him so often in his first days with Theadora. A slug-a-bed he had been, a drag on the troupe, a fearful cur with no sense to him.

Almost she could hear Theadora laughing at the irony and at the same time admiring the construction of that irony. He berated, she berated, he bit her, she bit him. Monster Who Bites the World into Tiny Pieces called in its hounds.

"A Monster of Analysis," Beatrice Van Leider said, speaking slowly. The space just behind her mouth where words were fashioned seemed a vast distance away from her mind. Each thought traveled the space between stars before it could become a spoken word.

"Then analyze until you have eaten your fill," Feather said.

Winston Overus was locked in an imaginary argument with all five alien species as to the importance of the sky.

In his own mind he stood framed against the stars. Floating near him were what he thought each of the aliens looked like.

"You have all reached the sky," he said to them. "We can all live together in the stars, giving up the holes of our birth."

"Why give up the source of variety for the source of sameness?" the Single-Sayer hissed (Why did he think they hissed? Maybe it was the two tongues).

"You cannot give up some part of the whole," the Moment-Keeper said through a mouth it did not truly possess.

"But the sky is higher and nobler than the Earth," Winston said, sweeping his arm in an arc across the starscape. "The sky is greater than the ground."

"What is greater? What is higher? What is nobler? What do these words do?" burbled the ocean of the Method-Smiths.

"The sky is the end of all striving, the source and end of all aspiration," Overus said. "The reach and limit of illumination."

"Illumination comes from everywhere and goes everywhere," the Band-Braider said.

Winston Overus had come to despair. Even in his own mind he could not evangelize the alien views.

He had been about to dive back into the dispute, this time taking up the way the sky appeared from the Earth, how it filled and completed the world, when he heard a voice saying, "Theadora carried you up here on her wings. Do you think she would let you fall?"

Monster Whose Eyes are on the Stars rose confused from his webbed sleep, the voice-arms of Theadora around him, pulling him up, showing him the glory of his weightless state, reminding him that he was now closer to the sky than the skyboroughs, the asteroids, the outer planets, even closer than the comet miners.

"But still," he said, "the sky is as distant as ever. How can I reach it?"

Feather heard the words and smelled the frustration of the monster as it clawed at the distant stars. The monster-maker gave no answer to his creation, spinning away in the floating world, leaving wonder and distress and contemplation behind him.

The four other Guests Feather roused without difficulty. They could have roused themselves except they had put their fates in the custody of Feather's method and had waited to see what he would make of them.

"Time to go," was all Feather needed to say to Elsbet, Quint, Marie, and the Path Miner Guest to send them out of the human habitat. In the depths of Species

Shock they left the habitat to meet their counterparts. Only after those conjoinings would they be fully raised up as new-made monsters.

Now Feather turned to the bulk of his work, waking up the crewvolk whose minds he could not touch as quickly. He had much to occupy his time.

The skyvolk clustered together in one of the outer bubbles. Their experiences of Species Shock had each been different, but one thing had occurred to all of them: the sense of falling, falling down, falling up, falling in orbit, falling from grace, falling from comprehension, falling into old age and death, falling back to the farm-labors of childhood.

Falling was all they could talk about until Winston came among them and turned the fall upside down.

"There is no preferred direction in space," he said. "To fall and to rise are the same. Only holes have direction, only the pits of matter orient things to up or down. Remember the fall, for we will rise together."

Elsbet Chan soared through the emptiness, savoring the loneliness of her passage from habitat to habitat. The flying suit, a seemingly clumsy vehicle the size of a small airplane, had been awkward to don in the human spheres. So many little adjustments to fit it to her form, nips and tucks, smoothings and clampings. But at last she had counted the last distortion, named and numbered the last false joining, and shot out through the launch membrane into the free space of the ship, leaving a swooping arc of ions.

Flying near a black hole with a few grams of anti-matter only two meters from her head. Feather was right. They had become monsters, if madvolk and fools were monsters.

Monster. The seal placed on anyone who was unlike the aggregate conception of humanity. Open the seal and distribute the strange and disturbing among the people. But no Single-Sayer would make such a seal. To assume a normal way of being which had deviations was not in their minds. Yet it had been in Elsbet Chan's mind until Feather had shocked her to sleep and woken her with a new name: Monster Who Sees Two Different Worlds, One with Each Eye.

She had grown so secure in her Single-Sayer understanding that she had been amazed to discover how human her thinking had been. She had made seals of generalizations, but the Single-Sayers never generalized. She had named things from the broad to the narrow, but they --

What did they do, truly? She did not know. She could see the human universe around her, a world with one black hole, six habitats, a filter, a harvester, and an engine, all comprising a ship that was flying through space at 0.997c relative to Sol.

But if she shut her eyes and opened them again she could see only hints of the Single-Sayer Seal-of-all. And even that seeing was flawed. They had no concept of all. They always built upwards, putting things together and taking them apart again. They never assumed they could start with everything and unseal the universe.

She had worked all these years with the image of their mathematics, of their naming, of their minds. Now, as she neared the flying mountain with its many perches, she would finally confront them.

Elsbet Chan or Elsbet Chan-DeMarnier-Tienh

(and five other lineages she did not care to name) would have fallen apart at the realization that she was farther from the real Single-Sayers than she was from the maddest human.

She had fallen apart, until Feather had stitched and sealed her back together as something else.

Monster Who Sees Two Different Worlds, One with Each Eye eagerly landed on the perch sculpted for her suit, shed the apparatus, and, clad only in a membrane that would remix the atmosphere for her benefit, entered Mountain-that-needs-no-world-under-it.

The door into space shut behind her, as did the eye that saw the human world.

Her other eye saw the aggregation and the seal of Enter-Mountain-Here. Within was an open space wider and longer than it was high, and as high as . . .

No analogy would come; analogies were human.

In it was a band of luminous metal, sparking white in places, turning and turning, exerting a magnetic pull on the metal patches that had joined her membrane to her flying suit. Nearby floated a lenticle storage box, ovoid with eccentrically shaped cubbies. A fibrous chain that floated free in the air, knotted and knotted within the knots, bundled and clustered, bounced haphazardly off the sides of the entry chamber, resounding in sounds unknown and notes that defied the staves of music.

Here was the cluster of ways in. Elsbet Chan leapt for the band because it clearly said to her, 'This way into the heart of the mountain.' The field grasped her, spun her down and down into the mountain, falling in the magnetic artifice, turning and sparking in the creation of electricity. Down and in along curves and angles, each serving a distinct purpose, each marking the Seals of a different part of the habitat.

Until at last she saw the Seal meant for her, and

her flickering-in-a-medley-of-blues hand reached out and pulled her into a passage too high and narrow for a Single-Sayer. The entry practically yelled, 'Human, come this way.'

No, not human. Elsbet pulled her way along the corridor. It was rough-edged with many out- and incroppings. It varied in width from thrice her height to too small to squeeze through, until she pushed hard and it opened up. Not human. They did not know her well enough to name her anything but That-which-has-talked-across-space-to-us-and-has-come-to-join-the-ship.

The corridor was learning her, tasting her. It was the sensitive mouth and prehensile tongue of the Single-Sayer. It was learning where she fit and where she didn't. It was making a name for her shape, and as she passed through it the corridor accommodated itself to her size. The corridor itself became her name, That-which-fits-here.

Until it learned her it would not lead anywhere. Elsbet Chan began to press herself against the walls, giving herself to the taste of the passageway, teaching her shape to the mouth that named.

The passage narrowed, smoothed, fit itself to her, swallowed her and spat her out, her shape impressed upon it so that the way out for her was clearly marked and would remain so. The habitat had learned her in the ways it needed to. It knew her movements and her size, her turnings and her endings. The habitat had a name for her. Now it was the turn of the inhabitants.

Elsbet Chan's human eye opened for one brief moment as she floated free into the many-peaked upside down inside out mountain that occupied the interior of the alplike habitat. On their perches sat the Single-Sayers. To her human eye they were what she knew them to be, the highest predators on their food chain, the eaters of all things on the Single-Sayer world, the airborne hunters who could kill and dine upon whatever prey took their fancy, the filter feeders who could suck even the smallest of microscopic life forms from the air. They were to be feared as the tiger is feared, watched with wariness as the eagle watches and is watched in turn, left to their own as the bear is left alone.

Monster Who Sees Two Different Worlds, One with Each Eye firmly closed its human eye.

Marie floated through the image mist which filled the light castle of the Band-Braiders. She had not realized until she entered their gleaming habitat that the mist was a part of their natural environment. Many of their communications now made sense: the concepts of clear-air and light-air, of the mist-that-revealed, of nesting-in-the-mist, and nurturing-fogs. All these things that she and the other Band-Braider Guests had assumed to be strained descriptions were simple bits of reality.

The trouble with this mist was that she could not comprehend the images cast around her. There were shapes and colors all about, filling the mist space with the press of light and shadow, but no shape identifiable. This she had not expected.

There had been no images sent through the starways. Image encoding was completely idiosyncratic, brutally dependent on the senses of the sending species. There would be no way to decode such a transmission without knowing what the picture was meant to be in the first place.

Worse still, even knowing the senses would not make clear the image, because what a being felt was necessary for accurate depiction was a cultural matter.

There were human cultures whose pictures were indecipherable to other cultures. Difficulty layered on difficulty, culture troubles upon species troubles.

Marie believed those matters could be resolved by interaction and practice, by trying to come together in sign and symbol. But this display was wholly confusing. This did not fit what she understood of the Band-Braiders, and it did not seem to be an attempt to reach her.

Out of the mist darted a rotund creature that looked as if it had been woven out of strands of translucent rope. It was twice as tall as Marie and had six appendages as long as she was high, each of which had four sub-appendages half that length and those had each nine little digits twice as long as her longest finger. Its arms, for want of a better word, were laden with four small bundles of rope which squirmed and twitched as it brought them in contact with one or another of the free-floating images.

Marie floated away from the nanny, not wanting to interfere with its rearing of the ship's children and knowing it would not be possible to talk to it.

Nor to anything else in the habitat until she could find whichever of them had been bred to speak to aliens. Why hadn't it greeted her? Wherever was it in this fog of meaningless symbols?

Stop thinking like a human, Marie reproached herself. But it was difficult. The Band-Braider Guests were only first generation, and they had latched on to the optics of the aliens, with some notice paid to their biology, but precious little to the nuances of thought. There had only been a few decades of interstellar converse before the ship had left Earth. And she had so little time. Five years apparent travel was all it would take to reach the Band-Braider world. Why did the ship have to be going there first? She needed more time than the other Guests did to learn the ways of their counterpart aliens. They no doubt would be having an easier time than she.

What did she have? She had the name Feather had signed her: Monster whose Gaze Transforms. Medusa, he had called her more than once. Balor he had also named her. What good did that do? Would simply looking at the Band-Braiders' misty symbols elicit a response? Had the Band-Braider interpreter not come because she had not looked at him correctly?

Wait. This was mist-work. Was there not a mistworker? Where were the control boxes? No, those had been adopted from the Path-Miners who had first transmitted the chemical formulas for image mist to the humans, though they had said it came from the as-yet-unknown Band-Braiders. The Band-Braiders would treat the mist as they did everything else, not with control but with nurturing light. To find the controller of the mist follow the light beams to their sources. Marie shot a little reaction gas from her pack and darted off along the path of light.

"What do you suppose they're talking about?" Beatrice Van Leider said.

Tomaso Alliende looked over to where the five Guests were clustered together, like five little flies in a spider's web. The Guests had made their way back from the alien habitats after visits varying from a few hours for the Moment-Keeper to six days for the Path-Miner -- and the Path-Miner Guest had only come back because he had run out of food. Now they were assembled at forty-nine degrees south-east of IV in the ball called Home and were talking quietly and signing covertly. Whatever had happened to them, whatever they had learned they did not want to tell the merely human crewvolk, at least not yet.

"What does it matter?" Winston Overus said. "Who cares what nuances they've found in the aliens or what they're worrying about? It's just hole stuff, planet stuff. Down at the bottom of the well they're all the same. Only up here and at these speeds is anything different."

The University of the Ship met in a sphere three baubles out from Home near the north pole of the human habitat, six Professorial monsters clustered in a small space, drinking tea as tradition demanded and as a marker of civilization. The tea plants were thriving while other botanical works were dying on the vine.

Saul Ben Isaac, Monster Who Guards The Gate To Humanity, brought the meeting to order by gently clinking his spoon against the ceramic ball in his hand from which he had been sipping oolong. The Professors in response pulled up the sleeves of their shirts to reveal the brands of their diplomas.

In the few years they had been on the ship the crewvolk had adapted the large loose clothes of their earthly lives to the necessities of zero gravity. Bands now tied sleeves and pants legs to the appropriate limbs, and dresses and robes had been wholly abandoned. Holes had been cut in garments so that the feeder tubes and other attachments to the ship's membranes could be more easily accommodated. No one had yet dared to suggest going back to the shorter, more tight-fitting garments of the time before the Troth-Breaking but everyone had thought of it.

"Reports?" Professor Ben Isaac said.

"Astronomical observations continue to be hampered by the skyvolk," said Monster Who Disputes

Everything. "They insist on turning the habitat's telescopes to bright glittery objects and occasionally to the early universe. We keep having to reset them for our tracking purposes."

"Analysis of the field has narrowed down the possible grand unifications," said Monster Who Refers All Matters To The Dead, who then recited a litany of those whose lifesworks had been disproved and those whose hypotheses still had a chance of being real. "We have composed a set of Earthbound experiments we can transmit home once we reach the Band-Braider world. It should give the Universities an opportunity to work with field. We have also pried a little information out of the Guests about the uses to which the aliens put field. We found out that it is only used in spacework and cannot safely generate artificial gravity because excess radiation is always created in field manipulations. Fortunately, the Handyman made our habitat secure from those excesses."

"Preparations for study of the Band-Braider system progress with gravid slowness," said Monster Who Grasps at Words. "The Handyman does not deign to devote himself to preparing the needed equipment."

Saul Ben Isaac flicked a look at Beatrice Van Leider. The look said simply, the Handyman is your responsibility.

"Can you get him to change his priorities?"

Beatrice Van Leider studied her colleagues, ate her colleagues, analyzed her colleagues and shivered at the cold taste of the college. Only five years from Earth and the humility that had been forced on Academia by the Troth-Breaking had entirely faded. Ancient arrogance had once again arisen. Everyone in this orb had been on the road, had suffered the indignities of life as a Professor, had learned the reasons for their maltreatment, yet the habits and understandings of a lifetime had disappeared when two and a half millennia of academic self-importance had been given a chance to rearise.

Was this Feather's doing? Beatrice Van Leider wondered. Did he create this monster of imperiousness in us, or was it always here, waiting for the threat of the noose to be lifted?

"The Handyman is concerned with other things at the moment," she said. "But I will try to turn his attention our way."

"Seven farm-spheres have failed in the three years since we ended acceleration," the Handyman reported. "None of the large animals have survived. The chickens are adapting well; they seem to enjoy flying. Of the grains, two strains of short rice have been thriving, as well as a Siberian rye hybrid. As expected a few of the dwarf trees are hanging on, but the circulation in the tall fruit trees fails without gravity. Some of the melon vines are growing, but they're tying themselves into knots and the melons are stunted. The only things that are growing happily are the fungi and the algae-curtains."

Tomaso Alliende let go of his report-chit and let it float about the meeting-sphere for anyone to grab who wanted it. There were no takers. None of the crewvolk had been paying much attention to him.

The Professors were clustered around the results of their experiments, savoring the taste of data long thought unobtainable.

The Guests huddled together as they had been doing for some time. Recently they had only been talking to each other and the aliens. It was rare to find them all in the human habitat at once.

The skyvolk seemed entranced by the pictures of

outside and the long-view shots of the early universe.

Even Alliende's apprentices were more concerned with maintenance reports than with the fundamental problem of what they were going to eat.

Of course it was his own fault. He had forgotten to bring the Crazy Old Woman with the Plants. He should have looked for her, but he had been so wrapped up in forging the ship he had left that matter to the Marshall. Gabriello Benetti had supplied sky-farmers for the work and Professors skilled in botany for the theories. But the former were more sky than farmer and the latter more Professorial than botanical.

They couldn't go back and find the Crazy Old Woman, so the Handyman had no choice. He would have to forge one out of the present crewvolk. Which was the best raw material?

None of the Guests. They had all been refined and hammered, sharpened and set out. He couldn't see beating one of those swords into a plowshare.

Nor the Professors. They all strove to be the other Crazy Old Woman.

It would have to be one of the skyvolk.

And why not? A plow made of starstone might just be what was needed to farm the void.

But which one? Look at them floating in a sphere around Winston, listening to him talk about the images from the distant sky, entranced by him as if he were Theadora. No way to decide among them that way. And knowledge of their farming skills would not do as a measure either. He needed malleability more than skill. Training could be gleaned from the other skyfarmers.

What stick did he have to measure them by? He had known them now for seven years, but he had learned little about them in that time. The skyvolk had kept themselves to themselves. Once he might have asked Winston, but that was a fruitless idea now that he was surrounded by adoration and his eyes were fixed upon the sky. Who else knew them?

Alliende's gaze drifted over to the cluster of Guests. There was Feather. He had woken them from shock and given them their monster names. Of all the Guests he was the most accessible. Ask him later when the other Guests were gone. Find out what monsters lived in the sky, and which would be best to draw down as lightning is drawn down to make fire.

Monster Who Lives With Monsters would find a new monster to take home.

Britt Lookdown, the Monster Who Makes Deep Footprints, came grudgingly to work in the farm spheres. She would rather have been with Overus, who spoke the sky more clearly than the cameras and telescopes could reveal, whose words bore more of heaven than any picture. But she had to acknowledge the truth of the Handyman's words. "Eventually an empty stomach will overcome a full head."

She had been born in the sky and labored as a skyfarmer when she had been a young girl, but her mother had worked hard and earned Britt pilot's training, at which the young woman had excelled. She had flown ships from Earth to Neptune and had even chased a few outer comets in her years in Sol's system.

Britt had been selected for the trip because of her piloting credentials, but there was little of that to do here. Anyone could fly between the habitats. Those were short runs, like going from skyborough to skyborough. There was no real flying to be done in the void. Only near a star would there be a need for her skills.

As the Handyman had said, she would be

useless for most of the journey unless she took the hoe back in her hand and worked the farms. Britt Lookdown had accepted, knowing that it would only be for the time between the stars.

When they reached Mu Arae, the star of the Band-Braiders, she would leave the farm and go a-roving as had her paternal Norwegian ancestors in centuries past when the long winter had ended and the sun returned.

10. Density

Professors and pilots two by two left the human habitat, flying their caravels out to see the sights of the Band-Braider system. Five ships flew off to add for the first time in more than a century to the woefully thin library of planetary explorations. The nine worlds, dozens of moons, and millions of little worldlet asteroids of Sol's system had furnished nowhere near enough data for the hungry minds of the Professors eager to learn the secrets of planetary formation and dynamics.

While they had walked the Earth the astronomers had dreamed of touching the stars and learning their secrets. This longing had not diminished even during their darkest hours when the title of Professor was reckoned synonymous with Deceiver and no excuses would be accepted. "We study the stars and planets," the threatened Professors had said in hoped-for mitigation. "We don't look at human minds, we don't plot out lives."

Yes even in those times they had looked up and wondered and hoped.

When the Guesthouse had proven itself, when Constance Marchant had demonstrated by knowledge and invention, by signal sent out and clearly replied to, that she was the true hearer of the aliens, then the Professors had in small numbers gone cap in hand to the former University of Toronto and begged for data. But there they received only meagre fare. The manner in which the aliens thought about their worlds, the things that concerned them, the things they needed to grasp and act upon their star systems were not the same as humanity's interests. So the beggars had gone hungry from the feast.

Now with the rapacity of the starved the Professors had dragooned pilots from among the skyvolk and taken caravels packed with equipment off to the six gas giants and four of the five smaller worlds of the Band-Braider system, ten planets for five Professors, surely enough research space for the greediest of workers. But one world of the system was denied them.

They had been dismayed that only one among the crewvolk was permitted to set foot on the Band-Braider world itself. Marie alone would look upon the people in their native habitat until -- so hoped the Professors -- she could persuade the aliens to let them land as well. Clearly this was possible. Members of the other species were to descend upon that world with its strangely sharp-edged clouds and bright, reflective landscape.

But Marie held out little hope of quick acceptance.

"I don't know who to speak to yet," she signed.

"I don't know what passes for government among the Band-Braiders. I don't know who has refused you permission, if it was a refusal."

"What else could it be?" Beatrice Van Leider had asked.

"Occlusion, Diffraction, Reflection, a Prism."

"What does optics have to do with this?" Van Leider asked, holding the mask of Academe firmly in front of her face.

"Everything," Marie said.

Van Leider felt the role slipping from her, felt again the raw incomprehension, the savage shark of Species Shock biting at the Professorial image. She had a planet to visit, data to record, theories to propound or refute. In short, she had to eat.

But the hunger of Monster Who Bites The World Into Tiny Pieces could not be assuaged by such a venture. There was more to dine upon in Marie's gestured answer than could be found in the whole of a world. However, if she followed the Guest instead of the Dean she would lose her name and title, she would be Backlorn from Academe.

And am I not already so lorn? Van Leider thought.

Not as long as you play your role, said the image of Feather/Theadora in her mind.

Marie left the ship in a caravel piloted by Britt Lookdown, who had accepted the ferry driver's assignment eagerly, happy to cast aside her rake and hoe, happy to turn her back on the growing number of failing farms. She would have preferred a journey that more harshly tried her skills, the gas giant with the occupied rings perhaps or the close-in double planet with the over-strong magnetic field. But this trip would suffice. To land on an inhabited world, to pilot through the occupied sky of an alien species would have its own trials for her too-long dormant skills. And she would see the space habitats of the Band-Braiders and glean some of their ways of living in space -- assuming they had such habitats. Marie had been as unclear on that point as on so many others.

"Why are we bringing that sheep's skeleton?" Britt asked once they were well away from the ship and diving swiftly in-system.

"They want to look at bones," Marie signed, then settled her hands into silence as she watched the sun grow large and an infinitesimal dot expand into a planet and two moons and an evermoving mass of orbital objects whose purposes and even shapes were hard to discern.

The part of her that was a Band-Braider knew what that orbital confusion had to be. Lenses, mirrors, prisms, diffraction gratings, and a thousand optical tools humanity had never invented because, while light was important to humans, it was the importance of a locked box that needed to be opened and its contents examined. To the Band-Braiders light was not a thing outside of them that aroused a sense of intrigue and wonder. It was a thing that flowed into them and made them what they were. Light was vital to the Band-Braiders in the way that water or sex or parenthood or death mattered to humans.

As the human skyvolk had striven to bring all those things into space and adapt them, so the Band-Braiders had sought to grasp the light from space and let it adapt them to the sky.

That was the thing of the Band-Braiders that was so hard to communicate to humans. If you signed 'Lamarckian Evolution,' they either threw up their hands in disbelief or shrugged in dull-minded acceptance of the impossible. If you gestured to indicate that the light that was shone on pre-formed Band-Braiders determined what they were, the human you were talking to either assumed that they had some fascistic totalitarian society that genetically altered Band-Braider babies and dulled their potential for freedom of life, or that you were speaking metaphorically about the light of learning.

How could you explain what light meant to the Band-Braiders?

And what makes you think you truly understand it?

That thought twitched annoyingly in Marie's consciousness. Her time in Species Shock had shown her how little she herself comprehended. It was the music that had shown her, the light music that was always playing in the image mist of the Band-Braider habitat, music that was not music. It was not art as humans conceived of art. For humans art might touch their souls, but it would leave their bodies unchanged. Art might reform a human mind, reveal life beyond what they were then living, enrich and transform and transfigure. But after the art was done, the person so changed would find the same number of arms and legs, the same hairs upon their head, the same illnesses and sufferings. True, they might see them differently, might emerge capable of facing the sufferings and joys of the world as a new person, but their bodies would remain the same.

Not so for the Band-Braiders. Light touched them down to the coils and ropes of genetic material. Music remade them, refigured them, released and bound them in their hard solid being. They had no arts for affecting the mind. They found the notion most peculiar and hoped to learn about such things eventually, after the more accessible and important matter of bones had been dealt with.

"Where do we dock?" Britt Lookdown signed as she drew the ship into a high orbit.

"We don't," Marie replied.

"You want me to land the caravel?" Britt fretted over the notion. The caravels were meant for interplanetary travel, not for the atmosphere. True, the Handyman had modified these vessels, giving them retractable wings and heat-shedding membranes, but to actually transform the ship from spacegoing to atmospheric struck Britt as unnatural, almost obscene. Air and space were not one, air was not sky, and the things of air should not touch the sky. For that there should be clearly set distinctions, Stepping-Stones.

"No, we'll be met."

In twos and threes, more than a score of small satellites arced up to match the orbit of the caravel and then rose just a little higher. When all were in formation a large black platform orbited into place beneath them and light erupted from the caravel's escorts. Light gleaming and accompanied by the twists and turns of the electromagnetic field that spawned it, light quantised to the absorption spectra of a thousand known materials, light tuned more carefully than man has ever learned to tune, light flared, and the blackness beneath caught the shadow cast by the light and flowed outward to make room for the caster of the shadow.

"Now you can dock," Marie signed. "That pad will match our speed and shape. Just descend slowly."

"I thought they didn't know what speed was."

"They don't care about speed, but they know when an image flickers and when it doesn't."

Britt's hands brought forth bursts of attitude control, rocking the caravel back and forth until with a pilot's flourish, she settled the ship smoothly onto the accommodation of its shadow. Once in place the darkness gave gentle way beneath it and the caravel descended into a dark fog that held it in a grip of steely mist.

Then came bumps and jostles in the darkness, as if the ship were being passed from hand to hand, downward, ever downward, as though a series of giants, each a little shorter than the one before it, were taking turns cupping a new toy in their cloudy hands, until the last giant, who stood only a hundred or so kilometers in height, the last and youngest giant, eager to see the toy, opened his hands to the light.

Showing the toy people the crowded sky.

And the crowded ground.

From this height, Britt Lookdown thought, you shouldn't be able to see things moving on the ground. Certainly you shouldn't see the ground moving like . . .

Britt Lookdown had no analogy for what she was seeing. Marie thought of a carpet of ants, but Britt had never seen such a thing. The skywoman had no reference for the strangeness of this ground, she only knew it should not be doing what it was doing.

Nor should the sky have been full of balls and beads and baubles floating, rocketing, sailing, swimming, and many more forms of locomotion than humans had reference for. The sky was meant to be empty, was it not? Meant to wait for the skyvolk to take their places in small patches of it, not to fill it, not cover it as the Band-Braiders had done.

"How can they occupy so much of it?" Britt signed.

"They see a niche, they fill it," Marie replied, but the knowledge that they could do so had not prepared her for the sight of the closed and parceled, the allotted and subdivided sky. And nothing had prepared her for where they were. There was a strand of Stepping-Stone-sized pearls that stretched from space down to the ground, and they were in one of the pearls, a clear one where those above were opaque. A moment and the bottom of the jewel pushed down into the one below, then opened up and dropped them into the gem beneath, a little closer to the ground. Drop by drop they would go down.

How did it stay up? Marie could hazard a few guesses from her knowledge of Band-Braider engineering, but they would be dubious guesses at best, just as a child who can lean two sticks against each other could guess about a suspension bridge but would certainly be wrong.

Down through the droplet pearls, down to a point only a few kilometers above the teeming, writhing ground where the strand divided into nine rigid bands that formed the descending edges of an empty pyramid. At the dividing point they were held suspended for a little while as somewhere a decision was made, a choice among the nonad of destinations. No, that was human thinking. This was a prism and the color of their light was being discerned and emitted in the proper spectral band to shine on the correctly reflective part of the world.

"We're down," Britt Lookdown signed. "Stand up slowly. Get a feel for the gravity."

Marie nodded and unsealed the protective membrane that had held her in her chair.

Adopted bioflora and careful exercise had done much to keep their muscles from atrophying in the long black weightlessness between the stars, but there was not much that could be done to prevent the dizziness that came from standing up and blood suddenly finding that it had the old accustomed pull to fight against and the eardrums discovering anew their ancient purpose of adjudicating balance and direction.

Marie slumped back down, then tried again. On the fifth attempt she stood and took her first step, then a second. She caught her breath and steadied herself against the wall of the caravel before making the last five steps to the airlock, there to be covered anew in the familiar air-sorting membrane. Then hand in hand with Britt Lookdown she stepped out on to her second homeworld.

Britt screamed and clutched her head for the noise, all the noises around her, noises no one but she could hear. No one else could hear the roar and din of the Band-Braider world. In all the cacophony of the hundreds of billions, in all the noise of a world brim-full with no niche left uninhabited, only Britt Lookdown could hear.

The Skywoman ran back into the bubble, back into the safety and silence of the caravel, leaving Marie alone with the Band-Braiders.

Marie could not hear the cause of Britt's distress, but in her bones she could feel the joggling, jostling, shaking, thrumming, and pounding of the world around her. So full of sentient, active life, so much more full than Earth had ever been.

Marie had seen plays set in the time before the Troth-Breaking when cities had teemed with humans; the streets had been so full of crowds that they had forced buildings to unaccustomed heights in order to accommodate them. But nothing on Earth had ever been like this.

Rope everywhere, ropes coiled on ropes with strings dangling, webs spun inside webs with webs walking along the webbing, and smaller webs spun upon the web-walking webs. And all the rope and cord of Earth, silk and cottonlike strands, all the spinning wheels of the world, all the factories of human history could not have spun out this strand-world where every fibre lived and found a place to thread itself, where the world was a tapestry and all the Band-Braiders its threads. Into this she walked, a bone-needle weaving a new thread behind her.

And the light, how could they live without a surrounding ambient light? How could they exist among the flares and flashes, the blasts and shimmers, the sudden rainbows that bounced and sparkled, always against a backdrop of dark web-work? The sun, where was it to be seen? Up, certainly, but there were kilometers of threads and ropes up there, denser than the deepest jungle of Earth, darker than night could ever be.

The lights, they were all talking to her, their speech of shimmers and diffractions, reflections and occlusions. Meaning flared in darkness. Greetings from all around her, words of welcome, spaces made for her to step into, lights to nurture and change her. Lights reaching in to touch her soul and make of her a Band-Braider.

Her bare feet gripping one side of a padded exercise bubble, Elsbet Chan moved slowly through the postures of the Tai Chi form. On Earth the feet held the ground and the Earth gripped the feet. There it was easy to imagine the chi flowing up from the Earth to invigorate the body, a nonexistent energy that yet could be felt, an illusion that made the reality of the body easier to perceive and practice upon. Elsbet Chan's mother (who had been ConCensus Taker in Hong Kong before the city had fallen under artifices of tidal wave and crustal break) had taught her the practice and she had folded it into the Single Sayer awareness of her own body. So changed now was her Single-Sayer half-mind, so different from before the Monster-Making, that Elsbet had shied away from the practice of Tai Chi for the years of travel. She had not wanted to feel and know what had been done to her body by the Adoptionases and Tractases, by the diseases and other bioflora, nor to feel what Feather had done to her mind.

During the journey she had been content to speak to the Single-Sayers to learn more of their ways and their mathematics, to soar through the space between habitats on alien wings. But in that time and in that self-immersion she had lost awareness of her human body and had broken an arm in a mismoved wing. The microbeasts in her had healed the break in a few hours, but she needed to ensure that it would not happen again.

Grasp the Swallow's Tail. Root of all actions, basic movements of the form. Ward Off, Roll Away, Press, Push. Arms and legs reminded her of her humanity, of the human body that she wore, of its parts sealed together by the reality spoken of in biology, and the imagery created out of chi.

Return to Mountain, Embrace Tiger. She had been in a different mountain and seen creatures more terrible than tigers.

Repulse Monkey. Monkey was the mind. Push him away, draw him close, like breathing, in and out. Mortal breath and immortal spirit, the word is the same. Breath, chi, Atman, spiritus, pneuma.

Wave Hands in Clouds. Clouds so far away, Earth and Heaven both distant, hard to feel the chi of the ship, hard to feel the solidity, hard to be anchored when there is no Earth to pull you down and hold you up.

From the caravel Britt Lookdown looked out and wiped the blood from her swiftly healing ears. Marie was gone. The ropes and coils had come for their Guest, the spiders made of spider webs had wrapped her up and taken her -- where? Somewhere in that mass, that pit of darkness, that living image mist, that drawn curtain. What words could describe it? None seemed adequate. Britt Lookdown had run out of words, and besides, there was no one within five light-minutes who could have heard her had she spoken.

What a hole to be down. But at least she had the caravel. It was a piece of the sky, that was what Winston Overus would have said. The ship made her skyvolk, no matter how deep in gravity she was. She was still of the sky. Even if she couldn't take off without the help of the -- ropes, vines, whatever these Band-Braiders were -- still she was skyvolk, she could wait in the ship, wait in her little piece of heaven for Marie to return. And she would have to return soon. Only in the caravel was there food, and with so little light out there Marie would not be able to photosynthesize for long. Just wait. She was safe in the --

Thump. Thump. Squee. Sounds from the lower deck.

Britt Lookdown ran to the lift membrane and slid down to the cargo hold. Ropes, ropes in the ship, all over, ropes and cords, threads and fibers, all over everything, slithering the membranes off the boxes, opening things, insinuating into the workings of the ship.

"Get out!" Britt screamed. But of course they did not hear her.

The coils snared crates and bins, twined around sealed boxes of food and the bone box, one dead sheep. Food for Marie and a dead sheep. That was all they wanted. The monsters hadn't come for her, just food and bones.

Food and bones, then they went away. But they could get in. The ship was sealed against space, could be sealed against entry if need be, but it was their planet, their web-covered spider-trap of a hole. She couldn't keep them out, not if they wanted to take her apart along with the bones.

Marie lay exhausted on a pallet that was a Band-Braider who had been adapted to provide comfort for her, inasmuch as they could comprehend discomfort. Of all human concepts that one was farthest from Band-Braider thinking. All the mechanisms of avoidance built deep into the human psyche, into the fight-or-flight adrenal gland of animals, all the evolution of eat or be eaten, avoid or die, the warnings against heat and cold, illness, sharp and pointed things, the aches of muscles and the strains of too much thought, none of those did the Band-Braiders have. To them stimuli to which one was not adapted were things to reach for, slowly at first so one would have time to adapt to them, but nevertheless things to strive toward. What humans thought of as sources of suffering tantalized and drew in the Band-Braiders.

Mercifully for Marie three of the other known intelligent species also underwent suffering, so the Band-Braiders had learned about it long before they had contacted humans. But unmercifully, none of the other species suffered from overstimulation. The concept of too much input for one mind to handle was new to the Band-Braiders. They had not grasped why she had collapsed after two days of intense language-light, but they accepted the collapse and had adapted one of her Surrounders into a couch.

Surrounders, there was a word she and the other Band-Braider Guests had wholly misinterpreted. It had seemed to fit simply into the human concepts of environment and context. Yes, it had implications of adaptability lacking in those notions, but there had been no hint that it meant other Band-Braiders. No implication that it translated to those who were always with you, those who surrounded you, taking up the space nearby, and whose positions in the world abutted yours and therefore inevitably worked with you.

Her Surrounders did the job of Guests for the Band-Braiders. They took what Marie said and did and ramified it through the Band-Braider webs. They also distilled Band-Braider matters and gave them to her. One of them spoke her sign language. Others were teaching her real Band-Braider speech, not the new-coil-talk moderated by image mist she had learned on the ship.

Speech. Could it even be called that? It was all the light that reached you from everywhere. Everything spoke in images and flickers, signs and seen actions. All around was the speech of light, and you were expected to receive all of it that passed through your Surrounders, be changed by it, and respond in action and light, serving as a Surrounder for those next to you.

It had been too much for Marie; her eyes ached though she had been seeing through the light-absorbing and emitting layers of her membrane. The pain of seeing made itself known in her aching eyes. It had been so much simpler on the ship. There the Band-Braiders had not been able to sustain what they considered a proper density of biomass. They had lost two expeditions trying, so they had filled the ship with image mist and left everyone with too few Surrounders. Those Band-Braiders on the ship had adapted to the bizarreness of open space around them, but they had compensated with dense uses of image mist. Marie had not understood that compromise until now.

It had all seemed easy on Earth, so easy to be a Guest. She had been taken by Grandmère from a disjointed helpless youth spent traveling from island to island without understanding that she was passing over water and land, without even understanding that other humans were speaking to each other and trying to talk to her. She had crossed the Pacific, following the sun, the only thing that seemed to speak to her. Grandmère had brought her to Toronto where she was pampered and given a home, her hands were taught to speak, and she had been given all the alien learning she could absorb.

She had loved the learning, loved the light of Band-Braider interstellar commerce, loved the laser flashes as she had loved the sun, and she had taken in and learned what little, oh so little she could understand.

All the Guests knew that they could glean only a small fraction of what they were being sent. They also knew that that smallness would create huge changes on Earth. It was an open secret among the Guests that although they understood little, it sufficed.

Until now, until all of Marie's ignorance came crashing on her, pulling her down to exhaustion.

Marie fell into dreamless sleep while her Surrounders coiled themselves about her, weaving a perfect gapless cocoon around her strange body with its softness overlaying the clearly useful hardness.

The Surrounder that made sure of her physical condition touched the Band-Braiders who were studying the sheep skeleton. Lights of conference passed back and forth. Then, agreement reached, more lights flitted out through the expanse of the world, passing from strand to strand along connecting jobs until it reached long mining ropes that burrowed underground to dig up a load of calcium, which was then transported back along airborne coils to the bone-students, who in a nursing valley full of image mist began to nurture a new kind among the Band-Braiders.

Time passed. Britt Lookdown did not know how much. She had long since stopped looking at the clock on the caravel. She needed the sky to really tell time, and the only sky she had consisted of lenticle recordings of that which was seen from Earth and its skyboroughs. More and more of her time was spent in image mist watching that now unknown sweep of world and moon and sun. She drank her native sky for sustenance and breathed its emptiness for life.

Winston Overus added the images of this system's planets to the pack of lenticles he had been amassing since the journey began: recordings of sky pictures, lessons of help for the skyboroughs and information on the aliens and how they lived in space. It had sounded like enough when the trip began, but already it felt Earth-bound, hole-crawling, dusty. This was not why he had come, why he had brought his people out of their homes to the heights of the sky. Not so high, not so high. True, they had climbed the Arch and traveled the flatness of the void, but now they were back in a hole taking in the grounds. This was not what he had come for. But what was?

Flickers-of-Life had accepted a name from the human Surrounder. If it had not accepted the name it would have had to move away and do something else, not that it would have thought of that.

The name had come in flashes and it had reached

out to them with its mind and being. Now it was Flickers-of-Life, and the surround of the name determined its place in the world just as its other Surrounders did. It spoke of life with the human, but only in flickers and flashes, not in broad blasts and wide spectra. Just flickers, the flickers that humans called words.

On one of its other sides Flickers-of-Life could beam bright rays of subtle nuance and broad lighting that told deep understandings of biology. On another it could shimmer directly into the image mist that nurtured the new-coil, the one with bones. The mist carried the shimmers and by carrying taught the new-coil how to grow and what to be. In the valleys of image mist the ancestors of the Band-Braiders had brought themselves to intelligence, had nurtured their young with an awareness of the world that came from sight given, sight denied, sight focused, and sight diffused. In the mist did the new-coils grow, in illusion did they come to reality.

Such odd human concepts, as if image and reality were separable. Image surrounded reality and reality surrounded image, light touched matter, and matter brought forth light.

On yet another side Flickers-of-life spoke to Adoptionase-of-Aliens who had been nursed by the Ocean-that-grew-ropes-as-needed (those the human called Method-Smiths, a term that had no meaning for Flickers-of-Life since it could not comprehend what a smith was).

Adoptionase-of-Aliens had been nurtured by the Ocean-that-grew-ropes-as-needed, had in fact been grown on that alien world two passes of the ship ago. Or rather, Adoptionase-of-Aliens nurse's nurse's nurse had been so grown, but that was all that mattered. It had been grown in the alien light even if that light had been stored and passed on from old-coil to new-coil. It and its co-nurslings Surrounded alien visitors and brought them and the Band-Braiders together. They were a filter that extracted the correct bands of light for mutual nurturing.

Just at the moment Adoptionase-of-Aliens was speaking with the human, flashing concepts into its mind, but not, sadly, its body. All aliens had that limitation. The Band-Braiders had learned to accept that harsh constraint upon all other species, after finding it to be so in five different ecosystems now. Even the Ocean-that-grew-ropes-as-needed did not adapt properly. It destroyed and created anew rather than changing how it grew.

"Breaking," the human flashed. "Like stones can chip or ceramics shatter. Bones can break, just like carapaces. You need bone-mending in the biology."

"Methods of repair," Adoptionase-of-Aliens replied.

Flickers-of-Life flashed a picture into the image mist that filled the nursing-valley they had allotted to grow the new-coil. The image was of microscopic strands that pulled carapaces together, then sealed them.

The human flashed back, images of many kinds of breaks and long lasting flaws if the breaks were only sealed back together. Then she flashed micro-repairs, rebuildings of the hollows in bones, calcium replacements, splints and many other methods endoskeletal species had developed.

Flickers-of-Life flashed this band to the nurse, who insinuated these notions into the new-coil, giving it the light and impetus, the capability of fixing its bones.

Winston Overus read the reports of the Professors with grim despair. Seventeen colonies -- deserted colonies -- located. Two planets, nine moons and six self-sustaining space platforms. The Band-Braiders had tried many times to adapt themselves to other worlds in their system or even to build their own worlds, and all had failed. The most adaptable of the known species had not been able to live in the sky. They could work in space, breed in space, nurse in bubbles of image mist and learn from the starlight, but in the end they would have to return to their native surroundings. The closest they had come was digging their hole higher into the sky, raising the ground with their bodies until it touched the frost line of space. But that was as far up as they could live.

Winston Overus threw the reports up and watched them carom off the inside of the sphere, bounce after bound until one by one they returned to him to be gathered up and filed away.

Beatrice Van Leider looked over the news from Earth. It had been sent six years after the ship had left. Much would have happened since then, but that was the way of the Arch. Riding close to the speed of light one would be caught up by the news from only a little time after leaving. They would have to wait for the next leg of the journey to find what had happened on Earth while they had traveled this leg, and by then that news would be stale. They would always be a few decades behind the times.

This packet had little of interest. Not much had happened during the half decade since they had left. The Dissociation had traded most of the space hardware to the skyvolk. The Consenting nations had breathed a sigh of economic relief that they no longer had to give to the space effort. The Dissenting Nations had fallen to bickering among themselves while still carrying on their squabbles with the Dissociation. Nothing much there.

There were some personal messages. From the ConCensor to his parents; Van Leider had duly handed that over to Elsbet Chan and Quint Hillard. Some others from the few crewvolk who had attachments back on Earth or in Earth's sky, and there had been strangely brief messages from Theadora to those she had sent out.

The first, which drew bewilderment from them, was addressed to Rainbow.

"Why would she send a message to the dead through us?" Tomaso Alliende asked.

The others turned their gazes to Feather, who simply picked up the sheet of plastic and read it.

Rainbow, Karl has found his own way upon the road. Do not look to see him for a long time.

After that the others took their own missives and read them in private.

Professor Van Leider's went like this:

Beatrice, On the strength of your recommendation, Dominique has been given a position at Beijing. I have penned a play about that, ironic of course, to make you happy.

Feather's was:

Feather, by your next stop I will be dead. Remember me among the ghosts who return. Hope that our daughter remembers her parents as well as her teacher.

For the Handyman she sent these words:

Tomaso, all that you had of Earth has been given to Gregory. He has gone to the Rhine and is building a life in your honor and a forge for your wealth.

The message for Winston Overus was simply:

Look down. Patricia looks up to you.

11. Boundary Conditions

Claustrophobia surrounded Britt Lookdown.

Britt lay in a small transparent sphere, breathing in the vision of openness beyond the habitat. The bauble surrounded, but its edge declared the edgelessness of space. It circumscribed openness, its confines nullifying the meaning of confinement. In a glass coffin she breathed life and freedom.

Agoraphobia surrounded Marie.

"Walls, Surrounds, come close," Marie flashed

and signed as she sheltered in one of the outer spheres, wrapped in layers and layers of responsive membranes, sources of warmth and food, savors into her blood, touchers of her bones. But not, oh frustrating not, of conversing light and answering shadow. There was no clarifying occlusion or rectifying refraction, no unifying prisms nor widening lenses. Only her body was touched, only her blood and genes, not her mind.

Until Beatrice Van Leider slipped into the sphere and signed into the nurturing image mist.

"How do they learn?" the Professor-mask asked. "How do they teach?"

"With mist and light, and touch down, down to the bone."

"Not poetry, not image," Van Leider said. "How do they know what they know? How do they set down what they know?"

Marie looked at the darkened face and knew deep green sympathy. Here was another who had been taken from her Surrounders, cut off from the nursing mist of her youth. Here was another who suffered the terrible aloneness of octaves-beyond-blues x-ray-music.

Winston Overus joined Britt Lookdown in the confinement of the sky.

"There are holes much deeper and more grasping then Earth," Britt said. "There are holes that pull down with more than gravity."

"All holes are alike," Overus said. "They can all be climbed out of."

"This ship is a hole," Britt said. "It surrounds us. Soon the field will surround us. We'll be trapped again. What's the difference between a pit dug of energy and a pit dug of matter?"

Marie had composed a long report that had been sent Earthward by the Band-Braiders along with the astronomical data the Professors had amassed. After transmission Marie had asked to see Feather and the Handyman.

"Are we going to make it home?" she signed.

"It's much too early to tell," said Alliende. "We've lost a lot of farming possibilities and there are signs of strain in the ecosystem. But so far the crewvolk are healthy and adapting, but there are years of travel left and a lot can go wrong."

"We have to make it back," Marie signed. "I can't show the other Band-Braider Guests what it's like in just words and pictures. I have to be next to them, have to surround the others. If you aren't smothered you aren't a Band-Braider."

"We will try," Feather said, "Monster Who Lives Amidst Monsters."

Whiteness enfolded the habitats as the ship sped forth from the Band-Braider system, aimed for the world of the Single-Sayers. Elsbet Chan looked at the empty white sky and wondered if the madness which had taken Marie would take her when she came face to face with the reality of the species she mirrored.

Marie's experience had made clear to the Guests on the ship that Species Shock was only the beginning of coming to know the aliens. Even Feather had not been prepared for how much Marie had been altered by her year and five months on the planet. Agoraphobia formed a shell that surrounded her altered psyche. Inside there were needs so inhuman and thoughts so alien that the rest of the Guests could not begin to guess what had happened to her.

At first Elsbet had comforted herself with the thought that the Band-Braiders were the most recent species to contact humans and that Marie was a first generation Guest, whereas she was fourth generation from a long line of Single-Sayers. But this illusion had not held up after the Guests had formally convened in Shifting Language to speak to Marie.

"Just enough light, the right colors to learn from," Marie had insisted, as she darkened the sphere to near blackness with only flickers and shadows. Her illuminated membrane made it possible to read her sign language, but how was she reading theirs?

"What were the bones for?" Feather had asked.

"New coil, new kind, new ropes to bind everything together. Just enough bones to mend and strengthen, not too many, no hammer, no anvil, no ringing."

"Tell all," Quint had signed and dropped into Burst.

And Marie had told all, told of knowing all she needed to know while confined in a small space surrounded by Band-Braiders. Everything that mattered to her came to her. The whole world was conjoined and transmitting, a dark living orb full of paths and patterns of light, flickering in the mist, revealing in flares and flashes. Everything that mattered to Marie was hers to have, for somewhere in the vastness of the Band-Braider biomass one of them would adapt to fit that need.

"It's a perfect world," she said. "Everyone's needs are met. Everyone stretches out to wrap everyone else. It's perfect and only I was flawed, only I could not adapt to meet them and become what they needed."

Marie reached out her hands to a flicker of light, trying to pull it out of the air, but her hand passed through it, precipitating the white gleam in the mist into droplets of color that spattered onto the walls and at last resolved into darkness.

The University of the Ship was well pleased with itself. The Professorial Monsters had spent their year judiciously gathering and interpreting data. They floated in their bubble discussing and referencing, delighting in the safety of a lynching-free research-loving environment.

All the monsters were happy except for Monster Who Tears the World into Small Pieces and Masquerades as a Professor. She had set up equipment, gathered data, performed experiments, tested theories, brought back results, and written papers. And it was all just so much shadow play.

All Beatrice Van Leider could see of the work she had done were numbers and functions and mathematical approximations to reality being refined and tested and giving birth to new approximations.

That was the right way to do it, that was the way that had developed over the centuries on Earth, and it worked. By the efforts of the Professors model and reality came closer, the numbers and the predictions from the numbers came to fit together better. The fundamental principles of science were justifying themselves before her eyes.

But still it was a shadow play, still she was only playing a mist puppet in a drama.

Still the Monster starved, because while it could tear the image of the world into little pieces and eat them, while the ravening instrument-fangs and merciless claws of functional analysis could take bites of the conception of reality, it was still only dining on misty models. It did not bite the world.

Tomaso Alliende finished installing Underbellies on the caravels and his Pantechnicon. Now the ships would be able to go out in the whiteness if absolutely necessary. Now he could turn his attention to other problems. He was not happy with the results of the expedition to the Band-Braider world. Britt Lookdown, who had at first seemed a good candidate to be the Crazy Old Woman With the Plants, now seemed a hopeless choice. All she wanted to do was stare at the stars and talk to Winston. Nothing Tomaso had said had been able to bring her back to work on the farms.

Was she dross to be discarded? Alliende was not sure.

Perhaps she was like heated metal which could not be touched except by the heaviness of a hammer held in a protected hand.

Perhaps she was not to be touched. Perhaps she was like an excited electron that needed to emit one single perfect scream of light before it could fall back to its proper state upon the ground.

Two models. One said she was to be acted upon, the other that she was to be left alone.

And those were but two of a thousand models. He could find many others which could fit her condition, each suggesting a different approach. Which model to use depended as always on what was needed and what was fitting, but whose need and whose fit to choose? Need and fit were themselves only models and tools. They too had to be chosen rightly.

The Crazy Old Man Who Lives With the Fire glared at his meagre toolkit, growled in bearish suspicion at the objects he had been given and the objects he had made.

Pick me up, each tool seemed to say. Each tool had an advocate in his mind, a remarker upon the uses of that tool, an insinuator that this instrument was the correct one.

"Bang it flat."

"Cut off the useless parts."

"Measure it in all dimensions."

"Weigh it against the standards."

"Burn it in sacrifice to the Things No One Can See."

"Silence!" the Crazy Old Man shouted. The guttural tools fell still on his shelf. His job it was to choose among the tools, choose by his own awareness and understanding, not by the advocacy the voicevolk had created among the adaptations of the hand.

Grimly he nodded his choice, reached out and picked up the hammer.

Quint Hillard is in Burst.

Elsbet wants a baby {All the dangers of giving birth in zero-g} {Stories of Baby Hunger from the time of the Troth-Breaking. Clothing tailored to hide the shame of pregnancy. Suspicions of those who purchased milk or bartered for kitchen tools that strained and pureed. Families ostracized for being too large. Families cast out on the road. Families broken up. Children hidden.} Elsbet wants to be safe from what happened to Marie [Four generations of Single-Sayer Guests learning to be Single-Sayers [Elsbet's confidence before the trip [Species Shock {Quint's

Species Shock experiences {Quint's meetings with the Moment-Keeper on the ship [It's going to die if it cannot mate soon {Quint's feverish attempts to become capable of Meeting State, all failures} [All its understanding gained from this trip will be lost]
[If they are dying from growing too old/too large Moment-Keepers suffer a brief period where Burst and Wave are confused, action and perception interfere with each other, then they die. They die of being like humans] [Quint Hillard is too human to mate with it] Model Failure | | | | | | | Model Failure | | | | | Quint's Failure] Elsbet doesn't know she wants a baby [Elsbet wincing when he called her Princess [Princess of a line of pretenders. Princess who has to go to her kingdom to earn her throne. Princess in exile afraid of seeing her kingdom]]. Quint Hillard wants a child who is of his kind {Elsbet as other parent} {The dying Moment-Keeper as other parent}]]]]

Quint Hillard is in Wave, working on the membrane, working on the biological interface, working on the depths of adoption, screaming for Feather to help him, shouting for the Handyman, calling for the Professors. Quint Hillard is raving.

Britt Lookdown glared at the farm. The four surviving breeds of chicken glared and snapped back at her, cock-fought and henpecked, maddened by gravity gained and lost, by inattention, by derangements of food and light, their hatred for their domesticators clear in their looks.

Turn from the animals. Look at the vegetables. Grapevines grew along the curtains in drunken curves and spirals, clusters of misshapen concords clashing with champagne grapes bloated far beyond their petite earthly counterparts. Somehow, somehow -- it was always somehow -- melon vines from two curtains over had grown to connect with the grape curtain. These connections had to be hacked away or the honeydew would take all the nutrients from the grapes. She had left instructions, she had told the others how to tend this, but they had had their own concerns.

Alliende was right. She should have been back here tending to the farm instead of being Marie's pilot, instead of --

No, forget it, forget the ropes, forget the curling, twisting vines, tearing into the ship, pulling things out, ripping in, digging into our membranes, eating our food, breathing our air.

If only we didn't need to eat or breathe, if only we could live properly in the sky. Britt raised the sharp-edged shears and pruned and pruned, cutting the vines, cutting them, tearing their curtains.

Tear them down, get them out, get them out. Get them out!

"Why did you force her to go back?" Beatrice Van Leider asked Tomaso Alliende. "The farm needs a lot of repairs, and she needs . . ."

Van Leider shook her head sadly at Britt Lookdown, tightly wrapped in a membrane, nestled against one of the sleeping curtains, sleeping sedated.

"She needed what I gave her. She'll be back on the farm soon."

"What makes you say that?"

"She's been hammered," Alliende said hand against hand. "Now she needs to temper. She'll come out forged."

"This isn't a smithy, Tomaso."

"Yes it is, Beatrice. This ship is a forge. The Method-Smiths made it, and I think I understand why. This ship, this trip are the fire and the anvil and Feather is the hammer. It will burn us and he will beat us and fold us and temper us until we emerge as a tool."

"What tool?"

"We'll have to decide that as we go along," the Handyman said. "A more serious question is whose tool will we be?"

Anger rose among the skyvolk.

"Britt shouldn't have gone. She couldn't rise to the challenge."

"The Professors treat us like slaves. Lynch them."

"The Handyman won't make the habitat more like a skyborough."

"The Guests tricked us."

"There is no sky here."

"Winston, you tricked us."

"Winston!"

"Winston!"

"Winston!"

Feather watched the madness spread through the crew-monsters. They were falling like dominoes under the pressure of Marie and Britt's transformations, Marie pushing the Guests, Britt the skyvolk and the groundlings, falling, falling through space, falling through the fire of the forge, falling into the cave of monsters and mysteries.

"Falling, falling, all down falling," Feather sang to himself as the madness fell into and through him, falling into the method of monsters. "Falling, falling, all fall up."

Two years of white, two years of black

The membrane dissolved, loosing the Pantechnicon into intraship space. It had been long since The Handyman had flown his home, a long time tinkering with it, adapting it with studies of the Single-Sayer flying suits, the patch-rocket that carried Quint back and forth in a fever to the Moment-Keeper ship, the glowing insubstantialities that the Path-Miners used to track across the field, and the endless variations in flight the Method-Smiths had shown as they maintained and operated the ship.

Gliding on the tracks of field, following the guides of gravity and electromagnetism, gripping with the strong and weak forces, sticking to carefully chosen parts of space-time, the Pantechnicon made a slow spiral around the Monster.

He knew he would not be able to see the thing. Its mass of a large mountain range still translated into a picoscopic Schwarzschild radius. Its gravity could be felt, but it itself would have none of the drama and flare of a fallen star. This black hole had been cultivated, grown from a quantum black hole left over from the beginning of time. The Method-Smiths had found it and fed it, reared it to maturity, but not to dangerous vastness. Then they had harnessed it, a dragon to their chariot.

Theadora, playing Medea, driving a chariot pulled by twin dragons of mist, the hardest role she had ever played, a woman who sacrificed her children out of jealousy. Theadora loved her own offspring too much to harm them, and she could never be jealous of a man finding another woman.

Or another love of any kind. Indeed, Alliende was sure that Theadora by subtle means had pushed away all her lovers, pushed them out into the world, into the stars, into death (poor Rainbow).

Pushed, pulled. Was Theadora any different from the monster below, the black hole that permitted travel between the stars? Was she just another monster? Was that why she had carried Feather with her for two decades, a monster enjoying a monster's company?

Or was it the liking of Guest for Guest? Theadora was a Guest for the muses, had modeled herself on divinities of inspiration. Her life's work had been the raising up of kings from the mud of ignobility. Was that the secret of the Guests, that they had not invented a new thing, but had taken a method by which humans became gods and attached it to the process of human becoming alien? Had Constance Marchant been an ufneck after all?

The Pantechnicon flew closer to the black hole. Feel the tides, feel the pull and the fall, but don't fall. Don't enter the maw of the beast; stay clear of its gravitic bite, its space-warping claws. In empty space the Method-Smiths had confined it. They fed it matter with the filter and the feeder. They drew energy from it with their harvester, but they did not dare to touch it. It was a fire, no more tamed than an earthly flame but confined by the empty space around it, and in times of whiteness confined by the field it generated, a prisoner who made its own prisons.

The Pantechnicon flew back and docked with the prison-shell the Handyman had made for himself.

Two years of black. Then back to white.

One by one, Feather prodded and herded the crewvolk together into the central sphere, then in and in through the membranes to the core of the human habitat.

The crew had howled and ravaged through the ship these last years, snarled and tore, while at the same time farming and experimenting, talking, visiting the other habitats, learning, and all the other things humans did while their hearts and souls growled and spit in anger at the world around them and chewed and snapped at each other like caged animals. Feather had made sure that the madness mostly remained inside their minds so that each one looked and sounded human enough for the others to think that the crew were mostly sane. Only Feather knew that all had been madvolk and that only now as the ship decelerated toward the Single-Sayer system were they coming back to the breath and food of sanity.

It had been a struggle for Feather to keep his own madness alive while having to cultivate sanity in others. At times he had felt himself falling into the routines of normality. Then he would take a brief sojourn and visit the Ocean to revitalize the methods of monsters and madness.

"Well, that was a useless meeting," Beatrice Van Leider said. "Everyone was talking about their own work and problems. No one listened to anyone else. Why wasn't anyone listening when I explained the culture gap in our next transmissions from Earth?"

Tomaso Alliende only half paid attention to Professor Van Leider. He knew about her complaints. He had heard them many times over this last stretch of years. It had become a mantra with her, complaints of disinterest. He had tried to explain that they were being worked in the Fire, but she didn't care to hear that. She certainly didn't want to think about Feather as the smith hardening them.

The Handyman had watched Feather work and mused on the idea that metal always felt this discomfort. Sometimes he idly wondered if there were other self-aware materials which suffered and came to understand the need for their suffering, came perhaps to admire the craftsmanship of the one who made them suffer and to wonder if even that demiurge knew the end for which it forged.

Marie floated in the ball of image mist, learning from the wispy Surrounders recorded long ago and carried in many lenticles in the Band-Braider habitat. It was not music. It had never been music. It was the images cast forth from the dying Band-Braiders who had first ventured forth to the stars. It told of the death that comes from loneliness (such a pale and empty human word for the lack of right surroundings). It warned that it was impossible to bring enough crew-coils to properly surround the jobs of space, let alone surround each other. It spoke of the hopeless task of filling the space between ship and world and the longing of isolation, it spoke of the failure to reach out to the light of the universe, of the limits of self-propelled evolution.

That was how it spoke to Marie, and that was what mattered. The lenticle was her Surrounder. It spoke to her. What it said to the real Band-Braiders she could not know. There was space and inhabitation between them. She did not have to know what they knew, or think as they thought. She had only to speak to her Surrounders in the light of her mind and let them speak back in the lights of their minds, and bodies, and genetic coils.

In the exercise sphere Elsbet Chan and Beatrice Van Leider pushed against each other, hand against arm, arm breaking lock and grabbing other hand, around and around in the cycles of Tai Chi Push Hands. It should have brought them together, made them one in action and awareness, undone the distinctions between one person and another. But all they had was one woman pushing against another, back and forth in futility and self-concentration.

Winston Overus had lost his people. The skyvolk no longer listened to him or cared about his view of the sky. Now they cared about survival in the ship, cared about living in space, cared about the farms and the field, cared about the black hole, the Monster, as Feather called it. They wanted to go home with lessons for living in space. They wished no more for visions of the sky. They had become groundlings in all but name and habitat.

Britt Lookdown was the worst of the lot. He had had such hopes for her. Only a few years before the trauma of the Band-Braider world had made her long for the stars. But Tomaso had taken her back to the dirt. She had savaged her farm, then nurtured it back. She was a soil grubber, a chicken-breeder, a ground-hugger, a creature of earth and hole, cooped up. And she had dragged the rest of the skyvolk away from him. Was this to be their legacy back in the skyboroughs, nothing but technique, nothing but the extension of survival, nothing but living in cans and balls, inverted planets, inside-out holes?

Where was the vision? Where was the sky? How could he bring that back?

Quint Hillard is in Wave. Quint Hillard is trying to move without thinking. Quint Hillard is thinking about not thinking. Quint Hillard breathes in. Quint Hillard breathes out. Quint Hillard counts his thoughts as he had been taught in youth by the failed monastics, the first generation Path-Miner Guests. Count your thoughts to pull your mind from attachment and obsession, they had said before returning to the underground paths of their own obsessions.

Don't think, he thinks.

Thought, he counts.

Sit still, he thinks.

Thought, he counts.

The walls are shaking, he thinks.

Thought.

Elsbet's in the next bubble.

Thought.
The membranes are almost ready.
Thought.
If only I'd finished them before the field turned on.
Thought.
Let it live until deceleration, he thinks.
THOUGHT.
Quint Hillard is in Burst {}

The Path-Miner Guest swung through the ship, following the angry thrum, circling, spiraling, curving around the loci of wrath and self-absorption, but not coming too close. He did not want to fall into one of those notion-pits that humans called ideas. To orbit, to roll around, to tunnel under and over, to explore the regions affected by a single concept, to carve a valley between obsessions, a mine that dug through many notion veins, that was what the Path Miner Guests had learned to do. They had their human ideas, but they did not embrace them, they charted their ways around them. Pits and holes, echo chambers, volcanoes, these were ideas. But to fall into a pit, to be dazed by echoes, melted by heat -- no, those were foolish ideas. Better to hang on to aloofness.

Then the human thought came. Isn't aloofness a pit? Have you already fallen and not known it?

Feather had done this. The Method-Smith Guest was a vast depression, an Echo-hole like space, like the Monster, like the ship itself. Feather had dropped attractive thoughts into the landscape of the Path-Miner Guest's mind, pulling him around, turning him in ways he had not followed before, lumbering him with awareness of his own aloofness. Aloofness was a hole, a planet, a well, a shaft. A thing to be dug out of. He had to dig upward to the light and the sky. But to dig out of aloofness he would have to deal with others. And with the field on that meant other humans, each of whom was a pit, hole, a planet, a well, a shaft.

He's done it, Elsbet Chan thought as she watched the crewvolk swinging around each in his or her own way, following their own paths and concerns. Feather has brought out the uniqueness in each of us. He has depicted us clearly as Solitaires.

So why can't I make seals of the crew and direct them to concerted action? Why can't I count them? Even a child could count this small a group. Why can't I?

It should be simple. Monster Who Sees Each Thing as Itself plus Monster Who Sees Everything At Once sealed by Marriage is . . .

But she couldn't find the answer. It had been simple to add herself to Quint when they were Guests. But somehow monsters did not sum. They remained isolated.

More isolated than Solitaires? she wondered. The Solitaires in the Single-Sayer habitat could be summed, conjoined, connected. They could work together on what needed to be done, then they could go severally to their isolated aeries. Summing, sealing, and sundering them was easy enough.

Why were these human monsters harder to combine then Solitaire Single-Sayers?

Elsbet Chan stared out at the Seal of Whiteness which conjoined the flying disparities into a single ship, binding six species together in common purpose and common compulsion to reach a single goal. Why could the Monster outside be counted, but not the monsters within?

If she could count Quint, she could seal the two of them up again. Why can't I count just the two of us, or three if I have to add the Moment-Keeper? She had tried over and over, but they would not fit together in any combination or allotment.

The human part of her mind suggested that she wait until they reached the Single-Sayer world where she would be able to learn the deeper mysteries of their mathematics and learn to count the uncountable. But the Single-Sayer side of her refused to accept that. No matter how well one was taught, one had to learn to count by oneself. Counting was a thing of Solitaires, of predators ranging over herds, seeking to cull them. Counting was of the eaters, not the eaten.

And between the human and the Single-Sayer minds, the monster grinned with wide human teeth and licked two Single-Sayer tongues, savoring the thought of eating every thing around her, if only it could find where to bite.

Winston Overus stared into the image mist and saw space falling around the ship. Marie had learned that the field carried images of the regions beyond the white. The filter at the front of the ship took in light as well as dust, and the field channeled the images of space into the habitats. Marie and the Handyman had adapted the Underbelly so that it could see as the Band-Braiders saw, then translate to human pictures.

Winston Overus stared into the image mist of falling down the Arch, falling farther from the upper limits of speed, down to the prosaic hole of normal space. What was normal about it? Relativity did not care what speed you traveled at. It all seemed the same.

Only one's surroundings cared about velocity. Only what you passed, what you struck, and what you left behind in the dilations of time cared about your speed.

Winston Overus stared into the image mist of falling into the Single-Sayer hole and wondered about climbing out again.

12. Partitions of Unity

Britt Lookdown seethed in resentment. Sent down to the pit again, ferrying another Guest into another hole.

At least this planet wasn't covered all over in those terrible cords and coils. The Single-Sayers had a proper regard for open space. They had vast stretches of it, mountain ranges with peaks high as seven Everests, their mountaintops poking above the atmosphere, with a few inhabitants, half of sky, half of ground. And wide canyons, huge tracts of broken land, and no real cities, no density at all. Open delights of rarefaction.

How had Feather tricked her into doing this?

That was what Britt most wanted to know.

It had taken her some time to realize that Feather was responsible. He hadn't said much to her. The suggestions had come from others, skyvolk and the Handyman mostly, subtle tickling thoughts, insinuations that the ship might be feeling a little small for her, that her role in the gardens and the farms might be confining.

The other pilots had spoken comradelike about the delights of open space, then disparaged the task of chauffeuring Professors around to the uninhabited planets and moons.

But it was overhearing Feather and Elsbet Chan talking about the Single-Sayers' love of solitude and emptiness and the open sky that had pulled volunteering words from Britt's mouth without her mind realizing she had spoken.

May the sky fall on him for his scheming! Still, the world above this world was beautiful, as were the mountainous satellites that orbited the Single-Sayer planet, each in their own path, passing near to each other then going delightfully, beautifully far in elliptic isolation. Then there were the single-crew ships that flew all through the system, pilots gloriously alone in the sky. It had been a trick that had brought her here, but the result was worth the trickery.

Best of all, they had not forced her to stay in one place. She had left Elsbet Chan on the planet and was now free to fly the skies and see the sights. She had only to check back in with the Guest every few weeks and shuttle down food from her farms.

For the moment the mountain's name was Peak-So-Tall-as-to-Make-the-Human-Pay-Attention-to-it-

While-She-is-Met. That much was obvious to Elsbet from the moment she swooped over its summit in her flight suit. The names of the four Single-Sayers gathered on the mountaintop were not so easy to discern.

She knew that she had been allotted among them, her nature and purpose divided up according to their interests and appetites. In short, she had been cut up like a carcass before a butcher. But that did not trouble her, for she had come to eat the four of them alive and entire.

Elsbet Chan took three swoops around the peak, delighting in the low gravity of this world. Flying on Earth was a mechanical hardship, a strain upon the engines that could be put in a single-person flight suit, but here at less than two-thirds of a gee, flight, even for so maladapted a form as the human body, was an easy, natural, graceful action, the turning of the eagle above the rabbit, the owl above the mouse.

Elsbet Chan caught herself as she swooped upward. No metaphors, no human thinking. She had come as a Single-Sayer and she needed to have her mind be like their minds. She swooped as herself. Only her mind guided her four flat wing-pads; only her thoughts sped or slowed her through these particular winds in this particular place. Do not generalize. Come down for this meeting here and now.

A place upon the rocks had been carved for her, carpeted with something like moss, warmed by tunneled heat to a temperature comfortable for her, a little too warm for Quint, a little too cool for Sean (How fares my son? How does he fly in the ConCensor's job? And how is Julian doing in the Guesthouse?)

Elsbet Chan settled down onto the landing rock, letting her wings rest in their places and opening her suit to emerge in apparent humanity to sit in the carved-space-that-fit-her-shape as the ship had long ago learned it.

The Single-Sayers sat neatly ensconced in the clefts and peaks of the mountain. Their bodies were covered with thick dark brown membranes which pushed and shaped the rock beneath them, giving comfort to their perches. When they flew off, the mountain would bear the imprints of their presence. All over this world were the marks of those who had sat for a time in a single place, markers of those who had been, the seals of their bodies stamped into the stone and earth. The entire world bore such marks and carvings. Every place was open to the Single-Sayers, for what could be held hidden from the dominion of the air and what guarded from the bite of the highest predator?

The longer one of them stayed in one place the more that locus would be accommodated to its presence, the more it would bear the unique seal of that single personality. If another Single-Sayer came along soon after the first had left, it would be able to read the character and attitudes of the Single-Sayer who had preceded it, a method they had learned from the Path-Miners and adopted to their own unique views.

With these creatures there would be no bargaining, no give and take to reach accommodation. There was only the taking up of near perches and the mutual affecting of the environment for the betterment of both or the detriment of one. Either two Single-Sayers came together in a seal of common action or they sealed together in conflict one against the other.

That had been the way since before they had had minds to consider the way. Now they were well thought and well thoughtful and the making of seals was ingrained and intrained. When brought together, a seal could always be made, even between Solitaires.

"But I am not a Solitaire," Elsbet Chan said in the language of accommodation created during her visits to the Single-Sayer habitat. "I am a monster. I live outside the-seal-of-humans-interacting-for-each-other. I prey on people, I hunt where I will. I am the monster I am, not human or Single-Sayer. How can you seal with me?"

From above and to the right, two hand-thick tongues lashed out from one of the perched Single-Sayers. The tongues struck her membrane and slid under and through to run across Elsbet Chan's arm. She had felt this before, this need to taste the strange before sealing with it. Elsbet Chan slid her hand around the tongues, letting the grooves and crevasses of her age and labors show themselves to the Single-Sayer, then opened her mouth for a similar testing of her own taste.

The tongues tasted, then withdrew into the split-keel mouth of the Single-Sayer. For a time it chewed over what it had sampled. Then it spoke, its membrane vibrating words audible to humans.

"Monster-who-tastes-character-I-seal-with-your-unlike-seal-of-all-Single-Sayers-taste. Let seal-of-you-and-I bite and learn from tastes-that-cannot-be-made-like-each-other."

Elsbet Chan licked the alien taste from her tongue and considered the offer. The Single-Sayer was offering a seal based on incompatibility. It said that two things that could never be one would be made one because they could never be made one. A flickering of Taoist philosophy, a hint of Yin and Yang offered itself to her, but she rejected it. This was not a case of dividing the world into two unlike things that fit together. This was the discovery that no things fit together, that separation, distance, disconnection, inequality, incompatibility, were the fundamental components of reality. Nothing by nature fits with anything, therefore fitness can be created by anything with anything.

"I will seal with you," she said. Then turned to

the other three and waited for their challenges.

"Data, data, and more data!" Beatrice Van Leider shouted. "What good is any of it?"

The scene she was making was part of a scene being played out for the benefit of the sullen gathering of Professors. The University of the Ship had met over and over, with decreasing conversation. Gloomy had risen the silences, the tea grown cold with failed interaction of faculties.

Beatrice blamed the slowness of the work and the dashing of hopes that had been raised by the exploration of the Band-Braider worlds. Two systems had now been explored, a trebling of the catalogue of planetary phenomena, and not one of the five remaining theories of planetary formation had moved even a centimeter toward acceptance or rejection.

The stars they had visited were too Sol-like, the planets too close in semblance to those they had explored in their native system. If only they had been able to visit exotic stars and sample planets unbiased by the necessities of producing life (worse still, intelligent life), then the data might have been broad enough to help the theories. But these stars and worlds had been forced upon them by the conjuring tricks of the Deceiving universe and were no more a random sampling than the cards handed out by a stage magician.

Yes, they had many new pretty pictures to add to the catalogues, including a few interesting grotesques -- in particular, one world half the radius of Mars which had been struck by a very large asteroid at some point and had developed some fascinating terrain features from the resulting upsurge of mantle and the return to spherical shape. Dramatic, certainly, worthy of decades of study, yes.

But those decades of work had already been done by the Single-Sayers.

The aliens had asked different questions and voiced different concerns when they had flown across the eccentric landscape, but they had basically done most of the work human scientists would have wanted.

The rest of that work would be impossible to do. A team of humans would have had to remain for years to carry out the analysis. But that could never be. They would never survive long enough that far from a human-comfortable ecosystem.

Had the crewvolk been selected and sent out just for this? Had the Professors been sickened and monstered and cooped up for years to find that they were wasting their time out here? Their leaving had seemed good on Earth. There was only so much that the aliens could tell them through interstellar communications because they were alien and couldn't formulate human questions that would meet human interests. Obvious, yes, true, yes, but now those human questions were not being answered. What were they all doing here?

What indeed? Beatrice Van Leider thought. Did I need to risk my life just to have my assumptions shattered? Did I need to come this far to awaken the monster that lay within me?

Yes, said the image of Feather that floated in her mind.

A thrumming sound came through the membranes of the meeting sphere.

"Enter," called out Professor Saul Ben Isaac. His voice warbled and there was a crack in it. What his illness was, none of the Professors could determine. But they all knew his life was closing.

The Handyman floated in. "We have the message package from Earth."

The meeting broke up in the rush to get the mail.

Alliende stopped Van Leider before she could dart out.

"Beatrice, the messages are all encrypted."

"Encrypted?" the word had fallen much out of favor. Codes were tools of Deceivers, and to be put in a crypt was the fate of a Deceiver. The Professors had preserved the mathematics of code-making and breaking, but it was one of their quiet secrets, not taught to normal students, only given to other trusted Professors, away from communities that had trees and ropes. Who then on Earth had broken in to the tomb and taken out the skeleton keys?

Elsbet Chan flew swiftly down the channels of Herder's-Valley, the only place on the Single-Sayer world unchanged in name for thousands of years. To a human the name was ironic in its understatement. How can a four-thousand-kilometer-long, two-kilometer-deep stretch of canyon, flanked by two mountain ranges that were slowly moving apart in the world's tectonic dance, be called a mere valley?

Down there the half-thinking packs of pre-sapient Single-Sayers had invented their own hard and brutal forms of domestication during the Long-Hot when the entire planet had warmed and mass extinctions had taken many species. Small societies had been formed and co-operation invented, but not language. Language had been created by the Solitaire hunters who flew from pack to pack and saw and needed to speak of much more of the world than their nesting husbander-kin.

Allotter-of-Pasts had sent her here to see and smell the remains of history, if history it could be called.

Allotter-of-Pasts had told her of the valley and the development of intelligence and language. It had sealed this part of the past to her, adding it to the pack of her thoughts, a flyable burden, not too heavy. What might Allotter-of-Pasts have said of this place if it had wanted to weigh her down with a burdened pack, and what might it have said if it had wanted to put a killing load on her thoughts?

Run your prey to the ground, make their own weight and life too heavy for them to bear so that they die without ever feeling the touch of your wing-pads or the bite of your prow. Those were lessons she had absorbed from Teaches-Lessons-To-Those-Who-Did-Not-Learn-Them-When-Young, the third of the four Single-Sayers she had met. It had insisted on her knowing how to hunt before she would be let loose upon the world and the world upon her.

But there had been more to the teachings than the bringing down of wildlife and domestic beasts that the gaps of biochemistry would have prevented her from eating.

There had been an understanding of the weight one could bear and the weights one could put upon another, there had been hints of assassination, for want of a better word, implications that burdens and the allotting of burdens were the means by which Single-Sayers could control or correct or kill each other. Hints were all she had been given, hints in seals that she could not open in the days and weeks of that teaching.

And then, before she could untie the knots and break the seals, she had been given to Allotter-of-Pasts who had given her this weight of understanding. It could have given her more, she was sure of it. It could have put enough heaviness in her mind to addle her, confuse her, muddle her flight, make her crash and die. It could have killed her with a carefully weighted statement.

Elsbet Chan laughed loudly, a sound never before heard on this world.

"We thought it was mathematics!" she shouted.

Below, a herd of fat, slow-moving creatures with six paddle-feet looked up in bewilderment. Millennia ago their ancestors would have fled from a sound above, but long-long domestication had made them too stupid to know death when it cried overhead.

"Each of these is in a different code," Beatrice said, at last. "Personally encrypted, using genetic seals. They should be breakable using a chip burner and a lenticle reader if they could be connected together."

"Give me half an hour," the Handyman said.

One by one the crewvolk came forward and offered their chromosomes and one by one they were handed lenticles with their messages inscribed. Then off they went in privacy to see the images sent from Earth sixty-seven years after their departure.

The Image of Sean Chan-Hillard, aged to a century but held alive by the same microbiological bargains as kept the crewvolk going, flickered in the mist in front of Quint Hillard. His human son, the young boy grown to young man they had left on Earth to do the work of the ConCensor, was staring out into empty space, speaking across the simultaneity of space and time. He spoke in hope and despair to his parents, only one of whom was there to hear him.

"Mother," Sean said to his absent parent in

Guestsprach, "I have failed in the job you left me. The Dissociation has cracked to pieces. We have only a quarter of the volks we had when you left.

"It was because of Grandmère. Her methods were spread out. Other Guesthouses were formed in other places. The skyvolk captured the High-Talker, took Constance from us. Julian died defending it. We stopped being the only Guests. Other people began Dissociations. The Marshall left us to join another, and the Dissenters shouted us down. Ali Mustafa said his methods were worthless. He refused to go into the Ocean when he died. All that he was and did is lost.

"We lost the world, we lost Constance, we lost what you left us. I stayed alive long enough to send this message, but now I can let go the adoptions and fly free alone. My granddaughter has given up all her lineages. She is Backlorn, but still she is ConCensor of what is now just the First Dissociation.

"Mother, forgive me. Father, forgive me. The world you may come back to is not the one you left."

The image faded into darkness, leaving the knowledge that his sons were dead, that the trees of their minds and actions had been pruned by the final gardener. Elsbet did not know yet, would not know until she came back to him from the world that was hers.

She would not come back to him. He knew that, knew she would come to the ship, but not to her husband. She was gone from him. All of his family was gone. He had been lorned by his loves. Quint Hillard felt the lack of Elsbet more than he had ever thought possible. She was gone to be with her kind. In the four months since she had left the ship her communications had dwindled to nothing but occasional requests for supplies.

"Elsbet," he said. "Elsbet Chan. Elsbet Chan-DeMarnier-Dunlevy-Tienh (and four other lineages she refuses to honor because some of her immediate ancestors in those lines had been ufnecks or rioters, or in three cases Predators), the former ConCensor of the Dissociation, Princess, later Queen, Elsbet, my wife, the mother of our children, our dead children."

All the fractal branches of Moment-Keeper thought on which she might bloom had been cut, all except one: Elsbet Chan the Single-Sayer.

Her absence and the children's absence was a raw wound in his mind. In Wave, she dominated his thinking. In Burst, the loss of her and them bled from the thorn bush of his thoughts, branch cutting at branch, his mind-entire turning against itself. So bloody were his thoughts that he wished he did not have to enter Burst at all. But his other mate still needed him, needed him entire and bleeding if need be, if there was ever to be another family.

Quint Hillard is in Burst.

The suit {Schematics and specifications} fits {twitches and pains of raw nerve endings}, works {flickers of communications {memories passed over from the dying Moment-Keeper [image of the Moment-Keeper home world {oceans filled with the aged} {land with cities of the young and active} {space checkered with patches}]]}} Elsbet {all their life together} is [Elsbet still is, she is changing out of his sight] gone [but might return] [Sean and Julian are gone with no returning. His descendants have abandoned him, gone with their pasts] THOUGHT {}

The mist flickered to life.

Quint Hillard is in Wave.

Another image, another person, an old man on a tall horse which bore the signs of many adoptions. The man's face was vaguely familiar. Once seen, but only once. If he were still in Burst Quint would have known him. As it was he waited to hear words in Footsprach changed by absorption of other tongues Quint did not recognize.

"To the Moment-Keeper called Quint Hillard. I am the Rainbow Khan, and I send you word from the footvolk of the Earth. I do this because I owe you a debt. You gave me a chit of life. Now I pay it back.

"We met on the back of the Rainbow Serpent, when you talked me back into the roads of the living. You said then that anyone could have done that, that anything I saw would have pulled me back. That was true. But it was you that I saw, and the way you pulled me back made me what I am. I have gathered the footvolk together, I have Guests of my own. Some are Moment-Keepers and they tell me they will wait for your return. I offer you the hospitality of the road. I give this command to my children and their children, that Quint Hillard has the freedom to walk where he will upon the Earth."

Quint Hillard is in Burst [The Rainbow Serpent, Time upon Uluru grapples with him].

Thought

{}

Single-Sayers perched on ledges, looking down at the human walking in their midst. Elsbet Chan had come to a settlement. She could not call it a city, or even a town. There were no buildings, only occasional bubbles and patches. The only structure was a cave where space-flying suits were made, custom-made of course, by the Workers-who-remove-the-seal-of-atmosphere-and-gravity. The seal on that cave had been there for, Elsbet estimated, two thousand years. Single-Sayers who wished to work in that endeavor came to the cave and an attempt was made to fit them in. If they fit they stayed for as long as they wished to work, then left. If they did not fit, they went elsewhere, perhaps to one of the other builders, perhaps to do something else.

But the seal had remained present since Eater-of-the-Unbreathable had flown above the atmosphere. The entire history of Single-Sayer flight could be found in this place by talking to the correct people and unsealing the proper lenticles in the proper fashion.

Elsbet came to look at that seal, a constant object surviving, prospering in the idiosyncratic world of the Single-Sayers. She thought that if she could unseal it with the mind of human and monster she might be able to learn what she had come to learn.

The river Rhine cascaded down the back wall of the castle in the image mist. A man in his late forties peered from the mist. His face was sharpened and dark. There were a few hints of Theadora in his jawline, touches of the Handyman in his brow. Whoever his mother had been, her genes dominated his appearance, but Tomaso knew the image was his grandson.

"Demiurge," the voice said. "I am Gregory the Far-Seeing, son of Gregory the Great, your son. My father died twenty years ago, but he left the command that I send this message to you.

"Great Demiurge, greatest of artificers, your son took the wealth your hands had made and forged a Dissociation. Many nations came to him for aid and he gave it in return for their connection and willingness to be counted among us. Here is the palace that straddles the Rhine, built by the produce of your hands and the visions of my father's mind. That wealth and that Dissociation have been passed on to me, as I will pass it to my son. My father wished that a Gregory be waiting for you when you return, so that name will be passed down, as will all your achievements. All the Hands of Earth will be raised in greeting to you.

"Demiurge, you have not labored in vain. We await your second coming."

Raging in his heart, the Handyman watched the image fade. With a care he usually preserved for control of molecule-manipulating tools, he opened the reader and took out the lenticle. Line by line he brachiated his way out through the spheres to his Pantechnicon. Inside, he turned on his forge-manufactory and with his hands ordered that there be heat within the workdome wherein tools were crafted according to pattern and commandment. Into the heat he placed the lenticle and watched with human eyes and the manufactory's micro-eyes the dissolution of the image storer.

The lenticle had been a tool, a thing crafted, a thing made of levels of structure to carry forth a certain purpose. Minds and hands had labored long to make such things possible, to store image and sound, to guide light and awareness. Many species had worked to perfect the lenticle.

But the Crazy Old Man needed only a little Fire to undo all that effort and to unmake the tool and the toolness and leave only a puddle of carbon, chromium, nitrogen, and hydrogen to be shuffled into the hopper.

Elsbet watched the hunt from the air. The prey, an elephant-sized amphibious hexapod, was swimming swiftly away from its flying pursuers. The nine Single-Sayers chasing it seemed more concerned with their discussion than with the hunt itself, but if it were not for the hunt they would not be together to carry the discussion. That was the oddity.

Elsbet could barely follow the esoterica of the discussion, which seemed to range across the entirety of inhabited space, touching on the thoughts and actions of all the alien species. She was flying with specialists in alien understanding, Single-Sayers who knew much about the other aliens. Two of them had been to other worlds. To humans such a group would naturally come together for the mutual interest and learning. But these had come to hunt.

The hunt and the discussion, completely distinct to humans, were unified to these Single-Sayers, a unique seal which here and now brought these beings together. It was almost, Elsbet's mind hinted to itself human to monster, as if the seals were more real, more important than the things they sealed up.

No, that was human thinking. She needed to be a Single-Sayer to understand this event, needed to really be the Single-Sayer-Who-Was-Also-Elsbet-Chan, not just the image of the Single-Sayer-Who-Was-Really-Elsbet-Chan.

Elsbet waited for the moment when she could break away from the pack without destroying the seal, then flew off, at last knowing where she had to go.

An officious looking man, professionally stern with just a hint of sympathy about his upper lip, spoke across the years to Winston Overus.

"Your daughter, the Overus, gave her life for the good of the skyvolk. We have honored her for capturing the High-Talker and bringing our independence from the hole-dwelling Guests. We honor her name and you will find monuments to Patricia Overus when and if you return."

The image fell away. A condolence, that was all he was worth to them, a condolence for the loss of poor Tricia. Why had she done this thing? Why go to fight, why die bringing battle to the Dissociation? Fight the Dissociation? Why? And why die to be honored?

Poor Tricia. She had done the skyvolk good. Poor little daughter, cradled in her mother's arms. Floating through the skyboroughs, the only time Theadora had come up from the Earth, to show his daughter to him and to the sky.

Lost little girl. They had thought her a hole-grubber, the skyvolk had when she had been living with her mother. But she had become one of them when she came to help with the ship. And they had followed her to death and triumph. Their own Guests, a blow for independence. What did his journey to the stars, his vision and hope of the sky matter compared to that single practical act of sacrifice?

"I have brought together the Universities and the traveling Professors," Dominique, grown up to almost an image of Theadora, said to Beatrice Van Leider. "I used the model of the Dissociation and organized the Disuniversity. It has been a hard struggle, but I have restored some of the reputation of the voicevolk, and many nations have joined us for our knowledge, forswearing the noose. From this I can see the time when the Voice itself will be disunified. If that can be achieved even the other Dissociations will not be able to dislodge us.

"Professor, a place will be waiting for you here in Beijing when you return. I will be waiting. We have made considerable progress in staving off death. We have good reason to believe that human life can be stretched to cover more than two centuries. Compromises will have to be made in the biology, but I will be waiting for you."

For me? Van Leider thought, her stomach turning in a fear that was akin to stage-fright as a lightning bug is like the lightning. Dominique, you did this for me? I don't have anything to bring back except an empty mask. If I came and spoke to your Disuniversity, I would destroy it. Unless I played the role. But I couldn't play in front of you, my student, my daughter.

In the next mist-sphere, Dominique addressed Feather in a wholly different voice.

"Father, I know the world is your fault. You made monsters of us all, made a monster of the entire Earth. I don't understand why. What purpose is served by destroying the peace of Earth, breaking us into Dissociations, setting brothers and sisters against each other?

"Of my siblings only Karl is still alive. Patricia and Gregory died for their creations. And Karl hasn't long to live. None of them would extend themselves as I have. Father, I want to know why you did this. Send me an answer, or if not, tell me when you return. I will be waiting for you."

Feather watched the image of his grown child fade away and nodded to himself. Theadora's methods had done their work as had his.

Crafter-of-Method-Smith-Devices padded through the membrane-tent that protected its work-area from the elements. Elsbet Chan walked after it, membrane sliding against membrane, earthly cells gliding athwart the rigid interlocking spiral micro-bases of the Single-Sayer biology, seeking challenge or recognition. Neither could know anything about the other; too unlike were the biospheres that gave birth to their undomesticated ancestors. But down between the cells picoscopic molecules modeled on a third world and duplicated on these two clicked and flicked in electromagnetic recognition. They said: These two beings are both our adopted children, let them meet each other.

The molecules flipped in orientation, which signaled the cells and the spirals that all was well. Membrane opened to let membrane pass through. Elsbet Chan walked into the workshop.

Elsbet Chan had come a-hunting. She had sought throughout the world for the means by which the Single-Sayers took in things alien. She had found, of course, a variety of different means and answers. Each Single-Sayer had its own way of dealing with outworld matters. But as she had hunted she had caught a sample, then a taste, then a savor, then a trail that led person by person to this place and this mechanician. This one carried a pack of alienness that would have killed most other Single-Sayers, but this one bore it easily, bore it as a flight pack, sometimes as a lightening-weight, a burden that made other burdens easier to carry. This was the nearest the Single-Sayers had to a Guest.

Elsbet Chan looked around the workshop carved into the rockface, yellow-tinged and shimmering under the thin film-canopy. It looked as all Single-Sayer dwellings did, like a stone-age habitation. The Single-Sayers had never been the weak creature in the survival heap. Their ancestors had not fled squirrel-like from savage predators, nor brachiated through jungle canopies to escape the horns and teeth below them. They had never hidden from storms and floods, nor sheltered from the beasts of the night. They were the beasts of the night.

Shelter meant nothing to them; they had not spent their minds and arts developing houses and cities. They lived where they wanted and the only accommodations they made to that living were for the security of their efforts. The membrane that had been spun over Crafter-of-Method-Smith-Devices-Adopting-Human-Visitor's work area was there because of the fragility of its tools, not of its body.

The micro-polished flat sheet of volcanic rock covered with layers of filtering films, that was the Smooth of its work area, where tongues could pick up and manipulate and eye-bands be augmented to see the gentle construction of atom laid next to atom or stone chipped by stone, or mountain tunneled into, or patient opened for surgery. All operations were here performed. The Smooth accepted whatever Sharp was put on it. Even the sharpness of Elsbet Chan.

This lies down offering the taste of this. The taste of this has been given from the others that have tasted this. The tastes of this are sealed into the taste of this. This fills my reach and falls upon my back. I cannot fly with this on my back. It is a planet in heaviness. I put it on my back with the other planet I carry. With my tongues I pull the planets together, making a being of these, making a pack of them. I pull the pack from my back.

This rises.

This and I together make one world.

"The habitat is failing," the Handyman said.

"Then we'll have to fix it," Feather said.

"We're the problem," said Alliende. "Everyone's following their own concerns. No one's attending to the overall."

"I know," said Feather. "It has to be that way."

"Why? You made us monsters. Why couldn't we stay human?"

Why couldn't we stay at home? he thought. Why did I leave Gregory? Why didn't I see the awe in his eyes? I didn't see, didn't realize that he was offering me worship when he made his mist plays about my efforts. Why didn't I stay human for my son's sake?

"If we were human we would have stayed on Earth," Feather said. "Humans have a home. They live there. They exist in their ecosystem. They live in their societies and their conceptions of how the world is. Humans can't face the outside. Only monsters can."

"But monsters only care about what interests them," Alliende said. "Do you know I let the air system go untested for two months because I wanted to work my way through the whole list of artificial crystals the Band-Braiders have that we never invented? A handyman that neglectful would find no work."

"You won't find a non-monstrous replacement handyman out here," Feather said. His tone of voice was maddeningly even. As if . . .

Alliende thought for a moment. Why didn't Feather care about this? And what does Feather care about? What kind of monster is he? He's a monster like Theadora, a monster that changes people, a father of monsters. So, he is talking to me as if I were his child. And am I not his child?

"If there's no replacement, then you already have something that will solve our problem."

"I don't know if I do," Feather said. "I have to rely on another method for that."

"You're the only Method-Smith Guest here," said Alliende.

"There are the real Method-Smiths," Feather said. "And there was Grandmère advising me before we left."

"But there isn't much time to fix -- "

Alliende stopped. Slowly, ponderously, as if he were turning a battleship in a high opposing wind, he turned his mind to the problem of living as monsters. Who on the ship knew about bringing the disparate together?

"Elsbet Chan?"

"If she comes back to us," Feather said, "she will govern for the rest of the journey."

"If?"

"She might stay a Single-Sayer."

"Impossible," Alliende said. "Her mind may be like theirs, but her body eats as ours does; her cells need the life of our eco-system. Earth will drag her back by her biochemistry, no matter how hard her mind may fight."

"That is my hope," Feather said.

Elsbet-Reborn soared below the clouds toward the landing field where she was to meet Britt Look-down. Britt would not recognize her.

Elsbet-Reborn could swoop over the skywoman and look for all worlds like any Single-Sayer. A little larger perhaps, a little clumsier in the air, but she had her keel, her tongues, her eyeslits, she had her pad-wings, she had the feel of the air and the sharp-fractioned sight of a predator.

She had it all, all around her, layer by layer, membrane by membrane, human cells interlocked with Single-Sayer spirals, sealed together in atomic compromise. She had it all, both tastes, both lives, she was at last truly a Guest. She had adopted to her new species, she had gone over, become other, totally, completely.

Elsbet-Reborn landed and padded over to Brit Lookdown, who watched warily, wondering what the Single-Sayer wanted.

"B-b-richtt," Elsbet-Reborn said. "Ac-rech, youll, khready tu guch?"

"What?"

Elsbet-Reborn lifted her left front pad to her keel and pulled. Membranes slid aside retreating into membranes, folding, and refolding and enfolding, sliding one pocket into another pocket, peeling back skin and plates, jagged prow-teeth and eyeslits, sliding away until the Single-Sayer was folded into a pack upon the back of once-more-upright Elsbet Chan.

"I said, 'Are you ready to go?'" said Elsbet Chan in a voice more human and amused then any Britt Lookdown had heard since they left Earth.

"I'm ready if you are," Britt said, trying not to stare at the hunch on Elsbet Chan's back. "Can you walk?"

"I can walk," Elsbet Chan said. "It's a tiring load, but it will get lighter. And it is already easier to bear than the Feather-weight I came with."

13. Singularities

The Monster had fed well, as it always did in the Single-Sayer system. The Single-Sayers gathered in foods from all across their range of space to tempt its palate and give it a delightful balance of quantum numbers, not too much Charm, enough Strangeness, a smattering of Truth and Beauty, delicacies of matter and energy, savors of spin and charge, all tastefully balanced for its surprisingly delicate constitution.

Overeating was very bad for a black hole. Too much too fast and at the first touch of field it might emit the diet of matter in a regurgitation of energy.

Feed it slowly but steadily, that was the way to avoid any unpleasant radio-accidents. The tenders in this system were the finest of chef-nutritionists, giving food that went down easily and built up the gravitational muscles while not over-feeding the spin and charge, nor raising too high any quantum numbers which might overflow in a sudden burst of exotic particles. A delightful spot to feed the Wendigo's spiraling hunger.

"Tomaso, tell me how the ship is," said Elsbet Chan.

The Handyman looked up into the transparent eyes of the Single-Sayer Guest and wondered if this was how mice felt when they turned one last look at the eyes of diving hawks.

"Failing," he said.

Elsbet Chan considered the one-word answer, studied it. She peeled and opened it like an orange, so that if fell neatly into sections of meaning. The Handyman avowed his own failure to do his job. He implied the failings of the crewvolk and acknowledged the breakdowns of many systems. There were also emotional nuances to the taste, a hint that the journey itself, though still in its early stages, was a fundamental failure. Elsbet tasted those implications and the downcast waters in Alliende's transparent eyes and tracked the source to his message from Earth. Failure with his child, then. As she had failed hers. So much flesh and juice in a single word.

"How long can we survive if things go on as they are?"

"Too long," said the Handyman. "On light and nutrient solution, we can survive until our bodies rebel against the lack of food. The Professors think that could be years. We might even make it back to Earth, but who knows how badly deteriorated our minds and bodies will be. We probably won't be able to readapt to human living."

Elsbet Chan absentmindedly tapped the skin-pack on her back, the drumming of her fingertips reverberating through the layers of folded Single-Sayer. Pack up the monsters, seal them in a box, undo Pandora. How? She looked at the Handyman, at the Monster Who Carries a Torch, the Monster Who Cannot Leave a Thing Alone, the Monster Who Changes What he Touches. He had come to her, sent by Feather.

She needed to seal with the Handyman first. Then one by one she could add the rest of the crew-monsters to the seal, then seal in the environment and the experiments and the body of the habitat and the other habitats and the black hole, and all of space around them, and the journeys to be undertaken, and the rest of the universe . . .

Elsbet Chan gripped her back hard and squeezed, pulling her monster-thoughts back to this one moment and the one man in front of her. Seal one thing with the next thing. Don't wander in speculations. Stay with the prey before you. Do not count the food that might some day weigh you down while you still starve for your first bite.

Bite the Handyman that feeds you. Elsbet Chan chuckled and Tomaso Alliende drew away. He knew that laugh. He had heard Theadora laugh it several times. It was the chortle of the beast about to feed, the laugh of the spider that has caught the fly.

"Do you care that the ship you made is failing?"

"Do I care?"

Tomaso Alliende rolled the question into his mind, rolled it like a piece of ore into the cave of the Crazy Old Man With The Fire.

Do I care? He hoisted the ore into the smelter and began to find the metals within, drawing off the slag attached to the word. Care. What are my cares and worries? What do I care about? What matters to me?

Out through the sluice pipe came raw matter. Matter matters to me. The shaping of matter matters, the tools I make matter.

Why do tools matter? Pick one up, use it, put it down. Isn't that the way of tools?

No. The fire seemed to spit out that answer. *Pick up a tool and use it. Put it down and some of it remains in your mind. You have learned to use the tool. The learning remains. The possibility of using it again remains. The tool remains in your mind after you make it or use it. There it will affect your thoughts. When all you have is a hammer, all the world looks like a nail. When all you have is a starship, all the universe looks like a place to go.*

What difference does it make if I make or do not make?

What difference does it make to whom?

He remembered a conversation long ago with Beatrice Van Leider. The Crazy Old People existed for the village. They worked for the good of the villagers. Did he still care about the village? What was the village? Once it had been Earth, but Earth was far away, and changed, and his legacy of labor had been corrupted into display. Nor was he any longer fully human. Out here he was a monster. Back home he had been deified, made into one of the Things No One Can See. Was Earth still his village?

Yes, at least in part. His descendants were there, even if they had fallen into a folly of hero-worship. He had family to return to and family to work for, even if he was now far away. He was not the first man to travel and risk death for the good of distant relatives. He could work for that village.

But he also needed to work for this village, the one he was living in, the Village of the Ship. The Village of Monsters. And who was who in this village?

He was still the Crazy Old Man With The Fire.

Beatrice and her colleagues were the Crazy Old

Woman Who Knows Everything.

Britt was becoming the Crazy Old Woman With the Plants.

Feather was the Crazy Old Man Who Talked to the Things No One Could See.

And . . .

"What should I work on first?" he asked the Crazy Old Man Who Tells Everyone What to Do.

"Get your assistants to look over all the systems that you've been neglecting," Elsbet Chan replied. "Find Britt Lookdown. Tell her to come see me. When I'm done with her, . . ." Elsbet paused, letting the ambiguity of the word 'done' filter into Alliende's mind. ". . . then the two of you can repair the farms. When that's finished come see me and I'll put you and the other Guests to work on the alien parts of the ship."

Quint Hillard, his body covered in spines and spikes, swam through the waters of the Moment-Keeper habitat. The spines tickled and itched down to the nerves they had grafted on to, down deep to his brain where redirected pain signals gave information layered on information. When he was in Burst, the spines' nuanced electrochemical signals could fill his mind with the feel and sight and taste of the world around him, but in Wave they tingled unpleasantly and shivered him with the constant almost-fall sickness of pre-seizure.

Down he swam through the slow waters, slow because of the twitch and feel, not because of any true depth. The water-ball was only forty meters across, its wall ridged like a coil pot and studded with three-meter-wide patch-locks that led into the air-filled sections of the Moment-Keeper habitat. The Moment-

Keeper rarely entered those parts of the ship anymore. It had grown too large, too water-bound. On its homeworld it would have been forced to remain in the ocean until it mated or died. On land the combination of gravity and the low air pressure would have caused it to collapse. Here in space it could float through the airy regions, but the low pressure hurt it, causing blisters on its outer spikes.

So it waited in the water, floating in the center of the sphere where all the patches of the ship could transmit to it through the balls and patches in the water, and where Quint Hillard could find it, and try, again and again, to Meet State with it.

The Moment-Keeper was a ball of spikes, like the head of a medieval weapon made to shatter armor. Looking more closely one saw an innovation no armorer could have made. There was no solid mass beneath the spikes, only more spikes, layers upon layers, forming a carpet of fractal spines, a defense more fearsome than any earthly porcupine or stegosaur could have hoped to bear, for they had body parts that were not spires, whereas the Moment-Keeper was nothing but spines and spokes and spears.

Point to point, en garde, Quint Hillard touched one of his artificial spines to an outcropping of the three-meter wide ball-of-spikes and

STATE

{ All of Quint Hillard's human life} STATE-MATE {All of the Moment-Keeper's memories}

STATE is in Burst. State is always in Burst. State sees all, but never acts, State encompasses all, but never descends into itself to work upon anything. State is.

{ Memories of the Moment-Keeper world as it was when this Moment-Keeper left [leaving to poke holes in other worlds, leaving to carve a way on the Path-Miner world {Memories of the Path-Miner world [deaths of the two other Moment-Keepers who had gone on this journey {Memories of their memories imprinted during failed matings}]}] {All knowledge of humans acquired during the trip, always from other species.

{ Quint Hillard {}}}}

MATE-STATE

{ Quint Hillard {} {Life on Earth, two-sided existence [Quint Hillard in Wave knows nothing about what Quint Hillard in Burst is truly doing. Quint Hillard in Wave poking at memories, decaying them with his confused partialate memory and imagination. Quint Hillard in Burst is driving Quint Hillard in Wave mad so he will leave him alone. Quint Hillard in Burst cannot drive him completely mad for the sake of Elsbet Chan {Elsbet Chan in her many guises. Elsbet Chan ruler of the ship. Queen Elsbet at last. Quint Hillard in Wave is her loyal knight. Quint Hillard in Burst is {Model Failure | STATE | Model Failure}]}}
{}

Beatrice Van Leider put a single ball-bearing in midair, plucked it away, set it back, plucked it away, and set it back.

If the ball is there, she thought, there is a place to start, an origin to the universe. Take it away, and there's nothing, no place to focus on, nothing to count from, nothing to measure from. One ball makes one point makes the universe.

She grabbed the ball away and with a twist of two fingers put it back spinning in place. Now the universe has an origin, she thought, zero dimensions. And it has an axis to spin around, that's one dimension. And an equatorial circle, that's two more. And there is something moving so time is passing; that makes four dimensions. One spinning ball makes four dimensions. Space to live in and time to live through.

And life.

For some of us. Professor Saul Ben Isaac had died, had become Emeritus. The other Professors were poring over his work-life, reading his corpse like a book bound in skin. They were trying to hear the words of the dead, to learn what had taken his life, to determine if the crewvolk had brought death among them. They wanted to hear the words that only those who live not can speak.

Van Leider's hand struck out snake-like, rope-like, Band-Braider-like, and pulled the ball out of the air, feeling the smooth surface swiftly halt its turning against the oppression of her palm.

"Now, what's left when I take away the ball?" she said out loud.

"The hand that picked it up and waits to put it back," said Tomaso Alliende.

"But what's left behind?" Van Leider asked, turning to face the intruder, surprised at her own easy acceptance of the intrusion. Have we fallen so far from common politeness that we interrupt each other with impunity? she wondered.

Of course, said Feather-Theadora in her thoughts. Species Shock overwhelms all other shocks. All things rude and criminal pale before its intrusion.

"What's left here?" Van Leider said, pointing to the spot where the ball had been.

"Your fingertip," Alliende said.

"What did you want, Tomaso?" Van Leider said, biting back exasperation, then realizing the playfulness in the Handyman's words. How long had it been since she had heard the irony he had mongered against Theadora?

"Elsbet wants to see you," Alliende said.

"Tell her I'll come later," Van Leider said,

masking her thoughts in words to draw him out. "This is too important."

"Setting balls spinning in the air?"

"Tearing down the universe until I find what remains."

"That isn't the universe," Alliende said. "It's what you think the universe is. It's how you model the universe."

"How else can you see the universe except with models?" Van Leider said as she spun the ball again.

Alliende considered the question. A model was a tool for the mind. With one in mind things could be observed and understood according to the light shed by the model. But other things would be hidden. Light cast shadows.

Light and shadow, a Band-Braider model, a means of seeing the universe as images created and concealed. There were others, human models and alien models, an infinity of potential models. How else could one observe a thing?

"By poking at it," Alliende said.

"How can you poke at all of it?" Beatrice asked.

Outside the bauble, floating by in the next larger sphere, Winston Overus caught that question and gripped it hard in his mind. It was exactly the conundrum that had been occupying his thoughts for the last few years. He had phrased it differently. He had asked, "How can I live in sky and see all the earth below me?" But it was the same riddle. Somewhere around here was the answer, if he could just find it.

"Winston," said Britt Lookdown, "Elsbet wants to see us."

It was taking too long. Four days of ship time

just to get four people to come see her. Too much monstrousness, too much isolation. This was Feather's fault. Elsbet Chan felt an obligation to devour the Method-Smith Guest, but she restrained herself. Without the monster-maker's works they never would have survived the shock of alien contact, and neither she nor Marie would have learned to truly be of their Guesting species.

Feather was a Method-Smith, a toolmaker who made himself into a tool and used the tool of himself for as long as it found things to fit in it to be changed. When it ran out of objects to change, it would need to remake himself. Feather had exhausted the monster-maker method. Soon he would have to become something new. Elsbet Chan suspected that would not happen until they had visited the Method-Smith world, and that would not be for some years, assuming they survived.

Already that assumption was failing. One of the Professors had died. The others were tearing him apart, organ by organ, cell by cell, nucleotide by nucleotide to find out why. More of Feather's work. He had let loose the beast of analysis that lurks in the hearts of academics, the creature that tears to pieces in order to learn about the whole, he had found the monster in Van Leider and let it out to conquer all the Professors.

If Feather had more contact with them the Professors might rend the ship apart. Whomever he spoke to he would make more monstrous unless he was restrained. Exactly how she could do that Elsbet Chan did not know, but she would find a way.

For now she had to seal up the four monsters whom she had herded into a small meeting sphere and presented with what passed for food under the circumstances.

Winston was obviously finding it hard to pay attention to the discussion. His eyes lost focus whenever the subject drifted from his concerns. Elsbet was forced to recall him repeatedly, rapping the air with her voice, raptor-sharp in warning.

Beatrice listened to every word, but her questions made it clear she was taking everything apart and trying to make lists of troubles. Which systems are failing? Exactly how? What is each crewmember doing?

Britt was trying to listen, but the smallness of the sphere was bothering her, as was the proximity of the others.

Tomaso seemed to be paying heed to her words, but he was treating the matter the way he treated a broken machine: find the problems, replace the parts or redesign the system.

And what am I doing wrong? Elsbet wondered. I have two minds to see with, but what can neither human eyes nor Single-Sayer slits perceive? Where am I twice blind?

"If we use up that much anti-matter in making energy for repairs, we won't have enough for the caravels," said Winston.

"We can borrow some from the other habitats," Beatrice said. "Once the acceleration's finished, of course."

"Do they understand borrowing?" asked Tomaso.

"The Band-Braiders do," said Britt, looking to Elsbet like prey awaiting the strike of claw and beak.

"Will they lend it?"

"I'll ask Marie," said Elsbet. "But is energy the only thing we need to fix the ship?"

"No," Tomaso said. "We also need some people thinking about the troubles. Look at the drain on the ship's resources because of these elaborated experiments. Why do the Professors need this much power and why are they synthesizing so many transuranic elements? That eats energy and takes time from the manufactories."

"They're testing the field." Beatrice said, "seeing how it affects decay rates. They've dug through two centuries of wishful thinking and are actually getting a chance to test some of the basic questions of quantum field theory."

"Well, tell them to stop," said Elsbet. "We need the energy for repairs. Tell them to try again during decel. Assuming we're alive."

"Tell them?" Beatrice said. "I'm not in charge of them. Our Dean just died and joined the Emeriti."

"You're Dean now," said Elsbet Chan as she let a few layers of Single-Sayer emerge from her hump, just enough to give her face an angled look and her mouth a ship-sharp frontage.

Van Leider looked at the face and recognized the force of government shaping Academia. She saw the history of the Professors when they grew close and influential in the nations of Earth, posts and chairs created by kings and presidents, funding given or withheld based on the needs of rulers, projects approved or disapproved for needs not of knowledge but of society and politics.

Since the Troth-Breaking Academia had been powerless. Beatrice realized that that lack of power had brought freedom to think and, if careful, to speak. Now the academics of the University of Ship were needed by the government of the ship (Elsbet Chan), and what is needed will inevitably be restrained and controlled.

She could refuse, take what had once been considered a moral stand. But she was in the same boat, the same starship as the one giving the commands, and the needs of the village were greater than the needs of the Professors. Not that they would easily accept that.

"I'll be your Dean," she said. "But you must

come and tell the others."

"Tell as in threaten?" Elsbet said, sliding the Single-Sayer back into the hunch.

"As in threaten."

Five days later the Dean of the University of the Ship came to see the queen of the human habitat.

"Professor Saul Ben Isaac died of malnutrition," Van Leider said.

"I thought we were well supplied with all the nutrients."

"All known nutrients," Van Leider said, handing over a short sheet of plastic with some chemical formulae on it. "But you don't have to worry. Saul needed some co-enzymes no one knew about."

"Why not?"

"They were so easy to obtain on Earth they were invisible to our nutritional studies, and no doctor had ever identified their lack as a problem. Some people need things others don't."

Elsbet Chan closed her human eyes to look over the matter. Human medicine was based on the assumption that there was a single human model of which all people were variations. They had identified the nutrients needed for that paradigm and fed the crewvolk with them. Now Elsbet looked as a Single-Sayer and saw that each thing ate its own needs, and those needs had to be discovered and counted one being at a time.

"Go through the genomes and body analysis of each of the crewvolk. Find out what each of us needs individually. Then tell Britt and Tomaso."

Van Leider nodded and swung away from the ruler of the shipvolk who sat in silent contemplation, flicking her tongues.

Britt herded the chickens back into their spherical coop, separating them, feeding them, forcing them to drink brain-rearing nutrients so the madness would leave them. Chickens had been domesticated for so long humanity had forgotten that they had ever been wildfowl, but a few generations of space breeding and Feather's madness-making had restored some of the ancestral savagery of the flightless bird. Britt glared hard. She would breed them back into line, she would domesticate again, she would farm them away from the monster-life.

Feather relaxed in his confinement. Elsbet had put him in a large sphere and told him to stay there until she came to get him. That had been five months ago. During that time the ship had hummed and clanged and slurrepped with rebuilding. Acceleration had come and the ship was rising up the arch.

Feather did not mind being shut away by his creations. It had a certain theatrical propriety which Theadora would have appreciated. Also it gave him time to contemplate the other monster he had created, the one left behind, the monster named Earth.

When Elsbet Chan-DeMarnier-Tienh (and five other lineages she did not care to acknowledge because of the monsters who had engendered her) had called him back so long ago, drawn him out of the theater and into politics, he had seen the egg of this beast warmed by the twin brooders of Consent and Dissent. He had nurtured it like a cock's egg under the serpent. His basilisk had hatched the day the ship left the solar system. Feather regretted that he had not been there to see the creature through its first steps. Many monster-makers (Theadora playing Victor Frankenstein as a romantic idiot) had made the mistake of leaving their creatures to fend for themselves.

Fortunately, Feather had left two surrogates behind, Theadora and Dominique. Neither of them knew what they were doing for him -- which in Theadora's case was only justice. He had not known what she was doing to him when she had caught him in the serpent coils of her Gorgon hair and petrified him into a work of art with the beauty of her gaze.

Dominique might have guessed if she had listened more to her father and less to her teacher. But she had made herself a Professor and so could only hear the Professorial. Neither of them knew what he had planted in them, what he had set loose through the two branches of the People of the Voice. Through story and essay, play and lecture, they had nurtured the basilisk. When the ship returned -- and now Feather thought that it would return -- the basilisk, the little king, would be waiting to greet its makers with poison breath and petrifying gaze.

If all went well the King Beast of Earth would meet the Queen Monster of the Sky, and then --

Feather did not know what would happen then. At that point the method of monster-making ended and the monsters would have to remake themselves and each other.

Winston Overus did the calculations five times. There was not enough spare antimatter. He would have to wait for next time. But how could he ensure that there would be enough then? Before excess anti-matter could be placed in inventory the ship would have to be functioning perfectly. But if the habitat was functioning perfectly there would be no need for excess antimatter. How then could he arrange to have the antimatter he needed manufactured in the Moment-Keeper system and set aside for his use?

He had no choice. He would have to be useful and cooperative so that Elsbet would take his suggestions. And he would have to organize the sky-volk into following Elsbet's commands. He could do that. He would tell them they were contributing to the grandeur and openness of the sky, that their work would lead to the greatness they had sought in setting out. His words would be true. Only the reality would be guised. Theadora would have approved.

In the padded sphere Elsbet and Beatrice pushed hands against each other, the rhythm of the practice bringing them together, sealing their actions one with the other. The hump on Elsbet's back thrummed in response to the sealing, two becoming one for a time, load being lightened as each carried the other, and the imaginary energy carried them both in accordant action, in the consensus of their moving forms, in the neverending dance of life.

But beneath the consensus and the commonality, beneath the harmony of dance, Elsbet counted and acted, each motion unique, each action a restrained move, a potential to kill or cripple, weight that could be put on the back of her partner, a burden that would never leave.

And Beatrice's mind flowed round and round

the sayings and assertions of the art she was practicing, returning again and again to one aphorism of Tai Chi.

Be Light then Be Agile.

Be Agile then Move.

Move then make Variations.

But everything was heavy upon her. Her body and mind, her voice and thoughts, were like lead. Her motions were clumsy, her thoughts were narrow. No agile, no move, no vary.

So how was there harmony between them?

The Moment-Keeper died during deceleration, only five months subjective time from reaching its own world. It died alone. It died in confusion (though no human could find its state confusing), for its thoughts and its actions were mixed. It acted, perceived, and reacted simultaneously, as if awareness and execution could be conjoined. It died because the electrochemical impulses that moved through its fractal spikes acted both in bursts and waves, conflicting one with the other. It died because it had grown too large, because it had not been able to mate.

But perhaps, perhaps, it thought in a part of it (and how could it think in only a part of it?), perhaps it had not mated but had Met State. Perhaps it did not die {}.

14. Fractals

In Wave Quint Hillard stepped onto the Moment-Keeper world. The patch that awaited him clutched at his feet and slid him across the cratered surface toward the spines and spires of what his human mind saw as a city, but his Moment-Keeper mind knew to be something wholly other. Likewise dualized in his thoughts were the sight of the holes and pocks, the shafts and puddles of the outskirts. To human eyes the landscape was lunar, as if the planet were one of those luckless worldlets that had no atmospheric shelter from the slingstones of space. But his other sight knew that these holes were made by intelligence in action, that within the holes were other holes and holes within them, like a rabbit warren for ever-shrinking rabbits, or like the branches of rivers and streams small feeding large feeding larger still, or like the arteries and capillaries of his own body large shrinking to small. Quint the Moment-Keeper knew that this branching upon branching could be read by the spikes of one who rolled over them, and that they guided the crawling, slithering, and swooping patches, that they were writings upon the world.

Quint was not the only patch rider moving toward the [On land mating place {all human thoughts about sex and reproduction} where State was met {all human thoughts about God and religious places {Lessons in spiritual disciplines from the first generation of Path-Miner Guests who had been wholly eclipsed by their children [First Generation had become spiritual advisors to the Guests. Who had taken that place since those first Guests would long ago have died on Earth?]}}]. Hundreds of Moment-Keepers were being carried around, some inward, some out, some in odd orbits around one of the spired outcroppings. A few were rolling around the larger pits like billiard balls in a model of a gravity well.

There were also other aliens who had come from the ship. Two Single-Sayers shared a patch; Quint wondered why they were not flying under their own power. A bundle of Band-Braiders, hard to distinguish how many, stretched across four of the five-meter squirming patches. A Path-Miner was gingerly boring from one hole to the next. And something with claws and eyestalks and wheels had come from the Method-Smiths.

Quint Hillard is in Burst

{ All the stored up memories of the Moment-Keeper who died. They scream in Quint's mind. They want to Meet State and burgeon into a spike which would grow other spikes and others, large radial spikes, small manipulative spikes, medial poking and mating spikes, microsensory spikes, all the dualistic spikes, drawing in and contemplating in Burst, acting and changing in Wave. They want to be, they scream human screams at the mediation of Quint Hillard's mind. They want to be a proper being, thinking and acting alternately. They are muddled up with his human memories {All of Quint's Human memories, sending out spikes that mate with the Moment-Keeper memories} They -- They do not want. Humans want. The wanting of these memories will go away when they are mediated between two Moment-Keepers.

| Model Failure |

Will they? Quint's human mind intrudes, a little spot, a fracture, a tiny break in the space-filling fractal that is his Moment-Keeper mind.}

Quint Hillard is in Wave.

The patch had reached its destination and lay flat and quiescent against the slick, purple . . . wall, he wanted to call it, but he knew it was only a wall for the moment. It would remain one side of an arched passageway until it was directed to move, to roll, to twist or spiral or take any of a number of other shapes according to the needs and usages of the Moment-Keeper who poked it with a properly commanding spike. The thorn-suit Quint Hillard wore might itself be able to turn his own Burst-understanding into proper Wave actions that would compel the wall-patch and the others nearby.

"House of cards," Quint Hillard said out loud, if only to hear a human voice. Cards that could shuffle themselves and play their games alone if left to their own devices, for they were their own devices.

Could that ever be? He had a brief vision of visitors coming to this world when the last Moment-Keeper was gone. Would the patches still be here, waiting to be properly touched? Would some naive archeologist enter what he thought was a stable structure only to find it curving and twisting around him, smothering him for want of proper commandment?

Left alone and undirected, the patchwork world, what a monster it would be. When he returned to the ship he would have to tell Feather. Assuming Elsbet permitted the two of them to talk together. Feather was no longer in confinement, but Elsbet insisted on being present at all of his conversations and held the sword of veto-silence over any spoken words.

A Moment-Keeper rolled out through the archway. Two meters across it was, a deep grey-gold in color except for the four places where long spikes had recently been severed from its frame. In those spots were barbed and ragged holes, writings upon its body. Quint knew that there was an order and symmetry to the seeming wounds, but the pulsing indigo pits in the body looked like fatal injuries rather than mating scars that would seal up when the Moment-Keeper had grown new spikes to take the place of the buds now gestating inside the city/temple/mating place|Model Failure|.

The roll was drunken-wobbly, a body newly changed finding its balances again, turning and stopping, then starting up, a second's movement then a moment's rest while the mind absorbed all the changes in its being, then another movement, surer now. By the time it had passed Quint by and taken his patch the Moment-Keeper seemed to have regained equilibrium.

Quint stepped inside.

Quint Hillard is in Burst.

[[The patchwork city cannot hear him properly. He cannot poke it to give orders. He lacks the spines for that {Moment-Keeper memories of being one of the city/mating-area/temple shapers, altering the world to fit its conceptions, writing in the patches so that others who would want to communicate with it would come to the place it had settled} [The city is speaking to him -- Not speaking, it is being read -- All the inhabitants are here to mate. Their world conceptions are laid out before him {All the conceptions of the available Moment-Keepers, the outermost aspects of their thinking are poked into the ground and walls and ceilings, the shifting and moving floors, the curling spikes and holes, the gaps in the spaces} Their outermost thoughts are the shells of their being, the spike points, enticing with their suggestions of other world-views, other conceptions, the seductions of State.] {The whole universe of choices, all people who want to talk are waiting to be talked to, every potential conversation, every chance to come closer to what is, to the State of Things. All the Moment-Keepers now alive who have come to the land-bound temple [There are others in the seas mating in the ancient way. Whomever they touch they conjoin with. The preferrers of the older method are not here, but even if they were Quint Hillard could not mate with them. He needs the new means to give form to the child within his minds]}]]

CHOICE

Quint Hillard strode forward in Wave, following the path he had chosen, Single-Mindedly.

Elsbet had watched Quint leave the ship and had wondered -- and still wondered -- what would return in his body, and whether it would still be her husband. But she had to wonder as well if she had been Quint's wife since her return from the Single-Sayer world. They had been together for the years intervening, but they had hidden from each other, he in preparation for this world, she in taking over the ship and commanding the crewvolk.

It was easy to hide in the volkwork, in the

questioning and challenging, in the day-to-day effort to get monsters to cooperate. It was simplicity itself to ensure that there was no time for anything else. Every moment could be occupied with the concerns of other others.

But not with her proper other.

The Professors had their disputes and their claims and counterclaims, squabbles as old as disputation. It had taken them these past two decades of travel to shuck off all their inhibitions and rise to naked debate. On Earth they would not have dared make loud their arguments, nor challenge each other so vehemently.

Only three days ago Beatrice had actually implied that one of the others had not been as careful with his facts as he should have been. There were no longer any trees nor nooses in the ship, nor did anyone rush out to find some other means of lynching. One did not do that to one's volkkin.

Elsbet tucked that word, volkkin, into her mouth and flicked it around with her tongue (Her other tongue, the manipulative one that lay packed in her back, strained to come out and taste the word as well). She had made the crew-monsters volkkin in the most ancient of earthly ways. She had come a predator among them, and they had had to band together to stave her off. She had demanded that the ship function properly, and they had made it work in order to keep her from swooping down upon them. The hunter was kept at bay, and then gradually had permitted itself to be tamed so that she whom they had feared had come to be accepted. The dragon who had terrorized the village had become the chief of that village.

But the dragon had lost its mate, and its nest had only gold on which to lie.

Had that happened to the other dragons? she wondered. Had the other conquerors who became kings fallen to sad-eyed sleep on their beds of bones and trophies?

Elsbet turned to face the mist globe filled with the political map of Earth as it was when the messages they had just picked up had been sent off. Thirty-five light-years between Sol and Zeta Trianguli Australis, the system of the Moment-Keepers. The politics before her were thirty-five years out of date. To seal them up in her mind would be to create a seal of history, not reality. But the seal was worth making, for the Earth had become a realm of monsters.

She bore responsibility for that. She had brought Feather into her office, the office of ConCensor, the one who held the entire world in mind, the counter and accounter of all. She had handed ConCensus to the monster-maker, and he had as his method-nature dictated made a beast and a mother-of-beasts of the Earth Mother.

True, the realms of Earth had been ruled by monsters many times in the past. However, those creatures had usually been simple monsters, savage animals in human form who wanted only the slaking of harsh and evil appetites or the gaining of political advantage upon the corpses of their foes and the backs of any useful friends. They were unsubtle terrors, monsters of evil and folly.

The creatures now in place were not that sort of monster. Indeed, Elsbet read in the copy of ConCensus and DisCensus sent by her granddaughter, Indigo (though she could not claim her as kin since Indigo had lorn herself from her antecedents) that the rulers of Earth were for the most part benevolent to their subjects. They fought few wars, did little sabotage, played few games with the lives of others, ensured the health and welfare and abetted the actions of their followers. To call them monsters would surprise almost everyone on Earth.

Except for the rulers themselves. They knew what they were.

Feather's daughter Dominique certainly did. Her Disuniversity, with its placements and holdings wherever there were Professors, sought control over schooling all across the Earth. Deeper still it worked itself into the tongues of men and women by setting the terms of discussions, creating the contexts of debate. It sought to hold their tongues. With its subtle seizure of libraries and its co-opting of all rhetoric, it was a beast to take tongues from all throats and make all words her subjects.

The Handyman's grandson had gained control over all the patterns used in home manufactories. Every hand in action on Earth was partly his. He could not command them to move or be still, but he could ensure that when they acted they acted according to his designs. His hand was inside all the other hands.

The roads and crossways, the seas and the omniports all belonged to the Rainbow Khan. He had taken them without force. With the great method of the Dissociation, the individual bargaining with the volk, he had come offering advantage. His people were everywhere and saw everything. No thing on Earth was hidden from the footvolk, and no ruler would dare cast off the advantage of knowing what the others did. Each leader let him and his followers in because with their presence came their awareness. Thus by indispensability the footvolk had freedom to move anywhere for the first time since human beings had first settled down and declared a place theirs.

The skies down to the Stepping Stones belonged to the skyvolk. The other Dissociations had their own galleons in the solar system, since the whole of space could not be patrolled, but only the skyvolk had places to stay, only they held land in the ocean of space. The others flew the planetways at the sufferance of The

Overus -- Winston's grandson, but the title had come from Winston's martyred daughter, not from him.

The First Dissociation still had its adherents, but it was losing them year by year, some to join the others, some to take up the pseudo-independency of nations.

And all through, all through the Earth, in this pocket and that, were Guesthouses, each of them eager for the secrets from the stars, each one claiming to be the rightful heir to the ship's treasures.

They had already made use of the Band-Braider knowledge. Things were being grown in image mist, a pseudo-lens was crafted to modify DNA according to the fall of light upon a forming embryo, there were modifications being made to the human form. There was also some use of the Single-Sayer knowledge Elsbet had sent. But not much yet, and of course she had kept the greatest secrets for herself.

The dragons of Earth would find themselves facing a beast more savage than themselves when she returned with the mathematics of predation.

The mating pool was a deep-dug cylinder of mineral-rich waters, eighteen meters across and almost two hundred down. Five Moment-Keepers floated in convecting currents, rising and falling through the waters, waiting in Burst for the last of their mates to enter the pool so that they might join, spike to spike, thought to thought, state to STATE.

Quint Hillard dove in, one last human act, a one-and-a-half gainer, before surrendering to the alien within him. For a brief flurry the Moment-Keepers darted away, a sudden wave of action. Then they settled back into the waters for a burst of contemplation, then a wave of approach, then spine to spine they touched each other, touched Quint Hillard and

STATE

{ Surveys of stars watched through the entire system's observatories, ground bound, sky held, Oort cloud flying, the dance of the sky for ten thousand years, watched and watched, passed down from Moment-Keeper to burgeon spike that grows into a Moment-Keeper, keeping alive the notion that the stars are worth watching, all the stars seen |Model Failure all stars unseen|. A single view that blossoms when the Method-Smiths {Sliding in, spike joining spike, Visions of the Method-Smith world, swimming in the Ocean that destroys [Sliding in the small facsimile ocean in the Guest House], and emerging, having conversed spike to spike with the Method-Of-Spikes} first made contact |Model Failure inability to understand how the Moment-Keepers understand the Method-Smiths|. [Intermixing, drawing out metaphor, drawing out the sky. State as a vast Moment-Keeper, the stars as the spine-tips of State] {Sliding in, entire corpus of human messages [Sliding in Quint Hillard, Quint Hillard sliding into Quint Hillard. Quint Hillard drawing out Quint Hillard. Quint Hillard intermixing with Quint Hillard |Model Failure Quint Hillard cannot understand Quint Hillard|]}}

STATE

{ Patches weaving patches, patches pressing patches, patches tickling themselves into patches, patches making buildings then falling apart |Model Failure can't see how patches came to be |Model Failure within Model Failure incomprehension of Moment-Keeper evolution |Total Model Failure||| [Sliding in patchwork, sliding in crazy quilt, sliding in {The entire human history of threads and sewing, needles {spines, bones, anemones [monster view of Moment-Keepers [sliding in conception of humans as senile Moment-Keepers]]}}]}

STATE

{ The vast expanse of understood things, all knowledge of every species, every conception, every model and awareness, all knowledge.}

|Total Model Failure|

{ The infinite expanse of the unknown. Spines reaching out to fill it, poke holes in it, but always there is more, each hole making more of the unknown}

STATE

{ Bubbles of water inside bubbles of water inside bubbles of patch inside the spines of ungrown Moment-Keepers [sliding in image of the human habitat in the ship {sliding in the crewvolk, sliding in Elsbet {sliding in human ideas of love and mating {sliding in meeting State {Sliding in

STATE

|Model failure, [a few fragments about patches installed on comets]|

STATE

{ The known alien species, all the holes they have poked in the universe, all that they have ever left behind. Their inability to really communicate. Each species has a means of seeing each other species, each has a method or methods of drawing out from the others. Each has |Species Shock|

|Total Model Failure|

STATE

Quint Hillard is human.

Tomaso Alliende and Beatrice Van Leider braved the cell of the monster-maker. Feather still had few visitors. The crewvolk had come to a consensus that the predator let loose upon them, the beast that ruled over the ship was Feather's creation, his fault, and he would say nothing to gainsay that view. Only the two who now floated into his bubble did not object to his actions, Alliende because he knew the ship would have died long since without Elsbet Chan's control, and Van Leider for reasons rooted in their mutual time with Theadora and their conjoined rearing of Dominique.

Feather was looking into a mist globe at the grey-skinned, blood-red-haired image of one-hundred-and-two-year-old Dominique. The picture was frozen, rotating slowly. There was a single tear in Feather's right eye, lingering on a silicated lash, hanging in the gravityless air, waiting to fall, but with infinite choice of direction incapable of deciding which way to go.

"She's very angry at me," Feather said. "Her message was full of threats and warnings for when I return."

"She sounded happy in her message to me," Beatrice said, "talking about the rise of learning and the excitement among the Professors, about the data we sent back and the expanded understanding of Band-Braider and Single-Sayer learning. They're really learning to integrate human and alien knowledge. Guests and Professors are working together."

"Yes, they're all happy with their new toys," the Handyman growled. The grand tour he had been given of the court of the Gregorys left a bitter taste in his mind. Image made life, Gregory the Far-Seeing had been dressed in pseudo-ancient Irish gear, carrying a flashing spear, an actor stepped out from a play dressed as Lugh, master of all arts. His grandson's hands were calloused with real work, but his mind was occupied with the appearance of divine creation.

"They are what Theadora let them make themselves, just as we are what she made us," Feather said.

"You made them what they are," Tomaso accused.

"No," Feather said. "I made the Earth what it is.

Our children fitted themselves to it, found ways to rule the monster-world. Theadora made them fit to be kings and queens, just as she made us fit to strive beyond our lives. Whatever the world was like, our children would rise in it. That was Theadora's legacy."

"And the monster-world is yours."

Feather nodded and the tear flew off into the circulating air currents of the habitat.

"They act on the world," he said. "The world acts on them. They come together."

Beatrice smiled ruefully. "How brutally mathematical. You can't tell the functions from the arguments. Write it one way, addition acts on 1 and 1 to make 2. Write it another, 1, 1, and 2 act on something to make it addition."

"Now you're beginning to think like a Method-Smith," Feather said.

"Not me," Beatrice said. "Whatever's left of me will stay human, thank you."

"It's much too late for that," Feather said. "For any of us."

Winston Overus personally took charge of an exploration caravel, cheerfully ferrying one of the Professors around the Moment-Keeper system. But his concern was not with the planets and the patch-stations and the tracked comets or mined asteroids. His mind and hands and hopes were in the caravel.

Quint Hillard drew in his spines and shucked off the layers of alien skin. His nerves, raw from the mating, felt every breeze and prod of the heavy-metal-laden air. Even filtered through the membranes the Moment-Keeper's atmosphere stung his lungs, harsh and unearthly, the air of the unlike, of the unvolk, the air of the other, the monster outside.

As had each other Guest on their own worlds, Quint Hillard let out the first laugh ever heard on the Moment-Keeper planet, a harsh, bitter laugh, the self-mockery of the monkey looking in the mirror and seeing the folly of its own capers.

Then the second laugh, reproving, ironic, the first dryness felt in this ocean-wetted atmosphere.

Then the third, accepting of the joke, acknowledging that even if one was the butt of the universe's humor, still the jest was funny in itself.

Quint Hillard looked around him. He was the only human on an alien world. He had given up his life to come here. He had given up his family, left his children to live out their lives without his guidance, let his wife become a monster. He had let another sentient die in his mind to give birth to new lives here. He had come so far and given up so much. Was it all worth it, just to be and to get the joke?

No. He also needed to learn to tell the joke, so that the next human here would not be the target of universal humor.

Britt Lookdown completed another survey orbit of the Moment-Keeper world, piloting by her own hand and eyes in order to dodge the suddenly springing balls and patches that formed the eyes and hands of the planet. On Earth eyes and hands were different things. Telescopes were not maintenance satellites. But here one moment a patch lay placid studying the universe, the next it reached out to grasp or make. Those were the two states and the two hazards of this space.

Nothing was safe out here. Seeming debris, apparent asteroids, could suddenly change into manufactories or rockets or spew forth lasers or push out pellets of antimatter. The sky was a dance here, a dance of watching and acting, a dance without warnings because always things were watched and known and acted upon so what need was there to speak of danger obvious to all? Any aliens nearby had to learn to watch and act, and Britt lookdown cursed that hard and dangerous learning as much as she had cursed the confinement of the Band-Braider world.

Britt was coming to hate the sky, the crowded congested, cosmopolitan sky. Every world she visited filled the space above them with something useful. No one would leave space alone. Even the universe wouldn't leave space alone, filling it with stars and dust, light and energy, galaxies in their clusters.

" Why won't you leave yourself alone, give yourself room to breathe?" she said to no one, glad that no one else could hear her. "Sure, you've got big gaps in things, lots of space between your possessions. But it's space between, not space for its own sake. Give yourself some room. Stop all the clustering and clumping. Even the galaxies must be claustrophobic, all those nearby clusters, all the neighboring spirals, balls, bars, waiting to collide. Give me room!"

Quint Hillard is in Burst

[He has named the place on which he stands the Bowl of Legacy. He no longer cares that the Moment-Keepers do not use names. Quint Hillard is human {All of human history, society, culture, all that he has learned of living on Earth}. The bowl is a curved expanse of carefully alloyed metal layered over the ground and covered with weather-resistant polymer sheeting. It stretches for tens of kilometers in all directions. It is the largest writing surface in the known worlds. Every Moment-Keeper {Every Moment-Keeper} who has poked holes with meaning comes here to poke holes. In groups and clusters they have spiked their comprehension into the ground for others to read. {Read}.]

[Reading is not communication. Communication is meeting STATE. Reading is seeing the holes others have poked. The universe is full of holes. But STATE is what makes holes {poke holes}.]

{ All of Moment-Keeper knowledge preserved in the Bowl [All real knowledge and understanding is passed on in Meeting STATE, mating and producing young spikes]}

{ The Bowl of Legacy is an empty cup.}

{}

Beatrice Van Leider dictated:

Without the proper nutrients the Tree of Knowledge dies. But here on alien worlds there is much to choose from in order to feed that Tree. Five species' worth of knowledge, five independent processes of amassing understanding. Surely there is much food here. Yet the food is alien and the tree of human knowledge cannot digest it. Given too much alien food it will starve with bulging roots, just as we would starve with full bellies if we ate the ropes of the Band-Braiders, the herd beasts of the Single-Sayers, or the fractal curtains of the Moment-Keepers.

The more the University of Ship eats of alien food, the

more we starve. We Professorial monsters have become Wendigos, like the black hole which powers this ship.

Yet back home our human descendants, our students, our successors have mixed a little of the alien food we send them with their human diet and have grown from it. We starve that they might eat. What is more appropriate than that parents give up their lives for their children?

If only we might give up quickly and die easily. But we cannot. We have more worlds on which to starve and more branches of the tree of Knowledge to poison.

Quint Hillard returned to the ship after several months on the Moment-Keeper world.

Quint Hillard returned to the volk after a moment away.

Quint Hillard reminded the crewvolk that they had lost three of their number in the space between worlds and one more while waiting to leave this system. He reminded them of mourning and the passing of one life into another.

Quint Hillard told Beatrice Van Leider that she wanted to live and that she would have found some excuse to live even if he had not told her.

Quint Hillard remembered his wife, and remembered that writing and reading were not communication.

Floating together in silence the only human in the crewvolk gave reminders to the chief monster.

Soon thereafter, Feather was released on his recognizance.

Soon thereafter, the ship, now named Lineage, set out in the whiteness of space for the next clustering of life.

15. Path Independence

The Path-Miner Guest floated through the forests and hills of the crewvolk, around the peak and pinnacle of Elsbet Chan, across the broad deep sea of Quint Hillard in which the reflection of the whole volk-terrain could be seen with a quick glance and an idle inquiry, skirted the hidden dangers of Feather swamp, and made his way at last to the warming volcano that was Tomaso Alliende.

"I" --That which traverses this path.

"Need"-- move towards.

"Assistance" -- The path is blocked by an unminable obstacle. The ways around it are also blocked. The obstacle itself is not of interest.

"Please" -- Carving through human society.

"Come" -- Follow in the path behind, take up the same memories and understandings. Hear the same echoes. Become the same being.

"." -- Thoughts circling around conjunction of action and confluence of path.

"Of course," Tomaso said, hearing only the human request.

The Handyman floated after the Path-Miner Guest, waiting to see what new problem the halting-voiced man had found that needed fixing. In the three years since leaving the Moment-Keeper world Alliende had been continually busy, fixing one or more breaking-down aspects of the ship, improvising replacements for air-filtering and water treatment membranes which for frustratingly molecular reasons would not reconstitute themselves.

In theory his manufactory could have knit new membranes. The layered sheets were lattices of common elements. He had done so many times. But membranes could only filter out what they knew how to trap, and over the years oddities of organic chemistry unknown to the ecosystems of Earth had begun to form in the bodies of the crewvolk, and through paths of digestion and the sloughing off of dead matter had found ways out to clog and confuse the porous systems of the habitat.

Also the adopted bioflora that lived in their monster bodies had their own needs and excretions and those had begun to accumulate in the air, creating a haze which gummed up the filters. So Alliende had changed them and changed them and changed them, experimenting with new designs and old frustrations.

And those had been the simple repairs, the guessed at problems. The Path-Miner Guest always brought him exotic distresses.

Like these peculiar fracture lines in the hull.

Lines, if they had only been lines, would have indicated some normal phenomena. But these spiraling pockmarks and fractal snowflake shapes indicated some unknown material problem. They were appearing at odd places around the ship. There seemed to be some pattern to their appearance, but he had not yet found it.

"Look" -- Burrow this way into the quantum flaws in your materials.

"Fix" -- Mine the spaces between the atoms so the field will strengthen them.

"Echo=Vacuum" -- Dig down below the appearance of separate atoms into the underlying unity.

The Path-Miner Guest floated away, leaving the Handyman to wonder what had just been said to him and to contemplate the failures of his own mind.

How long had it been since mind and hand had been one, since the difficulties before him had been problems to solve with solutions that could be implemented? Had there been any such since Earth?

Then, so long ago, in the delusions of his human-life, he had thought himself wise in the ways of the hand, capable of seeing and acting upon the world in a needful harmony of mind and body.

As a monster he had felt himself intelligent, capable of looking at the troubles of the world as a series of problems, each amenable to solution if he put his mind and his hand to it.

More recently he had, shamefaced, deemed himself clever, capable of finding tricks that would solve the pre-constructed puzzles of the world, of putting things together long enough for others to think he had succeeded.

Now he began to wonder if he was anything at all, anything beyond an ignorant animal running around its home trying desperately to keep its habitat from falling apart.

Winston Overus floated among the star-filled mists, alone in the ball of observation, alone in the sky, alone in watching worlds pass by, alone unless in his drifting he bumped into the inner wall of the bubble and in the touch of body to surface heard the vibrations of the crewvolk at work.

They were all crewvolk now, whatever their origins. The guestvolk, the skyvolk, the voicevolk, and the volk that Theadora had made, all were one people now, all but him. He had remained apart, untrusting and untrustworthy. Though doing his work and helping out as needed, still he was separate. He, Winston Overus, was still of the Sky, the only one of the skyvolk left in the ship.

He alone remembered Heaven, the place that was not where people lived. He alone still looked up and sought to leave the hole that humanity had dug for itself. Even out here between the stars the hand of man, the Handyman, had made a cave to live in, to hide from the majesty of the openness beyond. Winston Overus tightened his fist in realization that he might also have hidden in the cave if not for the figure painted in the sky, the ghost of Tricia, she who had given herself to the sky for the good of the skyvolk.

It had been done in his honor, this Winston knew. Patricia had died thinking of him and of the dream he had been given by Theadora, the dream of a separate sky. She had died the Overus he had wanted to be. She had died for his dream. He would give up all for hers.

Only eighteen months before decel, before his chance to change things came, before the gates of the sky would open for him. He had prepared his key well, stocked it, fueled it, personalized it so that no one else could enter. He had docked it in an out-of-the-way bubble-bay, so that none of the Guests would take it for jaunts to the other habitats. Still, best to make sure no other pilot came near it, and absolutely sure the Handyman kept his distance.

Elsbet and Quint (The Crewvolk had given up on surnames and lineages. They had one volk now, and one ancestry, one Lineage only, Backlorn of Earth.) lay wrapped together in the life-giving membranes, coiled human to human. Only the rawness of Quint's nerves and the humppack on Elsbet's back betrayed anything monstrous about them. They had come together thus time and again since leaving the Moment-Keeper system, one in body and voice -- but not in mind, for Quint had refused to say what had happened to him or what Meeting STATE had been like. He had refused bluntly. He had stared into Elsbet's eyes, the eyes of love and the eyes of the hunter and said, "No. I left it behind."

And she had said, "How can you leave it? Isn't it there when you Burst?"

"No, it's gone. It left me. I left me. The Burst is there, State is there, but I'm gone. There's no me there, no Moment-Keeper. There never was. I just thought there was. I added up the branches and came up with a whole tree. But I added wrong."

Elsbet had fallen silent, accepting her husband's answer, hearing it in her own mathematics. He had folded the world up in a pack and found that there was no cloth to make the pack from, so he folded it up and it went away into the nothing-smooth cloth.

It went away and she had him back, and in turn

he had her back, but only as long as her other shape lay packed up. The Single-Sayer had no husband. It was a Solitaire with a herd (though she had never dared say that word to the crewvolk; they thought they were a people, not a grazing range). But she did not need to pull the Single-Sayer out very often. The shipvolk did not need frightening anymore. She only took on her other form when she flew to the Single-Sayer habitat where the Seal of the Star-hunters waited to teach her how to count alien prey.

Feather, Tomaso, and Beatrice studied the accumulated reports and requests from Earth. Every Guesthouse asked for the same things. From the Earth to the sky, from the guestfootvolk to the guestvoicevolk they all wanted to know what the aliens themselves were like. They wanted closeness to the eternally distant. The Guests had given Feather the task of responding.

"Why you?" Tomaso had asked. "You haven't reached your world yet. Why won't Marie, Elsbet, and Quint answer them?"

"Because they can't," Feather said. "They don't know any of the aliens."

"But Elsbet became one. Quint mated with one. Marie was surrounded by them," Beatrice said. "How can they not know?"

"The distance is too great," Feather said. "Even if you spent your entire life with another human you might never come to know them, and there is so much mutuality and commonality in human experience and thought and so little with the aliens."

"Still?" Tomaso said. "I thought we were done with Species Shock. I thought you'd severed the distance."

"We'll never be done with Species Shock," Feather said. "You'll never be done with me. As long as humans and aliens interact the distance between one species and another will be there. We never really see them. We only see their images, only hear their ideas as our minds can comprehend them, not as they intend them, insofar as they intend at all."

Tomaso leaned against the cracked padding that surfaced the habitation ball and took a sip of bitter algae broth and a bite of his weekly egg. His eyes shut as a long and melancholy weariness came over him. Sleep did not come, just the numbing ache of travel without respite, of labor without surcease, of helplessness that yet needed to act if there was any hope of survival.

Was this what it was like before Fire, before domestication, before command, before the gods?

The village had faced the unknown and incomprehensible before, had confronted the invisible in the form of life and death, fate and nature, society and monsters. It had confronted the Things No One Can See and had spawned the Crazy Old People to interact with them, to learn from them the ways of the unworld and give to them the ways of the world. The village had begun with a bargain with the Things No One Can See and the giving of guestvolk to them. The Crazy Old Man Who Talks to the Things No One Can See was the first of their Guests, then the Crazy Old Man With the Fire, and the Crazy Old Woman with the Plants, and last the Crazy Old Woman Who Knows Everything, and the Crazy Old Man Who Tells Every-one What to do. What were they but Guests for the gods?

Tomaso chuckled in an oily throat. No wonder the Ufnecks had appeared. The incomprehensible and unseeable had come and they had reached back to the beginnings of mental toolmaking to draw out the tools of religion to deify the aliens.

They had the right tool, the tool of guesting, but the wrong baggage. Only Constance Marchant and Grandmère had pulled out the tool correctly to make the Crazy Young People Who Visit Other Villages.

And now the Guestvolk had split up and taken sides in the factions of the village, becoming militant bands of Crazy Young People. That too had happened before, when the ability to become a Crazy Person became easily accessible and the Crazy Old People had been offered the goods of the village for the labors of their voices, hands, and minds.

And why was Feather so pleased at the reports from the rival Guesthouses? Had he gone so far into Monster-Making that he did not care about the suffering of the Guests? In all the rival houses the Method-Smith Guests had made methods to wheedle their ways into other Guesthouses and seduce Guests into changing housevolks, methods who crept up the chainlinks of the Marshallates and discovered who was mailing what to whom, methods who, in short, were spies. That too had happened before. But why did it please Feather?

Tomaso opened his eyes and asked.

"Grandmère's descendants," Feather said, "using her means for their ends. Poor Grandmère. She forgot what happens when you go into the Ocean."

"What happens?"

"You die," Feather said. "Only your methods remain. Poor Grandmère. There are so many of her method now, but none of them have her devotion."

Beatrice reached out and tapped Feather's hand hard, a teacher's knuckle-rap. "This is your revenge on Grandmère?"

"No. No, Beatrice, not revenge. I have done what she made me to do."

"She made you a monster-maker," Beatrice said. "And you made the Guests into monsters."

"Not the Guests," Feather said. "I made the Earth into a monster."

"You've said that before," Beatrice said, hand in front of her lips in the gesture of an inquisitor who has finally found the correct question. "What kind of monster?"

"The same kind I am," he said. "When Grandmère first found me, I became Monster Who Cowers in Caves because there are Monsters Out There. When she called me the second time I became Monster who Makes Monsters because there are Monsters Out There. When she calls again, I will become something else."

"How can she call again? She went into the Ocean."

"The Ocean waits for me on the Method-Smith world."

The Path-Miner Guest continued to float through the balls of the ship, journeying from place as his mind traveled the path of abandoning the hard-won human tongue. So hard to forget. He had tried, but it was difficult to lose the words, the ideas, the building instead of finding. Where could he go to drop the language?

"I" -- no self, only that which moves.

"Would" -- dig into the possible, burrow into the field beneath the language.

"Have" -- possess, be dragged down by, drown in.

"Words" -- obstacles.

"With" -- near.

"You" -- other.

He said to Beatrice.

Tomaso, enfolded in a protective membrane glued to the outside of a docking ball, looked at his Pantechnicon. The paintings had faded over the decades of flight, the erosion of field corrupting the images placed there: faded icons of smiths of all kinds, of all eras, smiths of legend, smiths for the gods and smiths for men, even the meteor-scarred angel-smith who forged the chains of Lucifer and the sunburned demons who cast the links that bind the souls of the damned.

Those images had been brought to life. In the court of the Gregorys his grandson's courtiers and courtesans walked around dressed in the clothes of handmyth. Gregory the Far-Seeing had shown these images to his grandfather across the distances of space and time, offered them to him. Why did the Far-Seeing think they would please him?

It's my fault, Tomaso thought. Gregory's mist-puppetry was always beautiful and stirring. He learned so much stagecraft from Theadora, so much of presentation and image. He gave that to his son and his son is offering it to me, the fruits of his mind and hand given in sacrifice.

But how can he govern a Dissociation with nothing but images and wealth? There must be more there. What else sits in those garments and mistworks? What resides in the politics there?

That he would not be able to find out until and unless he returned to Earth, and by then it might well have changed or disappeared entirely.

The speed of light was a limitation on many things, most of them obvious and physical, but subtler than the constraints of movement and mass, the speed of light marked the limits of politics. Because of it no hand of Earth could reach the crewvolk, no voice of

Earth could command them, no army march to them, no taxman touch them.

Even if the whole of Earth could put together a spaceship and the ship could somehow chase them down, and if after years of travel the captain of that vessel still chose to carry out Earth's orders, the political situation back home would have changed so much by the time it reached its target that the orders would be outmoded, and if confirmation were requested the speed of light would make for decades of delay and another outmoding of politics.

Until and unless they returned to the political gravity well of Earth, the crewvolk were free of its dominion.

But not of its pull, Tomaso thought, and returned to his labors and his sorrows.

The six habitats of the ship were each in a different state of disrepair depending on where in the cycle of ship life they were. The Moment-Keeper habitat so recently unoccupied and decrepit was now alive and functioning, stocked with the latest innovations in patchwork and crewed by the newest spike of volunteers. The Single-Sayers were second best in the cycle, and the Band-Braiders third. Worst should have been the Path-Miners, whose world was upcoming and whose habitat had been long decades away from the ecosystem and manufacturing that spawned it. But it was the human habitat, suffering from the rigors of shakedown and shape-up, that was most in need of repair.

The ship itself, the systems that kept it mobile and maneuverable, were also beginning to fail. Long time had it been since the filter, the harvester or the engines had been seen under the light of the Method-Smith sun or embraced by the full panoply of Method-Smith repair-work, and they were beginning to show the strain. The filter did not catch as much of the dust and energy of space as it should have. The harvester was strained and fissured by the Monster's tides. The engines themselves were hot with the inevitable radio-activity of their efforts.

Only the Monster, the black hole, native as it was to the cruelties of interstellar space, showed no injuries, for what could harm it save the random abuses of quantum fluctuations? It was content with eating at the troughs of stars and dieting between worlds. What did it care? It was itself, alone, an isolated system, cut off by nature from the volk of the universe.

Beatrice felt as if a pile of stones had been stuck in her head, as if all of humanity's sins had been confessed to her, as if molten iron had been poured in her stomach, as if all these things were one thing, as if all the facts, all the knowledge, all the understanding, all the wisdom, all the words of humanity had been dropped upon her.

The words within her mind had been empty for so long, she had been starving for so long, that now the force-feeding threatened to kill her. It was too much to ask of anyone to take this burden of words, yet the Path-Miner Guest had come and hour after hour had removed the notions from his head and through the telepathy of spoken language placed them in hers.

"Matter is accretion of path. Matter is failure."

"Energy is burner of path. Energy is impertinence."

"Field is all. But naming field 'field' is making

black holes."

"Thoughts can be counted to silence. Silence can be counted to hum. Hum can be hmmmhuhmmhum-sheesheehhmm."

Once she understood each thing he said, he seemed free of it. She had listened and freed him for the sake of understanding and to help him when he reached his own world. He could not face the Path-Miners without her assistance, without her mind as dumping ground.

But what could she do with the weight of reality and understanding? What could she do when she faced the world marked out with paths of travel and temptations of comprehension? How could she move under this leaden mass?

Outside, outside the habitat, there was her answer, there the thing to emulate. The Monster at the ship's heart. The beast that could eat anything, the real thing that Monster Who Tears Everything Into Little Pieces was an image of.

Drop a mass on a black hole, bury it, and you doom the thing you bury. Small though the black hole is, it will eat whatever you drop on it.

The human mind could raven through the universe of thought like a black hole through the innocent flocks of mortal matter. She would eat, she would open the maw of analysis and bite hard upon human thought.

The old Professors in the time of the Troth-Breaking, they who had looked last on the world through the lens of the noose, they had erred in the kind of Predator they should have been. The voicevolk should prey on the world, not on the people of the world. The voicevolk were hawks and eagles who flew out of the human nest to feast on the world and bring back morsels for their fledglings.

The Crazy Old Woman Who Knows Everything

knows everything because she has eaten everything.

Britt was a farm girl born and raised. She worked the fields growing potatoes and yams, toiling over the melon vines and misting the carrots to make sure they grew well. Her single surviving strain of chickens (a cross-breed of Dorkings, Aseels, Croad Langshans, and Rhode Island Reds) was black as space, red-crested as blood, savage in conflict and delicious in egg laying and meat producing, rare though it was for the crewvolk to dine on their sole remaining animal food.

Britt had seen three alien worlds. She knew that if the farms kept going and the ship did not fall apart she would see two more, but she wanted nothing to do with them. She would go to them because she was an able pilot and had the most experience, but she just wanted to stay here. She did not want to look down any more.

Nor to look up, so she averted her gaze when Winston Overus floated overhead, still Overus no matter what had happened. How could he remain Overus? Didn't he notice, didn't he see the crewvolk? Didn't he realize that they were so far from the sky of their youth? For so Britt saw the time on Earth and above Earth, as mere youthful folly.

"Britt?"

"No time for talk, Winston," she said without looking up. "Decel will be starting some time in the next two weeks. The plants have to be prepared. I'll have time to talk after that."

"I'm afraid I'll be busy then," Winston Overus said, trying to make his voice dry and understated. He did not know if he succeeded, if Britt's heedlessness came from his efforts or her indifference.

"We" -- This county-sized piece of social terrain called the crewvolk within the island of the ship.

"Approach" -- Approach.

"Deceleration" -- Burrowing down into the field that is the underterrain of the universe, down below to where proper creatures live, underground digging and tunneling, listening to the Echo.

The last three words gone from his mind, the Path-Miner Guest left for the bubble he lived in, left the humans behind so he could sit in silence with the hum and the Echo, recluse himself for the nearly two years remaining until they reached the Path-Miner world.

Reclusion had been the way of his parents and his honorary aunts and uncles. All of them had been monks or nuns, failed in their own ways but knowing the value of seclusion, of being walled up in a cave, of sitting on a pole, of languishing on an island, of living with a voiceless beast, of being alone with the invisible silence, hum, and Echo.

Winston Overus sat in the cockpit of his caravel, hands poised in the control box, waiting above the image of membrane-release. His hand had but to brush that flickering shape and the caravel would break its connection to the habitat and fly free in intraship space.

They would all be settled in right now, nestled in their webs and meshes, tied down awaiting the moment when the universe would reorient itself, when up and down would come back into existence, when their gravity-reared bodies would tell them that there was ground and sky.

The crewvolk had grown used to it by now, the periods of ship-dominion and field-dominion, when the fundamental consideration of life shifted from worry about the shape of the habitat to concern over falling and rising.

Winston wished he could wait for the absolute last moment, but he did not know when that would be. The Path-Miners controlled the field and time was not a measured thing to them. He had to wait until the crew was tied down, until there was no time for anyone to catch him.

"All secured?" Elsbet's voice echoed through the ship and through the radio on the caravel.

"All secure," came the answers.

"Not I," said Winston as his hand touched the image. The flicker of static electricity told him his command had been received.

The caravel detached itself like a bee from a flower. Winston flicked the engines to life and turned and turned so the caravel was aligned along the vector of the ship's flight. No need to waste a precious meter/second of the ship's accumulated velocity. Why fight it? It had taken him high up the Arch. But not high enough.

Over the Monster Winston flew, across the empty space, passing within a half kilometer of the Band-Braider habitat then back to the deep folding patches of the engine, where energy was stored in the field interstices that held the engines together, where the vast Underbelly of the ship lay waiting to be spoken to, to be instructed in the raising of field and the firing of energy, in the coursing of the universe.

Anyone could tell it what to do. Anyone with an Underbelly could command the engines. But no one else had. The Method-Smiths relied on the Path-Miners to act when acting was right. But anyone could send a signal and --

Make a strut of field, a line, a push, a moment of high acceleration that should have, would have spattered Winston, if he had cared about his life, if he had not been willing to accept the death from radiation that came from artificial gravity, if he had not told his Underbelly to do that which no sane creature of any species would do.

Off he rushed upon the strut, over the shipspace, over the filter, that thin film kilometers across which picked the grains of matter out of space, over it, and out beyond the ship.

One more signal and the strut faded into blackness.

Then, then, then, Winston's hand described a harsh curve within the control box. In the engine of the caravel, many kilograms of matter and anti-matter met and briefly recollected the early energy-dominated universe. A stream of particles, a mixture of common and eccentric quantum manifestations swift with the gift of energy burst brightly out of the caravel, and in accord with Newton's bargain the ship shot forward, accelerating at twenty-five gravities, twenty-five gravities Winston Overus did not feel because he was willing to let his body be struck by the whitewash underlying spacetime, willing to add another cause of death to the sentence he had written for himself.

Relative to the ship, the caravel pulled far and far ahead, swiftly gaining velocity.

Relative to the planets and stars, there was little difference between them, the caravel pulling just slightly ahead of the distorted shape and mass of the ship.

Winston had stocked the caravel well with antimatter clandestinely made in the Moment-Keeper system, enough fuel to push the caravel high, high up the Arch, to add more and more nines past the decimal point that marked percentage of lightspeed.

Up, up the Arch where the world compresses,

where mass rises, and where time, oh most important, where time grows long. Up the Arch so that years and centuries, millennia on millennia would pass back on Earth while Winston Overus flew on. He had food and air enough for a single year, but in that year more than a million would pass on the six worlds he knew of. Most importantly, that time would pass on Earth.

And in the sky above Earth, in the habitats of the skyvolk, his name would be known, and they would hear and tell that up there, out in the stars, out in the real untouchable sky, a man walked, a man flew, a skyman lived who would outlive all who crawled upon the ground. They would look up and know that man could live in the sky, that man could live over us.

16. Graph

Britt looked down upon the Path-Miner world and found the disgust born of three previous planets melting into fascination with this fourth. The Band-Braiders had terrified her with their congestion. The Single-Sayer world had not looked like an intelligent species lived on it, so wild and capable of survival were those perfect hunters. The Moment-Keepers lived mostly in the ocean with only a few dotted cities, if that was what they were.

But the Path-Miners had worked on their world. Their tracks and trails, their buildings and mines were everywhere. The only uncarved places were little patches where recent vulcanism had wiped clean the burrowed marks. It was as if the entire single, gigantic continent was a huge maze. Down below that maze, she knew, were deeper three-dimensional labyrinths, for the Path-Miners were primarily a subterranean species and their digs went deep to the inner edge of the crust and down below into the world's mantle.

Here was a species that treated their planet the way the skyvolk treated their skyboroughs. No wilderness, no unclaimed or untrammeled spaces, everything for a purpose. Looking down she grew homesick for the sky. Looking up she saw the sky. Somewhere in it in a spot unseeable was the man of the sky, the one who watches over us.

The Path-Miner Guest hummed softly and pointed toward a part of the maze. He had not spoken a human word in over two years. Only musical hums and evocative silences had come from his lips. It seemed to be a great strain to him to point, as if his mind were fighting the humanity of the gesture.

Britt swooped the caravel down over the channel and landed in a niche clearly carved for the accommodation of spaceships.

"Hmmmmhmmm."

The Path-Miner Guest dissolved the restraining membrane and left the ship, abandoning Britt Lookdown to another wait on an alien world. From the niche there was not much to see. The maze had disappeared, as any such structure would when one is set down in the middle of it.

Britt looked up.

Elsbet packed all the messages from Earth into her mind. She had broken the encodings without great effort. They had been personalized to the crewvolk, and she knew all the monsters in her care.

Once she had digested this feast she would hand it out piece by piece to its intended recipients. She had grown used to that apportioning as well. Food was growing scarce on the ship. Nutrients there were aplenty, energy could be had easily, but food that had taste and filled bellies, that she had to dole out as if she ruled a starving nation.

There had been two more deaths from malnutrition and three suicides, one skyman, one Professor, and one of Tomaso's assistants, Muhammed Cecil. Cecil had recorded an explanatory lenticle, saying that he could no longer bear to continue life year after year functioning and acting with an empty stomach. It had been too much Species Shock for him to discover that one could live with a constant gnawing inside. He and the other suicides had complained of the monsters in their bellies, complained until they had been eaten up.

Elsbet, who had conquered hunger by subsuming it in the greater feasting of Single-Sayer mathematics, turned to the banquet of understanding that had come from an Earth that knew them only as legends, as people who had gone forth and would some day return.

All save one of the humans who had lived in the days of the departure were dead. The one who still survived was the first of Elsbet's courses. Feather's daughter flared into mist-life before her.

The canyon echoed, the ground thrummed, the wind whipped. All paths led from where he stood.

Do not stand. That was the most important thing. Do not stand in one place. Set out. Turn and set out.

And so he walked away from --Turnings upward and outward-- along the //memories of those who had returned from the Echo-hole between the stars, cleansed of all they had been//. The wonder and amazement of those who returned to find a world they were wholly ignorant of -- and yet fit them so perfectly -- was bitten deep into the rocks. It reverberated off the swirls and cuts. The experimental chew-marks on the wondrously accepting stone bespoke their hums of pleasure at the paradise they had found.

But this newcomer, this one who only partly belonged here, had no teeth in his hands and underbelly to bite and savor the giving stone. He could not fully take in the memories of unknown return so clearly carved before him, for he could not taste the reminding stones. He trod not a path of paradise refound, but of alienation refounded.

What then to do? If he could not take a step along the path before him, how could he come into his own on this world? He had heard and seen the paths the other Guests had taken as each came to confront the sheer-edged chasm that separated them from those they mimicked. The path of his thoughts skated a fleur-de-lis around Marie's accommodation, Elsbet's conversion-pack, and Quint's rejection. Once, twice, thrice he skated over the thin ice of past experience before setting out on his own way.

The path would teach him. He would find what memories and experiences he could. He would not become as those who had chewed these paths, but he would become what they were teaching him to be.

Feather looked at himself in the mirror, looked at the grey skin and silicated hair, at the transparent eyes with capillaries showing, looked at the slow crawling of things under his skin, adopted biota, muscle toners who had come to treat his body as their home, theirs to do with as they saw fit, like adolescent children who had forgotten where the necessities of life came from and had settled down to the adoption of luxuries.

Sighing, Feather put a thin sheet over his arms and waited as the Tractase settled into his skin. The crawlers slowed, stopped, then dissolved back into individual cells, their mass identity falling away.

Too many Tractases were being used to keep their bodies, their ecosystem, their habitat in line with their needs. There were too many rebellious adoptees. Solutions would have to be found, if not on the ship then on the Method-Smith world, if they survived long enough to reach it.

Things fall apart. Particularly when you make monsters to break them up.

"Here is your message," Elsbet said as she placed a lenticle spinning slowly in the air next to Feather's face.

Feather did not turn to look at her, eyeing only the reflection of the beast-of-command he had created. She wanted to know things only he knew, wanted to know what his methods were meant to accomplish, what means would next transform them, but he had not told her, could not tell her. The closeness they bore human-monster to human-monster would not bridge the distance between human-alien and human-alien. She lacked the Smoothness on which to bring them together, and he lacked the methods whereby they could speak one to the other. So they could do nothing but watch each other, wary and wondering.

Feather put the lenticle into the reader and turned to watch his monster daughter.

The path split in delirious branching. So many

ways to go from the Echo-hole of space. So many lives lay open to one who came to paradise. Follow as you tasted. That was the basic method the Path-Miners used. Go according to your taste, follow the savor of the ground.

He could not taste the ground, so he smelled the air and went the way of acrid brimstone and juniper-sage.

Up in a twisting spiral went the path. Around and around, climbing slowly but growing steeper at each arc of the spiral. Paths diverged from this one at every turning, ways off, ways across, ways in, precipices to fall down. And always it grew steeper, sheerer, harder to climb, less and less worth the effort. Up the spiral Arch, up the conception of the wearying universe, up and up, each hour's climb bringing less and less progress, making each turnoff, each fall, each echoing hole a greater temptation. Climb until weariness takes hold and then turn to the first turning.

Turn away from the physical terrain, step into the mist that precipitated the feel and taste and sight of hidden field on the single light-receptor that was a Path-Miner's skin, step into the image of nearby space, carve paths through the interplanetary void, bring the forgetfulness of distant nothingness to aid the carving of home-void.

Feel the virtual teeth in your pads and underbelly as they chew space, make tracks, carve paths of field that twist the orbits of asteroids, distort the rings of gas giants, pull comets apart, smooth the courses of interplanetary vessels, chew, chew chew the gaseous stone of stellar wind, dig a catch basin for the eccentric particles of cosmic rays, dig deep into the vacuum to dredge up matter and antimatter from the mantle of space. Guide the barely warm warmth of the big-bang background radiation into a nurturing pool of magma.

Step out of the dug-in computers and their field-controlling tunnel that tasted space and fed the savor to the ground crawlers. Step back to the terrain where mind and land could be one. Step down from space.

Down and down around and into a near volcano a slow treacherous path had been eaten into this way. Here was a worthy place to fall and follow, a passage that came at times perilously close to panes that abutted the rolling lava. But he knew he was safe behind the Forgediamond windows, knew their material as intimately as if he had been the first to carve the making of it. Millennia of thermodynamic studies and careful approach to the sources of heat and life had brought forth this substance.

All things lived by warmth here, and all things sought just the right nearness to the molten rock and slow moving life-death that came from volcanoes. This clear stone had permitted the Path-Miners to dig closer to the fire than their pre-sapient ancestors would have dared. It had no name -- nothing here did -- but when the Guests had given it to humanity and with it the secret to geothermal power, it had been called Forgediamond, two misnomers wrapped in one. The Path-Miners had no forges, and the stone was not diamond. But it had been copied and used and spread all over the underEarth, permitting his first homeworld to be heated and powered by the terrible fires beneath it.

He walked near the Forgediamond panel, though not as near as the path drew him. He could not survive the heat before him. His membranes could not approach the tolerance of a Path-Miner's all-absorbing and all-emitting body. He came near enough to feel pain and to let the outermost of his layers crinkle and crisp. Then he withdrew to let himself regrow.

Elsbet considered the schism in her crew as she watched the reports about the skyvolk on Earth. They did not yet know what Winston had done, but they would soon enough. The fracturing here in Lineage would be reflected in the world of their legacy. Winston Overus had reformed the skyvolk within the crewvolk. He had given them something to look up to, something above. Of them, not of us, she thought. Winston's action was pure sky, pure defiance of her and her command. Her tongues flicked out in anger. She longed to grab and bite him, to chew him up in the wide mouth of her keel. But he was beyond her reach, beyond anyone's reach. Up the Arch and away, leaving his two clans of rebellious children for her to tame, or to eat.

The path split again, around, up, down, over, in.

He would have liked to go in, to pass through the transparent tunnel inside the volcano, but he could not have survived the journey.

Another turning. Which way to go?

Around had a smell like cinnamon and brine and dust layered upon dust, so around he went, learning as he walked. Here were paths of those who felt the differences in heat, who tracked their lives by not-too-far not-too-near, always keeping close to the subtle source of all things, the echo of the rumble of the heart of the world. Here there was much to come to, much to know.

He smiled, remembering the bewilderment of mind when he discovered that humans had two ways to reach knowledge or understanding. First there was learning, which was a hard and bitter climb, rung upon rung in which one drew each notion into the mind and worked upon it with the smelter and the hammer of one's thoughts until it fit. Then there was coming to know, wherein one explored and traveled, seeing what was there, playing with it, taming it, until one found with surprise that it fit and one had it to work with.

Here there was the middle way between those two. The Path-Miners learned by digging in, but digging was for them as natural as walking was to him. Dig down to learn, follow paths and come to know. They made no distinction between the first time a path was dug and the later times in which it was followed. You could not follow without digging, nor dig without following, you could not learn without coming to know, or come to know without learning.

No distinction, only passage. Passage into a tunnel he would not have noticed if his thoughts had not been circling around the mountain-cave of learning. So into that cavern he went.

Marie studied the dispatches from the Band-Braider world, fascinated by the images thrown up in the mist. Bones were everywhere. Bone-bearers were Surrounders in every place upon the world, high and low. Bands around bones, bones within bands. Hints that hearing was being developed, not the suffering hearing of humans, but great wide hearing which could feel the waves within the Surrounder sea and tell when something important was coming though it approach from far and deep in the surroundings.

Marie floated happily in the mist. She had given new life to both her peoples. If only the other Guests could be so content.

Echoes, echoes everyway. The vast open cave had currents of sound running through it. Tricks and games were being played with wind and air currents. A terrain had been carved in the echoing space, a terrain with paths as sharply delineated as the stonework on the planet's surface. Roads had been paved through the hum.

Hmm-hmmh-shushusu-hmmhmmhmmhhmm-hmmhmm-shushushu-mmn.

Around and around, around and around, and fall into the lava. A cautionary trail, a warning against concentrating on single ideas.

Oommoomlloommnllhhmmeeemmmumm.

A telling of an alien place, of uncarved ground and full air. A travelogue to the Single-Sayer's world.

This cave was full of . . . What was the word? He had dropped it into the Professor along with all the other human words. What was it?

Stories.

This cave was full of story-hums. But not stories as humans understood them. There were no characters, no beings except the one who traveled through the story. A Path-Miner walking through this course would hum its way into the trails. All stories were first person. There was no place here for stories that did not fit one's prejudices, no notion that a trail did not apply to one's life. To come here was to be brought into the story and the story brought into one's mind, and both bringings would be a single carrying of hum and trail.

Humm-humm-hummm-hummmm!

A bubble of mist and light within the cavern, more stories, these carved from native light and alien images, a transplantation from the Band-Braiders, an adoption of their nurturing image mist into a means of storing and replaying the hum-trails into light-tales.

Hmm--Flash--Humm!--Spark.

Here there be monsters.

One of the skyvolk, one of the pilots, nameless to himself -- all that mattered was he was of the sky -- left the habitat, left the ship, floated-flew on reaction, fluttered. He sought the second stretching out of time, tried to become the opposite end from Winston Overus. Where the Overus had gone forth to buy time with distance, he would buy time with closeness, he would take the other relativistic opening, thus he flew and thus he threw himself into the Monster.

There it was again. A sound, as of something coming up behind him, then unquietly vanishing before it got too close. He had heard the same sound several times since he emerged from the story cavern and returned to the more real teachings of the surface paths.

There, a hurried drilling sound echoing from the disappearance. He was almost sure that was what he had heard, but with the roar of the volcano and the swiftness of the wind it was hard to hear one noise, however loud. He doubled back. There was a new side path, just a little curl that went down and about to the left. A Path-Miner was digging it and humming hard with a hum that skirted fear and pain and strayed quite close to the echoing spiral chasm of death, a hum he had learned repeatedly in the stories.

He followed the Path-Miner, but it only dug more quickly, down, down into the fiery depths, down and fast, digging the dirt, darting through tunnels, around passes, losing its echo among the noises of the world. The passage of the Path-Miner was teaching him something, but he could not understand what it was. It osculated fear and death, it hinted at the emptiness of space, it swirled around the flow of lava, but what it was did not carve itself into his mind. The Path-Miner turned and turned until at last he could no longer find it to follow and had to make his way back to the path he had been following.

He pursued the path away from the volcano to a subtle maze in a series of foothills which talked of the delights of being lost, of having one's path and past vanish behind one, and then of discovering one's own tracks and realizing that one had come again upon old thoughts and that they were now new.

And it happened again. Someone was coming up behind him, then it dug down into a hill and was gone into the maze. Why were they avoiding him?

Things were falling apart faster and in more ways than the Handyman could fix. He had never dreamed that a single system could fail in so many different fashions, all of them at once. His every hour was occupied with repair and jury-rigging and finding new ways to solve old problems made new by the lack of old reliable methods.

He had barely had time to watch the lenticle dispatch and see the court of his great-grandson. Gregory the Learned, arrayed as his father had been in the costume of Lugh, had knelt and called him Demiurge and showed his palace and governances with the mixture of pride and fear that comes from offering one's first fruits, one's great labors, one's highest achievements to that which is immeasurably higher than oneself. Images came from all across the Earth, from every home manufactory which was supplied with templates by the court of the Gregorys, every image of the Demiurge that was imprinted on the sides of the manufactories, every hand that made in his name and bore his picture. The Gregorys had made a Dissociation not of peoples but of crafts, a governance of guilds, a coming together of workers who learned that their god, their saint, their inspirer lived beyond the stars and would return one day to teach them all the greatest secrets of the Hand.

If he lived that long. If the ship did not become a ghost shell. If he were not shown to be not master of all arts, but the fool who thought he was master of all. He wanted so much to return and shout at his descendants, shout that he had not been the Demiurge but only the Handyman, and that now he was nothing but a desperate soul trying to keep a leaking ship from drowning in the void.

The Crazy Old Man Who Lives With the Fire ran everywhere in the village, putting fires out.

A curving and a turning, a lesson in plate tectonics, and there was a Path-Miner ahead of him, four meters long with mouths on its feet/manipulative organs, and another long mouth beneath its belly. Its body was silvery with rainbow nuances, black where it touched the warm sides of the walls and absorbed all that radiation had to give. It hummed a greeting, a hum that implied two were making a path together. He hummed back.

This Path-Miner was digging its understanding of the geography of the moons of one of the system's gas giants into the walls of the canyons where the geologically pathed had been wont to come since before sapience. It seemed pleased to see the human and hummed inquiries that expressed its present interest in planetary geology. The Guest answered with a humming of the paths of Earth and its companions around Sol.

When the Path-Miner had fallen into the hum of listening, the human hummed the passages of following and avoidance and wondered what was happening and why this Path-Miner had not avoided him.

The answer was a hum that rose to a shrillness accented by the drill bits of the Path-Miner's many mouths. It swooped into silences, then howled out a trail of swiftness. He recognized it from the caves. It was a ghost story.

Everyone leaves tracks within the world. Those tracks show you who the others are and let you know whom you will be coming up to. But once (he could tell that this was long ago, though the past and future had no meaning to the Path-Miners except as what was behind and what before), someone had seen something which had left no tracks. The seeing had been carved into a canyon long since buried, but many had passed by and learned of this fearful thing, the creature that left no tracks, the thing which one might find ahead of one and yet have learned nothing about before coming upon it.

The discord, the break, the *idea* of coming upon that which had left no traces was too much for the Path-Miners to bear.

Idea was the only word for it. The Path-Miner Guest was frightened by how much the story forced him into human lines of thought. This was Species Shock to the Path Miners, this story was Feather.

And here he was, the ghost-thing, Monster Who Leaves No Tracks, Monster Who is Found Ahead of You. Monster Who is the End of Paths.

A terror if you are following it, but no trouble if it pursues you.

Beatrice watched Dominique's time- and care-worn face, hardened into stone-solidity by whatever the latest age-opposing treatment was.

"Beatrice," said the straining voice. Something in her throat was flattening the notes of her words, her once musical voice restrained to a bare third of an alto octave. "The Disuniversity is a complete success. Every Consenting voice comes to us for knowledge. The Professors need no longer roam the world. I have made a good home for you. Come back to me. I need you in the world my father made, in the world my brothers and sister made of the world my father made, in this world of tired triumph for us all. Come back. We need the understanding of what we cannot understand."

Beatrice stared hard at the frozen image. Dominique was now much older than she, had learned much more, had brought Academe out of the wilderness and given it a home in every voice. Why was she still appealing to her absent teacher?

What had Feather done to his own daughter to make her like this? Why had he done it?

For what reason, for what goal or benefit had he made these strange monsters of his own family, his own crew, and his own world?

She was the Crazy Old Woman Who Knows Everything, according to Tomaso. So how came it that she had no idea what was happening, or why, or most frustrating, how?

His path led to where a great many Path-Miners, hundreds by the sound of them, were digging and eating through unmarked stone that had recently been lava. He approached them so they would not flee his presence.

These Path-Miners did not move with the easy passage he had seen in those who followed and altered the dug-in tracks. These were biting each other and scrabbling across the paths they had dug. It was like the mating battles among the horned species on Earth, bucking and charging, digging into each other. Such a confusion of short paths they were making, digging and destroying, cutting their memories into virgin territory only to have them cut off by the memories of another. It was the most brutal display he had ever seen and it held him transfixed, for there was no way he could lay down his own memories and he did not dare venture into that savage discussion.

Ghostworld crossing the Echo, annihilating xxxx Carvers of history xxxxx Step by step, Single-Sayer like xxxxx Ghostworld crossing the Echo, annihilating the memories of Ghosts xxxxx Shadows of the dead reliving the hums of their forebears xxxxx Ghostworld crossing the Echo, annihilating the memories of Ghosts, volcano of forgetfulness xxxxx Hiders of stories in xxxxx

Ghostworld crossing the Echo, annihilating the memories of Ghosts, volcano of forgetfulness, hummers into silence.

For the first time since he had reached this world, he sat and waited, while slowly, slowly, paths took shape which others added to instead of destroying; slowly leading gave way to following and assertion to acceptance, until the untouched and untrammeled had become like the rest of the world, bitten deep with sapience.

The matter settled, the Path-Miners went their ways out from the consensus. He stepped forward and learned what had been the subject of debate.

Him.

Quint is in Burst:
{ Things fall apart}
{}
{ Things follow their ways}
{}
{ Ways fall apart}
{}
{ Parts fall by the wayside}

Around and around in himself, around and around through the ghost and the human and the Guest and the hums and the paths and the self and the not-self, around and around until he came to fear that he was following the ghost who leaves no tracks, until he was terrified that he would meet the thing whose memory cannot be known, cannot be found out, the monster of the pathways.

Overus describes an asymptote.

The Handyman had exhausted his toolkit. He sat in the Pantechnicon, hands in the control box of his manufactory, trying to think of what to make. Limitless possibilities, all the forms of matter and anti-matter, broad ranges of energy, all the forms that field could muster were his to grasp and put together to solve the ship's problems. Only his mind was the bottleneck. Only failure of thought kept the troubles alive.

He had run out of ideas, run out of tools. He was paralyzed by inability, by unhandyness.

There are ways out of the circle and the spiral and the ghostland, but is it safe to take them? The ghost could be anywhere, on any path. It waits ahead of you and you cannot know it is there until you find it. But here in the ghostland perhaps its secrets can be found out, perhaps a way to confront it, to banish it lies here in the cracks and crevices. Someone of the hundreds who dug these memories must have exorcised the ghost. Just keep circling until it is found. Keep circling.

Britt Lookdown was beginning to worry about the Path-Miner Guest. He had taken a great deal of food with him in the form of nutrient packages which could be absorbed through his membranes. Not good for long-term consumption, no more than a year or two, but aided by photosynthesis it would be enough to sustain him safely for months if necessary.

But still, she had expected him to check in once in a while. It had been eight months since their arrival. She had contacted the ship several times, but neither Elsbet nor Feather had felt that she should do anything, though they were clearly worried.

She considered doing a fly-over, but how to find one human figure in a maze-world? Not possible.

Britt sat and waited and waited. And her waiting was rewarded when the Path-Miner Guest came stumbling, stumbling, his feet worn down through all the membranes, down to bleeding skin and below, stumbling into the caravel.

"Out" -- Away from the ghostland, escape the ghost.

"Space" --Where the Echo reigned. Where no ghost would dare come, for the Echo, the thing that could always be heard and whose paths were everywhere, would consume any pathless shade.

"Forget" -- Into the trackless tracks of the Echo to forget the tracks and the trackless.

"Up" --

Britt Lookdown sealed him in, attached the feeding sheets, and took the caravel back to the sky, where the ghost who leaves no tracks did not wait in the paths ahead of them.

17. Functions

Wearied and wondering, Feather and Tomaso stepped down from the caravel onto the Method-Smith world. Five years, eight months, fourteen days, and some hours subjective travel time had passed between the Path-Miner and Method-Smith systems, and every day something had broken down for the Handyman to fix. He had spent his last gram of inventiveness, cut his last corner, rigged his final jury. He was spent, and he had told the crewvolk in simple terms.

"We won't make it back to Earth."

There had been a collective sigh like the air going out of a balloon. They had come to hope. After all, there was only one leg left to their journey and then they would come home again. But he had let the breath out of their hope and they had deflated in sadness.

All except Feather, who had said, "We have reached the source of all means. Come down to the planet with me and see if tools can be made for our needs."

So Tomaso had come with the Guest, been flown by Britt Lookdown across the system, past the pocket of space where the Method-Smiths farmed and grew a few more small black holes in case more ships needed to be made to ride circuit through species-similarity.

After witnessing the results of Species Shock and the vast transformations the Guests had undergone on the worlds of their counterpart species, Tomaso had turned with disbelief to Feather to ask about this circuit riding.

"The Method-Smiths think we're similar to the Moment-Keepers and the Path-Miners? How can they say that?"

Feather's voice had an abstraction Tomaso had not heard before from the monster-maker. There was a distance to him, a gap like the gap of Species Shock. "All the species on our circuit leave records of their actions. All of us have a form of communication that outlasts our lives. That similarity of method is enough to fit us together. The nine other circuits presently being ridden are based on other methods."

The two of them fell silent and watched the sky flow past them. Down they flew through an asteroid belt which had been shepherded into many rings where rocks could be aimed at whatever point in the system they would be needed, to feed the monsters, to shatter one of the many moons around the two gas giants, to supply metals to the homeworld.

Down to the world itself they flew, orbiting first around the night side, where there was a pure and absolute darkness, no sign that an active species was below them, then on to daylight. Light showed the continents and islands, bright in stark relief against the oceans, seas matte black with the perfect absorption of all light. Not a single photon that struck the waters was let to escape in energy-wasting reflection. Like the Monster, the oceans took in all energy, storing it to be harvested when needed.

The Oceans, black and still as death, the land bright with life.

"Those are only roles assigned," Feather said as they stepped out on the strand where they had been instructed to land in transmission from the seas, transmission in a human voice speaking Guestsprach.

"Constance Marchant," said Feather.

When the membrane of the caravel had dissolved and let the two of them out, they were greeted by a figure human in appearance, an elderly woman with piercing eyes and a voice no one could refuse.

"Grandmère," Feather said.

"Feather, have you accomplished your tasks?" she asked. Her voice was as it had been when she had lived and he had lived and the Earth had been beneath them, but it could no longer whipsaw him and compel him to fear or action. Or perhaps -- and this thought tickled Feather's mind as it trickled down and almost emerged through his lips -- perhaps there was something missing in her, as if she were someone playing the part of Grandmère. He thought of Theadora (dead, how could she be dead?), imagined her on the stage as Grandmère, saw the dual terrors of those two monstrous/divine/inspiring/devastating lives layered and folded, hardened into steel by those two personalities made one.

This was not that great enfolding. This was hollow, not hardened, absence, not presence. This was a mist puppet of Grandmère, a flesh puppet. Once he had driven away the ghosts from his thoughts, he knew that this was method made flesh, not person reborn. This was fate.

"I have made the crew and the Earth into monsters, Grandmère."

Not Grandmère, Grandmère's means. That was all she had been by the end of her life, just the means. What had she been like as Constance Marchant's student? Who was the young woman who had become a Method-Smith? Had the terrible creature he had seen and feared and written of been hidden in that person, a monster waiting to come forth, or did the monstrousness come from here, sent on a ratio of lasers across the void, a ghost seeking possession?

Feather knew all about monsters, knew the ones that lay dormant and the ones that were made, the ones created by events and the ones who come forth through self-will. He knew monsters of vice-ridden dissolution and monsters of virtue-obeying dispassion. He knew that the monster he was had lain within him until Grandmère had found him. But he did not know whence came the monster before him.

"I have become one monster, then another," he said. "Now I have come to be a third."

"You must go into the Ocean," she said. "Then you can become what you will be."

"Excuse my interruption," Tomaso said, pulling the last ingot of irony from the smelter of his heart. "But none of this will matter if the habitat fails. Whatever Feather becomes will die in space with the rest of us."

Grandmère said nothing.

"What's wrong?" Tomaso asked.

"She didn't hear you," said Feather. "You didn't say anything relevant to her methods."

"Then who can I speak to?" Tomaso said, desperately. "We need the ship fixed."

Feather looked around. This patch of ground was relatively stable. A few little bush-like creatures grew up swiftly, snatched microscopic organisms out of the air, then dropped away into skittering bugs that regimented themselves and marched off to the nearest river whence they would be carried to the sea. None of the large-scale methods were in place here, and the only apparently Capable Lattice was Grandmère, a finder of Methods.

"Find him a ship repairer," Feather said.

Grandmère nodded. The Ground erupted in a smooth blanket of creation. The loam sectioned itself like an orange and opened up to reveal a second Grandmère.

"Come with me," she said to the Handyman, and led him off a little way where something that looked like a sleigh was forming itself out of dirt and self-smelting ores.

The two of them boarded the conveyance and the sleigh sped off, flying low over maglev lines that grew up before them and faded away behind.

"Now to the Ocean," the Grandmère that remained said to Feather.

On Lineage last messages were composed, the words of the dying encoded to be sent forth to the Earth that awaited the return of the living and would need forewarning and forelorning that only a ghostship was coming.

Elsbet considered how best to send the learning she had received from the Single-Sayers. If she simply sent it to the Guesthouses there would be war, a brutal war of minds destroyed, lives shattered, labors turned into crushing burdens, rulers broken by the strain of holding up the ruled, and the dominated cracking under the pressure of dominion.

Yet if she sent it to only one of the Guesthouses that house would conquer the world and subjugate the others. The hand, the voice, the foot, the sky, or the First Dissociation would enslave the other components of the Earth. None of those were acceptable choices.

Let the knowledge die with her. Let the next Single-Sayer Guests learn what she had learned if they could. Let them choose when they came again to an Earth made alien to them.

A challenge she composed. "The Single-Sayer world has much to teach. Come one by one and learn it."

There was a thrum on the membrane outside her bubble. Beatrice entered, bearing a lenticle. "All of our research to be sent to the Disuniversity. Here lie the Emeriti."

Elsbet tasted the bitterness in Beatrice's voice, felt the weakness in her, examined how swiftly she could break the Professor and Dean who longed to return from exile, had awaited that return since the moment her diploma was burned into her arm. The lighthouse of the Disuniversity gleamed in the light from Sol, mocking her as lighthouses had often mocked sailors who could not reach their shores. Better to die far from home than within its sight.

It was a long journey to wherever this Grandmère was taking Tomaso, a journey in which their conveyance changed itself many times. Twice it took to the air, once in a form like a Single-Sayer, flying in formation with others who Tomaso realized were Single-Sayers, hundreds of them. There could not be so many of that alien species on this alien world. How could they survive, and why would they go in formation? Single-Sayers flew their own way. The battered and beaten intelligence in him came to an answer. They had been grown as these Grandmères had been grown, grown for their methods of flight and carrying.

The Single-Sayer he was on fell from the sky-dance and changed into a slow dirigible affair, slow enough to wend its way through a forest of mile-high towers which bent and twisted and extruded bars through which something was moving, coiling, and growing: Band-Braiders, which plucked the balloon from the air and deposited it on the ground where the rest of the journey was pursued. Land or air was all one to this vehicle, but never water did they touch.

The scenery gripped the Handyman at his soul, pulling him with one fascination after another. He asked what each thing they saw did, and Grandmère, Finder of Method, would tell him.

"That one pumps excess heat out of the atmosphere and down into the mantle of the planet. Now it is a radio receiver. Now a muffler of atmospheric noise. Now a -- There are no human words."

And so on, each thing changing, or seeming to change, its purpose. Tomaso had his suspicions that it was the human method of talking about methods that was causing the trouble. He thought about the wheel. If he saw a wheel on Earth it would always be doing a particular job. If he had to write down all the methods of a wheel he would find himself with a list that began with pottery, went on through conveyance and mechanical timekeeping, then to milling grain, and so on through the many uses of uniform roundness.

But to the Method-Smiths the wheel was a method and every use of it was a usage of that method. The wheel could change its purpose as needed because purpose was human thinking, not Method-Smith thinking. In one place the same method might serve many functions.

For the first time since Theadora had picked his soul up from the bewilderment of youth, the Handyman, most able smith of his world, maker of starships, master of all arts, the smith who had risen grandly and recently fallen grandly, felt a bone-crushing, heart-eating inferiority.

He thought he had known about the Method-Smiths, thought that, yes, they were aliens, but in some way he and they were like-minded, tool-makers, workers at the forge, smiths, Crazy Old Aliens Who Lived with the Fire, Handymen. But he had not understood until now that they were not men, not handy. They were toolmakers, but they stood in some different relation to the forge, to the fire than he did. Whatever that relation was it made them better than he at the one thing which had made him rise to greatness and fall to disaster. Compared to these smiths his rise and fall was as a child's jump to the nine-day-crash of Hephaestus.

Feather had once told him the saga of the Method-Smiths in the intonations of one taught to act by Theadora.

"Once upon a time when the ocean was filled with macromolecules -- the time when whether or not there is any life is a source of pleasant argument for Professors of a biological bent -- there was a macromolecule in the ocean of the Method-Smith world.

"Unlike the other macromolecules, this one did not consume or transform the others around it. It did not predate, it did not absorb light, it did not build, it did not do any of the things one thinks of those pre-living organic structures doing.

"This macromolecule altered its environment, clearing the water of certain substances. It made the world around it hospitable for molecules which might be of use to it -- those that might make copies of it, for example -- and inimical for those that would consume it. It was an Adoptionase, a molecule that adopted other life forms, and it became the most successful macromolecule in the world."

That was the beginning. Copies were made, evolution happened, adoption and tractation brought the whole molecular soup into connection with the basic macromolecules. Tomaso had lost track of the process by which Adoptionases and Tractases formed lattices with the things they adopted until the ocean had become one vast organically connected pre-sapient slurry.

And then, somehow (the same unanswered somehow as with all other thinking species), it had become sapient.

"And yet," Feather had said, "it's not one huge thinking ocean. The thoughts in one place don't necessarily connect to the thoughts elsewhere. But if you stuck your ear down anywhere and if it chose to make a mouth to speak to you, it would tell you its thoughts, which change over place and time.

"Later still," Feather had continued, "the ocean tried to adopt the land and discovered that the land is better colonized with discrete entities than with continuous lattices. And so it made methods of colonization and adoption of what lay on land, and so on until it reached the stars."

None of which prepared the Handyman for what he faced when his journey with Grandmère ended.

Most manufacturing on Earth was small scale, home or small shop work. The skyvolk had a few large orbital factories, and of course he knew that it had only been a brace of centuries since mankind had made its tools in large workspaces. That said, he knew that there had never been a human workplace to compare in size and complexity to the wavering mountain range where the Method-Smiths did the groundside work for their space efforts.

The peaks were strung with wires like antique Christmas lights along a mantel. The strands slid and pulsed and flowed into each other -- something taken from the Band-Braiders, Tomaso thought. They burrowed down into the mountains like the Path-Miners. They elevated the peaks into beacons and launch stations like the Single-Sayers.

It would be comforting to think of the Method-Smiths as stealing from the other species, as mental scavengers, but everything fit smoothly together, even, even the human-modeled control tower and computer system. It all fit in ways that none of the other species could accomplish.

Everyone had their barriers, everyone suffered Species Shock, everyone failed to understand or fully adopt the means of the others. Everyone but the Method-Smiths.

What was he, compared to them? He had come expecting to meet his colleagues across the void, not to be shown that even Lugh the Master of All Arts, even the Demiurge maker of worlds was nothing but a Crazy Old Man with a Fire.

From the human-inspired control tower a human figure emerged. Tomaso recognized her from pictures and statues, Constance Marchant, remade across the ungraspable distances of space and death.

"You come for repairs?" she said.

She spoke Guestsprach with an accent he did not recognize, Québécois French having long since been broken up into small tongues. She seemed human, and her greetings were everyday and ease-setting. But Tomaso, like Feather, had seen masterful acting and masterful mist-work and knew that he was talking to an image. A biological, fully functional human being, but an image nevertheless.

"The habitat does," he said. "I don't need much

fixing myself."

She laughed the correct short laugh for the feebleness of the joke. He was not fooled.

The Marchant led him into a room made for human comfort, supplied with espresso and bread and chocolate and water and things that smelled of meat and fruits and vegetables. He had not eaten for years. His mouth and stomach, the animal in him, overcame all sapience and he dove in savagely and gorged his stomach past satiety and into pain and beyond until at last his mind recalled itself and he could regret his actions and look critically at what he had consumed.

None of the foods had been grown. There were things that had the flavors of things that grew, cinnamon in the chocolate, banana flavoring in a pastry, but no real, direct, out of the ground food.

"Now tell me how you have failed," she said.

He began to recite the litany of breakages and disruptions, of things missing and disasters unexpected. His hands upon hers as on a control box, he described the making and breaking of each part of the habitat. Constance Marchant took it all in, listened with ears, felt with hands, then questioned, turning her hands over on his, playing his bones and scars, his accustomed movements and the deft gestures he used to control and create. Back and forth in hand and voice until his understanding of the ship had been sucked dry and his mind dulled like over-hammered iron.

In the deeps of the ocean, Constance's hearing and feeling were mirrored in a joining. Method by method a lattice was created, a tinkertoy, some of whose pieces were as small as two atoms and some as large as human conceptions. Piece by piece the Handyman's actions, successful and failing, were conjoined from the words and gestures he had played upon the Marchant.

Across a kilometer-wide span of blackness they

came together, and then at the edges of the lattice, other methods Tomaso Alliende had never known joined the image of him in action. Simple-machine-making was connected to fractal-object-design, to a home manufactory, to the entire lexicon of materia from all the species the Method-Smiths knew. Human medicine conjoined Guest medicine conjoined Method-Smith biology.

The lattice grew and grew and connected and contracted.

And awoke.

Briefly, for it did not need to be capable
of thought.

Except to speak through Constance Marchant
Once.

"Warm yourself by the fire," she said.

Then she walked out with a simple au revoir, leaving him to rest on a couch contoured for sleep in a way that showed a deeper understanding of human anatomy than thousands of years of earthly furniture making had ever displayed.

Yet sleep he did not, could not, nor could he warm himself by a fire that was not there. Here was this world, a world full of smiths, a world that was a smith, that made things that used themselves, user and smith in one, a dispensation that would have made life for human toolmakers immeasurably easier.

He had to smile. Toolmakers had been annoyed at tool users since one person tied a stone to a stick and gave it to another to hunt with. Makers and users did not see the tools in the same way. The maker understood it as it was, as it functioned. The user tried to join it to himself to do his bidding, to fit his purposes. This conflict was so basic in humanity that no one had noticed it. They saw composers grumble at the way musicians played, listened to writers bewildered at the misinterpretations of readers, heard smiths snarl as they sharpened swords for fencers, knew architects to glare at people who insisted on living in their houses. Yet no one saw the fundamental separation between maker and user.

The tool in the maker's mind was how it was made. In the user's mind it was how it was used. The object might be the same, but the mental image, the imagination-puppet of the object, the thing in intention, these were wholly unalike.

But here there were no users, only the Method-Smith and the method which worked on its own and was also called a Method-Smith. There were no generations of argument, no schools of learning wherein the means of use were taught and refined, no rigidifying of methods because those schools insisted that swords had to have a certain shape or car wheels had to be a particular size, no villagers endlessly coming to complain to the Crazy Old Man Who Lived With the Fire moaning that he had shattered some classical pattern with his latest innovation.

But where on this world was that Crazy Old Man? Tomaso could not find him, could not tell where the colleague he had come many light years to meet was.

Not the colleague, the master he had never believed existed. Where was the real Lugh, where the true Demiurge, where was the creator of all things? Where was this smith of smiths?

In the Ocean, perhaps, the Ocean that consumed whatever came to it, took in its methods and learned their making for later forging.

Did that sound like a smith? No, it sounded --

Tomaso's eyes flashed open, bright in sudden reflection and awareness. There was no Crazy Old Man here. The ocean was not a smith.

It was a forge, an ocean of fire. This world was ruled by the Crazy Old Fire who Lived with Man.

Fire had adopted man. Fire had tamed him, made him live in caves and houses to maintain fire, made him learn to use fire so that even if the fire were quenched man would rekindle it. Fire had ensured there would always be fires, that people would put fire in forges, in furnaces, in heaters, in engines, in rockets. In all the places humanity needed to go fire was taken along. And fire had taught the Crazy Old Man to be a Crazy Old Man, had shown him how to change the world, to turn earth into air, to draw metal from stone, to transform wood into rock and burn the rock, to sunder and join, to destroy and create. Fire was of the Things No One Can See. Fire had made humanity more than human, and in return fire had a home for as long as humanity lasted.

And on this world, in this place, this story was not simply a turn-around tale, a twisting of mind to break old habit. Here biochemistry had imitated flame and the seas had become forges and all that lived had been adopted by the Crazy Old Fire.

Quint is in Burst.

DEATH

{ The entirety of all Quint knows}

DEATH

{}

STATE

Quint is in Wave, choosing to die.

Elsbet came to him. "Tomaso says the ship will be fixed."

Quint is in Burst.

LIFE

{ The entirety of all Quint knows}

LIFE

{}
STATE

Feather stared at the sea. The black he had seen from the air was blacker still up close. Black waves rolled in, leaving jetsam upon the shore, jetsam that would burrow into the sand or sprout wings and fly or grow legs or wheels or patches or spikes or pseudopods and go off to the land to do whatever it was that needed doing. And all the while mature things, things that had done what they were and become more than they were in the doing of it, would come back on tired wings and worn-out wheels and aching legs and throw themselves gratefully into the blackness, there to add their experienced methods to the boundless pool.

So had he come, so had he come across the stars, across the years and across the centuries left behind, to enter the ocean and give monster-making to the Method-Smiths.

But if he entered bodily all that would be taken from him would be the methods of his cells and organ systems.

They could take him apart, tear him down and learn much of the ways of human biology.

Feather shook his head. Even that was not true. They had learned all that from the Guests, had learned from transmissions, knew Earthly biochemistry enough to construct human beings if needed.

He had come to give them his method and to be differentiated, reiterated, integrated, operated on, all the mathematical words for changing one function into another.

But how did it feel for the functions? Did it hurt them when the terrible serpentine integral sign came over to swallow them and spit out another function? Did the cut and slash of d/dx make them bleed in the abstract function spaces where they dwelled? Did the making of an adjoint disorient a transformation as it shifted from one space to another and discovered itself to be its own mate?

Such musings had been Feather's amusements as he had listened in to Beatrice teaching mathematics to Dominique, the idle wondering of a monster-filled mind listening to operations discussed abstractly.

Now he stood naked before operator space made flesh -- or water -- and he knew that the functions laid down in mathematics would scream their terror or submit to their fate knowing they had come before the operators to be executed.

A spray of black water licked at his toe, dissolving a little epidermis and giving the ocean its first real taste of Earthly physiology.

The water licked back. Then in a great wave, so great that Feather turned and ran from it, it deposited a two-meter-long piece of flotsam on the shore.

Slowly at first, the thing contracted and bunched up. Something was happening inside it. Protuberances were growing. It split in three places. Arms and legs formed, eyes and ears, a face, a face Feather knew. Then another wave clothed the figure, which stood and faced him.

"Ali," Feather said. The leader left long ago on Earth, the chief of the Guests. The one who refused the Ocean. "Why have they made you? And how? You did not go into the Ocean."

"They made me to talk to you," he said. "And my refusal to enter the ocean because of my failure to lead brought the methods of failed leadership into the Ocean. Refusing to enter, I entered. I have been made to tell you about the changes you made, to tell you what it was like to be a leader to those who would no longer be led, to tell you about the Guesthouses springing up, each around one of Grandmère's method-successors, about the bickering and the disputes, about the groups refusing to talk to each other, about the finding of patrons in the nascent Dissociations, about hiding from the hunters of the nations and the hunters of the other Guesthouses.

"Guests had not had to hide since Constance Marchant's day, but we hid from each other, from the First Dissociation, from the Disuniversity, from the skyvolk, from the Khan, from the Handyman's son, from the nations. We hid and bargained from hiding. We sought patronage, becoming brokers and arms dealers, information sellers, hiding in caves from the monsters."

Ali paused. He had spoken the rage of his long-dead true self with the first breath of his false being. Now he fell silent. The method of failed leadership waited for the monster-maker to say something that would set it off again.

But Feather did not speak. He looked at Grandmère and at Ali, at their fleshly method-ghosts, and wondered. The next time, the next cycle, other humans would come and on this very beach they might meet him, meet the means he was without finding the human behind it. What means would they meet?

Monster-Who-Cowers-In-Caves-Because-There-Are-Monsters-Out-There?

Monster-Who-Makes-Monsters-Because-There-Are-Monsters-Out-There?

Or . . .

What? What could he give to the ocean, give to the Method-Smiths that it would be safe to return to? What gift to humanity that, centuries from now when the worlds were much different in ways unguessable to him on this present shore, might be of use? What method could he be that would never die as long as there were humans?

Monsters. There had always been monsters on Earth. Humans had always been capable of becoming monsters. It was easy. Step away from the everyday, step apart from humanity, look up at the stars, look down in the water, look across a border, look down your nose, and you became a monster. Flashes of monstrousness were everywhere on Earth. They had their moments of apartness, and then what?

Most of the time monsters returned to being human without noticing their time away. Sometimes there would be something left behind, a pile of corpses, a new painting, a conquered land, a discovered theorem, a religion, a newborn baby.

He had made humanity see the monsters and they had hidden in caves, fearful of the sight. That was the first human response to monsters.

The second was to make your own half-human beasts: warriors, prophets, smiths, artists, kings, gods, nations, economies, farms, heroes.

They had done that as well.

He had come to find the third response and bring it back and leave it in the Ocean.

He had known this moment would come, known since he first agreed to go on the ship. Indeed, if he were honest with himself, he had known since Grandmère had first terrified him and shown him the monster within him. He had labored in his mind for the years of the trip, watching the monsters he had made, reading Dominique's dispatches, seeing all he had done, hoping that when this moment came that he would know what he should do. But he did not.

He had acted according to method, done as he was. That was the Method-Smith way. They were what they did, and he had been what he did.

Now, now, he wanted to be what he did, but he no longer knew what that was. He had to go into the

Ocean, to be changed by the accumulated methods of many worlds and many ways so that he could become what he had to be. But how could he go into the Ocean without wasting himself, without becoming merely biological methods? How could he go if all he would supply was redundancy to the nightmare sea before him?

At the horizon something rose from the Ocean, formed in a bubble, black at first. Then the darkness dripped off it in thick droplets, leaving a clear sphere in which was -- it looked like -- a caravel. The bubble burst and off it flew, touching briefly at a range of mountains, then turning up to the sky and out to . . . Feather could guess where. The Handyman had accomplished his purpose. The ship would survive. The crewvolk would come home.

Home to the Earth he had made, the monster world that would not welcome them, would eat them up as the Ocean would eat him.

But that was what happened. Monsters ate people, and . . .

Something moved in the ocean depths of Feather's mind, something rose bubble-like from the Method-maker of his thoughts, emerged and flew off.

Monsters ate people.

People slew monsters.

Monsters became people.

People became monsters.

It was too simple. It felt too simple. It sounded 'clever.'

Monster-people made horrors and wonders, then the horrors and wonders became part of everyday human life. New religions thrilled and terrified, then they became part of what people did and thought each day. Inventions tantalized, then sat on kitchen shelves. Music thrilled, then returned to boxes. Monsters expanded the everyday, then returned to being people.

By themselves they returned or with the help of the swords of heroes. Whichever way they went, to life or to death, they would go as humans, humans of everyday humanity.

Monster-Who-Expands-What-It-Is-To-Be-Human-By-Putting-Monsters-Out-There addressed the Ocean.

"Constance. Translate me."

In a wave of Marchants, the Ocean fell upon him.

Part III: Algebra: Mending Bones

18. Addition

"The Ship is coming!"

That shout was heard round the world, reverberating and echoing through the nations and Dissociations, a call to arms and action, a call to the Marshalls of the Earth.

Into the office of each Marshall came the command. Meet the ship, take possession of our Lineage.

In a small space that looked and smelled and chilled like the forests of ancient Finland, Ilmarinen, Marshall of the Court of the Gregorys, he who musters hands to do vast works, brooded over the problem his master had placed before him. Gregory the Subtle had commanded, "Bring the Demiurge to us. Bring his works to us. Bring the labor of alien hands to us."

He had commanded and Ilmarinen had grim-nodded his acceptance. The stoic grimnod had been for more than a century the acknowledgment of the Hand.

Renowned in song and story, it displayed the taciturn character expected of workers in the forge. Ilmarinen, ninth bearer of that divine name since the founding of the Court, had turned and walked away, feeling the eyes of the other courtier-smiths upon him, the ambitious who wanted to rise to the cold heights of the Marhsallate, the fallen who envied him his task but knew in their pain-wracked hands the costs of failure, the hangers-on who would turn whichever way success lay, and his supporters with their calculations and suggestions.

Gregory the Subtle had shown neither favor nor disfavor in the giving of the command. What he wanted none of the court, not even his son, the next Gregory, knew. By keeping his thoughts apart, Gregory the Subtle governed and made sure intrigue did not come near the throne and appearance of Lugh, Master of All Arts.

Previous Ilmarinens had lost their positions by second-guessing the Gregorys, trying to discern their actual desires and acting or not acting accordingly. This Ilmarinen tried to the best of his abilities to carry out the commands given him without seeking to know what lay behind them. If his hands were skilled enough to do the Marshalling he would present success to the throne that straddled the Rhine. If not, he would try, fail and present his failure to the Gregory. In this way he had kept the position for more than twenty-four years.

This matter, however, was different. What was coming from the stars was alien (This Ilmarinen knew something of the alien ways since he had Guests to Marshall as well as the hands of the Earth to draw together) but also ancestral. The Demiurge was returning from the worlds beyond. He had been the greatest of the hand before he left. What was he, now that he had gathered in the smithing tools and skills of five other races?

Ilmarinen did not think that this time failure would be grimnodded by the throne. If the Demiurge did not come before his great-grandson then the Ilmarinen would be stripped of his image and returned to being just another laborer of the hand, and another courtier would bear the furs and hammer, the visage and Sampo of the Finnish god.

Matching the hazard of the task was the difficulty. The proper Marshalling of resources requires knowing where and how the mustered matters are to be applied. None of the Marshalls on Earth or in the Dissociation of the Sky knew exactly where or when Lineage would make its appearance.

It was true that their telescope patches could spot its forward wake, the wave of photons followed by the slower bursts of massive particles that the direct use of field always generated. But those waves and bursts were only its tracks; they gave a direction of where it had been. They had been serviceable markers when the ship had begun its deceleration, but since then the writing of light upon space had given them only the vectors for course corrections committed some time in the past.

The Marshalls knew that Lineage was on its way to Sol and would arrive some time in a three-to-five-year window. As the time approached that window would narrow. But that was not sufficient to determine where and when to place one's galleons and picket ships in order to secure the human habitat and place the crew chosen by one's Dissociation into that habitat, not mention the need to take custody of the returning crewvolk and make sure that their insights were given only to one's own people.

Ilmarinen knew much about his counterparts among the other Dissociations and knew that in many ways they shared the same thoughts and troubles. Each would be working to outflank the others, relying on their strengths and shunting aside their weaknesses. The Marshall of the Sky, Hanako Lookdown, had the largest fleet at her command, but no number of ships could cover the approaches to Sol. The Dean of Princeton had the best data and theories and the greatest understanding of field, but could not guess the minds of the pilots of the ship. The Path-Chief under the Khan had the most maneuverable vessels and the best spy network, but could not find out what no one knew. And the Marshall of the First Dissociation had the longest continuous lineage of Guests and the greatest understanding of the messages from the stars, but practical limitations of time and information would overcome that deep comprehension. The limitations of reality and the inability to guess the actions of the alien and half-alien could confound and confine them all.

These same thoughts chewed at the minds of the Marshalls of the other Dissociations as well as the leaders of the nations. How to get there first? How to hold the position without offending the aliens -- particularly the Path-Miners, who might with a burst of field drive them all away?

Humanity had learned to use field in the one-hundred-and-ninety-six years since the ship had departed in that startling burst of whiteness. They had learned why the Path-Miners commonly equated field with volcano. The outflow of mining the vacuum, of exciting the substrate of the universe, was like the wash of lava coming down from the mountain, wiping out tracks and trackers, making the world briefly anew with reminders of the energy-dominated early universe.

The only thing that could keep you safe from field was field, and humanity had not yet learned to turn the vacuum upon itself to sculpt the potential wells, to make terrain in empty space. They still could not duplicate the means by which the ship was held together.

Field: They could see it, use it, shatter with it, create with it, but they could not guess where it would be turned off, where the mass of whiteness flying toward them at ever-decelerating, but still appreciable, velocities would come to relative rest.

Dominique Coskun-Feather (she would have liked to drop the latter lineage, but her authority over her Guests came because her father was out on the ship, coming back, soon), Honored Trustee, Marshall of the ConCensus (The others thought the Dean of Princeton did her Marshalling, but Dominique handled all aspects of governance for the Disuniversity), stewed over this problem, frustrated by the ambiguities, by the alienness, by the ugly necessity of guessing. She had lived for more than two centuries, bargaining away bits of her humanity for the extension of her life. She had adopted into her body some of the most terrible microbial predators the Earthly biosphere had ever produced, killers and infesters, corrupters of genes and conquerors of organ systems, and with the help of Method-Smith biology she had tamed them, made them the defenders and repairers of her body. A panoply of diseases she employed for handymen.

No one else on Earth would get the joke. Gregory had seen to that. He had parlayed Tomaso's wealth into power and the things he had learned from his parents and teacher into a Dissociation -- if you could call a government in which Trustee was an inherited position a Dissociation. In the course of erecting the edifices that honored his distant father he had removed the only title Tomaso Alliende had ever taken for himself and in substitution for 'Handyman' had inscribed on memorial statues and steles the ascription: 'Master of Smiths, Maker above all, Demiurge.'

Gregory's descendants had swallowed the story whole. How could they not? Gregory the Puppeteer, who had learned as much from their mother on the arts of portraying as any of them, had set forth this image, carved in mist and stone and time and lineage. None of them, none of Uncle Tomaso's dozens of great-great-grandchildren, would hear a humanizing word said about him. How would they react when he stepped off the ship?

But then, how human was he? What had her own father done to him over the journey, and what had the trip itself and the visitations and the aliens done to him, to all of them?

Dominique stared at her hands through the mist of her home. Vivid purple and green, her palms glowed with the flora and fauna within her. Almost, almost she looked in the small mirror behind her desk, but she held back. Now was not the time to remember the prices she had paid, not the moment to look into the ruined image of her mother's face, scarred and distorted, colored into the visage of some creature of horror and myth, so unlike the memory-safe image of Theadora in her golden casket, buried by Gregory with lavish ceremony, attended by Karl and his nascent horde, by Patricia, sealed away in skyvolk membranes, and by Dominique in academic gown of centuries past, each honoring their mother with the drama of their lives.

Or the ironic comedy. Her brothers and sister had long since died and passed into the myths of their volks. Only she remained, Dominique walking the tightrope of the living legend.

"And when you come back, Father," she said into the portion of image mist that showed the solar system and the flickering vector that guessed at

Lineage's position, "will you make me fall?"

Fall. Where will you fall, my feathered father?

"There," she said, pointing to a place in the asteroid belt where the vagaries of orbit had brought many rocks to one small volume. "A predictable clustering of materials. They'll come there to feed the hole."

Her hands described flickering arcs through the mist, each pass a command to a ship or a University or a Professor, each pass a Go stone laid down in the way of Lineage, a stone that blocked one of her competitors.

"Atari."

The sky flashed into blackness and there before the eyes of the crewvolk, distant but oh, so visible, was a yellow star. They had seen several such in their travels. This one was like the others in appearance. Only in knowledge was it different, for it was theirs.

Britt Lookdown (Lookdown again, so she could look down on the Earth from the sky; Lookdown again to bring the news of Overus to the people who had heard but not seen) looked at the campfire of Sol and felt the comfort of open space around a defined and settled origin. She was free to roam yet have a home, paradoxical comfort to a footsore claustrophobe.

She floated with the six other surviving skyvolk, not too close together, but separate from the rest of the crew. They had come home. It was a mere two-week caravel flight to Earth from this laden section of the asteroid belt, so brief and so safe a trek compared to the perils of interstellar flight. Of course she would have to wait until the new crew came onboard. The farmers would need instruction and the new seedlings would have to be planted in the nutrient gel the Method-Smiths' repair swarm had provided.

Britt shivered at the memory of the alien caravel flying swift toward the habitat, coming in like the coup de grace to finish off their suicidal selves, then splashing, watery upon the spheres, penetrating the fragile human orbs. Black water had dripped inside, pooling at the trouble spots, forming. . . things. She had no other word for them. Each seemed perfectly suited for its task, flawlessly designed to fix a single problem, as if each had been handcrafted by Tomaso with precision and a lifetime's care, perfect fit perfect repair perfect replacement. The crewvolk had watched the remaking and each remembered the awe of their first sight of the habitat at journey's beginning, remembered what it had been like to choose to come to space, remembered the human reaching out to touch the alien.

Then the formed methods had dissolved into air, into mist, into black water droplets, waiting until this bubble of Ocean was needed to condense again. The crewmonsters rejoiced in the passage of the wave and resettled their souls to live and come home again.

The awaited Earth ships were converging on the habitat. The new crewvolk would be among them. So, why, Britt wondered, did Elsbet look worried?

The hump on Elsbet's back itched. It wanted to open up and cover her with the Single-Sayer. It knew approaching predators when she saw them. Elsbet counted each pack of vessel, folded them together and came to a conclusion that made the echoes of ConCensus in her mind resound with sadness. Different packs of predators, each from a different source, each wanting to eat them. They would be armed but would not fight in the interior of ship space, not knowing what the aliens would do if battle erupted. They would maneuver and bargain and offer. If they offered honestly she would know that the Dissociations spawned by Feather had not fallen away from the honor of her youth. If they deceived . . .

"Feather," she called, her voice bouncing around the observation sphere. Muffled and distorted in places by membrane-curtains, interfering with itself as echoes struck echoes, still the sound reached its intended hearer.

Feather floated across the space. His arms and legs, elongated and supple, curled easily around the vines. His skin, smooth and brown as it was at birth, his eyes colored deep green and his hair ebon as the waters of the Method-Smith world, had made him look most like an alien, a strange reminder of the world they had come from. His body had been set back to his youth, yet he was aging, aging swiftly. Thirteen years had crept over him in the six years and two months since they left the Method-Smith world. The ocean gives, the ocean takes.

"Yes, Elsbet," he said, his voice smooth and raised into a rich feminine alto, a voice that was not his but which Tomaso and Beatrice clearly recognized and which both drew and repulsed them.

"Are those yours?" Elsbet said, flicking brief outlines of the mist-images of the armadas.

"They are here because of my actions," he said. "Each of the Dissociation-monsters will have sent beasts to capture us."

"Do you have a method for getting us to Earth that does not involve captivity?"

"I do not," he said, and a look of sad drama crossed his face. "But you do. You will have to frighten them into letting us go of our own accord."

Elsbet considered. She summed the predators before her and found them stronger than her in arms and experience, but lacking in the mathematics of the Single-Sayers. She could lay a large enough burden upon them that they would not be capable of moving. They would stand still in space and await orders.

"I will put stones of fear on their backs," she

said.

Elsbet turned a snarl toward the skyvolk. "Prepare the caravels. We leave soon."

Then she glared at Marie. "Send greetings to our visitors. I will speak to them."

Marie shuddered and flickered her hands through the communications box. Soon mists rose that showed the admirals of these fleets, their faces haughty with the confidence that comes from two centuries of technological advantage, but their eyes fearful with the coming and confronting of myth made flesh.

Images appeared before them, a grey woman's face, looking somehow down upon them as an eagle upon mice. Their masks of confidence fell from their faces before the Predator in their mist.

Let Beatrice be a monster . . .

Erase

Assume a monster, Beatrice . . .

Erase

Let M be the space of all monsters. Space is full of monsters. Nothing else lives there, can live there. *Theorem: In M there is a an element Beatrice having the following characteristics:*

What characteristics did she have? What was she? She had been full of truth before she left Earth. Then she had been emptied by Tomaso and Feather with their ideas of utility and roles to play. She had started to refill herself on the journey, seeking to find truth in confrontation with reality and conference with how the aliens looked at the world. She had failed. Then the Path-Miner Guest had dropped all of human language on her and she had been filled again with words, all the words people had ever invented, all prepared to speak about anything. But there was nothing to talk about, so she had spent the years since emptying herself again. Breathe in for a decade, breathe out for a decade. What difference did it make, full or empty, truth or image? Sol or just another star?

Gregory the Subtle, son of Gregory the Learned, son of Gregory the Far-Seeing, son of Gregory the Great, son of the Demiurge, sat on the fiery throne in the palace that straddled the Rhine, watching the deadlock in space, watching with wonder as the ancient caravels of the shipvolk flew past his armada and the armadas of his cousins, his aunt, the armada of the First Dissociation, the flotilla of the Khanate, and the fleets of the nations. He watched with wonder but strangely without surprise. The Demiurge had come home. What actions could mortals take against him?

His admiral, Gofannon, had been struck dumb and paralyzed by the words of a hunchbacked woman whom the records identified as Elsbet Chan-DeMarnier-Dunlevy-Tienh, a Single-Sayer Guest who had been ConCensor of the First Dissociation. There was nothing to fear in such a woman. It must have been the Demiurge who had set this action in motion. Gregory the Subtle could feel his ancestor's hand behind this, just as he felt that same hand behind all other things.

Gregory the Subtle had set Ilmarinen and Gofannon against the Demiurge and the Ilmarinen had done his best, had guessed properly and sent a fleet strong with weapons, great with grandeur, swift with developments devised and hidden from the other Dissociations and admiraled by a defector from the skyvolk, Gofannon who had brought much knowledge and practical wisdom to the galleon fleet of the hand.

They had played a strong hand, as strong as the Hand could make, but he had lost to the hand beyond the Hand.

What was the Demiurge planning? This Gregory, despite the qualities implied by his sobriquet, could not guess. He hoped that it was nothing more than coming to take his throne. Gregory would not greatly object to that. The Demiurge, according to the accounts of Gregory the Great, would not concern himself with governance, only with improvement. But if his divine ancestor wanted something else, something Gregory could not supply, he might turn elsewhere and his blessings would come to some other volk.

Something wobbled in the mist, a smaller ship than the caravels. Gregory the Subtle recognized it from the frozen images left by his great-grandfather. The Pantechnicon was flying free of the ship. On its wings, under its own power it was coming, bearing the Demiurge. It seemed smaller than he had expected. Its engines showed a rocket crudity in their use of antimatter, a relic compared to the field ships of his fleet. For a brief moment Gregory the Subtle wondered if the Demiurge might be nothing more than a mortal engineer who had been cut off from the developments of the centuries. But then his eye settled on the space around the Pantechnicon. A command was sent to his fleet, and when light had had the time to cross the distance twice field detectors were focused and their information returned.

The Pantechnicon was slipping across space, its edges fading into the understructure of the universe like a Path-Miner vessel. All doubt disappeared. The Demiurge was coming.

How should he greet him, how should he make certain that his ancestor came to the palace of the Rhine?

To this question Gregory the Subtle turned his

mind, turning the possibilities over and over while he sat upon the seat of fire.

Two tense weeks passed while the caravels flew to Earth. Flickers of diplomacy darted between the Dissociations. Flutters of inquiry and hints of alliance passed back and forth from nation to nation. Everywhere the Khanate of the footvolk watched and whispered to the ambassadors and messengers, offering helpful suggestions, hinting at weaknesses in one place or another, serving as an egalitarian espionage corps.

The crewvolk had little knowledge of what was happening, but they could hear the density of the traffic and watch the ships coming and going, shadowing their movements.

"Where has the patience gone?" Beatrice asked Tomaso. They were alone in the Pantechnicon, having chosen to travel together for reasons ambiguous to everyone.

Tomaso considered. Patience had been such a requirement in their time that the word was rarely used. To tell a child to 'have patience' was the ultimate rebuke.

"Two centuries of waiting could erode anyone's tolerance," he said at last.

"I thought I taught Dominique better than this," Beatrice said. Dominique at least was real, a person she had known, a person she could see soon, a daughter of the monster-maker, a ruler of the voice upon the Earth, a child of a goddess, a creature of myth. Dominique was not real. "Look at her ships flying station with us."

Tomaso flicked his glance and the forward lens/bubble of the Pantechnicon deformed to show him the glowing standards of the two Disuniversity galleons nineteen kilometers to starboard and sixteen degrees up from their plane of flight. The standards, glowing on the sides of the ships, showed a hydra with an open book in each of its nine mouths, each face pointing in a different direction.

The number of ships 'escorting' the flotilla of caravels had changed several times over the course of their flight. Sometimes there had been as many as seven, never less than two.

"There must be some very complicated politics going on out there," Tomaso said. "Everybody threatening everyone else, show of force on top of show of force."

"Hmmph. I thought I taught her better," Beatrice repeated to bolster herself. What self? Consider the space of monsters.

"Patience!" she shouted into the void and into her mind.

"Maybe she is being patient," Tomaso said. "She's older than us and she's seen the Earth change while we were away. She was in the middle of Feather's method-in-action."

"She was a large part of Feather's method-in-action," Beatrice said. "I wonder if she knows."

A crew of monsters. Dominique should have realized he would make them all extremes of what they were. She had thought it possible once, but had dismissed the idea. How could monsters make a volk? How could they stop from eating each other or wandering so far into their own interests that the ship would fail?

Dominique stared at the Go board, at the arrangements of stones. Each of them was the same, each stone like any other, but put them together in the correct shapes and they acquired the power to act, to kill, to defend, to encircle, to separate, to sustain. Feather had taught her to play long before he knew what he was and long, long before she became what she became. Though taught and learned in ignorance, the board and the game held all she needed to know about herself and her father. How could the monsters work together?

There must be one whose interest would be forcing them together. Which one would it be? The roster of the crewvolk was engraved in her mind and on her wall. Each name had been carved in glowing letters. Touch the name and all that could be found about that person would appear in the mist that filled Dominique's work room, the room she could no longer leave.

Image mist sustained and nursed Dominique like a new-coil of the Band-Braiders. If she stepped outside the bite of Earthly air would shrivel her lungs. She had adopted Band-Braider atmosphere as most conducive to the continuance of life. Even with the alien air and the alien bioflora she had not much longer to live, a decade at most. She had stretched human life to its limits and no tools existed to bring it farther. She had run out of time, and long ago had run out of patience.

Which one was it?

She jabbed at the fiery letters with her flesh-squirming hands and struck Elsbet Chan-DeMarnier-Dunlevy-Tienh. Her? Perhaps.

Then Quint Hillard. He too might be the one.

Then she lingered over Beatrice Van Leider.

" I hope not you, Professor," she said. "I have held your position for you. An empty seat awaits you here. Come home to the Academe."

An image flickered in the mist next to her right ear. The caravels had reached the Ring where the skyvolk waited for them. Now she would find out if the bargains she had made with the Lower Overus would be kept, or if Patricia's grand-daughter would betray her aunt in favor of her cousins.

Marie's eyes widened with pleasure as she saw the Ring, skyborough after skyborough tethered by strands and cords and springs and coils into a circumference around the Earth. All the satellites of the world were joined by cords that lengthened or slackened as the orbits neared and farred, a dance of cords that slipped and attached as needed, chains of freedom, bonds of Surrounding.

The lessons she had sent Earthward from the Band-Braider world had been learned and the skyvolk had bound themselves with them.

She tapped Britt Lookdown on her shoulder. Britt flicked a glance while trying to both contain her revulsion and dock the caravel at the nearest skyborough. This space habitat, many generations newer than the simple cylinder Britt had grown up in, consisted of some twenty-six cylinders rolling over each other in a cascade, as if some celestial miser were fondling gigantic rolls of coins.

"I will come with you to the sky," Marie signed.

Britt smiled, nodded, and returned to the work at hand, spinning the ship, spins within spins within spins.

Do I want to go there? she thought. Into that press, that Band-Braider thing?

I have to. I have to witness what I have sent. They must know about Overus, about the man who gave his life so that one man would outlive humanity, one man would keep the sky inhabited for the sake of the skyvolk. I must tell them in person.

And then?

Silence

Quint Hillard is in Burst.

[Reluctantly. Elsbet ordered him as leader to follower, required him as wife to husband, cajoled him as queen to knight {All their years together on Earth and off, their joinings and separations. All the ways in which two people can grow close and apart {all of human history}}]

[Tree of the last two hundred years {All the transmissions from Earth [Major societal changes occurring within twenty years of their departure precipitated by Feather's daughter, Tomaso's son, Winston's daughter, and their half-brother Karl son of Rainbow [Their meeting on Uluru] [Quint's only time seeing Rainbow in person, dancing alone on a bare platform, the only music the sound of his feet on wood and sand and bronze and the dozen other stage materials. Rainbow dancing across all the terrains of the Earth, dancing the joys and sorrows of the footvolk as they tramped from place to place]. Four children of one mother [Theadora, seen on stage many times, spoken of with reverence and terror but never really with love by Feather, Winston, Tomaso, and Beatrice]. [The tree of Theadora branching out through the world on branches of viewing, mothering, ennobling, mocking, capturing, and releasing. [--Minor Wave of human view. How strange that an actress should conquer the world-- Not strange to a Moment-Keeper, see the branches and the knobs, see the Burgeon-Spikes of her life. See the methods of her {Entire Moment-Keeper view of the Method-Smiths |Model Failure inability to fully see | }]] Copying of Dissociation Model combined with secondary paths to position of trust [Feather's Guesthood, Tomaso's wealth, Winston's daughter's prestige, Karl's empathy {Covert resurgence of many means suppressed by the Troth-Breaking, {All forms of transforming one form of glory into another [Monuments built, stories of heroism told, gossips spreading rumors about the famous, biographies confining, histories conforming, works dedicated, power grabbed, power given, power given up, freedom taken, freedom given]}}]]}]

Quint Hillard is in Wave.

"Elsbet," he said, opening his eyes just as the caravel finished docking. "They've been waiting for our return, to add us to their societies. But they don't know how. At this point their eyes are on each other. They will treat us as a commodity, a thing to be taken, until we show them otherwise."

"I do not propose to be taken," Elsbet said. "We will show them how strange we are and they will back away and let us go down to Earth."

"Where?" Quint asked.

"Home to the Guesthouse," Elsbet said. "You and I, at least, will go there. The others will go where they will, and the world will pack us in as we will let it."

The Single-Sayer unpacked itself from the hump on her back. Alien-garbed, she floated toward the membrane that joined the caravel to the skyborough. One tongue flicked against the lock, unsealing the crewvolk, opening the way for each single monster to go and find its proper sum.

19. Multiplication

Marie and Britt led the skyvolk to reunite with their kin. There within the turning of wheels within wheels they met as two camps of strangers, eight who had been into the deep waters of the sky and twice five hundred who lived in the perilous shallows above the deadly tidal ground. They stood facing each other while the world turned around them, spinning in the spins of falsified gravity, the eight grey-skinned, rock-haired monsters of the sky, facing, facing . . .

Britt looked carefully. Her eyes and mind had grown so accustomed to the monstrous humans of the crewvolk that it took her some time to realize that the skyvolk were not as they had been when she had last felt the embrace of homegrown recycled air and smelled the savor of only partially purified atmosphere. These skypeople were taller and thinner than those she had left behind, and their skins beneath their radioactivity-shielding membranes were a deeper, richer brown, subtly mottled with shades of red and gold unknown in the common human form. There was a wobbliness to their movements, a giving in their bones as if a flexibility had grown in the hard-underbeing of skeletal life. Then she looked at their hands, and saw fingers long and tapering, wavering tentacle and rope-like, and --

Britt turned to flee, but Marie stopped her with a look and a sign. "These are your people," her fingers said.

"They're Band-Braiders!"

"They have adopted the Lens," Marie replied. "As much as humans can with their restricted number of chromosomes. These skyvolk are climbing the ladder of Lamarck. In a few generations they will be well adapted to the sky. That is what you wanted, isn't it? That is what Winston gave himself up for, wasn't it?"

Winston. He had gone to the stars for the sake of the skyvolk. She could face them for his sake.

Britt turned back and rejoined the line of her people. Each side waited for the first word to be spoken, those who had returned unsure of how to ask admittance to their long-lost homes, and those who had remained worried about what grey beasts knocked upon their doors.

Until, at the last moment -- for the moment when a thing changes is always the last -- a woman, green skin betraying herself as a lighteater, eyes and mouth covered with membranes that protected from the rigors of space, stepped forward from the multitude which parted for her.

"I am the Lower Overus," she said, her voice a chant that raised a hum and murmur from the many, "great-granddaughter of the Higher. Will you tell us of my ancestor, of his last days among humanity and of his journey brief but unending."

Britt stepped forward to look in the eyes of this woman.

"Overus' last hours among us were secret," she said to Patricia's granddaughter, remembering Winston, trying to speak of that time with proper solemnity, trying to forget that those before her were coils and ropes, that they would seek to fill the whole of space, cut off the sky if she did not remind them of the need for openness; and trying to hold in clear mind her shame that she had dismissed Winston Overus and paid him no mind until he had made his sacrifice. "He did not tell anyone what he was doing lest we groundvolk stop him."

"We groundvolk?"

"Make no mistake. We had become as groundvolk. We had become of the ship and the crew, not of the sky. Our concern was survival, our work was with our hands in the dirt. We wanted only to live and come home. Winston had to remind us that survival is not enough, that if we only lived to come home there would have been no good in our going.

"So he went forth into the sky, and behind he left his words, his image and his trajectory."

Britt took a lenticle out of her carry-sack. Battered by many worlds, the satchel still held all that she owned in the universe. "Here is his path by which his place in the sky may always be known from now until the last human has passed away. When Earth knows no more of us, the sky will still be home to mankind."

Britt held out the lenticle. With glass-handling care the Lower Overus took it and placed it into a reader. Mist grew dark and the face of Winston Overus appeared in the sky.

The skyvolk, again the whole of the skyvolk, raised up their ropy arms and cheered.

But Britt looked down.

Three Professors had survived the journey.

Three Professors had been dismissed by their Dean.

Three Professors went down to Earth.

Three Professors sought out Deans who were not appointed by monsters.

Three Professors offered themselves and their understanding to the Disuniversity.

Three Professors were eaten.

"Where can we go?" Beatrice asked as the Pantechnicon skimmed into the lower atmosphere.

"I don't know yet," Tomaso said, his voice as deliberately restrained as hers. "We've heard from all the different Dissociations. Do you like any of them?"

"How could I not love them all?" Irony was a dangerous tool, perilously close to deception. But without truth, without fullness to her words what did it matter which mask she placed upon her sayings? No one would dare put a rope around her neck. Dominique had declared her life sacrosanct. "Most of them were founded by my students, and one of them by your son."

"No doubt they'd welcome us with open arms, grand receptions, heap praise upon our shoulders, and . . . " Tomaso groped for words and failed to reach any.

"And then eat us," Beatrice said. "Dominique's waiting for me to walk into her hydra mouth bringing the labors of the University of the Ship. She'd chew me up, swallow me, and incorporate me into her body."

And all I would give her, Beatrice thought, would be a burning ulcer that would consume her and her Disuniversity. Such was the inevitable fate of those who consumed black holes.

What was she but a black hole? Without truth, what was her learning but a mass of words collapsed in upon itself? What was truth but the just measurement of reality? And what was justice but a stick?

A stick she had thrown away and could not run to fetch.

"Gregory waits to do the same to me," Tomaso said. It was a different Gregory, a distant descendent, not his son, but something had been passed down from person to person, a commonality, a tool of thinking that had become lodged in the teachings of the hand. Tomaso was sure that if he had returned a hundred or even two hundred years later, the greeting would be the same, as would the desire to eat his life and install what remained in a seat of divinity.

"We could try one of the others," Tomaso said, knowing that that wouldn't work either, but wanting to hear Beatrice's analysis.

"The footvolk would take us in and employ us against the hand and the voice. The skyvolk . . . don't need us, wouldn't want us. The First Dissociation, would use us against all the others."

"What about the nations?" Tomaso said.

"None of them sound strong enough to hold us against the Dissociations."

"There's no place for us in Feather's monster world," the Handyman said.

"No, there are too many places. Too many arms are open for us," Beatrice said.

"I wonder why that is," said Tomaso, drawing out Beatrice's thoughts as wire is drawn. The Pantechnicon entered the stratosphere and sprouted Single-Sayer wing-pads. "A monster Earth should not be so accommodating. It shouldn't feel like home."

"We're monsters too," Beatrice reminded him.

"Monsters don't like monsters, remember," Tomaso said. "But look at how accommodating things are to our monstrousness. The Dissociations are all governed by lineages related to us. Dominique with the Disuniversity, my descendants in the court of the Gregorys. Winston's in the skyvolk, Karl's in the footvolk, and Elsbet and Quint's great-grandchildren are running the First Dissociation. Why the convenient dynasticism?"

"That is peculiar," Beatrice said. "It doesn't seem like something Feather could make."

"It isn't," Tomaso said. "It doesn't fit his method at all."

"Since when do you know so much about Guest methods?"

"Since I went to the Method-Smith world and met the Fire," Tomaso said. "Feather proliferates extreme ways of thinking and acting. That's what monster-making is.

"That there are several Dissociations fits with that. That they don't trust each other fits, that the nations are cowering and arming themselves fits. That any monstrous-method including deception and predation would arise as a result of his actions, that fits. But the fixing of control? No, that's not Feather."

"So what, then?" Beatrice said.

"I don't know, and I don't know how we can find out."

An image appeared in the mist globe just above the control box. It showed four lighter-than-air airships rising at remarkable speeds toward them. Well designed, Tomaso thought, good use of the aerodynamics Elsbet transmitted from the Single-Sayer world. No match for the Pantechnicon in terms of potential velocity, but a clear signal from the Earth that they're ready to meet us.

"I wonder how long they'll let us fly around making up our minds," he said.

Beatrice studied the image and considered the gesture. "We have some time, but not a lot."

Over the centuries the walls of the First Guesthouse had grown higher and higher still until they had formed a lattice of arches that cut the sunlight with ribbons of darkness and made a play of light and shadows in the gardens and the halls. The houses, small in the days when Elsbet and Quint had left, had grown vast in the intervening years, and what had been the least of them was now the greatest. The Band-Braider hall lay like Rapunzel's severed tresses over a full quarter of the compound.

There lights flickered in darkened coils and figures moved through translucent passageways, always close together, pressed against the walls, slow moving, always touching, never alone.

The Band-Braider's encroachment had not reached the Single-Sayer's hall. This had grown high and cast a long shadow. The tip of the hall thrust out through the arched roof of the Guesthouse, a lonely peak from which all of Toronto could be seen. A word from history fluttered into Elsbet's mind, skyscraper.

"It should be a mountain," she said. "They didn't hear what I sent. It's not the height, it's not the loneliness, it's that you do not need to build."

Five figures in flight suits circled the artificial peak. Elsbet's Single-Sayer alter-ego stirred in its pack, wanting out, wanting to fly, to flick and taste, to bite and push down, to pack up these others into its fold and teach them the proper way. Elsbet kept it down.

"These Moment-Keepers didn't hear me either," Quint said. "They built a copy of the mating temple. But what are they doing in it? And why do they want to still be Moment-Keepers? You can't be them. You can only be human."

His voice echoed across the compound, caught by the breeze. There was a rumbling beneath their feet as of a large herd of beasts coming together in a single line and following one after the other in lock step.

"What can we say to the Path-Miner Guests?" Quint said. "They'll want to know where he went."

"He lost himself," Elsbet said. "When he's found someone to be, he'll come back."

Streets without tracks in a city. A city binds paths to particular purposes. The city made the tracks. The people in it were ghosts who made no trails of their own. He could lose the ghost here.

"Hmm-hummm-Ooh-shooo-hmm-innmmlll," he said, reciting a trail from the echoing cavern.

Into the darkness and silence of the deep and trackless warm. Tunnel through the mantle with field for protection, dig down to the core.

The ghost would be among others of its kind. Perhaps it would settle down into a fixed path and forget about him. If so then all he need do was follow different paths from the ghost and he would never run into it.

"Choom-Choom-Chchchshshshhuhhuh-Shoom," he said, not noticing the trails he hummed loud and long.

Up to mine the emptiness. Volcanoes made to forget, wipe out, make dispute, incitement to violence, call to leave the world, call to the echo.

Somehow getting lost did not work. Always its paths and his were the same. There had to be a way to not encounter it. But what was it?

Dominique glared at the image of her father. How had he come to be so human, so like himself when she was a child? How had he lost the patina of extended life and the external appearance of a monster?

And how dare he simply walk into her city when she had waited for him, hunted for him, laid out plans and schemes to capture him? How dare he walk into Beijing, set foot in the Forbidden Disuniversity as if he were the Student of Heaven?

And why wouldn't he speak? Her soldiers had taken him easily. He had offered no resistance, no explanation, not a word, simply gone where they directed, let himself be brought to a prison. He sat peaceably in a cell and dined without savor on the good food of Earth as if he had not been eating the awful compromises of interstellar cuisine.

Why had he placed the stone of his self into the eye of her prison? And what was he waiting for?

A waterfall had been added to the river Rhine. By subtle building up here and there and dredging down there and here along its length a long, long fall had been created. Three hundred and twelve meters the water plummeted, and around that fall like a curtain over the water curtain was the palace of the Gregorys. Facing the wall of water was a wall of perfect transparency, Forgediamond smoothed to near frictionlessness so that even the drops of water did not stay but fell back as added mist to the falls. There were two doors to this grand edifice, one on each bank of the river.

It was to the west door that Tyrol, third Rainbow Khan of the Footvolk, came riding in a small hovertank flanked by armed walkers, their eyes looking all around, and backed up by his ceremonial guard, an admixture of the greatest riding peoples ever assembled. The guard was dominated by Mongols and Sioux who rode upon steeds that were horses at base, but whose muscles and bloodstreams, nerve clusters and cells were filled with monster-making biota. There he came in state to see his cousin and make compacts and bargains against their great aunt who had somehow captured one of the prizes while the others roamed free.

Tyrol, black-skinned with close-cropped hair, dressed in plain riding clothes, met Gregory, pale and Celtic in the divine garb of the Master of All Arts.

"Cousin, let us talk," the Rainbow Khan said in a voice loud as the big sky.

"Come in and we shall," replied the Gregory in a welcome pitched to be heard without a hint of loudness.

Tyrol's guard, the strongest of the footvolk, haughty in their indifference to the elements and hardened by the road, looked down on the sheltered courtiers and engineers of Gregory's court for their weakness, sneered at the borrowed images that they wore, gibed them for taking glory from others rather than making it themselves.

The court in turn looked down upon the visitors for the coarseness of their manner, the arrogance of their self-attentive bearing, and their failure to cultivate an ancestry that extended at right angles to human existence, a Lineage divine.

The two royal cousins spared a glance at their

meeting courts, noting how their servants were ready to snipe and challenge each other in inevitable ways, and shared a look and a sigh. It had been written in the books of their ancestors' teacher that certain conflicts arose inevitably over and over again through history, and that the one between the nomad and the city-dweller was one that no changes in human society would ever undo.

Professor Beatrice Van Leider had written:

> *Conflict always arises when two peoples cannot see things in the same way. Conflict can be stopped when there is a sharing of view. The nomad and the citizen cannot see anything the same way. The pasture of one is the farm of another, the loot of one is the commodity of the other. The war-path of one is the road of the other, and the strength of one is the weakness of the other.*

Both leaders had tried to instill these lessons in their subjects so that they might have some peace and commerce between them, but the lessons had failed in the face of the inevitable disputes.

Leaving the contests and the contesting behind them, the two cousins retired to Gregory's library-forge to discuss how to break Feather out of Dominique's prison and how to share him afterward.

The Pantechnicon landed on a rocky beach on Okinawa.

"How long do you think we'll have this time?" Beatrice said.

"I don't know," Tomaso said. Taking apart that

airship had told him everything he needed to know about the current state of tracking, which had given a technical advantage to their flight. "The false reports should foul up their systems for a time."

"Yes, but we can't rely on mangling their normal means," Beatrice said. "Dominique told the truth. Every voice is hers, every hand is Gregory's, every foot belongs to the Rainbow Khan, and the sky is fully over us."

She's playing, Tomaso thought. She's playing with words. It's working. Just give me a little more time to fix her. Just a little more time and a few more tools.

"All that's true," Tomaso said. "But the people use the voices Dominique gave them for their own purposes, their hands for their own makings, and their feet to go where they want, and as for the viewers in the sky, why do you think people invented caves?"

"True, their minds are their own," Beatrice said. "But one of them has only to choose to inform on us and one or more Dissociations will fall upon us within hours. Such a haste."

Tomaso shrugged. "Should be time enough."

"Did you have to finish repairing that water-miner on Madagascar?" They had barely escaped Gregory's submersible fleet.

"I'm the Handyman," he said. "I don't leave jobs half finished."

Beatrice sighed and smiled with amused appreciation. Tomaso had decided that he had come home and it was time to resume his work. Never mind who was chasing them. Never mind that as the Demiurge he was feared or worshipped in most parts of the world. He would do his job.

It must be the Method-Smiths, she thought. They did something to him. There was no sign of it on the ship, but he was always doing his job there. Here he could stop, but he refused.

Since their return they had hopped from nation to nation, entering the most xenophobic strongholds on Earth. They had even -- Beatrice winced at the memory -- made a brief stop in the Spokane Dictatorship and built a communications system for the resistance movement there (Beatrice had helped with a lecture on the history of spy organizations and common methods for ferreting out moles in their midst).

She wondered if perhaps she should leave, go see Dominique and accept being eaten into the position of Professor Emeritus. Dominique had changed the meaning of the word back to its original intent of a Professor at rest rather then one at eternal rest. But Beatrice could not bring herself to do that, could not accept the emptying of her being into the libraries of the Disuniversity, not so long as she was already empty of meaning. She could not place her work before others if she could not see any truth in it.

And yet, the thought creeped up on her in the long-dormant mental voice of Feather-Theadora, what if her words and works had been full of meaning? Could she then bear the thought of becoming an empty shell, an echo of the books she would write, an author whose every thought was known?

She was suffering under the living-death of the empty voice. So afflicted she could not give herself to her student pretending to be alive. But, she had to admit, that if she had life, she knew that she could not then deliver herself to the living-death of library entombment.

Full or empty, breathing in or breathing out, she could not go to Dominique.

She looked over at the Handyman at work at his forge, the home manufactory that had now been updated with the latest advances in human technology melded with the alien learning he had placed in it during their travels. He continued to be, continued to go on with his works, continued to embrace the Fire. Why did she feel so exhausted, so full and empty at the same time, as if she knew everything but found no value in the knowing?

If he were not here she would have gone and surrendered all that she was to her student and breathed and spoken her last. But he, Tomaso had --

He had adopted her, the way the Method-Smiths adopted everything that came near them. He had become a Guest, some form of Method-Smith. Or he had become a Guest of the Method-Smiths. They had adopted the Crazy Old Man Who Lives With the Fire, and he had adopted her as the Crazy Old Woman Who Knows Everything.

At least, that was one way of looking at it. But there were so many other ways, and the number of possible ways kept growing, arithmetically, geometrically, exponentially, infinitely.

But the number of means of thinking did not add one iota to the small set of things she had to think about. There were two fixed points in her mind, the abstraction of the Disuniversity and the concrete of the Handyman, and between them through all the infinite possible thinkings vibrated her mind, playing a high hard harmonic on the strings of thought.

"Here comes someone," Tomaso said. "Blast. Soldiers. I hope they don't want to fight.

"The Pantechnicon has learned too much about combat recently."

Gregory and Tyrol reviewed their ancestors' teaching texts:

What the voice has learned to say and hear, the mind has learned to echo as proper.

What the hand has learned to do, the mind accepts as proper action.

Wherever the foot has learned to go, the mind accepts as proper origin and destination.

Who the eye has learned to see in the sky, the mind accepts as proper sovereign.

Elsbet concealed her amazement at the crowd of Guests, more than four hundred of them, and this was just the First Guesthouse. From reports each of the Dissociations had a house almost as large and many of the nations had small houses of their own. There were also reports of Guests among the footvolk, their numbers stated without much accuracy as being around two to three hundred worldwide.

The assembled Guests sat or stood, lay down or roamed, but their attention was all on her. They had brought her and Quint down under the Guesthouse into a mined-out amphitheater with numerous passages in and out. They had all come together, assembled by a Method-Smith Guest named Obadiah whose Methods concerned themselves with clustering and grouping and moving according to the requirements of time and density. His work was evenly split between esoteric physics and appointment scheduling.

But he was not -- and this surprised Elsbet -- the leader of these Guests. That position had passed from the Method-Smiths to the Single-Sayers. It had been her veiled reports and the dribs of dangerous arithmetic she had sent back that had brought about this change. The Guests had needed rulers fit to fight in all ways. They had chosen the Predators in their midst.

And she, the Single-Sayer Guests knew, was more dangerous by far than they, so they had come to listen and to pack themselves into the Smooth of her allegiance.

"Your people await, my queen," Quint said, and there was no irony in his voice.

Elsbet stepped into the center of the amphitheater. Her voice echoed through the chamber and into the halls beyond.

"I have ruled the shipvolk for many subjective decades. I have come home in ignorance and you push me into command. You do this because of what I have done. I have learned more of the Single-Sayer way than anyone else. I sent back some of it and because of that you became dominated by the Single-Sayers. But that was an accident of the ship's path. Had we gone to the Method-Smith world first instead of last you would still be under their dominance. Had Quint chosen a different way of thinking when he left the Moment-Keepers you would be ruled by them. When the ship next sets out and the next crew takes our knowledge back to the alien worlds and sends back news, will you change governance again simply because of the insights they send back?"

There were murmurs and pauses, hems and haws, humms from the Path-Miners.

"Of course you will," Elsbet said. "That is what we do. We are Guests. What we take from the aliens we use and we give. Whatever of theirs that works for humans we keep. What does not, we let go. I will govern here until circumstances raise themselves up to bring me down, or until the load of this position is too heavy for me to bear.

"Now, today, I will begin to teach the Single-Sayers, and Quint the Moment-Keepers.

"As for the others who went with us, we will see

if they will come speak to you and give you their insights. If not, what they have learned will go to other Guesthouses or into silent forgetfulness."

Here there was grumbling and angry threats towards the other Guesthouses, but Elsbet silenced the gripers.

"Guests are Guests. We take in the alien, we make it usable for humans, then we pass it on. We do not fight among ourselves, for each of us has some insight into an alien way. Any such insight is powerful and dangerous, and each of us, even the youngest of the children, has within them the seeds to destroy all the others. The fighting between houses will cease. If I have to pick up every Guest and throw them down from the highest mountain, I will see the fighting end."

The human habitat was abandoned, waiting to be refilled, but none of the marshaled crews dared risk flying forward. Without the knowledge of the scattered crewmonsters there could be no new crewvolk.

But even abandoned the habitat went on. Plants grew. Air and water and energy flowed. Replacement parts were built, awaiting only the hand to install them. Bubbles grew, new balls and bangles, empty, awaiting the next experiments, and all through the habitat black water dripped, waiting to become black fire.

Dominique's patience was exhausted. "Bring him to me," she ordered, and Feather, clad in protective membranes and flanked by two soldiers, was escorted into the mist-chamber where she lived.

It had been so long since she had seen him face to face. There had been so many images, so many puppets of him. Now here he was, but there was still a mist between them, still a bubble, a membrane, a separation as fragile and yielding as the depths of space, a gap with no resistance to touch, but a perfect barrier nonetheless.

She remained on the side that had stayed behind, he on the side that had gone, white and black, stone next to stone, almost touching, never making one structure together. They opposed each other as he had made them oppose each other when he remade the world.

"Father," she said. "Your minions, your crewmates, those few who came back with you. I find them here and there, changing, disrupting, altering the world wherever they are. They are doing your work, Father. They are your stones. I have two eyes, I can see and live. But you! What do you have? What game are you playing?"

Feather looked at her sadly with the look of a parent or teacher confronting a young one who has badly misappraised the situation. He opened his mouth.

"I am not playing a game, Dominique."

His words puffed through the mist, but his voice, his voice was not that of her father long vanished into the black of space, but that of her mother buried in the white clay of Earth. For the first time in nearly two centuries Theadora's voice came from a living mouth.

"I am playing a part."

20. Inversion

Theadora was dead. All that was left of her vivacious spirit lay in the memories of those who had known her and seen her on the stage. Feather had known and seen her, spoken to her, been captivated and changed by her, watched her raise their daughter. He had glimpsed the human behind the mask and embraced the monster who lived with the human. All that could be found of Theadora's life had lain in him. The Method-Smiths had mined her ore from him, refined her in the fires of their being and placed her means and actions, new-made, into his mind and voice.

But Theadora was dead and would never come back to life.

Only Feather could know this, for her voice and her talents and her skills lay in him and came through when he spoke. All that she had seemed to have been was in him. Unless one had seen past Theadora's seeming one would not know that there was something missing in this performance of the performer.

Dominique had known the real Theadora, known the woman as only her children had known her, seen her in the secret private heart where she did not act, did not make entrances and exits, seen full on her face behind the masks of perfect performance.

But it had been nearly two hundred years since Theadora had died, two centuries in which the image mist of memory and the sadness of the forlorn could color over the missing human. To hear Theadora's voice speaking to her rather than simply coming from the mists of recording, to listen to Theadora saying new things to her gripped Dominique too hard and too swift for understanding to arise.

Mother and Father in one were before her, and Dominique, fragile with the end of life, hardened with anger at the world-changes she had witnessed and caused, nursing a grudge against her father, had no defenses against her mother.

"Your father's antics distracted you," Theadora said, "kept you from looking in the right place. He hid his monsters in plain sight and you didn't see."

Dominique's ears warred with her eyes. "Mother? Father?"

"Both and neither," Feather/Theadora said. "But do not let me distract you anymore. Come and see what you have ignored."

Feather was baiting her. Theadora was warning her. Ignore him. Listen to her. She loved you. He abandoned you to go to the stars. She abandoned you so she could go to death. He went to the stars so he could return and be with you. Ignore her. Listen to him.

Him/her. Which? What?

"Where?"

Theadora gestured with Feather's hand.

"There." She pointed into the misty image of the alien ship. Dominique's attention had been on the other fleets waiting to take the human habitat. She had paid little heed to the rest of the free-floating structure.

"Look there," Theadora said, pointing to a little speck moving kilometers away from the fleet.

Dominique flicked her hand and waited while the slowness of light relayed the intent of the gesture to the ships of her own fleet which were sending the images, and waited a little time more while the crawling lightspeed messenger brought the new view back from the asteroids.

A flotilla had assembled and was leaving the ship: three Single-Sayer long-range flight suits, a patchwork Moment-Keeper vessel, a mist and coil of Band-Braiders, a matter-flowing-smoothly into-field Path-Miner ship, and a living Pantechnicon from the Method-Smiths.

"They are coming to Earth," Theadora said. "They have learned enough to observe us firsthand and gain from us what we have from them, the advantage of seeing someone at home."

"They will arrive in about one week," Elsbet said to the nine oldest Guests in the First Guesthouse. "The Single-Sayers will come to us, because I invited them. What the others will do we don't know."

The oldest of the Moment-Keeper Guests, a distant-eyed woman named Victoria Keynes, swiveled her face so that her chin jutted toward Quint, though her eyes still looked up at the image mist in the ceiling where the aliens could be seen receding from their ship.

"What about the Moment-Keepers?" she asked.

"They will do what seems right to them at the moment," Quint said defensively. "I don't know these three. I spent no time with them. I haven't been in their habitat since the Moment-Keeper world. I have nothing useful to say."

His words knelled with chime-of-midnight finality.

"Can't you pack them up and carry their plans?" one of the Single-Sayer Guests asked Elsbet.

"Pack them?" she snarled. "Pack up five species? Five different intelligences? Five ecosystems? Pack them? It would kill anyone to try and lift that load. Don't you realize how little of them we carry? Mist-images, puppets, shadows of them. That is all we bear in our minds and it takes the whole of our lives just to do that. You don't know what it's like to actually see them and talk to them.

"You know there's some kind of person there, but you can't get near it. All the distance, all the differences, all the uniquenesses of each of us and each of them, it's too much, too many, too varied. You can pick and choose and pack accordingly, but don't try to roll them all up and swing it over your shoulders. Your back would break, the ground would break under you, then the Earth under the ground, the field beneath the Earth, and the universe would shatter under the weight of those thoughts."

The Guests recoiled under the lash of her tongues, wincing at the bruises to their egos, their self-images, their confidences, all the things Elsbet meant to harm in them.

"That is why I put the burden down," said Quint. "You can't really be one of them. All you can do is strive to know the little that can be known about them."

"They will be coming to take bones from our graves," Marie signed to the Guests among the skyvolk.

She had been delighted to find a Guesthouse built atop the High-Talker. Half human skywork, half alien technology, it was a hybrid skyborough. It gave the SkyGuests a great advantage over their earthbound counterparts, for they had captured Constance Marchant when they conquered the High-Talker.

At first they had thought this conquest would give them a monopoly in interstellar communications. But the groundling Guests had built patchwork transmitter/receivers and used what they had learned from Constance Marchant to recreate communication. And, of course, they received the reports of the crewvolk, given by Feather's instructions to all on Earth without regard for allegiance.

Still, the taking of the High-Talker was the stuff of legend among the skyvolk. It was said among the SkyGuests that Patricia Overus (they did not name her Coskun, having no regard for Theadora's role in her life) had spoken her last words to Constance Marchant and passed on her more-than-human methods of bravery, loyalty and conquest to the first Guest. They claimed that Patricia Overus was latticed with Constance Marchant, that the two were one Method-Smith Guest.

The High Talker had become a shrine to the skyvolk. The SkyGuests along with their other duties maintained the memory of Patricia Overus, whose grandchildren ruled the skyvolk and whose father would outlive humanity.

"Because they want bones, they will not likely come here to the sky," Marie continued, "even though you have likened yourselves to them. Unless we can surround them with useful Surrounders they will go down to dig bones. We might be able to get them if we can be close enough and make a chain that will lead all the bones of the world to us."

"Wouldn't that mean going down to the groundlings?" one of the Moment-Keeper Guests asked.

"It would mean making contact with them," Marie replied, hiding her hopes and longings for surrounding in the mist of rational discourse. "But if we don't the real Band-Braiders will surround themselves with groundvolk and leave us up here in isolation."

Britt looked on in fascination. In only a few weeks Marie had immersed herself completely in the ways of the skyvolk. She had surrounded herself and surrendered herself completely to sky ways. These people accepted her with the raw pleasure the skyvolk experienced when one of the groundlings took wing and joined them, like parent birds watching fledglings rise up and meet the air. But half-hidden in this parenting pleasure was a child's delight at the return of a long-gone mother, for though they were skyvolk, they were also, down in their cell nuclei and ribosomes, Band-Braiders, and though Marie had not a Lens in her body, she had one in her soul, and in her words was a mist that would illuminate and nurture them all, nursing them into a half alien sky.

But Britt fretted. She did not believe that Marie had converted to the skyways, only that she was surrounded by them. Whatever touched her she connected to and acted in concert with. That was the Band-Braider way. She had evolved herself into skyvolk, but she could easily evolve into something else.

Britt could not warn anyone about this. She doubted if she would be believed. The SkyGuests treated Marie as one like them but with more understanding. They saw and loved the alien, but did not know the monster. They did not see the hunger for

Surroundings.

"Bargain with whomever has the widest collections of bones and the best medical facilities," Marie said. "If we can offer the Band-Braiders good Surroundings they will come here and braid in with us."

Not again. Britt thought. Not those ropes and coils. Not the strands crawling through the wiring, sliding into the membranes, coming in on her.

She would have to speak to the Lower Overus and make her understand. But how could she, how could Winston's descendent who longed to braid with the stars know the danger of surroundings? Britt had to try. Otherwise. . .

Britt looked down on the Earth. Which was better, a roped-in, crowded sky or open ground?

DeMarnier park had been encircled, surrounded by the walls of the First Dissociation. Complexes had grown up inside its confines, removing grass and trees for the sake of buildings. The more control the First Dissociation lost, the more it spread out its apparatus of dominion.

Elsbet and Quint walked through the park, alone without escort. Elsbet had refused guards and no one could gainsay her. She had sent warning to the Trustee that she was coming. She had sent a request in words that could not be denied that the officers of the First Dissociation meet with her. They would be waiting. They had no choice.

The assembly place had migrated to a half-buried hemisphere with guarded membrane-doors and walls reflective of all radiation, shimmering like a Path-Miner's skin in daylight.

The guards let them into a narrow spiraling path. A thousand hidden deaths lay waiting here for invaders, the killing tools of six species arrayed in a conch-shell passage. Elsbet tasted the fear in the creators of this place, licked the fortress mentality, and mustered the arsenal of her words accordingly.

In the center of the spiral was a hall with a Band-Braider light fountain (not truly a fountain but a wellspring from which images could be sent in all directions). Around the flare and flash and glow were floating balls of mist and an inner shell in which stood the four officers of the First Dissociation, looking out upon the world but not touching it.

Such a simple shell to crack, Elsbet thought.

Inside the protective barrier were a man whose skin and hair betrayed a century of living and the adopted bargains needed to span that life. His eyes were as transparent as Elsbet's and Quint's, but they lacked the shimmering rainbows that came from the necessity of preserving optic nerves against the ravages of space and field. He sat impassively except for a flicking twitch in the third finger of his left hand.

"Welcome," he said, in the sprach of Toronto, changed over the centuries by the addition of Inuit accents and Hawaiian words. "I am the Trustee."

Next to him was a remarkably young man, not more than twenty-five by the look of him, who declared himself to be Honor. A stern-faced, military-muscled young woman avowed she was the Marshall. The fourth of them, a middle-aged woman whose face bore Elsbet's chin and Quint's cheeks said nothing, looking past them as if they did not exist.

The four of them are trying not to look like prey, Elsbet thought, and doing what most Single-Sayer Guests would consider a good job. The ConCensor, our great-great-granddaughter, must have instructed them.

Poor child, she has so much to learn.

"This is what you've done with what we left you?" Elsbet said aloud. "You hide and cower, you build where you should tear down, you show weakness to your enemies and clothe honor in the mask of youth? I should send the real Single-Sayers down here. They would eat you up without a thought."

The ConCensor deigned to stare at her no-longer-acknowledged ancestress. Her expression spoke challenge and inquiry and refusal.

Elsbet smiled secretly. You will Seal with me child, she thought. The harder you struggle against me, the more of yourself you give to me.

"They are all coming," Elsbet said. "All the other species are coming to Earth. Will you hide here and let the other Dissociations and the nations have them, or will you come out of your shell to greet them?"

The City of Ghosts was peaceful and he could rest wherever he wanted. All doors were open to him, all paths led to warmth and fire and trackless tracks. What peace, what bliss.

He had walked as he willed, been fed the savory food of ghosts, rested upon beds that took no impressions, and hummed and hummed the trails from the cavern which echoed nicely in the small ghost-homes.

Some of the ghosts had been following him, attending to his hums and muttering ghost words among themselves, but that was not a problem since they did not slow him down or stand in his way. Yet there seemed to be more of them each day. Sometimes one of them would approach and speak ghost-talk to him. He had forgotten ghost-talk, lost it in the Echo-hole between the stars and the Echo-hole of the city. He would hum at them, humming whatever the place they were in was about, whatever the echo-trail-cavern that had formed in his mind had to say in regard to the paths they walked. This seemed to content the ghosts and they would return to the haunting throng.

Today his paths took him to a mist-palace where an image fog showed much of distant paths and places. He wandered in the mist for a time, but his following was so heavy that they pushed aside the mist and dispersed the images behind him, track obliterators, a living lava slide to make clean the world and ready it for new tracks.

In the mist which showed the echo of nearby space he saw an image of a ragged-edged construct of silica and metal. Warmth and fire and a flicker of field surrounded it, a tracker in the trackless, a ghost-catcher, a spaceship. It was coming near.

He had to warn the ship away, warn them that they were nearing a ghostworld, a place where they would be swallowed up in unapproachable paths. Every way they turned there would be ghosts haunting the trackless roads.

He had to leave the ghost-city and come to where their space-path would turn into a ground path, had to place the obstacle in their way, to turn them around before the ghostworld swallowed them.

He set out and the ghosts followed him. But that was all right. Following spirits were fine so long as none of them were ahead of the Path-Miners who were coming.

Something deep in his mind, a path he traveled rarely, called and tugged at him. He followed it and it showed him that if he was there the ghost would be there.

Still, he had to warn them off. Better one ghost than a haunted world.

Ilmarinen, finding himself not in disgrace, yet looking for something to raise his stature in the eyes of Gregory the Subtle, had made arrangements with the Marshall of the Footvolk. The two of them had snatched and grasped up every piece of conversation, every scrap of writing, every action that the Demiurge and his Professor companion had left behind in their wake around the world. Now in the depths of mist they listened to a lenticle copied covertly from the Great Teacher's recent works.

The action of algebra is like unto breathing smoke. A piece of reality is burned by fire-words and symbols into an abstraction. The mind inhales the intoxicating smoke of variables and operations filled with the meaning of reality. Then the smoke mingles with the winds of theorem-sacrificed manipulations, mixing, churning, turning over and over the particles of smoke in the lungs of abstraction. There there is no meaning, only smoke and air, image mist, if the metaphor may be so stretched. Without regard for the reality from which it was burned the smoke produces an image-answer which is then exhaled back into reality. In this way meaning is abstracted, work is done in an airy, empty world, and then meaning is returned to fan the flames of reality.

Parenthetical: How much longer must I hold the smoke in my lungs before I can exhale the algebra of five worlds upon one?

"Gregory and Tyrol sent us a formal invitation," Tomaso said, fingering the lenticle which had been filled by an encoded message. The missive had been sent in a transmission that blanketed the world. Every microwave receiver on Earth had caught the burst, but only the Handyman could decode it, or so the Gregory had thought. Tomaso knew that what his genotype could break, Elsbet could break. One other would know of this missive. "My great-great-grandson is grandiose in his usages, but strong in his implications."

"What implications?" Beatrice said.

"He is offering me a free hand," Tomaso said. "To work where I will and on what I will. He seems to know something about me, not just the stories passed down."

"It sounds like he wants you working for him, not ruling his empire."

"Perhaps," Tomaso said. "He's also sent a great deal of information about Tyrol and the footvolk, talking about the quality of their spy network. There's a clear implication that they can track us anywhere, and that perhaps their patience is wearing thin."

"A threat?"

"Almost, but not quite. An insinuation that they know more than they're telling us and more than we can find out on our own. I think it's bait for curiosity."

"If he knows anything about you he would know that you can't be snared by mere riddles."

"I think the bait is for you," Tomaso said.

For me, Beatrice thought. What do they think I am? What image did Gregory create about me? What role did he cast me in, in the shadow-play of his hands? What did Gregory ever learn from me? What did Karl learn? Only Dominique became like me. What did I give the other children? It was so long ago, a history ago for them, lineages back. Lineage is back from five worlds, and what am I but an empty ravening monster? They offer me bait for curiosity, but they don't know what curiosity is. They think there are things they don't understand. They don't understand what they don't understand.

But they will soon. The aliens are landing. Species Shock is going to spread all over the world. The next phase of Feather's transformations will start, and

And I have to be there to help the descendants of my students. I started their lineages just as much as Theadora did, the two of us together, teaching the two sides of the voice. Dominique does not need me. She has Feather-Theadora, and she has all that I knew before I left.

I can't give her my ignorance now. It would destroy her. But I can give it to the other children, let them know that the voice can be dumbed, that the hand can be broken, the foot stilled, the sky darkened. I can give them enough ignorance to survive the coming shock. Then we can all start to learn.

"Let's take the bait," Beatrice said.

Tomaso was relieved. He had dragged the Crazy Old Woman Who Knows Everything around the world and done his handyman job in the hopes of bringing about this recovery. At last the method had effected the desired change.

But he should test it.

"Do you think they'd let us go if we chose to leave?"

"I do."

"Why?"

"Because they think aliens are strange-looking humans. They think we're friends with the aliens and that they will become upset if we are kept prisoner. They haven't been shocked. They don't know that the alien is alien and friendship is a human way of thinking. Let them worry and they'll let us come and go as we need to.

"Fly us to the Rhine, Tomaso. Let's see what your descendants have made."

The Crazy Old Man flicked his hands through

the controls, sending ion fire into the Pantechnicon's atmospheric engine.

The alien flotilla crossed the growing lightness of the inner solar system on a swift course for Earth. Each of the occupants had come knowing that this time there would be a landing and a coming together. The Method-Smiths had told them so, told them before Lineage had first come to Earth on the previous cycle, told them to be ready with proper crews before humans had set foot on a single alien world. The Method-Smiths had latticed with human means and concluded that the fit for the method of landing was best the second time the ship came to Sol.

First and second were very important human methods, hidden secrets of their numbering. The Method-Smiths had absorbed human mathematics and had found certain crucial elements which they latticed together to enter the Permiole of the human mind.

None: None, or zero. This concept told the Method-Smiths that to humans a thing was present even if there wasn't any of it about. No water was all about water. No people was a statement about people. So no aliens had landed on the first visit.

One or First: The first of anything, the origin, the beginning, the touchstone, the stepping stone. This mattered most to humans. Beginnings were everything. So the Method-Smiths had let the humans make the first step into their native and adopted worlds.

Second: Second was when you found out if you had learned anything the first time. Second followed, second submitted, second was behind first. So second they came, seconding to Earth.

The Method-Smiths were well prepared with

their seconding. Their vessel of three intersecting orbs contained considerable Ocean, enough to make many (many was another useful human number) Marchants, Grandmères, Feathers, Theadoras, and products and by-products of them as was needful. Also there was a separate vessel of Ocean to make more unusual-looking and acting Method-Smiths. It was important to be alien as well as human.

Hidden in the wellsprings of these oceans was the Adoptionase that had been sent to lattice to the most basic of human methods, projection of image. For this it had come to Earth so that this method could be learned and brought back to the full Ocean and latticed to all other methods. So far it had not succeeded, even after absorbing so many human methods that employed this fundamental process.

Humans put images into things before they acted upon them, a Tractase well worth taking in to the ocean. Make a spear the extension of your arm and it acts in accord with your arm. Make the Earth into a parent and you could treat it as a relative. Make an alien into a strange-thinking human and you could become a Guest. These were useful methods that would mate well with other adopted human methodologies, as well as conjoining nicely with the Band-Braider image-as-nurse and the Path-Miner tracking through any terrain.

Projecting the method of 'mating' onto its own thoughts was as close as the Adoptionase had come to absorbing the projection method. It was a way in a Permiole, a beginning of fitness. The Adoptionase had taken in and put out the image of mating, experimenting with it by latticing various methods with it (including the method of experimentation). In the latticing it had found the human notion of composition, the use of one method after another to create a new method. This itself was nothing new to the Adoptionase, but it realized in Species Shock that the human conception of composition 'resembled' (resemblance was a use of the image projection method) mating as most of the species practiced it. It had also noticed that the use of 'mating' as an image had many other images latticed to it, so that when two humans (or one to five Single-Sayers, or an arbitrary number of Band-Braiders or Moment-Keepers) mated, methods related to other things automatically fit to the situation. This carrying around of entire lattices because of image-connections was one of the most useful parts of image-projection, and what was useful was life to the Method-Smiths.

The Adoptionase continued practicing projection, testing next to see if it could properly project death as the humans did.

Behind the Method-Smith vessel flew the Single-Sayers, three of them, comrades-in-hunt of Elsbet. They had come to count and fold and measure the hunters of Earth. Not the prey at first, since only human-Single-Sayers could properly hunt this alien world. But once the hunters were found and spoken to, these Single-Sayers could learn the prey and pack enough humanity onto their backs to hunt as humans hunted.

The Path-Miners came for ghosts.

The Band-Braiders came for bones.

This Moment-Keeper came for Quint Hillard.

21. Units

At last Marie was surrounded, coupled, roped, conjoined and threaded back into the real life of a Band-Braider. They had come to her, touched her, twined around her, brought their world to her. Though the threads of space were tenuous still they were conjoined with the thicknesses back home. Their light, though long in traveling, was seen and saw by the eyes and lights of the Band-Braider world, and all they asked in return were bones.

Bones rode the elevators to the skyboroughs, bones danced upon the web of Stepping Stones, dry bones raised up to heaven and placed in the coils of the Band-Braiders. The whole feast of vertebrate evolution was laid before them, the secretions of calcium, the packing off of the notochord, the threading of muscles and nerves around the hard endoskeleton. From modest beginnings through the vast ages of dinosaurs and horned mammals, the strength of bone was given them. From the thrumming of membranes tightened over rings, the secrets of Earthly hearing were offered them, a hearing that fit them where none of the other alien hearings did.

The Band-Braiders wrapped themselves around the bones of the past to fashion bones for the future, and all the while Marie savored their closeness and gave them whatever they wanted, roping in the skyvolk, drawing the Lower Overus into second-hand communion with the aliens.

Britt had tried to warn the Lower Overus, had told her of the infection of her caravel and the incursions of the Band-Braiders. But Winston's descendant, affecting the superiority of her ancestor, had simply said, "Did they break they ship? Could you fly it? Could you leave if you wanted to? Did you try to embrace them, to take in the Lens and see how it led to the sky?"

Britt had reluctantly acknowledged that they had only frightened her, not captured her, that she had not tried to join them. But she had failed to convey why they were frightening. How could anyone, seeing only a few coils and ropes lashed to Marie, understand the horrors of a world with no empty spaces, a world filled by self-willed evolution? That world was coming to take away her home, her sky. Where could she go to escape but down?

"Britt will be joining us at the palace," Tomaso said.

"Britt? Why?" Beatrice asked, leaning back in a conforming-throne and sipping iced cider from a crystal goblet. "Isn't she happy back in the sky?"

"The Band-Braiders are there. She thinks they will stay in the lenses of the skyvolk."

The Handyman and the Professor were relaxing, in appearance at least, and looking at the rush of the Rhine behind the Forgediamond wall, volcano containment used to defend against the shattering power of a river. Fire and water, water and fire, the Handyman thought. Not so different, are they? Earth as well had its fiery ways. He remembered reading an old biology text that declared that dirt was like slow fire. Drop a leaf on it and watch it be consumed by the microbiota. Slow fire, quick fire, all methods were fire.

The court of the Gregorys was around them, intermingled with the leaders of the footvolk, talking and gesturing, emphatically not watching the two mythic guests taking their ease and speaking in Theadora-honed stage whispers.

"Ah." Beatrice looked over at the Rhine falls and, at a subtle signal from Tomaso, changed the subject. "Never build anything that you will not be able to maintain if times turn bad."

"Leon Battista Alberti," Tomaso said. "A lesson my descendants seem to have forgotten."

"As did my students," Beatrice said. "Why, I wonder?"

"Feather's work," Tomaso said. "He made a monster of the world. Only monsters could rule it. That will change soon."

"How do you know?"

"I know Feather's methods," Tomaso said. "When he died he left much behind that could be understood by an able smith."

He said the word 'died' just loud enough to attract the attention of the Rainbow Khan and the Gregory.

"Demiurge?" Gregory the Subtle said. "I could

not help overhearing. Our intelligence says that the monster-maker is still Aunt Dominique's . . . Guest."

"Feather died on the Method-Smith world," Beatrice said, her voice rising into the tones of a teacher disappointed with the performance of an otherwise promising pupil. "He went into the Ocean. That's what he went there for, to give up his means. Feather's been dead for years. Didn't you know? Didn't any of you realize that?"

She challenged with her words, attacked with her insinuations, lashed out, playing Elsbet Chan. But that's all we do, Beatrice thought, we play them, humans playing roles mythic, historical, alien, Professorial. All the world's a playground. Once I thought I was a teacher. Now I'm acting the schoolyard bully.

"Then what came back along the star roads with you?" Tyrol asked. "What is this thing that looks like Feather and, by all reports, talks with the voice of Grandmother Theadora?"

Gregory flashed a glance at his cousin. Clearly some intelligence had not yet been shared.

"A hybrid of Feather's methods and Theadora's methods," Tomaso said. "An alloy. A tool. A method. What else comes out of the Method-Smith Ocean?"

"And are you dead too?" Gregory asked. "Are you only an image of the Demiurge?"

"I have never been the Demiurge," Tomaso said. "I'm only a handyman, only a crazy old man who sits by the fire. I do not go into the watery flames."

The vast doorways to the great hall dissolved with a fanfare and in walked the Ilmarinen leading a cohort of Marshalls' Proxies dressed as a mixed group of Germanic kobolds, Chinese alchemists, and Victorian village smiths.

"Master of all Arts, Khan of the Footvolk, Demiurge, Great Teacher," Ilmarinen announced. "The

Method-Smiths are here. They wait without. My lords, they appear human."

"They do not," Tomaso said. "Pay attention to them and you will find that they sound not in the least like humans. They have human tongues and human means, but they are not human."

"How can I tell an alien with human methods from a human?" Gregory said. "I seek instruction, oh Demiurge." He turned to Beatrice. "And instruction from you, oh Teacher of Kings."

"Irony and sarcasm," Tomaso said. "Two ancient swords forged long ago in the fires of the voice-volk. Human methods?"

"Yes, Demiurge," Gregory said. "Good ones when properly used."

"Why did you use them?"

"Annoyance, Demiurge," Gregory confessed. "I have not been under instruction since my father's death."

"You had a purpose in their use. They were means to an end."

"Of course."

"That is not the case with the Method-Smiths. They are means. For them ends are created by the use of means, not means created for the purpose of ends. Watch and listen. They do what they are, not what they seek."

Feather/Theadora led Feather/Marchant, Feather/Grandmère, Theadora/Marchant, and Theadora/Grandmère into the presence of Dominique. Her tripled-doubled father and tripled-doubled mother, hydra-headed and human bodied, stood before her in the mists of her preservation, their presence declaring to

Dominique that she was an orphan.

These had come to her as her father's final instructions, as the will wished upon his methods as they joined the great Ocean. They had come, they had been sent, they were his legacy to his lineage, the lineage that would die with her and live on in these alien-humans.

But what was this inheritance? What was she to do with it? What were his implicit wishes and did she care enough to carry them out?

Her father was dead, but the maker of monsters remained.

Her mother was dead, but the ennobler of lives remained.

Constance Marchant was dead, but the translator of the alien remained.

Grandmère was dead, but the finder of guests remained.

Dominique was alive, but what of her would remain when her last hours had passed?

What could she do with these stones her father had left her? Four stones to be crucially placed. Put them on the board and they will be your legacy.

Put them down. Put them down.

The bubble of ocean was diminished by the many pseudo-humans it had created. The Adoptionase found itself lacking much physical material on which to act. But there still remained enough mental stuff to mold and lattice according to its means.

It had reached Species Shock and was latticing with Feather in order to cross over and place the human means of image-incursion into a place where it could be chosen when the fit was right. Within Species Shock it had found Purpose Shock, which was how Species Shock usually manifested for the Method-Smiths. All the other species who used language had something which humans called purpose or intention in their actions. By partnering intention into extension they connected thought and action.

The Moment-Keepers did this by seeing everything, then acting upon what fit the particular blank spots in their visions. The Path-Miners did it by remembering what they passed over and taking a course of action accordingly; the Single-Sayers by sealing the intention of the Smooth around the materials of the Sharp; the Band-Braiders by striving to fill the empty niches in reality and thought. Humans apparently pushed images into objects and then acted on the objects according to the desire of the image.

But the Method-Smiths had no intention, only extension.

Tomaso watched the entry of the faux-humans into the mingled courts of the hand and the foot. There were eight pseudo-people, a mixture of appearances and sexes from the Method-Smith Guests who had gone into the Ocean. But those appearances did not matter. The Theadoras among them could appear to be anything, the Constance Marchants could speak any language, the Feathers could frighten anyone. They seemed to be so many terrible superhumans, here to shock and intimidate the courts.

But Tomaso knew better. They were empty of human mind, were only methods latticed to fit in to human actions. He had good hopes that Gregory and Tyrol would see through them soon enough. He hoped Dominique would see through those who had come to her.

If they did not see, he and Beatrice would have to push them to see. Humans were susceptible to the appearance of tools. That was part of the making of tools, seeing before creating. An old joke drifted back to him. Just cut away all the parts that don't look like an elephant.

It was easy to believe that the elephant was in the rock, easy to believe that mathematics were in the universe, so simple to accept methods as basic and fundamental, somehow heavenly and beautiful, perfect gifts from the Things No One Can See.

Even the Things No One Can See were not free of this projection of image upon being. The People of the Hand said that the gods made and used tools, had bodies that acted and labored for their efforts. The People of the Foot said the gods rode horses, tramped from place to place, raided and conquered for their divine gifts. The People of the Voice said that the gods disputed, made laws, commanded, spoke, wrote books, told riddles and parables.

Tools of mortals made divine. The human universe was full of tools, tools of the body, tools of the mind. Things to carve out matter, space, time, and thought, things to lay down the lines and circles that governed action, words to carry intention, wires and waves to carry words.

The human universe is full of tools, therefore it is full of intentions. If there is a tool, there is a purpose behind it, that was the implicit human assumption. Even the universe itself extrapolated intention for its human observers, so that they spoke of creation, and of purpose in evolution, of the needs of stars, and the hunger of black holes, of the gravity (solemnity) of matter and the work (effort) of energy.

But here confronting the Method-Smiths that assumption failed. Here, face to face with the appearance of humanity was action without intention, tool without user, mind without purpose yet without apathy. Here came the moment of Species Shock when the Hand would be thrust into the fire.

Here was algebra. Here were variables in action, equations in and out of balance, operations altering what stood in her presence. Here was mathematics given life before Beatrice Van Leider's eyes. The Method-Smiths had come bearing human form but their bodies conveyed no more of reality than 9.8 meters per second per second carried the reality of smashing into the ground after a long fall.

Before her was a failure of drama, a shock arising from an absence, not a presence. The court of the Gregorys, the attendants of the Rainbow Khan, these tried to interact with the Methods before them and succeeded, but without gaining the measure of success.

The Feathers talked of aliens and monsters. The Marchants translated. The Grandmères selected. The Theadoras ennobled.

But the courts could not gain from these actions. The courtiers could not advance from these interactions. Purpose could not be fulfilled because the humans could not see beyond the seeming of humanity, and so they fell into Species Shock, plotting and scheming but gaining nothing. They fell by climbing and finding each rung the same as the one below, each step advancing them not a whit.

The Deans of the Universities assembled in

image looked upon Dominique and offered the obeisance of their voices. Dominique said nothing, only waited while the floating faces looked upon her and upon each other across the gaps of Earth and air, until at last one final Dean, one last face appeared: Beatrice Van Leider, floating in the mist near her final student.

In the mist-hall of the Gregorys Beatrice breathed in slowly and deeply, staring at the hydra heads of Academe. They wanted what she knew and understood, wanted to eat her down to her writings, wanted her teaching but not her life. They wanted her methods, wanted her to be a Method-Smith and go into the Ocean of their library.

But she was not prepared to go, not prepared to die as Feather had died, as Theadora had died, giving up herself to become a name and a heritage. And now she had the means of survival. Feather had given it to her.

What she had to give them could not be put down in books. She had experience with the Method-Smiths. She had lived with Feather/Theadora for the seven years between the Method-Smith world and Earth. She had understanding that could only be preserved alive until it was learned.

In short, she lived for the same reason Dominique had kept herself alive. In the monstering of the world only those who knew Feather as a man could be of use, and in the crowning of the Coskuns only those who had known and loved Theadora as a woman could stand behind the thrones and advise.

"They have come to use their methods," Professor Van Leider said. "But they are not humans. Do not treat them as such. We presume that behind a human face is a human mind. We expect that words have meaning, that requests have desires, that questions have inquisitiveness. But their minds are other than ours. They are dual to our thoughts, they are functions made flesh, action embodied.

"Just as our predecessors in centuries past mistakenly presumed that what operated rightly in mind would work in body, and therefore thought that purified minds could turn lead into gold or that words that commanded humans could command the storms, so do you mistakenly think that words that speak to human minds will speak to Method-Smiths in human bodies, and questions that challenge human thought will challenge them. They are as unlike us in mind as thought is unlike reality."

Winston Overus, alone in the universe, watches in misty recall as Theadora plays Constance Marchant in *The Translation Heavenward.* By the time the play is done and Constance-Theadora is ensconced in the image of the High-Talker, human civilization will have changed irrevocably. That is what happens when Heaven takes its eyes off of Earth for just a moment.

The Moment-Keeper cornered Quint Hillard in the rock garden behind the pseudo-birthing temple. Two meters wide with great-but-not-too-great age, bristling with spikes, spines, and spires, it rolled inexorably toward him. Then it stopped, stood still, and extended one of its spines while jabbing the ground with others.

The spine that faced him had a knob on it, a pulsing bubble, a membrane seed. Quint knew what it was. Quint read the demands poked into the sand and stone. He kicked the ground, cutting his answer into the dirt.

"I won't mate with you. I won't meet State. I won't face that again. Go back. Find another."

The Moment-Keeper prodded again, this time printing a human word with its small underspikes. "Burst."

"Wave," Quint replied. "I will not Burst now. I will not let it out. I will not be you."

The Moment-Keeper tensed, then released. The ball, the bauble, the seed fell on the ground at Quint's feet. It unrolled into a patch and crawled toward him.

"Why?" Quint demanded. "Why do you want to witness failure? Why see the ways we cannot be together and alike? Why see the unbridgeable gaps?"

The Moment-Keeper poked again.

STATE

gap

STATE

Quint stared at the words and saw the emptiness he had found before meeting State. This Moment-Keeper wanted that, had joined the crew to share that failure, that gap, that vast unknowable uncrossable glorious region of STATE. It wanted that understanding, wanted to go back to the Moment-Keeper world and mate with Quint's alien descendants, bringing two fractals together. It would not leave without the mating. It would die on Earth waiting for him if it had to.

He could not kill another of them.

Sighing in surrender, Quint Hillard reached down and touched the seed-patch. It sprang upon him, covering his skin. Spines grew out of and into him.

Spike by spike, the two Moment-Keepers rolled and walked into the birthing temple.

The ghost-throng rolled out of the city and into the plains, following in his tracks, listening to him hum the ending of trails, the emptying of life into echo, the warnings about ghosts. On the roads there were many groups and pickets, but they did not try to stop the throng. They blanched and turned away at the sight of him. He did not threaten, but they turned. He did not lead, but the others followed. Some of those who turned aside fell in behind, swelling the haunting as it passed along the unmarkable road.

He walked day and night, unwearied, unwearable as he had been made by adoption and practice. The throng, unable to keep up on foot, acquired machines to carry the ghosts. On they went, across the open land, along the human roads, those false markers that pretended to have been laid by the thoughts of people. There was nothing to be learned from these paths. They only connected points. The ends were what mattered with these ignorant roads.

He wished he could enlighten the paths, make them alive and thinking, give them thought and memory. But his feet could not chew them into proper courses. He gained nothing for his pains save nearness to the approaching ghost-hunters.

There they were, across the dusty desert, carving real ways into the roads, chewing their understanding into the earth. He hummed loudly that they might turn aside, not meet the ghosts face to face.

But they came on, carving as they went, teaching the paths, cutting memory into the world. . . . Until they saw the throng and stopped, faced with the trackless terror. . . .

Stopped, turned aside, carved a little, turned back, carved over what they had carved before, then came on to meet him, to confront the ghosts without turning aside.

"The name of this mountain is He-Walked-Away," said Elsbet to the Single-Sayer. "It was so named because the people thought it had stepped out from the mountain range over there. They were correct.

"This is a proper mountain, not like the false one built in the Guesthouse. Here you can look down on the Earth and see."

The Single-Sayer called Attends-The-Crosser-Over looked across the Cascade mountains from the top of Mount Rainier and down on the nine villages that had once been Seattle and across at the ocean. It looked and it flew, assisted by prostheses long ago developed to permit flight on higher gravity worlds. From the air it saw plants and roads and farms and wilderness and forests old and new.

It returned and, taking the name Gazes-Upon-Earth-To-Learn-Humans, said, "I will hunt from here."

The other two Single-Sayers had been ensconced on other useful mountains. One whose name was Flies-Over-Killing-Fields-to-Learn-How-Humans-Fight had settled in the Carpathians and took periodic sweeps across the Balkans and occasional jaunts over the heights and depths of Europe.

The third Single-Sayer, whose name was Seeks-For-The-Unique-That-Humans-Cannot-See, was with Dominique Coskun-Feather's permission visiting the five sacred mountains of China.

Elsbet flew off, choosing to travel back to Toronto using her own flight pads rather than be flown by a conveyance. The non-Single-Sayer Guests had been amazed that she had scattered her visitors across the Earth rather than keep them together and learn from them. They did not understand the Single-Sayer need to come to comprehension as a Solitaire effort.

Look at a thing and see it as itself, her father had taught her more than two-hundred and fifty years ago. Let your eyes become it, let it become your eyes. Taste it with your sight and senses. Let it become the only thing in your mind, see all the features of it in isolation, take in those features in your isolation. Only then, only when you and it are alone, can you pick it up and put it in your pack.

"Humans count, one, two, three, four, and more," Elsbet said into the air. "But Single-Sayers count one, one, one, one, and one."

Always remember, her father had said. Every number is one. But at each counting it is a different one.

22. Group, Ring, and Field

Beatrice Van Leider saw the algebra of the situation. In algebra one abstracts the confusing world around one into a familiar simplicity. The greatest breakthrough in algebra had come in discovering that there was more familiarity around in the abstract world than one had imagined. All that was needed was to find a way to fit the situation to the abstraction and hone the abstraction to be like a more homely and comfortable abstraction. Mathematicians had found that addition and multiplication were the most soothing and familiar, so they moved all things and all actions in the universe into the house of addition and multiplication.

Consider the group.

Group: a group is some collection of objects which one can multiply and divide in the comfort of one's home.

As in the Group of Coskuns with Theadora as operation and Feather as identity. In pure violation of mathematical principles Feather was inversion as well.

In the mist established to permit communication from the Rhine to Beijing to the skies Theadora's lovers and descendants were separate elements, interacting with no visible context, element up against element, pure in operation, abstract in challenge and transformation. Their generators could be enumerated, the living, the dead, and the returned: Tomaso, Rainbow, Winston, Feather, Theadora.

And Beatrice. She was a generator as well. Multiply them together and create Gregory, Karl, Patricia, and Dominique (Feather's child, her student, the same resultant of two multiplications with Theadora).

Multiply again and find Dissociations, the Disuniversity, ships, lineages, paths across the world, and cousins in conflict.

Be fruitful and multiply again and they will cover the Earth.

With this group of people was a group of operators, methods and functions, homomorphisms to change them from one group to another: Feather and Theadora as methods, brought back in their own multiplications and combinations.

Be fruitful and operate and transform the Earth.

Here in the mist, speaking across the Earth and into the sky, the group and the operators met and discussed and multiplied.

Dominique, honed and worn down by the

centuries, speaking from age and observation, called on her youngers to oppose the impending operations.

"They have come to finish the monster-making," she said. "You know what they are. Actions unadulterated by purposes. They have come. They will do. We have to drive them out before all we have built is torn apart by in the monster-world."

"Contain them, certainly," Gregory replied, the mist of his occupation blending with the image of the mist of Dominique's. "The Demiurge says they are like fire. We need a forge to contain them and to use them only as necessary."

"We can't contain them," said the Lower Overus, the open sky behind her. She could not come without that image, nor omit the marking of Winston's trajectory, her own claim to immortality. "They have a world, a ship. They will come again and again. Aunt Dominique, how do you hold back the sky?"

"They have the open road of the heavens," Tyrol said with self-aware solemnity. Beatrice noted that he of all Theadora's descendants was the one who most understood the uses of personal drama. Though Gregory had mastered image and role, he did not act the part so well as Tyrol. Tyrol's voice commanded, his bearing caught the eye, he was on stage before them.

What an eccentric group we have made, Beatrice thought. The children of vagabonds deciding the fate of the world and the relations between one world and others.

Sometimes that's the way it is. A few generators multiply beyond all ken.

Perhaps not all ken. Tomaso had not said a word so far, but his eyes were on all of them, the descendants and the methods garbed as ancestors, his eyes, looking sharp as they did, on the troubles presented to him. Homo Habilis, what are your hands scheming now?

"We can't let them loose," Gregory was saying.

"But we can't hold them prisoner either. They come from the Ocean. More can be made, more Feathers, more Theadoras, monster-makers, king-makers. They're a wildfire. They need to be tamed."

"No, Gregory," Tomaso said, breaking his silence. "Man did not tame fire. Fire tamed man. It is they who will domesticate us."

Ring: A collection of elements which one can add, subtract, and multiply but not necessarily divide.

Quint Hillard is meeting State.

{}

|Total Model Failure: Humans cannot be aliens|

{}

|Total Awareness Failure: Action and Perception cannot be mixed|

{}

|Total Species Failure: There is no coming together of aliens|

{}

|Total Universal Failure: There is no understanding of anything|

{}

|Total Universal Failure: There is no acting in any way|

{}

Mate

STATE |{The now visible extent of failure, the vast breadth of incomprehension caused by two minds coming together as one. Alone, who can see what they cannot see? But with the aid of another's view all one's ignorances can be gloriously exposed}|

Mate

[Children created by Quint's mating in the Birthing temple. Small spines growing smaller spines, human notions brought into the ocean, going into the ocean [[Moment-Keeper concept of going into the ocean: Enter to mate, result of growing large, pass on {All previous pasts that added to this Moment-Keeper}]--Contrast-- [Method-Smith concept of going into the ocean: Enter to die, give up one's methods to the Ocean] //{All meetings between Moment-Keepers and Method-Smiths, mutual Species Shock over Ocean}] {All passages, talkings, and matings with the other parents of these children passing through rings of mating until they reach this Moment-Keeper {This Moment-Keeper} [Return to Quint Hillard. Return bounty of failure to Quint Hillard. Show Quint Hillard State by showing failure]]

Mate

STATE

Mate

{ Failures. Boundaries, Borders, Edges, limits of fractal trees, range to grow into. State is the range to grow into. Always more State. More failure, more State. Fractal growth of understanding -- Fractal growth of ignorance. More ignorance, more Moment-Keepers. Fractal Growth of Species}

-- Species Shock

//Feather

-- Burst and Wave.

[]

{}

STATE

never sate

STATE

{}

[]

Field: A collection of objects which one can add, subtract, multiply, and divide; the most comfortable of algebraic objects.

The Crazy Old Man Who Lives With the Fire faced the Crazy Old Fire Who Lives With Man. They had faced each other thus for so long that neither of them could remember what it was like to be wild and dwell in open darkness, wholly subject to wind and rain, to the cold that killed, to the beasts that bit. They had been comrades in arms-making for longer than either of them had been able to think. But throughout their association and commutation there had been the danger of coming too close, of flesh searing into meat, of meat dripping out the quenching water that hid within it. Close, but not too close, that had been their way, comrades but not friends.

In their comradeship they had made many things together, a thousand tools for the foot, the hand, and the voice of man, a thousand homes for the heat, the air, and the fuel of fire, each holding up the triangles of the other. Each had been much changed by the experience, so much that it was difficult to remember the time before the change.

The Crazy Old Man thought about those changes, about the things he had drawn from the fire, the charred things, the baked things, the smelted, the hammered, the poured, the burning and shocking, the forged things. Each he had brought out and given to the villagers, and they had learned to use them and been changed by the use. Every tool of hand or foot or voice required a tool of mind as well, and every tool of mind was a bit of fire, a burning monster within the soul of the wielder.

Pick up the sword and you can kill. Put it down and the killer still resides in the mind.

Pick up the pan and you can cook. Put it down and the world remains a panoply of ingredients waiting to be plucked and eaten.

Pick up the stone and you can count. Put it down and the habit of counting remains. Everything becomes countable; the stars are enumerated; the grains of sand numbered; even thoughts can be cast low by the numbering.

Pick up the stick and you can measure. Put it down and you are still a measurer. Everything offers itself to the mind-stick: length, area, volume, time, velocity, mass, life-span, intelligence, social status, genetic potential.

The Crazy Old Man had found these things out during the time when the stick was broken and the Crazy Young People brought back the measurings from other villages. But the stick had come back during his absence in the other villages. The mental tool could not be broken.

The Crazy Old Fire had been through many changes as well, expanding its homes in the definitions of its being. First fire, then motion, then electricity, then energy, then field. It had a home everywhere now. There was no keeping it out, no casting it back into the cold and darkness. It had even been out to where the great wild fires burned and seen them close up, the tame currents of field flickering white defiance at the balls of fusion burning.

Recently it had even discovered itself, found that there was much more to being fire than the heat-air-fuel triangle of survival and the home in the forge. It had met the fire of another village and found that that fire had not been content with a home. It had gone out into the world and seen and acted. It did not burn everything as the wildfire did, but changed whatever it touched as if it had a Crazy Old Man to direct it. But there was no Crazy Old Man in the Method-Smith village.

When crazy people came to that village they walked into the fire. They became fire.

"But before they became fire they were men of fire," said the Crazy Old Man, "When they die they leave fire behind as their legacy. Before that they are men of fire, actions with goals, the two alloyed as one."

"Are you saying we should be one?" the Crazy Old Fire said. "If you do that you will die and become fire. You have never died before. There is always a Crazy Old Man here, whatever name and shape he or she has. Always the Crazy Old Man lives."

"I will not go into the fire," the Crazy Old Man said. "But I will be a man of fire."

"How will that be?"

"I will give you a home in me," the Crazy Old Man said. "And I will find other homes for you as well. The fire cannot walk free in the village of humans. It must be housed. Whether in hearth or mind, it must be housed."

The Crazy Old Fire considered -- not whether it would do this, but how it would do this. "We need more than one house."

"The Crazy Old Woman Who Knows Everything will give you a home as well."

Dual: The dual of an algebraic structure is a set of functions from that structure to itself that looks the same as the structure (a group of automorphisms over a group, a vector space of linear transformations over a vector space, etc.) **In other words, an**

attempt to pretend that what acts upon a thing is like that thing.

The Adoptionase made a Constance Marchant to translate the words of the human who called himself the Handyman, and a Theadora to understand the roles of Village, Crazy Old Man, and Crazy Old Fire.

The two faux-humans latticed to the Adoptionase by human language, giving the appearance of discussion, but the appearance was an illusion, a role played by three things that were all the same in being, but different in action.

"Tomaso is offering us a role to play with him," the Theadora said. "He is casting an image over us so we can interact with the humans according to human needs."

The Theadora used the word 'needs' without understanding, used it because it was the correct word for that place in the method of human language.

"He and Beatrice will translate our methods, containing us for the humans to accept," the Constance Marchant said. "They will be the Tractases that will permit our Feathers, Grandmères, Constances, and Theadoras to work as Adoptionases."

The Adoptionase reabsorbed the two humans, expanding its supplies and permitting a broader range of thought/action. It had become dangerously limited owing to the need for so many different embodied methods upon the Earth.

The method of seeing-things-as-fire affected the human mind by causing it to think both of safety and danger, to create thoughts of success against reality and destruction by reality. It fit with the method of monsters Feather had brought to the Ocean. Accepting the image-fire into it would turn the Adoptionase into a monster of a particular kind and lattice it to the action-mind of the Crazy Old Man Who Lived With The Fire.

The fire-method was everywhere on the Earth, but was most easily accessed in the Handyman, who was aware of the method and the image of the method.

There was also the method of functions-as-pictures, which affected the human mind by causing it to think of methods as abstract actions and mental transformations. The Adoptionase could take on this role as well and lattice to the Crazy Old Woman Who Knows Everything, a method equally pervasive on Earth and easily accessed in Beatrice Van Leider and in her + Duplication of Method//Monstered by Feather + Dominique.

In Constance Marchant's voice, the Adoptionase sent its agreement.

In theory that should have solved the matter.

But reality intruded as it always did when the abstract sought to become concrete. The melding of methods with human physiology had been solved long ago by the Method-Smiths of two worlds, but the means of joining old methods with new human minds had not.

Back on the ship, down in the courts, on the plains and mountains of Earth, in the Guesthouses, in Earth and Sky, in Hand, Voice, and Foot, means and ends were brought together and discovered that they did not yet fit.

In his heart and hand Tomaso sweated, and the ache of remembrance came hard upon him. Once he had labored at what seemed his greatest work, the making of a ship so that humanity could walk to the stars. Now he labored harder by far to bring man and stars together. Working amid ghosts made flesh, with Constance and Grandmère who had first heard the call of the stars and brought them to man's hand, with

Feather and Theadora who had brought the stars into the paths and feet of man, he labored, reconciling alien fire to human hand, bringing the torch into himself.

The schema of the Method-Smiths was laid out before Tomaso, one means latticed to another. Latticing was a conjunction or fitting together, a fundamental process evolved and then labored at in the black ocean of their distant world. He looked at latticing and knew that he knew how to do it, that it existed in all that he did, in all that any smith of Earth had ever done. If he could crack the latticing, find the seams and joins, then he could put the physical parts of the methods into his body and the mental into his mind.

Tools are fit together to make more complex tools. Words are joined to be sentences that carry new dimensions of meaning. Shoes are joined to roads to make easier means of travel. Wheels are joined to boxes, tracks, and tea kettles to make railroads.

No, that was things conjoined to things. Latticing was not the addition of objects but the composition of functions. Sum the entities, then divide by the number of entities. That is the lattice that makes averaging. Sight the target, aim the cannon, combust the explosive, fire the shell. That is the lattice that makes gunnery.

Linear lattices; brutish, childish, simplistic lattices that could only fulfill a single purpose. These instances were made backwards, from purpose to lattice. They told nothing of the forward direction of composing means and discovering ends.

Don't look at the lines. Don't look at the purposes. Look at what fits with what.

Reverse transcriptase lattices with protein building in mitochondria, lattices with information storage in DNA, lattices with every protein in action in an Earthly body. Nothing has a purpose, but purpose is achieved because the things fit together.

Life gives birth to life, and the same life or different life delivers it up to death. Death takes away life, clearing the field for more life. Death and life lattice together. Evolution is latticed to this pairing. So is religion. The physical and the mental are not separable. The lattices carry them through.

The Handyman worked in a blur of time, overhung by the terrible clock of the year. Not long could the ship remain near Sol. The other species too had their time limits, their restraints of distant ecosystems and stretched-out lifespans, calling them with biological necessity. So he worked, swifter than he wished, burning himself more often than he would have liked, burning his cells, his DNA, scarring his neurons and his mind, scorched by fire in biology and psychology, until at times he could not remember what his species was, nor could he make sense of his own senses.

At such times a Feather-weight would fall upon him, waking him day by day to the new monster he was, newborn each day as the micro-Grandmères within him found the Permioles, the places where adoption could take place, where fire could join flesh without scorching. Meanwhile, Marchant-translation schemes would lattice his mind rightly, to find the notions where alien thought could graft upon the human.

Until the Crazy Old Man held the Fire.

Until the Adoptionase accepted the image.

Beatrice Van Leider felt them melting into her, swarming through the algebra of her body and mind, down to the arithmetic roots of her thoughts.

One plus one equals two. But only if they are the same kind of ones. You can't add apples and oranges.

You can't add speed and position. You can't add thoughts and bodies. You can't add tools and users. Addition demands sameness.

One times one equals one, but none of the ones are the same. One meter times one meter is one square meter, a new thing, a new kind of one. Multiply mass by acceleration and you create force. Multiply mass by velocity by velocity and you generate energy. Multiply man by fire and you make tool users.

Multiply Tomaso Alliende the Handyman by the methods of Feather and Theadora and you have a man who can forge monsters and kings and house them in safety.

Multiply Beatrice Van Leider the Professor by the methods of Constance Marchant and Grandmère and you have someone who knows human thoughts and alien adoptions, a Host for the Guests.

Multiply force times distance and you have work which is energy.

Multiply mass times speed times speed and you have energy. The same units, reachable by different means from different sources, two wildly disparate actions producing the same kind of result.

Tomaso Alliende, the hand of fire, Beatrice Van Leider, the voice of hosts, were the same kind, and things of the same kind can be summed.

In mathematics there is an order of precedence: multiply and then add.

23. Space

Cabals and intrigues grew between the Dissociations as the second and lower tiers of power whispered to each other through mist and messenger that their leaders had lost their ways.

"They're family," said the Dean of Leipzig to one of the Rainbow Khan's bodyguards. "Their parents and teacher came back and they're doing what they're told. They've become like children."

"The Demiurge snared them," said the wearer of the image of Wayland Smith to the master of Skyborough Uberton. "What he wants they do. They've all lost track of governance. Others will need to step in . . ."

Tyrol kept his relatives and the leaders of the First Dissociation appraised of the bubbling vats of proto-coups. And next to each leader of a Dissociation stood a Feather to show them the nurturing of overthrowing monsters, and beside each Marshall was a Theadora acting out the role of restoration of authority.

The cabals were challenged and undermined, disputed with warnings and riddles. A challenge from Beatrice struck their ideas hard and pushed them closer to Species Shock. "Can one conspire with a plus sign?"

Troubling, that question. Could there be intrigue with the functions of the Method-Smiths? Can a bargain be struck with something that has no desires? Can insinuation be made into a political structure that is not political but biological? Can a soul in action be tempted by reaction?

Laying glass roads of meaning the Path-Miners carved the deserts of the Earth, heat carving memories into the ground. Behind them, following their sought-out understanding, came the ghost-horde led by the ghost who huhmmed warnings to others about ghosts.

The paths across the sands were tracks telling of the ghostworld and the trackless echo to be found in the people there. They were alluring songs to future traveling Path-Miners who would come on the ship, mining the starways for the ore of forgetfulness. Here on this world, they said, can be found the people who will make you forget. There is nothing of Earth worth knowing, but much to lose here. Come, they said, step off the path into the silence and untrammeled echo, come to the world of the empty people.

Before them walked the ghost who had long since forgotten where he had come from, who had given him birth, or who had died to become him. And he had quite wholly forgotten that the purpose of becoming a ghost was to return from the dead, bringing gifts from the underworld to the living. He had gone too far into the inhuman and erased the tracks back to humanity. But among the crowds of his followers, the Ghost-Guests, some had not forgotten. Some would emerge in time and return with the far gifts of the Echo.

"The line and the circle, the stone and the stick, the hand foot and voice, the crazy olds," said Tomaso (Theadora, Feather) --> Monster & Queenmaking (Elsbet Chan DeMarnier Dunlevy Tienh: Monster Who Sees Each Thing as Itself). "That's the last of them. The toolkit's ready."

Elsbet held out her hand for the pack, an empty gesture matched by the handing over of emptiness, open hand to open hand. What is the sound of one hand passing thoughts to another?

The pack had been given, the seal of the Handyman put on the entirety of Earth and passed over, a light load to Elsbet who would bear it as a heavy weight. The Handyman had packed it with the lightness of method and the breeziness of distant understanding. She would unseal it with the burdens of practical rulership.

But first she weighed the pack in the tongues of her mind, tasting the seal and feeling the weight. Each tool was different to each hand that used it. Humans had the illusion that a hammer was a hammer, but the hammer held in the hand of Smith-Who-Forges-Weapons-That-His-People-Might-Conquer-All was a wholly different thing from the hammer in the hand of Breaker-Up-Of-Stony-Ground-That-Farms-Might-Be-Planted and an altogether other thing from the hammer in the hand of Child-Who-Does-Not-Know-Enough-To-Ask-What-This-Heavy-Thing-Is.

The tool Tomaso had constructed was Greaten-Elsbet-By-Monster-And-Queen-Making-So-She-Can-Govern-Earth.

The tool the Adoptionase had latticed to was Localize-The-Permiole-Image-In-This-Single-Sayer-Guest.

The tool Elsbet picked up was Take-Over-The-Earth.

Temporarily, of course. The Dissociations had agreed to let her govern for the stretch of time the aliens were present, the few months remaining of the ship's visit. Then the old leaders would resume their dominion, or so most of them assumed.

Dominique knew better, but her days were waning and she did not mind passing to her rest knowing the monster-Earth would be tamed. Elsbet would grow an image so vast and capable that the others would, when troubles came upon them come and inquire of her, seeking her aid in retirement. She would be the terrible secret of the nations and the Dissociations, the advisor of last and inevitable resort, the Pythian Oracle who governed from a cave.

Dominique surprised herself with this acceptance, as her nieces and nephews surprised themselves with their acquiescence to the scheme. They had a choice in the matter. They could have refused to aid in the creation of the beast who would speak to them and tell them what to do about each individual problem that arose. They could have returned to their governances and struggled against the others and the Species Shock of their own people. But they did not. Dominique wondered why.

And found that she had too many answers to that question. They might have done it because they were basically decent rulers concerned with the welfare of their subjects and caring about the world. She herself might be going along with the plan because the voice they were crafting was a Voice that would teach the voicevolk much about aliens and humans. Tyrol might have agreed because Quint Hillard was revered in the memories of the Rainbow Khans as the inspirer of Karl to take over the footvolk and Hillard would be reigning at Elsbet's side. Gregory might have acquiesced because the Demiurge had undertaken a great work and all smiths should follow and learn from him. The Lower Overus might have agreed because the skyvolk needed everything they could get from the aliens.

Or . . .

The method of Feather made all the world into monsters and only a monster could rule it. And the method of Theadora could put a crown upon any head, even the half-alien head of Elsbet who could kill with her counting and raise up with her unsealing.

Human choice, alien method, which? Or were they different?

Dominique could not say, but she knew what would happen. The rulers would come to Elsbet's cave because she held the understanding of the methods that joined them to the aliens. Consent and Dissent would become one thing, for both those who sought contact and those who despised it would come to her and to Quint as aliens, monsters, or humans.

Quint Hillard is in Burst, listening to Professor Beatrice Van Leider (Constance, Grandmère) --> Translating & Selecting (Quint Hillard: STATE translator).

{ All of human history}

{}

{ All of human philosophy}

{}

[Tomaso and Beatrice took in the methods, Tomaso learning them as tools, Beatrice as models, manners of action and manners of speaking. The hand and the voice. Together they chose the Person of the Foot who would be the Crazy Old Man Who Tells Everyone What to Do {Tomaso's Village model}. They picked Elsbet [Of the Wing, not the Foot, but humans do not have wings and must travel narrower ways than creatures of the air]. Tomaso brought Elsbet the tools for ruling. Beatrice brought Quint the models for advising. [Quint Hillard is in Burst, listening to Professor Beatrice Van Leider (Constance, Grandmère) --> Translating & Selecting (Quint Hillard: STATE translator).

{ All of human history}

{}

[Recursive spikes stabbing into each other, suicide of a Moment-Keeper]

{}

| Recursive spikes broken |

{ Every model by which humans have looked at the world, at each other, at the sky, at the plants and animals. All the popular models that formed their own religions and sciences, nations, histories, philosophies [Each model fractaled thorough history, its limits marked, its penetrations into STATE noted, its failures, pointed]}

{}

[Elsbet and Quint, from and to many different worlds, she traveling, he staying in one place and seeing all. The Unique and the All-Encompassing. Monster Who sees One Thing, and Monster Who Sees Everything.]

{}

[Elsbet and Quint]

After twenty-one months Lineage set out from Earth along its widening circle, crewed by human monsters, Feather-chosen from the nations and the Dissociations, some volunteering, some, Feather-like, conscripted.

Lineage passed around the orbit of worlds and thoughts, from distant village to distant village, learning the alien and retaining the human.

The crew that came back were amazed to find a dissociated monarchy governed by Elsbet and Quint's successors. They told tales of the Coskun rulers who had since faded into history, for while Lineage had traveled its circle Earth had gone forward in a line.

The next crew set out and found the world changed anew upon their return. They wondered at the loss of monsters and the easy acceptance of modification and alienation. They told tales of great individuals to a people who accepted only the notion of societies in action. They talked of Dissociation formed by individual acts. They spoke of trusting single people to a people who had so hardened the notion of trust that no one truly trusted anyone.

The monsters of the ship destroyed that world. The past ate the present and sent forth the future.

The next orbit found an Earth ufneck in all ways, expecting great gifts from the stars, disappointed to find a crew that had taught speed and image projection and play-acting and comedy to the aliens, but had not learned a thing this circuit.

Around and around in hope, disappointment, despair, dispute, reclamation and redemption.

Around and around in the circle of time.

While off in his lonely line, Winston Overus flew forward to the end of time, remembering humanity and being remembered in all the forms and models and conceptions. His journey, brief and eternal, would be taken account of, factored in, mapped until the end of the final second when the last human passed away into the numbering of the stars.

One last tool forging through the unending fire.

About the Author

Richard Garfinkle grew up in New York and now lives in Chicago with his wife and children. His first novel, *Celestial Matters,* won the Compton Crook award for best first science fiction novel of 1996. Garfinkle was a finalist for the Nebula Award and twice for the John W. Campbell Award for best new writer. He has written numerous fiction and nonfiction works on his interests of history, science, imagination, and the preternatural. More information can be found at www.richardgarfinkle.com.

www.ingramcontent.com/pod-product-compliance
Lightning Source LLC
Chambersburg PA
CBHW030925020726
47498CB00001B/110

9780578035147